Harry C. Palmer

Sights Around the World With the Base Ball Boys
Comprising most interesting sketches of the famous sights of the World

ISBN/EAN: 9783337193973

Printed in Europe, USA, Canada, Australia, Japan

Cover: Foto ©Andreas Hilbeck / pixelio.de

More available books at **www.hansebooks.com**

Harry C. Palmer

Sights Around the World With the Base Ball Boys

Comprising most interesting sketches of the famous sights of the World

SIGHTS
AROUND THE WORLD

WITH

THE BASE BALL BOYS.

COMPRISING

MOST INTERESTING SKETCHES OF THE FAMOUS SIGHTS OF THE WORLD AS
THEY WERE SEEN BY THE GAY TRAVELERS ON THE

"ROUND-THE-WORLD" TOUR OF AMERICAN BASE BALL TEAMS.

INCLUDING

THEIR EXPERIENCES AS A JOLLY PARTY OF FUN-LOVERS AND FUN-MAKERS AMONG THE
JOLLY FELLOWS OF OTHER NATIONS—PRINCES, NABOBS AND ROYAL ENTERTAINERS;
ALSO IN EXCITING CONTESTS ON HISTORIC GROUND AND AMID STRANGE PEOPLES.

BY

HARRY CLAY PALMER,

*The Great Authority on Sports, and the Representative of the New York "Herald," Boston
"Herald," Chicago "Tribune" and "Sporting Life" in the "Round-the-World"
Tour of the Base Ball Boys.*

PROFUSELY AND ELEGANTLY ILLUSTRATED.

EDGEWOOD PUBLISHING COMPANY,
1892.

PUBLISHERS' PREFACE.

THE reader needs no introduction to the popular players of the Chicago and All-America Base Ball teams who, under the management of MR. ALBERT G. SPALDING, travelled around the world in 1889.

At the time of the famous tour telegraph instruments were ticking the whereabouts of the boys and the scores of their grand exhibition and match games all over the world, and the reports told in five figures the numbers of the crowds that thronged to see the exponents of our national game.

Successful as was the tour in the estimation of lovers of Base Ball, there was a phase of the trip which, had it been given the prominence to which it was entitled, would have been vastly more interesting to the thousands of readers than the details of the games.

The boys we sent around the world to show our European, Australian and Asiatic cousins how we pass our leisure hours and strengthen our brawn were, perhaps, more appreciative of fun and more capable of fun-making than any group that ever left our shores. They improved every opportunity for gratifying their love of the humorous, and they left behind them a glittering trail of joviality, festivity and sport that has made their names a synonym for all that is merry in the places they visited.

Our author, on account of his intimate knowledge of Base Ball, his accuracy as a reporter, and his ability as a writer, was chosen to accompany the boys on their tour as the representative of four of the leading papers of the country, and in this book he has faithfully written the most interesting and the most ludicrous events of that famous tour.

Mr. Palmer is an accomplished newspaper man and an accepted authority on sports. He is a bright and witty writer, and was never so thoroughly "in his element" as when, on the steamer's deck, in the railway carriage, or on the piazza of the hotel or inn overlooking the panorama of passing people, he wrote for American readers accounts of the feats and frolics of his fellow-tourists, the Base Ball Boys.

His camera was as frequently and as wisely used as his pen, and the result is a charming gallery of excellent portraits and sublime scenery, mingled with "snap-shots" of the boys or their mascot in ludicrous situations, that make brilliant pages which are already bright without them.

We feel that no apology is necessary for placing this book before the public. It has a decided mission for good. There is but one class of persons whom it could fail to interest. Those who have no appreciation for athletic manhood, no relish for innocent sport, no taste for witty humor, who would rather sigh than smile, and prefer the shade because they are afraid of the sunshine, should not read it; but, to those desiring to make a rapid tour of Europe, become acquainted with the strange people of several nations, go into their homes, learn their peculiarities and oddities, view the historic scenes and wonders of the Old World, and at the same time fill each day with fun and sunshine, we extend a cordial invitation to join this jolly, good-natured party, and accompany us in the following breezy pages "Around the World with the Base Ball Boys."

THE PUBLISHERS.

CONTENTS.

THE "AROUND THE WORLD" TOUR.

BY HARRY C. PALMER.

ILLUSTRATIONS.

THERE have been some noteworthy tours in the history of modern athletics—tours that have commanded the interest and attention of the English-speaking, athletic-loving nations of the world. England's cricket teams have visited those of Australia, and Australia has likewise invaded England—a fact that not a few of old England's representative batsmen and bowlers remember with feelings of mingled regret and pleasure ; Ireland has sent her cricketers to America and America has flashed her most promising colors upon the great ovals of the British Isles ; Ned Hanlon has crossed the Atlantic and Pacific to do battle with English and Australian oarsmen in their own waters ; and an American wheelman has encircled the globe with the track of his bicycle. All these tours excited international interest, and their heroes were in each instance the recipients of many courtesies and kind attentions during their stay abroad and upon their return home.

During all of this time, however, the national game of the Americans —save in a single instance—had never been carried beyond its own shores. It is a matter of history that in 1875 the old Boston and Athletic teams, embracing A. G. Spalding, Adrien Anson, Harry and George Wright, and others of America's crack professionals of those days, journeyed to England for the purpose of showing Englishmen the beauties of the American game. At that time, however, baseball had only just entered upon the remarkable era of public favor and prosperity that has since marked its development in America, and it is safe

* By Harry Palmer, the "Around the World" Tour correspondent of the *New York Herald*.

II

to say there was not one Englishman out of every ten thousand who had even the faintest conception of the theory of the game, for no information bearing upon it had ever been sent to England previous to the advent of the American teams on British soil. In 1875 sentiment was not ripe for the successful introduction of our great field sport into any foreign country, and this fact made itself apparent to these touring players before they had been long in England. They were most hospitably received, however, and did it fall within the province of this chapter to speak more fully of that trip, much might be said of the courteous treatment accorded the Americans by the London cricketers and their friends. That tour is memorable, even if only because of its pioneer character.

ALBERT G. SPALDING.

The great tour of the winter of 1888–89, however, causes our first invasion of England to be almost forgotten, for it stands to-day, as it must for many years to come, far and away the greatest, most successful, and most noteworthy tour ever attempted in the history of athletics. The leader of the English tour of 1875 was also the leader of the world's tour of 1888. The English tour, however, was in reality but a mutually agreed upon and experimental trip, undertaken with very vague ideas as to what the result would be, artistically or financially. At that time Albert Spalding was the young, popular and hard-working pitcher of the Boston Red-Stockings, with little more than his energy, ambition, and love of the game to draw upon for the success of the trip. But how differently he organized, planned and conducted the tour of 1888–89. As the possessor of ample means, absolute control of two well-selected professional teams, under contract to him for the faithful observance of his wishes, took the place of the mutual-arrangement aggregation of 1875, while the same great lubricator of all worldly enterprises—gold—rendered possible the employment of experienced assistants, the provision of comfortable, and for the most part luxurious accommodations, and in fact rendered practicable the tour of the world by representative American teams.

The financial outlay of such an immense undertaking was necessarily very great. Mr. Spalding thought of this at the time he conceived the plan. He also realized that the receipts from such a trip could not be figured upon as a factor in its success. Unfavorable weather might prevent no small proportion of the appointed games; thousands of unprofitable miles would have to be traveled; and, worse than all, a lack of interest or a failure of the people in Australia and in Great Britain to understand and enjoy the game, might result in financial disappointment in the only countries included in the tour wherein there were grounds for hope of receipts. The financial failure of the trip seemed not improbable. Indeed, it was predicted by many.

The projector of the tour did not, however, look upon it as a money-making venture, and it was probably because of this that unfavorable predictions did not discourage him or affect his plans. On the contrary, as the arrangements progressed the more liberal and broader-gauged they became. It was early determined that there must be no lack of means and no hesitancy in disbursing them, and there was none. Mr. Spalding for obvious reasons practically shouldered all financial responsibility, and at no time was money withheld or wanting when the welfare of the tour demanded its expenditure. The journey across America from Chicago to San Francisco, was made in special and luxuriously-appointed dining and sleeping coaches; the best hotel and steamer accommodations that money could secure were enjoyed throughout the journey, and the tour of England and Scotland was made in a style that attracted as much attention as did the players themselves. In a word, a deposit of $30,000 in a Chicago bank as a "tour fund," with almost unlimited means behind this deposit, gave the party every reasonable assurance that a lack in this respect would not detract from their enjoyment.

Associated with Mr. Spalding was Leigh S. Lynch, the well-known dramatic manager and formerly the associate of Mr. A. M. Palmer in the management of the Union Square Theatre. Lynch during his dramatic career had made the journey to Australia several times; was possessed of a wide acquaintance in the colonies, as well as valuable experience in the management of such parties; and was altogether the man to assume the business management of the enterprise. At this time nothing had been said of a tour of the world, Mr. Spalding's only thought at that time being to cover Australia and New Zealand thoroughly. As will be seen in the following pages, however, the journey had not progressed far before he had pretty well decided to return to America via the Red Sea, Egypt, Europe, and the Atlantic ocean.

LEIGH S. LYNCH.

Once decided upon, preparations for the big trip were actively begun, though for fear of possible rivalry in the field, publicity was for the time avoided. Manager Lynch started for Australia in February of 1888, to secure exclusive control, for baseball purposes, of the Australian and New Zealand cricket grounds. Drawings for attractive lithographs and announcement posters were at once begun, and this taxed the best skill of designers and lithographers. The outcome was indeed a work of art, picturing all the players in various attitudes of the play, and giving other attractive views calculated to arouse interest wherever seen. These posters preceded the party everywhere, and did much to arouse public interest.

The all-important work of selecting the teams was also taken under consideration. This was no easy task. On the contrary, it was an exceedingly delicate undertaking. Not only must the men selected be the best exponents of the national game, but they must combine with their ball-playing ability, intelligence, good address, good habits, and good morals, qualifications not easy to find combined in any class of men. Confident that the trip would develop into one of international import- ance and interest, and that it would attract the attention of all English- speaking nations at least, Mr. Spalding was determined to take no chance of bringing discredit upon the party through the careless selection of his players. This point he kept in view not only during the time of selecting, but from the time the party left Chicago until it reached it again after having completed the circuit of the globe. The result was that the splendidly proportioned, well-mannered score of ball players was warmly welcomed and greatly admired in every country they visited as a representative and typical body of Americans, while, at the same time, they gave exhibition after exhibition of ball playing that will rank with the best ever seen upon American soil, even during the championship seasons.

One would naturally suppose that an opportunity to see Australia would be eagerly seized upon by every clear-headed, intelligent Ameri- can who could possibly avail himself of it, and yet to Mr. Spalding's surprise he experienced serious trouble before the work of signing his men had been completed. The Chicago team, or rather ten of its ablest members, signed at once, and were eager for the trip. It was not so, however, with the All-American team, which it was intended should be composed of one or more players selected from the representative teams of the country. No difficulty was experienced in signing them, but after they had signed, visions of sea-sickness, of death upon foreign shores, and of disasters upon the ocean, began to arise before the eyes of some of the men, and two or three of them suddenly discovered insurmountable obstacles to their joining the party. Michael Kelly, of Boston, for instance, had entered into business in New York, and was consequently unwilling to leave, even though he had signed a contract to do so. Tiernan, of New York, sent a telegram, in which he declared his inability to go, as he was "ill." Others were afflicted with sick mothers, and still others suddenly determined upon hasty marriages, until, at one time, it looked as though no team could be organized to oppose Chicago on the tour. Those who were willing to be persuaded, however, finally tossed their fears over their shoulders, and those who would not be persuaded were left behind, their places being filled by equally capable men.

In April, Lynch returned from Australia, and the plan of the tour having long since been made public, it became a never tiresome subject for comment and discussion in baseball circles throughout the United States, while the Australian press began to show an interest in the enterprise that augured well for its success in the Antipodes. The games of the world's championship series between the New York and St. Louis teams prevented Captain Ward and pitcher Ed Crane, of the New Yorks, joining the party at Chicago, but they overtook the company before it reached Denver; Herman Long, of Kansas City, Ed Hengle, and Frank Flint, of Chicago, accompanying the party until the arrival of the New Yorkers. Thereafter there was no break. After a farewell game upon the League grounds in Chicago, on the afternoon of October 20th, the party traveled by easy stages across the continent toward San Francisco, playing en route at St. Paul, Minneapolis, Omaha, Des Moines, Hastings, Denver, Colorado Springs, Salt Lake City, Los Angeles and San Francisco, finally sailing from " Frisco " Sunday, November 18th, for the Sandwich Islands, New Zealand and Australia. The Chicago, Burlington and Quincy Railroad had provided for the party two magnificently appointed special cars—a dining and a sleeping car—and upon these the journey ide in truly luxuriant style as far as Denver. Special cars upon the Denver and Rio Grande, and Central Pacific roads carried the party the balance of the journey. After two weeks of never-to-be-forgotten attentions and courtesies, including banquets, theatre parties and ball playing upon the Pacific coast, we boarded the steamship Alameda for the first sea voyage of the tour. Leigh Lynch had preceded the party in order to prepare for its arrival at Honolulu, Auckland and Sydney, and the management promised to fall, for a time at least entirely upon President Spalding's shoulders. Fortunately for all concerned, however, " Jim " Hart, at that time the popular and energetic manager of the Milwaukee team, who had consented to accompany the party as far as St. Paul, was prevailed upon to continue his journey in a managerial capacity to the Pacific coast. Hart subsequently proved one Mr. Spalding's most valuable lieutenants, his ability, experience as a manager, and wide acquaintance proving of great service.

To a description of the charming tour across the prairies and through the mountains of America ; of the ova reception tendered the party

by His Majesty King Kalakaua in the Hawaiian Islands; of the generous hospitality of the Australians; of the adventures and experiences
of the Americans in the spice-scented island of Ceylon, in Egypt, in
Arabia, through a delightful section of continental Europe, and in the
British Isles, the following pages are devoted.

THE PARTY.

On the evening of October 20th, a few days after the close of the season of 1888, two magnificently equipped railway coaches stood in the
Union depot at Chicago, their sides ornamented by long banners of
white linen upon which had been inscribed the words, "Spalding's Australian Baseball Tour." No other cars had ever stood in the great station similarly decorated, and yet no inquiries were made by the hundreds who crowded the platforms, for every well-informed traveler knew
that the Chicago and All-American ball teams had played their farewell game upon the Chicago grounds that afternoon and were about to
take their departure for Australia. Hundreds of baseball enthusiasts,
including scores of the personal friends and admirers of the departing
players, crowded the station, and it was not until a few minutes before
leaving time that the members of the party bade a final farewell to
the crowd, and, together with their more intimate friends and relatives,
passed through the gateways and sought the neighborhood of their
train, where they said their last farewells to mothers, wives, and sisters.
Perhaps no time could be more favorable for the introduction of the
reader to the individual members of the party than when, having stored
valises, uniform bags, and su. dry packages away in their respective
sections, the boys awaited the signal for departure.

Inside the car stood Captain Anson and his wife; she, tall and fair-
haired like her husband, with big blue eyes and a complexion typical of
this particular charm in American women. Near them were seated
Mr. and Mrs. Ned Williamson, the curly face and big muscular body
of the famous short stop bending over the fair head and pretty face of
the Southern girl he had made his wife six years before. Further on
stood Tom Burns, the quiet-mannered man-of-many-friends among ball
players, in conversation with George Van Haltren, the well-propor-
tioned and active Californian who has made an enviable reputation with

2

the Chicago Club, "Van," by the way, accompanied the party only as
far as San Francisco, his home. At the far end of the sleeper stood
Tom Daly and Mark Baldwin, inseparables, and as we afterward
learned, the leading spirits of the party in mischief and practical joking.
Out upon the forward platform, blonde "Jimmy" Ryan leaned against the
break-wheel conversing with two pretty girls, whose faces shone under
the prismatic rays of the center-fielder's magnificent scarf-pin; while
just beyond, Fred Pfeffer, faultlessly attired, stood looking alternately
at the toes of his patent leathers and admiring the faces of half a dozen
Chicago beauties upon the other side of the railing.   Out-fielders
"Mart" Sullivan and "Bob" Pettitt, both "Yankees" from the hills of
New England, and both fair-haired, muscular, and splendidly proportioned, pressed against the railing for a last farewell.   Catcher Fred
Carroll, broad-shouldered, muscular as a blacksmith, and handsomely
dressed in a light traveling suit, together with Tom Brown of the Bostons, chatted and laughed with George Wood and Captain Fogarty as
the quartette stood beneath one of the big electric lights of the station.
Wood, a blonde, and Fogarty, dark-complexioned, dark-haired, and dark-
eyed, are, like Baldwin and Daly, chums.   Both are members of the
Philadelphia team and both are typical ball players of the higher class,
in manner and appearance.   Fogarty is an Irishman possessed of an
inexhaustible fund of wit, a cheery presence and a handsome face.
Save upon two occasions, once on the Pacific and once in crossing the
English Channel, he was one of the well-springs of life to our party.
Wood was more quiet, but as fond of life as his chum.   Frank Silvester
Flint, or "Old Silver," as he was known among the party; John Tener,
of the Chicagos, tall, dark, and slender; Captain Ned Hanlon, of the
Detroits; Manager Jim Hart; Hermann Long, of Kansas City, and
tall, blonde-headed John Healy, of Indianapolis, are comparing their
watches with the big clock on the station wall, while among them all,
passing from group to group of the party, with a kindly word here and
there and an all-seeing eye to the details of arrangement, is Mr. Spalding, President of the Chicago Club and projector of the tour itself.   He
came through the gates half an hour ago supporting upon his arm a
stately, handsome, venerable lady, nearly as tall, robust and fine-looking as himself.   This was Mrs. H. I. Spalding, Mr. Spalding's mother,

and through the many miles of travel, as well as among the many attentions and courtesies showered upon us during the tour, the stately presence, snow-white head, and kindly face of this honored lady ever swayed
a genial and restraining influence over the more impulsive members of
our combination, and lent that air of distinction which the presence of
a stately woman alone can impart.

Such was our party as it stood in the depot awaiting the first turn of
the wheels upon that memorable tour, and it subsequently proved a most
congenial and delightful party for all. It could not well have been
otherwise, in view of the principles which guided Mr. Spalding in his
selections, and during the entire journey around the world not an unpleasant incident, nor a serious difference of opinion occurred to mar
the pleasure of the tour. Later on, at Denver, the party was augmented
by John Ward, the well-known captain of the New York team; Ed
Crane, the genial "tenor-pitcher" of the "Giants," whose excellent
voice helped us to while away many a pleasant hour on deck ; "Billy"
Earle, the enthusiastic little catcher of the Cincinnati team, whom we
picked up at St. Paul, and James Manning, the popular captain of the
Kansas City. In addition to these were Newton Macmillan, correspondent of the *New York Sun*, Mr. Goodfriend, of the *Chicago Inter-Ocean*,
and the writer. Harry Simpson, of the Newark team, accompanied the
party as Mr. Spalding's assistant, and afterward, remaining in Australia, did much toward helping the growth and development of the game
there.

At Denver we were joined by Leslie Robison, Jr., of Peoria, Ill., who
accompanied the party for the pleasure to be had out of the journey.
Mr. Robison was a somewhat delicate looking young man, with a
plethoric purse and a generous nature. That he was made welcome,
goes without saying. At San Francisco the party was still further increased by Irving W. Snyder, of New York, and George Wright, of
Boston. Snyder and Wright formed the third brace of inseparables in
our party—"Two Dromios" in fact, who suffered and enjoyed every
hour of the journey in close companionship.

Perhaps, however, the two most interesting members of our combination—interesting not only to us but to the people of every country
we visited—were the "Professor" and the "Mascot."

For the edification of readers not versed in baseball lore it should be stated that the mascot has become quite an important institution among the professional teams of America. He may be a boy possessed of some special attainment or physical peculiarity, or he may be a bull-pup with a prominent patch over his left eye. It matters not whether a mascot be brute or human, so long as his presence upon the players' bench insures a victory—in the minds of the players—to the team with which he has cast his fortunes and in whose favor he exercises the influence he is supposed to have with Dame Fortune. We picked up our mascot, Clarence Duval, at Omaha, a little, slenderly built, impish-faced negro, with a remarkable talent for plantation dancing, "hoe-downs" and "walk-arounds," and the gift of baton twirling to a degree well calculated to make the average drum-major wild with envy. A French actress making a tour of the Western States, and with whom he had traveled for some weeks as an attendant, had discarded him in the wilds of Nebraska and we picked him up en route. Subsequently he was rigged out in a red coat, gold lace, tight-fitting white trowsers and high-topped patent leather boots, and other paraphernalia of a drum-major's make-up, and led the teams upon the field for their games, walking in front of the line and swinging his silver-tipped baton in a style that never failed to excite enthusiastic applause. On shipboard he danced for the party, his music being the rhythmic clapping of hands by expert members of our party. The little beggar danced for King Kalakaua, amused the Prince of Wales and King Humbert of Italy, and afforded his fellow-tourists no end of diversion. Subsequently, however, he proved a deserter.

And now a word about "Professor" Bartholomew. "Proff," as the boys soon learned to call him, was certainly as original, adventurous and queer-lingoed a resident of Michigan as ever went beyond the shores of his own country. The "Professor" was a balloonist who had broken nearly every bone in his body and gouged out one of his eyes by falling into a tree-top during his professional career. Nothing deterred, however, by his disastrous exploits of the past, he was still following the life of an aeronaut when he met our party in San Francisco. His proposal to make the tour with us to Australia was accepted by Mr. Spalding, and the "Proff" accordingly became one of the party. His specialty, that of parachute leaping, was comparatively new in the Antipodes, and his trip was a success, artistically and financially. It was indeed a thrilling sight to see him ascend, swinging to the trapeze bar of his balloon, until he became but a speck against the blue sky, and then suddenly leap from his perch out into space, clutching the bar of his parachute which trailed after his rapidly descending figure until the air caught its folds and spread it out like a big umbrella above him. The daring fellow, as soon as the parachute had opened, would then go through a series of nerve-thrilling gymnastic performances that rarely failed to make more than one of his spectators turn their faces away in fear. A typical Yankee, with all the characteristic curiosity of New Englanders, he was a source of much amusement to our party, and an object of real interest to the people on the other side of the world. We were all thoroughly sorry when in Ballarat the "Professor's" descending parachute hurled him against the zinc cornice of a roof and cut a big gash in both legs below the knees. He recovered during the voyage across the Indian ocean, however, and was soon as quizzical, curious and originally funny as before the accident.

THE " PROFESSOR'S " SPECIALTY.

Frank Lincoln, the American humorist, was one of us as far as Australia, but did not continue further. Leigh Lynch and Mrs. Lynch, *nee* Anna Berger, the celebrated cornetist, joined us in Australia, completing the party, which was but little changed during the remainder of the tour.

But while I have been introducing my readers to the members of our party, the big station bell in the depot has sounded the time of our departure, and the train moves slowly past the platform, while hundreds of handkerchiefs flutter a farewell, and the first mile, in our journey of thirty-two thousand miles, has begun.

ACROSS THE CONTINENT.

Many American readers have taken the trip across the continent to California and the Pacific slope, and will therefore be familiar with not a few of the scenes through which our party passed. Let me say here, however, that no American can form any adequate idea of the grandeur and extent of his own country until he has made this journey. The days of the bison, the Indian scout, and the red raiders of the immigrant settlement are over, it is true, yet on every hand one sees evidences of a life so entirely different, so crude, when compared with methods and surroundings of an existence in the large cities of the East, that the people, their striking characteristics, their broad Western accent, their evident thrift and enterprise, and the apparent, though as yet imperfectly developed, resources of the country, are as interesting a study as any to be met with in a journey around the globe.

Our party, too, were making the trip under exceptionally delightful conditions. With our magnificently equipped special cars we wholly ignored the hotels en route. Our coming having been well heralded at each point, as well as our intention announced of crossing the Pacific to Australia, local enthusiasm had been aroused all along our route, and we were the recipients of marked attentions which assumed a public character before we had progressed very far upon our journey. At each city our arrival was awaited with impatience ; the press, not only of the West, but of the entire country, watched our progress from day to day, the correspondents of our own party alone representing nearly thirty of the leading papers of the Union. It was pleasant to be thus anticipated ; to feel that timbrels were being sounded in honor of our arrival, and that thousands of honest regrets followed us upon our departure ; it was pleasant to be made much of; it was delightful to travel in such regal style, and altogether no lighter-hearted, more tho-roughly satisfied party than ours, ever crossed the continent.

We left Chicago Saturday evening, October 20th, at 7 o'clock, and arrived at St. Paul the next morning. The trip from Chicago was filled with pleasant incidents up to the midnight hour. At each station we found enthusiastic crowds assembled, anxious for a glimpse at the party, and each assemblage gave us a hearty cheer as our train pulled out of the local station. Had we left Chicago in the morning our journey to the "Twin Cities" must have been one continuous ovation. We took dinner upon our dining-car, the "Cosmopolitan," shortly after leaving Chicago, and with that meal our party became a unit of congeniality and pleasant anticipation. After the tables were cleared, it quickly became apparent that every man of the party was provided with an entire poker outfit. To those of my readers who do not approve of card playing this may appear as a reflection upon the moral tone of our ball players. But it should not. The games entered into by our party during our long tour of the world, were played rather for the interest and enjoyment they held for us, than for gain. During such a journey there are hours that cannot be passed half so pleasantly in any other way, and if reference is made in succeeding pages to the games of "draw" indulged in upon our sleepers, or to our chances at "Calcutta pool" during our sea voyages, the reader will understand that the indul-gence was the outgrowth of a desire for diversion, and not of a desire for gain. The ladies of our company, with the consideration character-istic of American women under such circumstances, generously com-manded the boys to smoke whenever and wherever they pleased, with the result that the sleeper "Galesburg" became not only our sleeping apartment, but our smoking-room, our club-room and our quarters for songs, jokes, music—we having a mandolin and guitar in the party—and a good time generally. The ladies participated in our music and shared our fun, while we, in turn, enjoyed their society from breakfast until bedtime. Such was our party, and such our methods of passing time, with ample means and incidents for diversion even from this pleasant mode of travel.

Our arrival at St. Paul was the occasion of quite an assemblage at the Chicago, Burlington and Quincy depot, on Sunday morning, the

boys holding a levee in the sleeper "Galesburg" from breakfast time
until nearly noon. A game had been scheduled for that afternoon,
President Spalding having decided to adopt a policy on the Sunday
game question, according to the established customs of the cities in
which we played. Sunday games had been an established institution
in St. Paul for many seasons, and we consequently felt no hesitancy in
playing there on the day of our arrival. It was a bit chilly for ball
playing, but we put up our second game of the trip in good style, and
in the presence of two thousand people. Frank Flint (Old Silver),
caught for the All-Americans, in the absence of Kelly, who had
returned to New York under contract with Mr. Spalding, to arrange
his business affairs, and rejoin us in Denver. Kelly's name was
upon the score card, however, and it was some time before the crowd
discovered the fact that "Silver," and not the only Kelly, was behind
the bat. Flint might have passed for Kelly very well, but he struck out
five times during the afternoon, and this was more than the crowd
could stand. The weather was too cold for brilliant fielding, and the
game was cut short at the end of the sixth inning, that Chicago
might play the St. Pauls.

This last was the game over which the crowd became most enthusiastic, it being charged with a degree of local interest entirely lacking in
the game between Chicago and All-America. St. Paul, of course,
played ball for all they were worth, a natural and earnest desire to
defeat so strong a combination in the presence of a local crowd, inciting
them to their best efforts. Game was finally called at the end of the
seventh inning, on account of darkness, with the score in favor of the
St. Paul team, and Manager Barnes, of the local team, at once
challenged Anson to another game at Minneapolis, on the following
day. The challenge was accepted, and the visiting teams were
driven to their cars.

On the following morning our special cars were run down to Minneapolis, and here the importance and character of the tour was, for the
first time since our departure, declared with much pomp and dignity.
A parade in a dozen landaus drawn by horses with old gold plumes and

new gold blankets, behind a band of twenty-one pieces, led by a drum major with a scarlet coat and a big silver baton, emphasized our arrival, and although the day was colder than the preceding one, game was begun in the presence of 1800 people. The All-Americans turned the tables on Anson in this game, Tener being freely hit and none too well supported, while Van Haltren pitched an effective game for the opposing team. Meanwhile the crowd had been burning with impatience for the game between the Chicago and St. Paul teams to begin, and applauded enthusiastically when the players finally took the field. And what a game the youngsters did put up, to be sure. Tuckerman pitched and Earl caught for St. Paul, while Mark Baldwin, in the box for Chicago, proved a puzzle for every "Saint" who faced him. As inning after inning was played without a run being scored, the enthusiasm of the spectators knew no bounds. Pfeffer, however, finally made the winning run for Chicago in the fifth inning, reaching first on the play that put Anson out at second, stealing second, going to third on Tuckerman's wild throw to catch him off second, and crossing the plate on the play that retired Burns at first. It was a hard fight, though it lasted but five innings, and a credit to the St. Paul team though they did not win.

At seven o'clock that evening we left Minneapolis for Cedar Rapids, and after a turn at the cards, a bit of music, and the enjoyment of our cigars, the party retired—but not to sleep. It was Tom Daly's night for practical joking, and few of us escaped. He fished a piece of ice out of the water cooler and slipped it into Tom Brown's berth; he concealed himself behind the curtains of Herman Long's berth and filled the compartment with thick clouds of West Virginia "Stogie" smoke, until Long rolled from between the curtains, his eyes wet with tears, and vowing vengeance between his attacks of coughing; he artistically decorated with lampblack the good natured face of the sleeping John Healy, and perpetrated some similar outrage upon each of his fellow tourists whom he found asleep. Meantime word had been passed along among the wakeful ones that Mr. Daly was executing "a raid," and as a result a grinning and expectant face shone from between each pair of curtains, save those behind which Daly's victims slumbered.

Unfortunately for Frank Flint, his gentle snore reached Daly's ear through the berth curtains, and the joker, parting the drapings, stood

looking upon the slumbering form of his unsuspecting fellow player.
The opportunity was too choice a one to be treated in an ordinary way,
and Tom stood for an instant with an expression on his face which told
that his active brain was at work devising some crowning piece of mischief. What it would be was the absorbing question with a dozen
interested observers.

In an instant he dropped the curtains and started for the rear end
of the car, while a dozen pairs of eyes followed his movements. Our
sleeper was the last car in the train, and Daly, stepping out upon the
rear platform, detached one of the bull's-eye red lights from the railing

PRACTICAL JOKING—"SILVER'S" FEARFUL AWAKING.

and re-entered the car. The dozen watchers now divined his intentions,
and with difficulty restrained their laughter. Stepping carefully to
"Silver's" berth, with the lantern in his hand, the joker quietly parted
the drapings, and thrusting the lantern within twelve inches of Flint's face,
made the berth walls echo with a yell that would have done credit to the
lungs of a Sioux warrior. "Silver," who had been pressed into taking one
or two "night-caps" beyond his usual allowance, was startled from his

dreams by the awful screech, only to gaze into the great red eye which Daly held steadily before his face. The lurid glare of the light blinded the old player and scattered his terrified thoughts beyond all hope of re-collection. Slowly he raised himself into a sitting posture, never once taking his wide open eyes off the horrible thing before him, and then as the climax of his fear was reached, gave a gasping, terrified howl, and plunged through the curtains into the aisle, striking his head with a resounding thump against the top of his bunk as he went. There he sat for a moment until the choking sounds issuing from a dozen compartments caught his ear, and then sprang to his feet with a dangerous gleam in his eye, as an uncontrollable and simultaneous burst of laughter filled the car from end to end. Daly had suddenly disappeared, no one knew where, not to present himself until the steward announced breakfast.

The teams were tendered a great ovation at the city of Cedar Rapids, which we reached on the morning of Tuesday, the 23d. Our cars were switched upon a track just in front of the Union depot, and from the time the boys took their seats at breakfast in the dining-car, until they entered their carriages for the grounds, they were never lost sight of by the crowds that filed past our cars in such numbers as to impart a much better idea of the city's population than any of us had entertained before. Full half a dozen special trains were run into the city from adjacent towns, each train loaded, and by noon the city presented a holiday appearance. A more beautiful day for a ball game could scarcely be imagined, and fully four thousand people flocked to the grounds to witness the game, which was well worth going to see. At the request of many, Mr. Spalding acted as umpire. The score was tied in the fifth inning and again in the eighth, the victory finally going to Chicago when Ryan crossed the plate with one man out in the ninth inning. After the game, Mr. W. C. Beake and other gentlemen, who had arranged our reception at Cedar Rapids, together with their wives and daughters, supped with us in the " Cosmopolitan," President Spalding breaking a case of " Mumm " with the boys, in appreciation of the dash and spirit they had thrown into their game during the afternoon. We left Cedar Rapids at 6.30 P. M., with the parting cheers of the crowds at the depot ringing in our ears, and reached Des Moines, the State capital, the following morning. The game at Des Moines was witnessed by some 1500 people and was the prettiest contest yet put up by the touring teams. Hutchinson and Sage, of the local team, in response to a request made by several Des Moines gentlemen, filled the points for the All-America against Chicago, and did some great battery work, while they received excellent support in the field. We were joined at Des Moines by Frank Lincoln, the well-known American monologue artist, who accompanied our party upon a professional trip as far as Australia.

From Des Moines we pushed on rapidly toward Denver, stopping en route for games at Hastings and Omaha. At the latter point we picked up Clarence Duval. Tom Burns espied the little African as the teams were on their way to the grounds in carriages, with a full military band at the head of the line. A sorry looking little "nig" Clarence was, with his dusty and tattered garments, and his badly battered cap to one side of which a thread of gold lace was clinging, the only relic of better days the poor little darkey possessed ; unless, perhaps, it was the tarnished baton he carried. "Bless me!" said Tom Burns, as he caught sight of the boy, "if there isn't the little coon. Where in the world could he have come from?" and the third-base man beckoned to Clarence, who scattered the crowd in his desperate efforts to respond.

It seems that while the Chicago team were east upon a championship trip, Anson met the boy in Philadelphia, and being taken with the urchin's precocity, as well as his dancing and baton-twirling skill, had made him a proposition to travel with the team as "mascot," an offer the boy quickly accepted. He was accordingly togged out in a page's suit of navy blue with brass buttons, at Anson's expense, and promised to henceforth use his influence in favor of his benefactors. In New York, however, he came under the notice of M'lle Jarbeau, a French actress playing the country at that time, and the attractions of stage life held out to the newly appointed "mascot" were too great for him to withstand. He deserted the diamond for the stage, and the team had seen or heard nothing of him until Tom Burns caught sight of him at Omaha.

There was a merry sparkle in the waif's eye as he jumped out of the carriage at the grounds, and with prompt re-assumption of his

former authority, ordered the uniformed teams to " Dress ranks, dah !"
Then, as the band struck up a march, he tossed his rusty baton into the
air, and, while walking in front of the line of players, went through a
series of movements and tactics that caused the real drum-major of the
band to rest his baton upon his arm and gaze at his youthful superior
in astonishment. The exhibition caught the crowd, and it cheered the
darkey for his inimitable performance, as heartily as it did the players
when they drew up before the grand stand.

THE MASCOT'S MARCH TO VICTORY.

"Where'd you come from, boy?" asked Anson, in a gruff voice, as he
shook hands with the lad.

"Miss Jarbeau don gimme my release dis mawnin'," was the reply.

"Well," said Anson, "you're black-listed from this party; d'ye understand? We've got no use for deserters."

"I reckon you'se right, Cap'n," was the boy's philosophic reply,
"but," he added with a quick look for a bit of sympathy in Anson's
face, "I'se had a mighty hahd time ob it since I left you all."

"Ahey," said Anson, "I don't doubt it in the least. You look as though you had, and you deserve it. But we're done with you," and Anson walked off to the field while Clarence strolled over to the players' bench and sat down with a very downcast expression of countenance.

It all ended, however, by Clarence re-entering the carriage with Burns and returning to the train with our party, where I found him half an hour afterwards, sobbing at having been ordered out of the car by " the old man," as the boys soon began to designate Anson. We got together, however, and took up a purse for the little darkey, and then talked to Anson until he relented and decided that Clarence should accompany us as far as San Francisco, and further, if he behaved himself. It will be seen in the ensuing pages that he proved a great source of amusement to us during hours that without him might have been dull.

The game at Omaha resulted in a sweeping victory for the All-America team. Ryan took the box for Chicago, and his slow, easy-left-handed delivery deceived the opposing batsmen under Hanlon's captaincy, until the fifth inning, when Hanlon, Hengle, Van Haltren and Long suddenly dropped to his curves and pounded him unmercifully. The exhibition of batting pleased the Nebraska people immensely, and they howled themselves hoarse, as All-America made the circuit of the bases time and again.

At Hastings, however, Chicago turned the tables upon their opponents, and with Baldwin in the box batted out a pretty victory off Van Haltren's delivery. The falling of a section of the grand stand just before the game commenced, and the unexpected precipitation of a hundred or more spectators a distance of twenty feet to the ground, proved a serious though not fatal accident, but the crowd of three thousand people who had come, not only from Hastings, but from all surrounding points, were out for a holiday and a day's fun upon the occasion of the visit of the teams to their city, and soon forgot the incident in the excitement of the game. While at Hastings, some of the boys took Clarence Duval, gave him a bath, and arrayed him in completely new apparel, and when he returned to the car, the rest of the party scarcely recognized him. He sported a light check traveling suit with a natty hat to match, patent leather shoes, new underwear, spotless linen, and carried a cane. When he led the teams upon the ground that afternoon he was certainly as much of a curiosity as the teams were an attraction, and President Spalding, who had been absent from the party on a trip to Kansas City and who returned just in time to see Clarence's *début*, decided at once to take him with us to Australia. He was made to sign an iron-clad contract, in which he agreed to undergo all sorts of horrible penalties upon the first attempt at desertion. Anson, however, would not be convinced of the little darkey's sincerity, and said, that night upon the train, as he looked the mascot over in his new clothes, "this reminds me of the new suit I gave you in Philadelphia, last spring, in which you ran away from us two days afterward. It would not surprise me a bit if you should desert us at San Francisco." Clarence looked indignant.

"Ain't I done signed dis contrack?" he asked. "Ain't me word good?"

"I should say not," replied Anson, "didn't you run away before?"

"Didn't I done tell you I was kidnapped?" replied Clarence.

"Pshaw," said Anson, contemptuously; "I believe you would desert us now for Miss Jarbeau, if she happened to run across you."

"Well," said Clarence, philosophically, "dat's because you don't know me. I habn't de slightest doubt in de world dat if Miss Jarbeau seen me now," and Clarence looked at his new outfit with an unmistakable expression of pride, "she'd say to me, 'My gracious, Clarence, whar you been? come along wid me, boy, and don't let me lose sight ob you agin.' I know she'd say jus' dat."

"And what would you say?" asked Anson, with an amused smile.

"What I say?" said Clarence, and he looked the impersonation of pride and self-confidence, "why I just say, 'Go on, white woman, I don't know you now, an' I neber did know you.' No sah, Mr. Anson, I is done wid actresses de rest ob my nat'ral life, an' you hear what I say."

He kept his word and stayed with the party until we reached Chicago on our return, but he proved so utterly worthless and so trifling that, despite his dancing powers, we should not have been sorry had he been left in America.

While en route from Hastings to Denver, we met the St. Louis train at Oxford, Nebraska, and, while we were waiting the connection, Captain John Ward, accompanied by Ed Crane and Will Brown of the New Yorks, dusty and travel-stained, but none the less welcome, rushed in upon us. Brown was on his way home to spend the winter in California, and was still suffering from the broken thumb he received in St. Louis, in the World Championship series between the Browns and the New York team. Crane and Ward, however, had come to join the Australian party as members of the All-America team. President Spalding having brought Captain Manning with him from Kansas City and telegraphed for Earle at St. Paul, our party was complete at Denver, where Hengle, Long and "Old Silver," left us, to return to Chicago.

When we awoke for breakfast on the morning of the 27th, we were rolling over the beautiful prairie lands some fifty miles east of Denver. The air was clear and exhilarating, as it always seems to be at those high altitudes, and every man of the party declared himself in splendid condition, as a result of the cool, bracing atmosphere, and the anticipation of reaching the first really important stopping-place upon our journey across the continent. While at breakfast, the ladies of the party were the first to catch sight of the great snow-capped mountains, rising like a mirage in the distance, and as we drew near Denver, the outlines of the great piles of rock, with their beards of stately pine and fir, and their glistening summits, became more and more distinct, until one of the party ventured the opinion that they were not more than six or seven miles away. "They are forty-eight, sir," said the conductor, who happened to be passing at that moment and heard the remark, "they deceive nearly every one who looks at them for the first time and who is unaccustomed to estimating distances upon the prairies in high altitudes. It is no trick at all in this country to see from forty to fifty miles, and at some seasons of the year even further than that."

Denver is, in appearance as well as in fact, the metropolis of Colorado, and also of the entire country between that State and the Rocky Mountains. It is a beautiful city, inhabited by thrifty, enterprising people, who seem to make money easily and let it go unhesitatingly. They are great patrons of amusements of all kinds, great lovers of the good things of life, and consequently enthusiastic supporters of base-ball. That they had been expecting us was clearly evident on every hand. Our coming had been well announced, and the private cars which had been side-tracked for our use at the depot were surrounded by visitors during the entire morning of our arrival. The parade in Den-ver was a showy one, and when the teams passed through the gate into the grounds, Manager Hart was having all he could do to handle the crowd. Here, as at Hastings, Clarence Duval's drum-major perform-ance, as the teams came upon the field, was the signal for hearty laugh-ter and applause. The crowd soon showed that although it had not had the privilege of witnessing league games through the season, it was perfectly familiar with every player that made up both the Chicago and the All-America teams; familiar not only with his personal appearance, but with his record, his position on the field, and his especially good qualities as a player. It was the more to be regretted, therefore, that the boys should not have put up a better game than the first of the two games played at Denver.

The field upon which they played, however, was not the best in the world, being hard in one spot and soft and sandy in another, while the fact that the players were unaccustomed to playing in such a rarefied atmosphere had much to do with the exhaustion of the base-runners. Denver had been accustomed to seeing much better ball-playing than the Australian teams gave them an exhibition of; and as they expected much better playing than they had ever before seen upon the home grounds between the local teams, they were naturally much disappointed. On the other hand, the further the game progressed the more annoyed and the more discouraged the players got, and the more stubborn and erratic the spirit which moved the ball. For instance, the ball would be batted straight at Williamson, and Pfeffer, seeing a chance for a double play, would run up to take the ball from the bat, short-stop at second. Just before it got to Williamson, however, ten to one it would bound clear over his head, or shoot between his knees, with the result, not only that a double play was spoiled, but that what looked like a very stupid error had been committed, and both in-fielders would return to their positions very much out of temper, and consequently more than ever liable to make new mistakes. It was a big crowd and a very enthusiastic one

3

at the start, but the score of 16 to 12, by which the Chicago won the game, was a decidedly unsatisfactory one to the spectators, who had been accustomed to a much better rendering of the national game.

If we played a poor game on the day of our arrival, however, we more than made amends the following day, when, I think, the boys put up one of the prettiest contests that it has ever been my pleasure to witness. The crowd was perhaps not so large, but fully 4000 people gave their enthusiasm full vent, and at least half that number left the grounds with sore throats and with voices hoarse from cheering. Billy Earle, who had just joined the party at Denver, and Ed Crane and Van Haltren did the battery work for the All-Americas, while John Ward, playing with the team for the first time, covered "short" in a style that no one but Ward has mastered. That John was not unknown in Denver was clearly evident, for when he came to the plate in the opening inning the big crowd gave him a hearty welcome of applause. His clever and strategic batting pleased the spectators as well as did his fielding and base running, and he was cheered again and again as a reward for his efforts. Crane and Baldwin were both at their best in the box, and the former only gave way to Van Haltren in the eighth inning because he could no longer continue such hard pitching against the rarefied atmosphere. Van proved as formidable as Crane, and when the ninth inning was completed, with the pitchers working their hardest and the support of each man playing ball with their teeth set and bent upon winning the game, the crowd was in a state of suppressed interest and excitement that found vent at every opportunity, in the wildest cheers.

Some of the fielding work was superb, while the efforts of the base runners, despite their shortness of breath, kept the crowd howling through both of the extra innings played. It was Hanlon's catch, however, that caused the crowd to lose all control of itself. Almost out of sight into the blue air sailed the ball, and away across the field sped Hanlon at a rate that a professional sprinter would have been proud of; Sullivan, in the meantime, made the dust fly around the runways; just once Hanlon turned to look above, and then ran on again faster, if possible, than before. Suddenly, however, he stopped, turned his face to the crowd, ran backward for fifteen or twenty feet, then threw his hands

above his head; at the same instant his heel struck a hillock of sand
and pitched him headlong through the air upon his back. As he fell,
however, his right hand was held above him, and as he sprung to his
feet the crowd saw that he held the ball. For probably five seconds
that big assemblage held its breath, and then, as the famous outfielder
started in for the diamond and the balance of the All-America players
turned toward their bench, such a cheer went up as one rarely hears on
the ball field. For
baseball enthusiasts
and lovers of the

ED HANLON'S GREAT CATCH AT DENVER.

game it was, indeed, a scene for an artist,
and Hanlon was cheered and cheered
until he paused to raise his cap in front of the grand stand. It was a
magnificent game, and completely offset the disappointment which our
game of the day before occasioned.

We left Denver the same evening for Colorado Springs, where we
were announced to play upon the day following. Much to our regret,
our broad gauge, splendidly equipped dining and sleeping cars were

left at Denver, and our combination was transferred to two narrow-gauge sleepers especially reserved for us, in which we were to make our journey through the mountains over the Denver and Rio Grande Road. Compared with the spacious carriages we left behind, the narrow-gauge cars seemed like toy cars, but they were completely equipped for all that, and we had a world of fun in them before we left them at Ogden, in far-away Utah. Indeed, the only serious ground for revolt against our new accommodations that any of our party could discover was the narrow space of the sections, which crowded to no inconsiderable extent some of our four-handed poker parties who were desirous of wooing Dame Fortune in the same section. This reminds me that the poker element in our party had received an important addition in the person of Captain Anson's father, "Pa Anson," as we soon learned familiarly to call him, in order to distinguish him from his stalwart son. According to the old gentleman's theory there were but two sources of enjoyment in life; one was a ball game and the other was a good poker game. "Why," said the old gentleman, as his portly figure and ruddy face, despite his silver hair, told that he had enjoyed every day of life accorded him, "I would rather play poker and lose right along, than not to play at all."

We received a great send-off as the train pulled out of the Union Depot at Denver; every man seemed to have a score of friends to see him off, and every traveler about the Depot staid around our cars to get a glimpse of so celebrated an aggregation of ball players.

We arrived at Colorado Springs the following morning before day had fairly broken, and of all the delightful breaks in our journey across the country our visit to this Saratoga of Colorado was perhaps the most amusing and most prolific of pleasant incidents. Mr. Spalding had very thoughtfully telegraphed from Denver to have carriages and saddle-horses waiting our party at the depot by six o'clock upon the morning of our arrival, in order that we might enjoy a ride to Manitou and the Garden of the Gods, and when the colored porters awakened us, there was a scramble among the party to see which should first get into his clothes and out upon the platform for a first choice of horses and equipages. By seven o'clock, just as the sun was gilding the very top of "Old Pike," our party had entered three comfortable park wagons and mounted a dozen bronchos with enormous saddles, which really covered fully one-third of their sinewy little bodies. It was a beautiful drive, one that none of us will ever forget. Eighteen miles ahead of us and a little to the left, arose Pike's Peak, so massive and grand in its proportions that it looked, in the clear atmosphere of the morning, scarce five miles away. The bright sunlight brought out every crag and crevice upon its rugged old sides, and as we approached it it towered before us more imposing in its grandeur than all

IN A HURRY TO CATCH THE CONVEYANCES.

the descriptions we had read of it had prepared us for. To our extreme right we could just catch sight of the peaks of towering sandstone that form the Gateway to the Garden of the Gods, while before us twined the picturesque and well-beaten roadway through the valley.

Manitou was six miles distant. It is the summer resort of wealthy Western people, who have built attractive and Swiss-like residences upon the mountain sides and in the off-shooting valleys, that they might here enjoy the cool breezes and the mineral waters during the summer months. We dismounted at Manitou and drank of the delicious waters in the Silver Springs, after which we enjoyed a splendid breakfast at the Cliff House. Then resuming our horses and carriages we passed down the picturesque mountain road and a mile below turned off into a little valley which led to the rear entrance of the Garden of the Gods. The peculiar formations of sandstone to be seen in every shape and upon every side in this remarkable spot, have been described time and again by all travelers, who have doubtless felt, just as I feel, that their duty to their friends would not be fully discharged did they fail to write something descriptive of that spot which nature has so charmingly and fancifully designed. "Punch and Judy," "The Balanced Rock," "The Mushroom Rock," "The Duck," "The Frog," "The Lady of the Garden," and "The Kissing Camels," are all wonderfully true to the objects they are fancied to represent. The piles of sandstone reaching 330 feet into the air, forming the Gateway of the Garden, impress one as no description of these wonders could, with the matchless sublimity of the creative power. After admiring the many weird and remarkable things to be seen in this play-room of Nature, we passed through the Gateway, our equipages winding away through the valleys and then up the side of a hill for perhaps two miles, to the summit. Here we came out upon a broad plateau and, as we rounded the last turn in the roadway and stood upon the topmost ridge, a chorus of admiring exclamations went up from a score of voices as we caught sight of "Old Pike" rising before us in full view, and in all its impressive majesty, upon the other side of the little valley where nestled Manitou. Cheyenne Mountain lay, dark and sullen, to the left of the great snow-capped peak. Twenty-five miles away, distinct and clear as though but ten, there stretched the far-reaching ranges of the Rockies. Six miles away lay Colorado Springs, which we had left nearly six hours before, and for which we now drove at a brisk gait.

The ride home, over the hard mountain roads and in the clear morning air, was enjoyable, refreshing, invigorating. The Park wagons bowled along at a brisk speed, while Pettit, Carrol and Tom Brown, three of the best horsemen in our party, had a great race across the plateau, Pettit finally distancing both of his competitors. This reminds me of other equestrian experiences during the morning. Several of our party, a dozen, perhaps, rode bronchos, all of which were provided with the exaggerated saddles I have mentioned. President Spalding rode a bay gelding and, as he is quite a horseman, managed the hot-tempered beast admirably. Captain Anson bestrode a cross-eyed sorrel, which I afterwards learned had been the property of a Colorado cowboy. During the ride two or three head of mountain cattle became excited by the approach of our cavalcade and dashed on in front of us over the smooth roadway. Anson's sorrel, true to his early training, stuck his stubby tail out behind him, laid his ears back upon his head, and, with a vicious squeal, started after the now thoroughly-frightened longhorns. How "the old man" managed to stop his beast I do not know, but when we came up with him a quarter of a mile ahead, Anson was sitting down at the roadside and his horse was tied to a post near by. At Manitou the sorrel was turned over to Bob Pettit, and under Bob's master-touch the old ranger, who had plenty of spirit and bottom left, proved a better nag than all the others in the party.

Mark Baldwin rode a mustang which persisted in waltzing all over the road with his rider. The animal's antics and Mark's heavy weight finally broke the saddle-girth, and the big pitcher was pitched into the dust. He promptly turned his waltzer over to Sullivan, and the latter proved himself a horseman. Ed Crane rode a bay bolter, and rode so well that no one would believe his story that he had never been in a saddle before. Carroll and Tom Brown were both at home upon the sturdy little ponies, and the style in which they cut loose over the mountain roads caused the natives we met with to wonder at their recklessness. On the way back to the Springs Ward and Crane got separated from us in some way, and half an hour later, when the boys in uniform were seated in their carriages at the depot, ready to start for the grounds, two horsemen appeared away up on the side of the mountain, coming along the roadway, evidently with more regard for time than for their personal safety. Their sure-footed ponies brought them down all right, however, and a few moments later Ward steered his mustang into a post at the depot, grasped him about the neck with both arms, and took a slide over his head that would have won him a big burst of applause had he been able to get it off in the same style on the diamond. Crane could not stop his horse at all. The animal had evidently been out on such jaunts before, and was positively bent upon repeating an old and familiar trick. With the bit in his teeth, he kept on through the town for the stable, and Crane had to roll off of him as he finally shot through the low door of the barn. We could not wait for Ward to dress, and so drove to the grounds ; but John was equal to the occasion. He called a boy to hold his pony, and, donning his uniform in the car, remounted and rode

HOME RUNS OF A STARTLING SORT.

to the grounds *a la* Paul Revere, save that he wore the uniform of the All-Americas instead of the Continentals.

The Denver and Rio Grande Railway people had promised to hold the train for us an hour, if necessary, and had they done so we would have had ample time to finish the game in good style. We had scarcely begun, however, before we received word that the train could not be held over fifteen minutes, and this fact being communicated to the players they were at once seized with a desire to get through, even at the cost of good ball-playing. The result was that they became nervous. The glaring sun shone down from a confusingly "high" sky, and, to make matters worse, not a man could run bases without nearly dropping, from short wind, as the result of the rarefied air. As at Denver, the crowd knew what good ball-playing was, and naturally felt dissatisfied with such an exhibition, but there was no help for it. The boys could not have put up a better game, under the circumstances, to have saved their lives, and at the conclusion of the sixth inning, with the score 13 to 9 in favor of Chicago, we piled into our carriages amid the jeers of the crowd, which, by the way, was an extremely fashionable one, and cut loose, amidst a cloud of dust, for the depot. So great was the hurry that we might easily have left two or three of our party and not have known it. However, all the players managed to keep our carriages in sight, and our party was intact when we reached the depot.

"All right?" shouted the conductor, questioningly, as he looked at President Spalding and prepared to wave his hand to the engineer.

"All right, I guess," said Mr. Spalding, doubtfully. But just then he happened to catch sight of a cloud of dust away up the roadway, and, looking anxiously towards it, he called out to the conductor to hold on for a moment, at least. The cloud of dust rapidly became larger, and as it neared us we could see that it surrounded a horseman who was sparing neither himself nor his beast to lessen the distance between himself and our train. As he came nearer we recognized Jim Hart. Jim, it seemed, had remained behind at the grounds to settle the question of finances with the local ground authorities. When he had finished counting his cash he discovered that the party had left him. With two bags of silver, weighing probably fifteen pounds apiece, with three miles between himself and the railroad station, and with the time of departure but a few minutes off, the situation was certainly a serious one. It was by no means too small a hole for Manager Jim to pull out of, however, and, seizing the first mustang that he could lay his hands on, without regard to the arrangements of the owner, he slung his twin saddle-bags across the neck of the mustang, and commenced his race for the train. When Jim reached us he was covered with dust, the perspiration was streaming down his face, his collar was in a state of complete dissolution, his trousers had worked half-way up to his knees, and his silk hat, badly in need of an ironing, was jammed down over his face, while he clung desperately to the sacks with one hand and endeavored to guide his by no means mild-spirited mustang with the other. His appearance was too much for the risibilities of our party, and we howled with laughter as we drew his exhausted form upon the rear platform of the now moving train. I am very sure no member of our party will ever forget Colorado Springs, and it is not at all likely that Colorado Springs will ever forget the Australian Baseball party.

Soon after leaving Colorado Springs we entered the mountains, and about the hour of sunset we steamed into the Grand Cañon of the Arkansas. At the mouth of the cañon, an observation car, with a seating capacity of about 100 people, was attached to the rear of the train, and into this we crowded. Then right into the heart of the mountains plunged the puffing pair of engines that drew us. Immense walls of rock rose hundreds of feet upon each side of the track, and the head waters of the Arkansas river boiled and frothed in the mountain gorge below us, while the narrow-gauge line of railway twisted and turned upon its way through the grim chasms, so narrow, so deep, and so dark that at times we wondered if we should ever emerge from them. Soon we swung into the Royal Gorge, over the suspended bridge that spans the torrent at this point, and then on through the bowels of the mountains where the sunlight has not reached, mayhap for centuries, and as I looked upon the massive piles of rock that lie in awful disorder, or rise in towering spires,—the thought came unbidden—how fearful must have been the convulsions, and how terrible the throes through which old "Mother Earth" passed ere these imposing masses were piled in such wild confusion. We stopped at little mountain station of Solida for supper and then steamed upon our way for Marshall Pass, which may, without doubt, be classed among the grandest stretches of mountain scenery in the world. Our train was divided into two sections, of which the sleepers constituted one. Each section was drawn by two powerful engines and up the sides of these towering mountains we climbed, our trains being, perhaps, a mile apart. The moon had not risen, and the great cliffs and gorges were shrouded in impenetrable darkness.

Across the chasm on our right moved the lighted train of coaches forming the first section, four hundred feet above us, the furnace doors
of the engines wide open, the smoke-stacks sending forth showers of
red-hot sparks and smoke, which looked like liquid fire as they plunged
into the precipice, along the edge of which the train was running.

"Is there any bottom to this chasm?" asked one of our party of the
conductor who had joined us at the window.

"Well, there is no telling that," replied the officer; "a freight train
rolled off there a few months ago and we never heard of any of
them since, but we could see bits of the cars sticking to the sides of the
cañon, not bigger than so many pieces of kindling wood. If there is
any bottom to it, I never have seen the man that has found it."

Silence, like a mantle, fell upon the little group at our window as the
conductor spoke, for we all knew that within a few minutes our train
would be passing that identical spot, with a mass of towering granite on
one side and an impenetrable chasm on the other. The wheels of our
little sleeper hugged the steel rails closely, however, and ultimately
we stopped on the back-bone of the great dividing range of America,
10,858 feet above the level of the sea. As the train stopped we all
jumped from the coaches, and stood knee deep in the snow along the
side of the tracks. Imagine it. Six hours before we had been playing
ball under a hot sun at Colorado Springs, and now we were indulging
in a game of snowball on the top of the Rocky Mountains. From
Marshall Pass our journey was down hill, of course. We had left the
country of the Missouri and the Mississippi and were descending the
Pacific slope. The views of mountain scenery we had enjoyed thus far
had surpassed anything that any of our party had anticipated, but the
greatest of all was still to come. We were due at the Black Cañon of
the Gunnison at midnight, and a goodly number of us determined not
to retire until we had seen it. Ned Hanlon, Manning, Earle and myself clung to the hand-rails of the rear platform of our sleeper, and
gazed in silence at the wonders of this world-famed chasm as they were
revealed to us by the ruddy glare of the furnace and the light of the
stars which peered through the crevices of the giant rocks. Rounding
a curve suddenly, we came upon the great Currecanti Needle, a slender spire of rock that rises from the centre of the cañon until its point

seems to touch the very stars above. Winding past its base our train shot into a narrow crevice, and the great needle disappeared as suddenly as it had burst upon our view. Impressive in the depth of its solitude, overpowering in its grandeur, and terrible in its suggestions as to the causes which produced it, the Black Cañon of the Gunnison is most appropriately named.

CURRECANTI NEEDLE.

It was nearly three o'clock when we left the cañon, but no one of those who remained awake to witness its grand scenery will ever regret the sleep they lost. We awoke for breakfast at Green river, and after leaving that point entered the mountains of Utah. All day long our train wound round the base of big mud - colored hills, stopping occasionally at little settlements, the inhabitants of which were Indians, Chinamen and rough-looking frontiersmen. How they live or what they live upon, the passing traveler cannot imagine. On the evening of the 30th we reached Salt Lake City, and that night occupied beds for the first time since we left Chicago. Captain Fogarty, Tom Daly, Tom Brown, Mart Sullivan, Billy Earle, John Healy, Leslie Robison and myself were up bright and early the following morning, for a horseback ride through the environs of the Mormon stronghold, and, as our horses were fiery and eager to go, we did some tall riding through the picturesque country, finally drawing rein before the Parade Ground at Fort Douglas, in time to witness the dress parade of four companies of troops. After watching their evolutions for a while, we rode through the officers' quarters, and admired the pretty wives and daughters of Uncle Sam's soldiers as they sat upon the balconies of their residences, becomingly attired and enjoying the fresh breeze from the mountains. The view of the valley in which lies the city is a grand one from this point.

We found a good ball park at Salt Lake City, but a heavy storm interrupted our first game, and rendered the grounds unfit for our second. This prevented any model exhibitions of ball-playing, although the conditions under which we played were productive of any amount of fun for the spectators. Some twelve hundred people attended the first game. But a drenching rain stopped play in the first half of the fifth inning, just as All-America was beginning to bat the cover off the ball. It rained all night, and the mud in the streets and on the runways of the ball park was very soft and affectionate. Indeed, the conditions could not have been more antagonistic to good ball-playing. The outfield was in places covered with water, and the black muck on the runways was only hidden by two or three inches of sawdust which covered it; yet in spite of all, the game was full of interesting situations, and afforded two hours of good sport. Wood, Van Haltren, Manning and Ward did some beautiful infield work, and the All-America team entire had their batting clothes on from the time the game began. The black mud on the runways gradually worked itself up through the sawdust, and soon had our boys looking like a lot of street laborers in rainy weather. The white traveling suits of the All-Americas suffered sadly from the desperate base-sliding of their owners, while Tom Daly's swimming feat in centre field caused the crowd to double up with fits of laughter. It was a good game from the start to the finish, with as much kicking and warm rivalry as anybody could ask for, notwithstanding that the score was a jug-handled one in favor of the All-Americas.

We left Salt Lake the same evening, and as we assembled in the rotunda of the hotel for supper, fully two hundred people were present to shake hands with our party and bid them farewell, the boys having made scores of friends and admirers, notwithstanding their brief stay in the Mormon stronghold. While waiting for departure time, Clarence Duvall entertained the assemblage by his "baton performance and the

plantation walk-around," John Healy and Fred Pfeffer acting as his orchestra. Salt Lake City had never witnessed a similar performance, and a storm of applause, together with a handful of silver, rewarded the Mascot's efforts. We got away from the Walker House in a big omnibus that was long enough to accommodate our entire combination of thirty-five people, and as we rolled through the streets to the depot, shortly after nightfall, we sang the favorite chorus of "Old Silver:"—

> "Hide away; hide away;
> Dere is no use to try to hide away.
> Get your baggage on de deck,
> Don't forget to get your check;
> For dere's no use to try to hide away."

THE MASCOT IN REPOSE.

And as we drew up to the station platform, Jim Fogarty, with a preliminary call of three cheers for Salt Lake City and the people in it, led the party in an ear-splitting yell that startled a sleeping baggage-man off his truck, and caused an old lady to drop her band-boxes and make for the station, screaming "Help!" "Police!" at every jump, while the station-master for the moment seriously contemplated turning in the fire alarm.

"It is only them consarned, frisky baseball people," yelled a hackman, and then everybody but the old lady laughed. Our train was twenty minutes late, and during this interim Clarence danced for us, and somebody getting out the banjos and mandolins with which our party was supplied, we soon had the populace of the vicinity running to the station to see "the minstrel company that had just come to town," as a small boy put it. Of course, the mischief makers of the party were not idle long. John Healy stood apart from his companions with his grip at his feet, gazing at the top of a distant mountain and seemingly absorbed in reflection, possibly of home, or of the thousands

HEALY'S DAY-DREAMS RUDELY BROKEN.

of miles of our journey yet incompleted, when Tom Daly crept up behind him and dropped upon all fours. Just then Fogarty slapped the big pitcher vigorously on the shoulder, and John's heels went up in the air as he did a back somersault over Daly's back. John's training had not been neglected, however, and one of his long legs flew out in time to catch Tom under the coat tails, sending him sprawling into the crowd.

At Ogden we found two special sleepers awaiting us, and departed at midnight for San Francisco. The following day seemed an unusually long one to every member of our party, for the three thousand miles which we had arranged to cover between Chicago and the Pacific slope was becoming just a bit tiresome. All day long we rolled over the prairie lands of Utah and Nevada, the great mountains looming up in the horizon, twenty and even thirty miles away. Looking from the windows of our cars we saw droves of big jack-rabbits jump from their hiding-places and cut off across the prairies. Now and then a gaunt wolf or coyote would skulk from beneath a sage bush and draw sullenly away from the train. We caught sight of one pack of half a dozen of these brutes during the afternoon. Away they ran for a little distance, and then sat with their lips turned back from their fangs, snarling at our train for having disturbed them. Great cattle ranches stretched away up the broad valleys through which we were passing, and thousands of sleek-looking animals browsed upon the grasses which grew so luxuriantly along the streams which crossed the meadows. It was, indeed, a grand section, and until one has traveled it he can form no conception of how broad, and rich, and unequaled by those of any other in the world, are the great pasture-lands of the United States.

Upon the following morning, that of November 3d, we found upon awakening that we had entered a section of country vastly different from that over which we had ridden during the preceding day. The views were not of barren rocks and mud-colored hills, like those in Utah, nor like the broad valley lands of Nevada, but of lofty mountains rich in verdure ; and, as we proceeded, the elevations widened into beautiful valleys and the mountains gave way to lovely hills adorned with thousands of green trees. As we neared Sacramento we seemed to be in a veritable Garden of Eden. We partook of a delightful breakfast at Sacramento, at which the tables were loaded with rosy apples, delicious pears, yellow and red streaked peaches, and great bunches of grapes, all the product of that rich fruit-producing district. We had been expected by the baseball enthusiasts of the city, and there was quite a crowd at the depot. The cheers they sent up as we pulled out of the big station twenty minutes later reminded us of our departure from Denver and Chicago.

Beyond the city, we rolled through the rich valley of the Sacramento, through prosperous fruit ranges, and past grape vineyards that stretched away as far as the eye could reach, until our train pulled up at the little station of Suisun, thirty miles from San Francisco. Here a pleasant surprise had been prepared for us. Manager Hart, together with Frank Lincoln and Fred Carroll, had gone on to "Frisco" in advance of the party from Salt Lake City, and together with a score of Pacific coast baseball managers, and representatives of the entire San Francisco Press, had come out to bid us welcome. The first intimation of their presence was a chorus of cheers that went up as our train stopped, followed by a scurrying of feet across the station platform and the jarring of our sleepers as the delegation sprang upon them. Among those who had come to welcome us in addition to Hart, Carroll and Lincoln, were Tom Mackay, the ubiquitous and widely known passenger-man of the Burlington ; Messrs. D. D. Robinson and J. F. Moran, of the Greenwood and Moran Club; Eugene Vancourt, Al Foreman, and Messrs. Dressler, Batchelder, Cory, Crawford and Bannett, representing the San Francisco Press ; together with Managers Harris and Finn, all good fellows, and prominent representatives of the newspaper and baseball fraternity of California. At Port Costa the following telegram was handed President Spalding :—

"San Francisco, November 3d, 1888.

"A. G. Spalding, of Spalding's Australian Baseball Tour :

"We welcome you to our city and to the Baldwin Hotel. You will find carriages waiting at the foot of Market street. E. J. Baldwin."

At Oakland we took the Steamer which bore us across San Francisco Bay to the great metropolis of the Pacific coast. We found carriages in waiting, and fifteen minutes after we landed we were quartered in our rooms at the Baldwin Hotel, but not to rest. Manager Hart had notified half a dozen of us while on the Steamer to don our dress suits immediately upon our arrival at the hotel. At six o'clock, that number of the party, in evening dress, had assembled in the rotunda, where we found awaiting us representatives of the San Francisco Press and the California Baseball League. They escorted us to "Marchand's," where we partook of a dainty supper, topped off with most delicious California wines. Those present were Mr. Spalding, Captain

Anson, Captain Ward, Frank Lincoln, Newton MacMillin, Manager Jim Hart, Managers Harrison, Robinson and Finn, Messrs. Cory, Dressler, Crawford, Bannett and myself. Lincoln's wit and the baseball reminiscences of Jim Hart and Mr. Spalding shortened the time between the courses most delightfully, and at 8.30 we arose from the table, having had our first experience of San Francisco hospitality.

Repairing to the Baldwin Theatre we joined the balance of the Chicago and All-America teams, in full evening costume, and occupied the two proscenium boxes at the performance of "The Corsair." It is needless to say that the party were objects of interest to the audience. We reached San Francisco on the evening of the great parade of the Republicans of California, and the city was fairly alive with people. Market street was a long line of colored fire and pyrotechnics, while cheers ascended in such volume as to almost deafen one. The entire populace of the city and of all California seemed to have joined in the demonstration, and it was well on toward morning before even honest people went to bed. Were the members of our party among the revellers? Well, in all probability most of them could have been found very near the centre of the city, as long as the glare of the parade, the crowds and the handshaking of friends kept them there. With our arrival at San Francisco, most of us felt that the first stage of our trip was completed. Here we were to stop for two weeks before starting on our voyage, so we felt that we were at home for a time, at least. "Two weeks," did I say? Never before did time pass so rapidly to any of us, and when the day came for final adieus, and the big steamer cast off her cables and started upon her journey of 7200 miles, there was not a man among us who would not gladly have extended his stay indefinitely.

In no section of the United States possessing the same population to the square mile are Baseball enthusiasts more numerous than at San Francisco. They can play ball there all the year round, and their championship season begins when the seasons of the League and Association end. They have turned out some of the greatest ball-playing talent in America to-day, such men as Fogarty, Brown, Van Haltren, Brown, of New York, and others of equal ability and reputation, having come from the Pacific slope to don the uniforms of the great Eastern Clubs. In San Francisco they like close scores. They want no errors, and they would rather see a sixteen innings game than shake hands with the President. The clubs of their own League, through several seasons past, have put up a wonderful number of closely-contested games, in which it has been the exception that the combined runs of both teams in a game has exceeded eight or nine in number. They seem to gauge a player in California rather by his ability to stop runs than to get them. Yet, at the time of our visit to California, many of the most brilliant, skillful, and difficult-fielding players of the ball field were comparatively unknown in California. Indeed, it was not until Jim Hart took the Louisville Team there, in 1885, that Californians were enabled to understand just what degree of perfection in team-work and fielding a ball team could attain. When the Australian party visited the coast, the infield work of Williamson, Pfeffer, Ward, Burns, and Anson was a revelation to most Californians.

Something over 13,000 people turned out at the Haight street grounds to witness our initial game in San Francisco, and it has never ceased to be one of the regrets of the tour that the game did not prove a contest, or even a creditable exhibition. The day was perfect, and thousands lined the streets through which our carriages passed in parade on their way to the grounds. Cheer after cheer welcomed the players as the gates of the grounds were thrown open and the carriages filed upon the field. The great crowd arose to its feet and shouted itself hoarse as the band escorted first the All-Americas and then the Chicagos on to the grounds. The practice work of both teams was brilliant, and had the game been anywhere near as good, the expectant and good-natured crowd would have been entirely satisfied. The boys, however, were tired out with travel and the late hours they could hardly have avoided keeping after their arrival in San Francisco. In addition, every one of them was over-anxious to put up a strong game of ball, and their over-anxiety made them the more nervous as the game progressed. I never saw men work harder or try more determinedly to play good ball; but it was of no use. Anson himself "fell down" at first before two innings had passed. Baldwin, who had pitched such a grand game at Denver, seemed to have little or no command of the ball, and Chicago's stone-wall infield seemed unable to field a little bit. The crowd was disappointed but good-natured, and generously ap-

plauded the occasional bits of good fielding that shone through the long
series of errors. As for the players themselves, I do not think I ever
saw a more completely disappointed lot of men. Had each of them
been out a hundred-dollar note as the result of the day's play, they
could not have felt more dissatisfied ; but they sensibly put a bright face
upon the situation and determined to show Californians what kind of a
game they could put up before they left.

The second day after, the All-Americas faced the Greenwood and
Moran team at the Haight street grounds and suffered a crushing defeat. Crane was unsteady in his delivery, and although his support
worked hard, it made errors at critical points, while the local batsmen
rarely failed to get in a hit at the proper time. Unfortunately for the
All-Americas, Anson acted as umpire and gave Captain Ward's men
a long way the worst of it in most of his decisions. But for this fact the
score would undoubtedly have been less one-sided.

Two days later the All-Americas met the Pioneers and John Healy
pitched. It would undoubtedly have been a winning game but for the
poor fielding support accorded him. A total of eleven errors, most of
them costly, were divided up among Hanlon, Crane, Manning, Van
Haltren, Wood and Fogarty. The absence of Ward, who had yielded
to an inclination to run up the bay for a day's quail shooting, made a
big hole in All-America's infield, and was, no doubt, responsible to a
great degree for the poor work that resulted. Purcell pitched a fine
game for the Pioneers, and to his work more than to anything else was
due the victory which 3000 spectators applauded heartily at the end of
the ninth inning. Meantime Anson's men had gone down to Stockton,
and while the All-Americas were losing a game in San Francisco, were
engaged in one of the prettiest games of the tour with the Stocktons.
Tener did some pretty work in the points for Chicago, Stockton's batsmen failing to get more than two clean hits off Tener's delivery. It
was too dark at the end of the ninth inning to play off the tie, which
stood two and two, and the game was consequently never won.

Stockton came up to San Francisco the following day, November 9th,
to see what it could do against the All-Americas, and the latter, stung
by two successive defeats at the hands of local California teams, turned
upon the champions and gave them such a beating as doubtless left a

lasting impression of the fielding and batting abilities of Ward's team. Ward himself covered short and his presence made a wonderful difference. The Stocktons pitched Baker, who at that time was one of the promising pitchers of the coast, and he was simply pounded all over the field. The game was certainly a beautiful exhibition of the strong points in baseball. Crane pitched a great game, and little Earle caught him in a style that won him many hearty bursts of applause. Hanlon covered third, while Van Haltren fielded centre, and smoother team-work than that done by the entire combination is not often seen. The base running was particularly good. Just how hard the boys worked, and how determined they were to make the Stocktons feel their power, can be seen by reference to the score, which shows a total of 17 stolen bases, of which 7 were taken by Fogarty alone. In a word, All-America taught the Californian champions a good deal that they did not before know about the game, and after that, neither the Stocktons nor the Pioneers would meet either the All-America or the Chicago teams during our stay. On November 10th the crack Haverlys had a try at Anson's men and were well beaten in a pretty contest. Incell, the star pitcher of the coast, and one whom many of the Eastern clubs were after at that time, filled the box for the Californians and pitched a good game, although his support was weak. The Californians, on the other hand, could not hit Baldwin, and the big lead Chicago had secured in the third inning, was not thereafter broken.

The work of the visiting teams against the local talent had served to offset the rather unfavorable impression created by the character of our first game in San Francisco, and there were nearly 7000 people present a week later, when, on a beautiful day, the Chicago and All-America teams met upon the Haight street grounds for their second game, which, while not without a dash of poor work here and there, was marked by fielding of a character that I have never seen surpassed for brilliancy. Tener and Van Haltren were the opposing pitchers, and each pitched effectively, although Van Haltren's in-field support was at times faulty. Chicago's in-field, however, at no time during its entire existence ever put up such a wonderful fielding game, and the enthusiasm of the crowd knew no bounds at half a dozen stages of the contest.

The following week the teams went to Los Angeles, where, upon

November 14th and 15th, they played two games in the presence of several thousand Southern Californians. All-America played all around Anson's men in both games, whitewashing them in the first game, with Healy and Earle in the box and Baldwin and Daly as the opposing battery, and beating them by a score of 7 to 4 in the second game, with Crane and Earle in the points against Tener and Daly for Chicago. The teams returned to San Francisco on Friday morning, the 16th. It was intended that a farewell game should be played the following day, on the eve of our departure for Australia. The elements decided otherwise, however, and a steady rain killed all plans for a farewell contest. Our steamer, which was to have sailed Saturday afternoon, was delayed twenty-four hours by the non-arrival of the Eastern mails, however, and we did not get away, in consequence, until the afternoon of Sunday, November 18th.

It must not be inferred from this account of our stay in California that we did nothing but play ball. On the contrary, the boys were simply overwhelmed with attentions from so many different quarters, that it became impossible to accept all the invitations extended, or to find time for sleep between the many pleasant entertainments arranged for us. The little supper which some of us had enjoyed at Marchand's on the night of our arrival, was simply a forerunner of the long line of banquets, dinner parties, receptions and theatre parties which extended over the entire period of our stay. Nearly every member of our party managed to take a tour through the Chinese quarters, and Bob Pettit, Captain Anson, Tom Daly and myself enjoyed not a few delightful rides on horseback around the picturesque environs of the city.

The remarkable sights to be seen in Chinatown proved so attractive that many of our party made two, and some of them three, visits among these Children of the Orient. I made the journey the second night after our arrival at San Francisco, in company with President Spalding, Manager Robinson and President Mann of the California League, Manager Hart and Newton MacMillan, the *Sun* correspondent, our escort being Sergeant Burdsoll of the San Francisco Police Force, and I feel that I am quite safe in saying that no pen, however clever, could adequately depict the revolting, and yet fascinating, sights we saw. The illustrations of vice and crime prevalent in the Chinese quarters of the city, which have appeared in our illustrated publications from time to time, have not been exaggerated—indeed, they have fallen far short of depicting the horror of it. Chinatown is perhaps six blocks long by three wide, and it is steadily growing. The Celestials have crowded all the white people out of their district, and have their own government, their own mercantile houses, their own water works and their own courts; and although they are under the City Authorities, to a great extent they live independently of the municipal laws. It is almost impossible to apprehend a criminal among them, and equally difficult to convict him when apprehended. They have established their gambling-houses within walls of impenetrable steel plate. The sentinel stands at the doorway, and in dangerous times gives signal, that they may shut out intruders. As we passed one of these houses Sergeant Burdsoll pointed out to me the picket on duty in front of the brilliantly-lighted passage which entered the building.

"That fellow," said the Sergeant, "looks half asleep, doesn't he?"

The Chinaman was leaning against the doorway, his hat pulled over his features and his hands tucked way under his blouse.

"Yes," replied our party, "he certainly doesn't look as though he is attending to his post."

"Well now, you just watch him," said the Sergeant, and pulling his hat over his eyes, he sauntered slowly across the street until he reached the curbstone, where he made a sudden dash for the doorway. The seemingly sleeping Celestial, however, started as though suddenly touched by an electric wire. He threw both hands across the doorway, barring the officer's progress, and at the same time uttered a peculiar cry. Ten feet beyond the doorway we could see the heavy steel-plated inner doors close with a bang, and almost at the same instant the outer doors came to with a crash, and the Chinese sentry was left standing upon the pavement in the presence of the officer. The Sergeant returned to us, and remarked, with a smile, that a Chinaman is never so watchful as when he appears to be asleep. "That fellow as he stood there," said the Sergeant, "was sweeping the street with his glance in both directions for half a block."

"Can you not batter down their doors and make prisoners of them?" I asked.

The officer smiled. "My dear sir," said he, "it would take three hours to enter these places, and when we got in, not a Chinaman would be inside. What would be the use of it, any way? No power on earth can check the crime and vice that exist in these quarters to-day. I might have arrested that sentinel whom the closing of the doors left upon the sidewalk, but what good would it have done? I could have brought him before a Police Court, and might have arraigned him upon the charge of resisting an officer, or of vagrancy, or upon some other convenient charge, but he would probably have been fined and let go; and even though imprisoned, his fine would have been paid and he would have been let go, and even while he was imprisoned there would have been hundreds of Chinamen to take his place at the Gambling House door."

The methods of living and the crowded conditions of the dwellings in the Chinese quarter are simply beyond the power of human conception until seen. Many a Chinaman, for instance, will lease a building four stories high and by deepening the foundations will make a six-story building of it. Then he will construct partitions in the rooms and hallways until he has secured accommodations for about four or six hundred Chinamen in a building which could not accommodate more than thirty or forty Americans comfortably. These apartments he rents to Chinamen for twenty-five or fifty cents a week. One room which we entered was eight by ten feet in dimensions, with a ceiling perhaps eight feet high, and in this room, reclining upon bunks arranged like the sections of a sleeping-car, were thirteen Chinamen. Their bunks are practically their rooms—their dwellings, in which they keep their personal effects, their clothing, their little tin box in which they cook their rice, their chop sticks, their slippers and their opium outfit, without which no Chinaman could exist. The streets of the entire district swarm with Mongolians, the only Caucasians to be seen being the officers of the law, or tourists like ourselves. Into foul-smelling lodging-houses, into opium joints thick with sickening vapors, down through underground passage ways, where it would be death for a white man to go alone, into Joss Houses, with their hideous idols, their burning tapers and their weird-sounding drums and tom-toms, into the din and through the fantastic surroundings of the Chinese Theatre, with hordes of almond-eyed, villanous-looking, and at times murderous faces peering at us from every nook and corner, our little party threaded its way. We grew dizzy from the overpowering odors, and were anxious to again breathe the air of a Christianized and civilized community. No religion save idolatry is known in Chinatown; virtue is unknown there. The people have brought the heathenish customs and horrible practices of their barbarous country with them to San Francisco, and cling to them with a tenacity that shows the hopelessnes of converting them to our views of life and religion and of their ever becoming desirable citizens.

The attentions of which our party were the recipients did not, by any means, come from the baseball element alone, although to the officers of the California League we are indebted for much of the warm hospitality that made our stay in their city so pleasant. The journalists of San Francisco and the merchants were equally attentive and courteous. Mr. Waller Wallace, of the California *Spirit of the Times*, entertained President Spalding, Captain and Mrs. Anson, Mr. and Mrs. Ed Williamson, Captain John M. Ward, Captain Hanlon, Newton MacMillan and myself, in charming style, at his Oakland residence; while the Press Club, on the evening of November 12th, entertained the Press representatives of our party, with President Spalding and Captains Ward and Anson, in a delightful entertainment and banquet at the Press Club rooms. Upon the following day a number of us were entertained at the Merchants' Club, by Mr. Frederick Stratton, the law partner of Ex-Congressman Miller, the Hon. Charles Alexander Bird, of the California State legislature, Mr. Al Evans, Secretary of the Bonanza and Consolidated California Mining Companies, and a number of merchants of high standing upon the coast. All seemed to be as familiar with baseball as they were with mining stocks, mercantile methods, briefs and depositions, or legislative affairs; and a more congenial company, capable of more thoroughly enjoying the many reminiscences and stories of old-time players, certainly never sat down to a two hours' dinner.

On the evening of November 17th, the day prior to our departure for Australia, Mr. Spalding tendered a farewell banquet to the members of the San Francisco Press and California League at the Baldwin Hotel.

Covers were laid for seventy-five guests, among whom were many prominent, well-known citizens. The banquet hall and tables were magnificently decorated with designs in which baseball paraphernalia and implements were a prominent feature. Perhaps, the menu card, which was the result of Frank Lincoln's ingenuity, was among the most remarkable ever laid opposite a plate. On the inner side of the " Score Card," as Frank had designated his production, was printed the list of viands, headed with the timely injunction, " Play Ball." Among the courses were " Eastern Oysters on the Home Run," " Green Turtle, a la Kangaroo," " Petit Pate, a la Spalding," " Asperges, a la Willow," " Petit Pois Française. a la 'Over the Fence,' " " Stewed Terrapin, a la Ward," " Frisco Turkey, a la 'Foul,' " " Mashed Peaches, a la 'Soft Ball,'" " Baked Sweet Potatoes, a la 'Hot Grounder,'" " English Plum Pudding, a la ' Hard Hit,' " " Brandy, a la ' Hot Ball,'" and other equally remarkable dishes. The menu card was circular in form, its exterior representing the cover of a baseball. There were many delightful evenings spent before the tour of the American team was completed, but I am sure that none was more delightful than that of our farewell banquet at San Francisco.

The speech-making was of an impromptu order, the remarks of the speakers being filled with baseball nuggets, happy sayings and humorous incidents. " Early California ball-players," by Judge Hunt, of the Superior Court, fairly bubbled with quiet humor and bristled with quaint allusion ; " The National League Champions—the New York Baseball Club," was responded to by ex-Senator James F. Grady, of New York, who paid a magnificent tribute to the great team that won the championship of 1888. " The San Francisco Press," was treated by Mr. W. N. Hart, of the San Francisco Press Club. " The Good Ship 'Alameda,'" brought Captain Henry G. Morse to his feet and gave our party our first view of the good-hearted, clever commander of the steamer which carried us 7000 miles across the Pacific. " A. J. Spalding and the Australian Trip," was responded to by Mr. Samuel F. Shortridge ; " Old California," by Mr. Durkee ; " The Chicago Nine," by Captain Anson ; " The All-Americas," by Captain Ward ; and " The Baseball Cricketers," by George Wright. In a happily worded address, President Spalding thanked the Press and the Baseball people of the Pacific coast for the magnificent reception tendered us, and for the warm. hospitality that we had not failed to find in every quarter since our arrival at San Francisco.

On the afternoon of the day of our departure a number of the boys went down to the dock to inspect the "Alameda." She was by no means a large ship, but was neat and trim-looking, perfectly equipped, and with room enough to accommodate 125 passengers. The decks were spacious, and in the warmer latitudes were to be protected from the sun's rays by an awning. A well-stocked library and saloon was located just above the dining-room, and forward and aft of this were the deck state-rooms, the most desirable upon the ship in tropical climates, also a big smoking- and card-room, where the boys congregated many an evening during the voyage or spent the lazy hours of the afternoon. Altogether, we were favorably impressed with our steamer and our captain, and despite our regret at leaving the hospitable shores of California, we were anxious for the novelty of starting upon our voyage to Australia.

The day of our departure finally arrived, Sunday, November 18th, and it dawned gray and sullen, with the rain still descending in a generous shower. Toward noon, however, the clouds broke and we began to hope for fair weather. None of the boys breakfasted at an early hour, it being fully 11 A. M. before they began to show up in any numbers in the rotunda of the hotel. About noon, myself and my fellow correspondent, Newton MacMillan, or "Mac," as I shall hereafter refer to him, accompanied by several San Francisco journalists, entered a carriage and drove to the steamer. The wharf-house and the steamer itself were crowded with friends of the tourists, and a chorus of shouts went up as our party of newspaper men emerged from our equipage. Not over eighty passengers had been booked for the voyage, but several hundred were upon the steamer's deck, friends of the departing tourists, and fully a thousand more crowded the wharf. At the rail, near the staging, stood Manager Jim Hart, Captain and Mrs. Anson and Ned Williamson and his wife, chatting with scores of friends, while President and Mrs. Spalding were the centre of another group near by. The boys leaned over the rail and chatted, and joked, and laughed their farewells with friends on the dock. All was noise and confusion up to two o'clock, the hour at which the steamer was to sail, when the last call for visitors to leave the deck was given. Shortly after that hour Captain Morse took his post at the starboard end of "the bridge," his big figure set off to advantage by his gold-laced uniform of navy blue, and raised his hand to the sailors on the gang-plank, and to those who stood by the steamer's moorings on the dock. There was breathless silence on board, the quick rattling of the chains, the splashes of the cables as they fell into the water, the thud of the gang-plank as it dropped on the deck, and then the "Alameda" began to move slowly from the dock. Every passenger pressed toward the rail, and cheer after cheer went up from the deck, to be answered by those on the wharf.

FROM SAN FRANCISCO TO HONOLULU.

The big ship swung slowly out into the bay, and within a few minutes all we could distinguish of our friends on the dock was a dimly outlined aggregation, and now and then a flutter of a white handkerchief. Presently the ship headed for the Golden Gate and we were off upon our tour of the World. Ah, it was delightfully invigorating—the motion of the ship, the refreshing air that came from the headlands and rushed through the rigging as she glided rapidly over the smooth surface of the Bay, past the shipping, and around the peninsula upon which San Francisco is located, our party still lingering at the larboard-rail, loath to relinquish their gaze upon their country's shores. As we neared the bar the ocean swell became perceptible : and when we passed the bluffs that form the Golden Gate, and steamed out upon the bosom of old Ocean itself, the "Alameda" began to rise and fall with the long swell that characterizes the Pacific from coast to coast. The sun was shining when we left the dock, but the weather was erratic, and before we were fairly out of sight of the coast the land was hidden by a fog which settled around our ship and rendered necessary the frequent sounding of the whistle. Some ten miles out we stopped to let off our pilot, and then proceeded on our journey, bound for Honolulu, a distance of 2100 miles.

In addition to our own party, which numbered thirty-five, there were perhaps twenty-five others. Among the most conspicuous of these was a big, broad-shouldered, dark-complexioned man, who looked as though he would be a perfect terror in a "free for all." This was Prof. William Miller, the wrestler, whose name is known in professional circles and

among lovers of athletics all over the world. He and his wife were
bound for Melbourne. A somewhat effeminate, sandy-haired young
man, with a weak-looking red moustache and still weaker-looking eyes,
was known to our party during the first week of our voyage as Sir
James Willoughby. He affected an English accent, and let it be quietly
understood about the ship that he was simply out for "a bit of a tour,"
and expected to return some time during the course of a year or two,
by way of India and Europe, to England. He was very much addicted to
champagne and cigarettes, and before the trip was over afforded us
considerable amusement. A tall, loose-jointed, awkward-looking man,
with a gray beard and bronzed complexion, and with an eye that seemed
to look through you when it looked at you, was Major-General Strange,
of the English army. He had for years been quartered in India, and had
taken part in that most memorable of the world's revolts, the Sepoy
Insurrection. Frank Marian, and his trim-looking wife, with their over-
precocious baby, were a pair of American light comedians upon their
way to fill their first engagement in Sydney. Both Marian and his wife
were accomplished banjoists and guitarists, and their ability as musicians
contributed much to our entertainment and enjoyment.

Colonel J. M. House and a Mr. Turner, stock-yard men of Chicago,
were both hale, hearty, jolly fellows, a little beyond the prime of life,
and were taking a trip to Australia for business and pleasure. House
was really a good fellow, and did much to afford that diversion and
excitement so much needed and so much appreciated by the voyager.
Before we had been out many days he instituted the old game of "Calcutta Pool," in which we all took a warm interest until the winning
coterie narrowed down to so small a number that the "lambs" of the
party got tired of the game and drew out. "Calcutta Pool" is simply
the selling of auction pools upon the distance traveled by the steamer
for twenty-four hours, ending with noon on the day in question. For
instance, fifty tickets consecutively numbered from 291 to 340, this
being the probable minimum and maximum of the ship's record, are
issued and distributed to as many holders, in return for what is practically an entrance fee, at $1.00 each. The tickets are then put up at
auction and change hands according to the degree of confidence felt by
the respective bidders in their numbers. If a man held 302, for instance,

and was convinced that the ship would sail 310, he would sell to some one who wanted 302, and himself bid for the latter number. The auction is, therefore, likely to increase the pool of $50.00 to $200.00, or even $300.00. Our first pool, with an entrance fee of 50 cts., was in the nature of an experiment, and was consequently a small one, aggregating $105.00; $45.00 of which went to the holder of ticket 307; $30.00 going as a second prize to the holder of ticket 302, and an equal amount going as a third prize to the holder of ticket 312. The numbers of the tickets 302 and 312, the second and third prizes, being five above and five below the number of the first prize. The pools were sold every morning after breakfast, and it was great sport until the boys began to be too much in earnest over it, when for fear of unpleasant consequences we mutually decided to drop the practice.

It took our party some time to become accustomed to the sailors' method of dividing the twelve hours of the day, and of being able to distinguish the hour by the number of bells which were sounded regularly amidship every half-hour. To the sailor the twelve hours are divided into three watches, namely: from noon to four o'clock, from four o'clock to eight o'clock, and from eight o'clock until midnight. At 12.30 P. M., half an hour after the noon hour, the ship's bell rings once; at 1 P. M. it rings twice, at 1.30 P. M. it rings three times and at 2 P. M. it sounds four times; at 4 P. M. it rings eight bells, this being the greatest number. Then it begins over again, ringing one bell for 4.30 P. M., and continuing every half-hour until it rings eight bells at eight o'clock, after which it begins at one bell again and increases up to eight bells at midnight. Our party were quite startled the second afternoon out from San Francisco, when at three o'clock the ship's bell began a horrible clanging, and we saw a lot of miscellaneously clad seamen running up from the ship's steerage and galleys, springing upon the top of the cabins and boiler rooms, where they quickly unrolled the reels of hose and attached them to the ship's hydrants, while a score or more of men stood by the life buoys and the long rows of water buckets which stood near the deck. The performance caused more than one pale cheek among the passengers not accustomed to sea-voyaging; but we afterward took a great interest in the performance, which we found, upon inquiry, to be the daily fire-practice of the ship's crew.

It requires just about a week to make the journey from San Francisco to the Sandwich Islands, and to quote a much traveled English gentleman whom I met upon the voyage, it is perhaps the most delightful sea-journey, in every way, that one can take. The great ocean, as indicated by its name, was as quiet and peaceful during those days in November, when our party crossed it, as an inland lake. The sun shone down upon us from a cloudless sky. The salt air was pure and healthful. The breezes that came to us from the spice groves and sugar plantations upon the Sandwich Islands, were warm and gentle enough to remind us of a June day at home. The surroundings and conditions of our new life upon shipboard were just novel enough to be delightful; and in looking back over our journey around the globe, I can recall no part of it that was pleasanter than those days upon the Pacific.

An ocean steamship is a world in itself, wholly apart from the rest of the world, and to the space within the limits of its hull must the voyager look for all in the way of comfort, enjoyment, entertainment and diversion. After the first four days the novelty of ocean travel is gone, and one grows a little tired, perhaps, of looking out over the rolling waters. His mind then seizes upon everything and anything that will relieve the monotony. It was so with our party. The fondness for games of chance, of all kinds that ingenious brains have hit upon, took possession of the "Alameda's" passengers before we were three days out of San Francisco. After that, it was ten to one that any man who made an offer of a bet within hearing of one or more of his fellow passengers, would not escape without having his bet booked. We bet upon everything and anything—water, wind, the kind of soup we would have for dinner, the last man to leave the table, and no one knows what not. As an illustration of the betting craze, the following instance is a good one: In the card-room, one morning, Fogarty cried out, "Twenty-five to one that the ship does not go down before we reach Honolulu."

"I will take you," said Captain Anson, plunging his hand into his pocket, and then looking foolish as he realized what he was about to bet upon.

No more interesting event can occur at sea than the meeting of another vessel. The first instance of the kind that our party experienced occurred upon our fifth day out. Ed Crane, Tom Brown, Fogarty, Daly, John Ward and myself were seated on deck near the saloon, about eleven o'clock that evening, when the entire ship and the surrounding waters were suddenly illuminated by a powerful calcium light on the top of the wheel house. We leaped from our chairs and went forward to find that we were signaling the steamer bound from Honolulu to San Francisco. She had left America before the Presidential election had taken place and so knew nothing whatever of its result, as the Hawaiian Islands have no cable connection of any kind. The signal agreed upon was one rocket in case of Harrison's success and two in case of his defeat. Two miles of ocean rolled between the two ships, but we could clearly discern the lights and hull of the "Australia" in the bright moonlight that flooded the ocean. The mate brought a big rocket from the wheel house, leaned it against the rail and touched it off. There was a flash of light, a downward shooting of yellow fire, and the great rocket ascended into the air, leaving a fiery trail across the sky, until it burst into a hundred colored stars. There is something wonderfully impressive in signaling a vessel at sea—a sort of red letter event in the voyage, made all the more remarkable by surrounding conditions. The "Australia's" lights gleamed over the waters for perhaps twenty minutes, during which time beautiful rockets crossed the heavens with as many lines of light in answer to our signal, and then the ship and her lights vanished from our sight.

Before leaving San Francisco, President Spalding was fortunate enough to meet with the English Agent at Liverpool, of the Chicago, Burlington and Quincy railroad, over whose line we had traveled from Chicago to Denver. The result of this meeting was a lengthy discussion between the Englishman, Mr. S. S. Parry, and Mr. Spalding as to the advisability of our party's returning by way of Europe. The outcome of this discussion was an arrangement between Mr. Parry and Mr. Spalding, by which, upon his return to Liverpool, Parry would visit such European points as Mr. Spalding was desirous of playing games at, and cable the result of his investigations to us at Australia. If he found that indications were favorable to our reception in London, and throughout Great Britain, in which country Mr. Spalding was most desirous of giving exhibitions of the American National Game, Mr.

Parry was to wire us to that effect, and Mr. Spalding would then deter-mine upon a future course of action.

To return by way of Europe would necessitate the expenditure of thousands of dollars for transportation through a section in which little or no interest would be felt in Athletics. Yet Mr. Spalding did not know but that the expenditure would be a wise one from a business standpoint. The press correspondents had been taken into his confidence and given his views before leaving San Francisco, and Parry departed for New York and England about the same time that our party left for Australia. By mutual arrangement the papers represented by the special corres-pondents of our party were placed in possession of all the details of Mr. Spalding's plans, with the understanding that they were to be pub-lished on the Sunday following our departure from America ; and no member of our party save the correspondents, Mr. Spalding himself, and Captain Anson, were apprised of our possible return by another route. After we were upon the high seas, however, the matter was allowed to leak out, with a view of learning how the members themselves felt upon the subject. The mere mention of such a possibility aroused much enthusiasm and during the balance of the voyage, and up to the time when it was finally decided, in Melbourne, probable routes were discussed with the pleasantest anticipations, and everything descriptive of the countries and people of continental Europe, Asia and Africa, that the ship's library afforded, was eagerly read by the boys.

Had we left San Francisco Saturday afternoon, the time set for our departure, we would have arrived in Honolulu the following Saturday morning. As it was, however, we were a day late, and Saturday, No-vember 24th, passed with our ship ploughing through the ocean, 150 miles from the Hawaiian Islands at nightfall. We had been scheduled to play a game of ball in Hawaii, where there is a very large baseball element, and as Harry Simpson, our advance agent, had sailed from San Francisco a week ahead of us to prepare for our coming in the Sandwich Islands, we could, in fancy, picture the disappointment of the Hawaiians, to say nothing of the despair of Simpson and of the Recep-tion Committee which we doubted not had been appointed to receive us, when the day dawned, and grew, and finally passed away without our steamer's being sighted ; and it can be truly said that the disap-

5

pointment was not wholly confined to Hawaii. All the way across the Pacific our party had hoped, against hope, that the ship might make up the day we had lost and land us in the Sandwich Islands on time, after all. This, however, could not be done, and we were compelled to content ourselves with the inevitable.

On the morning of the 25th of November, however, the lookout on the bridge of the steamer sighted land just as day began to break. Such an event on shipboard cannot long be kept from the passengers, and, while the morning was still gray, our party tumbled out of their berths and, having hastily arranged their toilets, came upon deck, anxious for the first glimpse of Honolulu. All that was to be seen at first was a faint shadow upon the distant horizon. As the "Alameda" continued on her way this began to assume more definiteness, and the rugged peaks of the mountains finally loomed up against the brightening sky. An hour later the bright green of the island's verdure became plainly discernible, and then the city of Honolulu itself, with its little fleet of shipping in the bay. Nowhere in the world, save perhaps in Ireland, have I seen foliage and vegetation of such a truly emerald hue as in the Sandwich Islands. The land is of volcanic origin, and the rugged sides of the huge mountains, which rise directly out of the sea, and between which lie beautiful valleys rich in the luxuriant foliage and verdure of the tropics, are covered by a seemingly unbroken mantle of beautiful green that is as pleasant to the eye as the sight of land, of any kind, is always delightful to the voyager. As we neared Diamond Head the ship's engine slowed down, and by the time we had left the ocean's swell for the placid waters of the harbor, all the passengers were clustered at the bow, anxious to witness · every incident of the landing.

As we drew nearer, a ship's boat put off from the dock and soon reached our side. It brought to us Mr. Geoffrey, the steamship company's agent, Harry Simpson, Mr. F. W. Whitney and Mr. George W. Smith, who is a cousin to President Spalding, a prominent citizen of Honolulu and chairman of the committee appointed to receive us. Three or four dark-skinned natives followed, each bearing a basket filled with wreaths of flowers called by the natives "Leis," and indicative of welcome and good will. One of these wreaths was placed about the neck of each member of our party. Meanwhile, the steamer's cables had been made fast, and our good ship was slowly drawn to her dock, while fully 2000 people looked upon us as though we were visitors from another world. In the centre of the assemblage stood the king's band, "The Royal Hawaiian," in uniforms of white duck, which contrasted admirably with their dark complexions, and, as a cheer went up from our party in response to that of the crowd upon the dock, they began to play "The Star-Spangled Banner," "Yankee Doodle," "The Girl I Left Behind Me," "Auld Lang Syne," and other airs familiar to American ears.

It was a beautiful morning, the rising sun gilding the mountain sides and brightening the plantations along the shore, while it distinctly outlined each individual of the rapidly increasing crowd upon the dock. The officers and crew of the U. S. Cruiser "Alert," which lay a few hundred yards away, were on deck and welcomed the "Alameda" with a hearty cheer as we drew alongside. Upon our steamer all was excitement and eager anticipation. The strains of the magnificent band on the shore, the crowds of Americans and government officers attired in white duck and white straw hats, the sight of land, and a strange land at that, after seven days of continuous ocean sailing, and the realization that we were expected and that great preparations had been made for our coming, had the effect of strangely impressing every one of our party. Cheer after cheer went up from the dock, and the boys responded, but in a spasmodic, discordant chorus, that told how little their voices were at command. They were big lusty fellows, with plenty of muscle and plenty of nerve, and eyes that probably had not seen tears since the days of their boyhood, but just at this time, when they wanted to cheer their loudest and to seem their happiest, did their voices choke and their eyes fill with tears that came unbidden. Only the voyager can appreciate the joy that our party felt at landing upon that beautiful morning in Hawaii.

The crowd on the dock was characteristic of Honolulu. The Hawaiians are dark-complexioned, straight-haired fellows, with regular features and bright, intelligent faces. Their attire of white linen is wonderfully becoming and added greatly to the attractiveness of the scene as it appeared from the deck of the steamer. Score upon score of pretty girls, for the most part dressed in white, chatted with their escorts and critically sized up the stalwart fellows of our party. Our arrival at Honolulu was evidently an event of no small importance. Upon his arrival a week before Simpson had been cordially received, and the interval up to the time of our arrival had been one of pleasurable anticipation for nearly every resident of the city. Without telegraph communication of any kind, the arrival of a steamer in Hawaii is an event of interest, even upon ordinary occasions; but a steamer was doubly welcome, upon which came a score of the greatest ball-players of America, who came, too, that they might give Hawaiians an exhibition such as they had never before seen, of a game already a great favorite with them.

We had been expected, as I have said, the day before, and on Saturday morning all Honolulu was awake early to welcome us, and a big crowd assembled on the steamship docks to watch for the signal announcing our arrival. The royal band was in waiting, and the government tug "Eleu" steamed up, ready to convey a party of prominent citizens as far as Diamond Head to welcome the coming guests. Arrangements had even been made to take the port physician with the party, so that he might board the steamer at the earliest possible moment. As time passed and no steamer came, the disappointment may be imagined. The day was a fine sample of Hawaiian weather at that season, warm and beautifully clear. Business had been suspended and everybody was upon the street in holiday attire. The band upon the dock allayed impatience by playing for the crowd which watched and waited for the steamer all through the morning, and indeed we were not given up until after three o'clock that afternoon. Not having arrived Saturday, it was, for some reason, imagined that we would not reach Honolulu before Monday, the 26th, and the programme intended for Saturday was, therefore, put aside in the mind of everybody until Monday morning. No such thing, as our arrival on Sunday morning, seemed to have occurred to anybody, and, consequently, when the ship was sighted at six o'clock, the town was startled by telephone messages which went over every wire in the city, to the effect that the "Alameda" was off Diamond Head. In half an hour the streets were astir with people, and again the band had assembled with the crowd.

While our party had been shaking hands with the members of the

Reception Committee the steamer had reached her berth. The companion-ways were let down and our party, descending to the dock, entered carriages in waiting. We were driven rapidly through the picturesque streets, along which grew great palm trees, banana, and stately cocoanuts, bearing their clusters of heavy-shelled fruit, and then passed on, by the palace of King Kalakuau, to the Royal Hawaiian Hotel, which, standing in the centre of beautifully-laid-out grounds, rich in every

THE "ALAMEDA" AT HER DOCK IN HONOLULU.

variety of tree, plant, and shrub known to tropical climates, looked more like the palatial residence of some Sandwich Island or Cuban sugar king than anything else to which I can liken it. Scarcely had we taken seats at the breakfast-table in the great, airy dining-hall, its windows extending from floor to ceiling and opening on spacious balconies that surrounded the house, than the superb band which had welcomed us at the dock began a concert at the music stand beneath the windows. This band is the musical pride of Honolulu, and is maintained at the expense of the Government. Under the leadership of Band Master Berger it has attained a reputation that reaches far beyond the Hawaiian shores ; and what harmony it does make ! The Hawaiian Band has few equals, and no superiors, in America. Ah, it was delightful, that breakfast in Hawaii ! The tables filled with great bowls of luscious yellow oranges and juicy bananas, the moisture even yet upon

THE ROYAL HAWAIIAN BAND AT THE MUSIC STAND.

the broken stems, which had been taken from the parent branch not half an hour before ; the air laden with the scent of tropical plants ; the grounds crowded with dark-skinned, dark-eyed Kanakas, in their cool-looking costumes of white duck and flannel ; the bright sunlight that warmed and beautified every growing thing around us, and the glorious music, all combined to make our experience more like a dream than a reality. Instead of the customary dish of oatmeal at breakfast, we were

KING KALAKAUA, THE QUEEN AND SUITE ON THE PALACE GROUNDS.

served with the native dish of " Poi," a pink-colored mush, which, when eaten with rich Hawaiian cream and a covering of sugar, is very palatable. The native method of eating "poi" is novel. The forefinger is plunged into the dish, given a peculiar twist, and withdrawn with a mouthful of the food clinging to it; the lips close over the morsel and finger, leaving the latter, when it is withdrawn, ready for another attack on the dish.

After breakfast we adjourned to the balconies and again heard the

A NATIVE FAMILY ENJOYING ITS NATIONAL DISH—POI.

sweet strains of the "Aloha Oe," or welcome song, that had greeted us at the dock. The prelude is played by the band, and then the musicians rest their instruments upon their arms, and sing with exquisite harmony their "Aloha Oe" in the melodious language of the Kanakas. Air after air was played for our amusement as we stood in the midst of our tropical surroundings enjoying every breath we breathed and every strain we heard. We were finally informed by the Chairman of the Recep-

tion Committee that His Majesty, the King, had extended our party an
invitation to call upon him at his palace, 11 o'clock being the designated time. At that hour the Royal Band stepped from the music stand
and formed in front of the hotel ; Clarence Duval, in full drum-major
regalia, taking position at the head. President Spalding and United
States Minister Merrill walked down the steps behind the band, and
the Chicago and All-America teams, together with the other members
of our party, followed in double file, the ladies accompanying in carriages.
When all were in line, Clarence tossed his baton in the air, Band Master
Berger raised his hand, and the band poured fourth a burst of harmony
as the procession moved down the walk toward the gate of the grounds,
and then along the avenue to the King's Palace.

The grounds of the Royal Palace are a picture of tropical beauty.
We entered the great gateway and proceeded up the narrow avenue to
the massive porticoed entrance of the palace, where the band stepped
to one side and continued playing, as with hats off we ascended the
steps, Minister Merrill and President Spalding leading. We were met
on the balcony by members of the King's Cabinet and were shown by
attendants to the blue room of the palace, where we deposited our
hats and canes and awaited developments. Presently Minister Merrill
took President Spalding's arm and requested the balance of the party to
fall in line. Mrs. Spalding, escorted by Mr. George Smith, followed
Messrs. Merrill and Spalding, and after them came Mr. and Mrs. Frank
Lincoln, Captain and Mrs. Anson, Ned and Mrs. Williamson, Captains
Ward and Hanlon and the members of the Chicago and All-America
teams and Press representatives. We filed across the great hall, past
lines of ancestral paintings that decorated the walls and throne room, the
latter an imposing apartment, perhaps 100 by 150 feet in extent.
The King, attired in citizen's clothes, stood before his throne at the
further end of the room, while a Gentleman of Honor, in court costume,
was on either side. His Majesty extended his hand to Minister Merrill
and President Spalding as the two approached, and then President
Spalding introduced each passing guest as the line filed by, the King
bowing in acknowledgment of each introduction. The fifty or more
visitors had all been introduced and had assembled on the side of the
room opposite the doorway as the King turned pleasantly to Messrs.

Spalding and Merrill and shook hands cordially with both. The three chatted and laughed for five minutes longer and then the American Minister and Mr. Spalding bowed and turned to the doorway, the entire party following them into the great hallway and saluting the King as they made their exit. Here we registered our names upon the court register, admired the royal paintings, viewed the spacious and splendidly decorated dining hall and reception rooms, and finally, assembling upon the balcony, were escorted back to the hotel by the Royal Band, which again reëntered the music stand and played airs from the popular operas and composers, while the members of our party sat upon the balconies of the hotel and enjoyed their cigars.

Upon the return from the palace, the question of a game for that afternoon began to be eagerly discussed. It was well understood that the Hawaiian law, a statute of the old missionary times, prohibited all forms of Sunday amusements, and President Spalding, in answer to questions put him on our arrival, stated that it was his purpose to respect that law to the letter. About noon, however, the members of the Reception Committee drew up a petition to President Spalding requesting him to have the team play a game of ball that afternoon, and setting forth that the signers would bear any and all expense incurred, of any kind whatever. Duplicates of this petition had been made and placed in the hotel and other public places, and within an hour half a dozen of them, bearing nearly a thousand names, were handed to President Spalding. He received them upon the balcony, glanced over them, and assured the eager assemblage that if a game could possibly be played in accordance with the municipal laws governing such matters, their request would be complied with, as both of the teams were quite anxious to play. President Spalding and the members of the Reception Committee then entered a carriage and were driven to the residence of the Marshal, where the situation was talked over and it was learned, beyond all question, that any attempt to play a game on Sunday would be in violation of the local statutes. President Spalding, consequently, adhered to his first decision, though when the fact was made known at the hotel, the crowd gave vent to its disappointment in groans and howls, and declaring that they would make an issue on the Sunday question at the next election.

That there was to be no game was a disappointment, indeed, to the Hawaiians. They had anticipated it for weeks before our arrival, and now that we were there, with twenty athletic-looking fellows fairly aching to play, the laws would not permit it. The situation certainly was exceedingly trying to the hot-headed Kanakas. They accepted it good-naturedly, however, and went to work in earnest to make our stay pleasant. Half a dozen park wagons and twice that number of saddle horses were placed at our disposal, and every member of the party took advantage of the opportunity afforded to do the city and its environs. Some of the boys accepted an invitation from the U. S. war ship "Alert" to visit the officers upon their vessel, and, from Fred Carroll's account, I imagine they must have spent a charming afternoon, all of the officers being baseball enthusiasts and admirers of the game's great exponents. Another party was taken charge of by one or two Honolulu gentlemen, and witnessed a "Hula Hula," a native dance, by a dozen graceful Kanaka women. Others of the party rode out to the Pali, perhaps the most wonderful piece of coast mountain scenery in the world.

SPLENDID COAST SCENERY ON THE PALI ROAD.

President and Mrs. Spalding and other members of the party entered a wagonette and drove south along Nuuanu Avenue, through the beautiful Nuuanu Valley; past the Royal Mausoleum where sleep the former

STATUE OF KAMEHAMEHA, THE CONQUEROR.

Kings and Queens of Hawaii, from Kamehameha, the conqueror, down to the Princess Like-Like, the last deceased of the royal family ;

past the residences of wealthy Honoluluans, the broad-porticoed houses being almost hidden by masses of foliage of palm, banana and other tropical trees ; on past taro and banana fields until a point was reached from which the rolling Pacific could be seen stretching away to

HAWAIIAN LADY IN RIDING COSTUME.

the horizon like a great burnished mirror, while the city, thick with foliage, lay in the valley below. Returning, the party made a detour that they might pass the Queen's Hospital, built by King Lunalili in memory of Queen Emma. From the Hospital the party drove to Wai Kiki, the Asbury Park of the Hawaiian Islands, finally stopping at the residence of the Hon. A. S. Claghorn, where they met the Princess Kaiulani, a beautiful Hawaiian girl of rare accomplishments and winning manners, the next but one to succeed to the Hawaiian sovereignty. Further along we found the residence of the Hon. John H. Cummins, one of the wealthy men of Hawaii and proprietor of one of the great sugar plantations of the Island. The house was festooned with American flags, and on the broad verandahs we were entertained with music and songs by a band of native boys with their guitars. A novelty to Americans was met with during this charming drive, in several horseback parties, the ladies of which, according to the custom of the country, bestrode their horses, being attired in a suitable and very elegant riding habit. Their grace and skill as riders were very admirable. From Mr. Cummins' house we were driven back to the hotel that we might prepare for the grand "Luau" or native feast given in honor of the Spalding party by His Majesty, and Messrs. Samuel Parker, John Ena and George Beckley.

The "Luau," or native feast of the Hawaiians, as it was given in our honor at Honolulu, was certainly the most novel, if not the most gorgeous event in which we participated during the tour. The feast took place upon the Queen's grounds, in the centre of which stood the Queen's private residence, and just as it began to grow dark our party started from the hotel and drove to the scene of the banquet. We passed the King's palace, and after a drive through an avenue of towering cocoanut palms, came unexpectedly upon the illuminated grounds of the Queen's residence, with their magnificent grove of banana, date, cocoanut, royal palm and many other varieties of tropical plants and trees. The grounds literally blazed with light. Flaming torches of oil had been set ten feet apart in one huge square around the outskirts of the park, while the softened glow of a thousand Japanese lanterns shone through the luxuriant shubbery, reminding us not a little of the *tableaux finale* in our great spectacular dramas at home. Moving about over the graveled walks and through the beautiful shrubbery we could see the figures of two hundred or more of Honolulu's residents who had been invited to meet the visiting Americans, while from all quarters of the grounds we heard the singing of bands of native boys and the sweet melody of their guitars. The scene could scarce have been more attractive, and certainly not more surprising.

The uniformed officers at the gates fell back in the most deferential manner as our party entered, and, with U. S. Minister Merrill, President Spalding, Captain H. G. Morse, and the ladies in the lead, walked toward a great tree near the centre of the grounds, beneath which stood His Majesty, the Hon. John Cummins, and members of the King's cabinet. In accordance with a very old custom in the royal families of Hawaii, a tree is planted upon royal ground at the birth of each member of the royal household, and as the tree grows in vigor, strength and beauty of proportion, or as it is destroyed by the elements or weakened by disease, the future of the child is prognosticated. The tree under which King Kalakuau stood had been planted at his birth, some fifty years before, and upon the night of our reception the King was present, in the prime of life and full vigor of manhood, while the tree towered above us, its branches far-reaching and covered with luxuriant foliage, while its sturdy trunk seemed capable of bearing the brunt of wind and weather for ages to come. His Majesty informally and cordially received his guests, after which the boys, in accordance with the royal mandate to make themselves perfectly at home, wandered away in groups about the grounds.

In one of the lattice-walled rooms of the Queen's residence stood a table bearing a hugh ten-gallon punch bowl, from which two dusky attendants were serving delicious beverage to all who requested it. Fogarty, Burns, and myself, together with several officers of the U. S. cruiser " Alert," entered to test the contents of the bowl, when, before we had reached the table, half a dozen pretty Kanaka girls, attired in gowns of some loose woven material of pure white, that contrasted beautifully with their dark hair and Italian-like complexions, approached us with a charming air of confidence, and, slipping their dusky arms around our necks, smiled into our astonished faces as they proceeded to fasten over our shoulders, "leis" of flowers—the wreath of welcome of the Hawaiians. We were all too much astonished for the moment to do much else than stare at the dusky beauties as they stood before us, their shapely arms exposed through the flowing sleeves, and the brown skin of their rounded shoulders only partly concealed by the delicate texture that covered them, and before we succeeded in recovering our self-possession the wreaths were fastened and the girls were extending the same pretty and hospitable, not to say affectionate, courtesy toward others who had entered. Outside, the scene was indescribably gorgeous, and after paying our compliments to the punch bowl a second time we joined one of the groups of Honolulu's fair daughters who had assembled in force to meet our party.

A short distance away, in the centre of a grove of magnificent royal palms, preparations for the "luau" were going on. The ground had been covered with dried rushes and native grasses to the depth of three inches. Upon these had been laid the table, in the shape of a U, the boards resting upon blocks which elevated them, perhaps six inches above the rushes. Upon each side of the table had been laid long strips of matting, upon which the guests were to sit—tailor fashion—while stationed ten feet apart stood a line of Kanaka girls attired in flowing robes of white, and waving to and fro over the table long-handled, brilliantly colored fans. The innumerable colored lanterns and the lurid glow of the oil torches which shone through the palm trees, the voices of the native boys and the sound of their guitars, the presence of a hundred white-clad Kanaka women, and the intoxicating perfume of the tropical foliage, all combined to make our experience a novel and delightful one.

An hour after our arrival the King arose from his seat beneath the branches of his Birth-tree, and offering his arm to Mrs. Spalding, proceeded toward the grove in which the tables had been laid. Following the King were H. R. H. Lilino Kalani, the King's sister; and Prince Kawanonakoa. After them came President Spalding, Captain Morse, and the remainder of the party. Thanks to the skill and experience of the royal ushers, the big party was gracefully handled, and within a very few minutes after the procession had formed we were seated, the King sharing with Mrs. Spalding a richly embroidered silk mat at the head of the table, while others occupied seats upon the native matting. Opposite each plate sat calabashes filled with "poi," while upon the platters and encased in long, coarse-fibred leaves in which they had been baked, were portions of beef, pork, veal, fish, chicken and all other viands to be found upon a moderate banquet table, but all prepared in native style. Fruit of almost every variety known to tropical countries was piled in lavish profusion from one end of the table to the other, and the usual wines were served without stint. Bands of native boys stationed upon the outskirts of the party played continuously during the feast, and not a few of us who were lovers of stringed instruments left neglected the dishes before us while we listened to the peculiar rhythm and exquisite harmony of their music.

Some of the experiences of the Americans with the native dish of "poi" were amusing. A pretty girl opposite me laughed merrily when

6

I transferred a spoonful of the pink porridge to my plate, and then, as if to impress me with my ignorance of Kanaka customs, plunged two rosy fingers into the dish before her, gave them an expert twist and transferred the clinging substance to her mouth. For a moment I wondered where the young woman had learned her table manners, and then as it dawned upon me that every one but myself was indulging in the same breach of table etiquette, I too fell into line and ate "poi" with my fingers, a la Hawaii, and what is more, I found it exceedingly palatable.

The "Luau" proceeded as nearly all banquets do. There was a continued hum of conversation mingling with laughter, merry badinage and the music of the native boys, until silence was finally requested by His Majesty's Attorney-General, who, speaking for the King, expressed the pleasure His Majesty felt at having been afforded the opportunity of entertaining so representative a body of Americans within his own kingdom. President Spalding responded briefly, his well-worded tribute to Hawaii and its people's generous hospitality being warmly received by the resident Honoluluans present. Some moments later the King expressed a wish to hear Frank Lincoln in some of his specialties, and in response the humorist had the King and his guests laughing heartily before he had fairly got to his feet. His satire on after-dinner speeches, his "A, B, C" oration and his artistic mixture of a "soda cocktail," which many Americans will remember, were never more cleverly given, and certainly never called forth more enthusiastic applause.

After fifteen minutes of uninterrupted laughter over Lincoln's remarks we arose from the table, the King and the members of his family and cabinet returning to the trunk of the great tree, beneath which a levee was held, the ball-players mingling with the crowd in the gardens, where scores of dark-eyed Hawaiian beauties flirted and chatted with a zest fully equal to that exhibited by the typical American girl.

It was perhaps nine o'clock—our steamer was to weigh anchor at ten—when the members of our party filed under the branches of the great tree to bid His Majesty farewell. Kalakuau had seen Clarence Duval do a plantation "breakdown" to the "music" made by the hands of Tommy Burns, Fred Pfeffer, Ryan and Ned Williamson, and after laughing heartily at the little darkie's " pigeon-wings" and "walk-arounds," had rewarded him with a ten-dollar gold piece. He had conversed pleasantly with many members of our party, and as we passed before him he shook each one of us warmly by the hand and wished us *bon voyage.* He has a fine face, with dark, expressive eyes and a kindly expression that grows more interesting as one looks into it, and more than one member of our party afterward declared himself as having been most agreeably surprised in His Majesty—to whose generous hospi-

CLARENCE CUTTING "PIGEON-WINGS" BEFORE THE KING.

tality we were so greatly indebted. Our farewells spoken, we paused at the outskirts of the natural pavilion which sheltered the King and gave His Majesty three American cheers, which brought a smile to his face and further good wishes to his lips. Three more were given for Our Friends in Honolulu, and then Fogarty made himself the target of half a hundred pairs of admiring eyes by proposing three cheers for The Ladies of Honolulu. It is needless to say that they were given,

after which we were driven rapidly to our steamer. At the dock a
great crowd awaited us, the assemblage at the Queen's grounds having
adjourned to the steamer's side almost in a body. The King's band
was there, and even now I can in fancy hear its beautiful strains in the
" Aloha " song, while the scene of the waving, cheering crowd upon
the dock, illuminated by the powerful rays of the ship's calcium, and
the farewells that came to us more and more faintly as the " Alameda's "
head swung out to sea, are doubtless still as fresh in the memories of
all our party as they are in my own.

Fair Honolulu. We strained our eyes that night to catch a last
glimpse of the disappearing lights upon its shores, with regret at
leaving, and hope of again seeing what many of us still remember as
among the most beautiful spots upon the globe.

> Fair Honolulu, City of the Sea,
>   On Oahu's shores, where stately mountains rise,
> To dwell forever there, with thee,
>   Would be to live in earthly paradise.

Upon leaving Honolulu, we entered upon the longest period of our
voyage across the Pacific; the distance between Hawaii and New
Zealand, our next stop, with the exception of a brief wait for the mails
at the Samoan Islands, being nearly 3900 miles. The trip from San
Francisco to Honolulu, however, had made good sailors of most of us,
and the novelty of tossing about upon the swell of the ocean having in
a measure worn off, the more active minds of the party soon became
restless under the inactive life we were leading upon the quarter-deck.
Anson was first in an endeavor to bring about a change.

" See here, George." said he to Wright, the afternoon following our
departure from Honolulu, " this kind of a life will never do for American ball-players upon a missionary tour. We shall all be as stiff as
old women and as fat as aldermen by the time we reach Australia, if
we don't take exercise of some kind. Can't we arrange to have a bit
of cricket practice ? "

George, a little later, held an interview with Captain Morse, and the
result was that on the following morning, half a dozen sailors set to
work to roof over and wall in with canvas the rear end of the quarter-

deck promenade upon the larboard side of the ship. This was done to prevent the balls from bounding into the sea, and when completed, gave us an enclosed cricket alley about eight feet wide, ten high and forty feet long. The wickets were set in the extreme end of the alley, and the bowler, facing the opening of the tent, twenty feet beyond it, found plenty of room in which to swing his arm, and ample distance in which to "break" the ball quite effectively, despite the smooth decks and the occasional roll of the ship. Through George Wright's thoughtfulness in providing the party with a fifty-foot stretch of cocoa matting, upon which to bowl, the obstacles which the smooth oak planking of the deck offered to good bowling were overcome, and a surface almost as good as genuine turf secured. The boys began practice almost as soon as arrangements were completed, and did not afterward fail to put in several hours a day. Indeed, it was just what they all wanted, for they had begun to get a bit stiff and heavy, just as Anson predicted, as the result of three hearty meals a day and no exercise, save,

CRICKET ON SHIPBOARD.

perhaps, an early morning turn on deck, and the bowling and batting either in the warm sun outside their tent or the high temperature inside of it, brought out the perspiration freely and landed the players in Australia almost in the pink of condition.

It was the expectation when the party started out that we would play almost as much cricket as baseball, particularly in Australia, but we afterward found that we had little, if any, time left for other than the ball games arranged for by Manager Lynch. We did play one game of cricket in Sydney, and while our boys gave an exhibition of fielding with which the fielding work of the Australians could not for one moment compare, our lack of bowling and batting ability gave the Sydney Eleven an easy victory in the partly completed game played. A few of our players possessed a fair idea of batting with a straight bat, but the majority would hold on to the idea of hitting the ball hard, with a cross-bat, just as they were accustomed to do in baseball. Had they schooled themselves to do more blocking and less hitting, eight or ten of them, with continued practice and the experience of half a dozen games against the Australians, would probably have developed into very fair batsmen by the time we reached England.

Time passed so rapidly upon the voyage that we had drawn near the New Zealand coast before we realized it. The weather became warm enough, soon after we had left the Hawaiian Islands, to permit of the boys sleeping upon deck, and between the hours of midnight and five in the morning, the comfortable cane-seated steamer chairs surrounding the deck saloon, were sure to be found occupied by slumbering ball-players, attired in their flannel pjamas, and wrapped in the blankets they had brought from their state-rooms. The sailors awakened all deck-slumberers about half-past five by washing down the decks for the day with half a dozen streams of salt water, and then the boys would retire to their state-rooms, and divesting themselves of their pjamas, would reappear, *au naturel*, for their salt-water baths, the water pouring from two big perforated nozzles near the smoke-stack, with force and volume enough to wash an entire regiment in half an hour. Then after a "sponge off" in fresh water, followed by a cup of black coffee and a soda cracker brought us by the cabin stewards, we would prepare our toilets for the day. The salt-water baths were a source of any amount of fun, and were besides great invigorators, the boys, when they had donned their flannel suits and straw hats, coming upon deck with hearty appetites for breakfast, and in good condition for their morning's cricket practice.

Contrary to our calculations on leaving Honolulu we crossed the equator somewhere between one and two o'clock on the morning of December 1st. Had we crossed in daylight we should have received Neptune and his suite as they came over our bow from the depths of the ocean, but as it was, we were compelled to rely upon our own resources for celebration during the hour of crossing, and our resources were by no means few. A really good literary and musical programme was given in the cabin after supper, under Frank Lincoln's supervision, in which the piano, a mandolin, two banjos, and a guitar provided very acceptable orchestra music. General Strange, the old English army officer, gave us a thrilling account of his experience in the Sepoy mutiny in India, he having been present at the siege of Lucknow, while Frank Lincoln wound up the programme with a series of his amusing specialties, after which our entire party moved our steamer chairs well up toward the bow of the ship, and under the light of a million stars, played and sang everything, from light opera to plantation darky ballads, until Captain Morse informed us, about one o'clock, that we had crossed the earth's girdle and were in southern seas.

CAPTAIN MORSE, COMMANDER OF THE "ALAMEDA."

Captain Morse, by the way, is an ideal captain. He stands six feet high and weighs 283 pounds. In his day he has been an athlete of no ordinary ability, and one of the rarest treats I enjoyed upon that voyage was getting into the big fellow's state-room, together with Ned Williamson, Tom Burns, and Ned Hanlon, to listen to the "old sea-dog's" stories of travel and adventure. He has been all over the world, and has sailed the Pacific for the past twenty-three years, until the record of his travels would make an exceedingly interesting volume. The captain sat at the head of the first table in the dining saloon, with

President and Mrs. Spalding at his right, and Mr. and Mrs. Frank Lincoln at his left ; his hearty laugh and his good-natured, jovial countenance leaving no room for any such thing as a dull meal at our table during the voyage. Others at table No. 1 were Mr. and Mrs Anson, Ned and Mrs. Williamson, Captains Ward and Hanlon, the Press correspondents, Tom Burns, Fred Pfeffer, Fred Carroll, and George Wright and his chum Snyder.

On the morning of December 2d, a few hours after we had crossed the equator, the wind began to blow great guns, and by noon the "Alameda" was rolling about like a log in a mountain stream, while, to the amusement of the boys, great sheets of water dashed over our decks. Tom Daly, Pettit, Sullivan, Brown, Carroll, Earle and Healy skirmished around from one end of the ship to the other, soaked to the skin and yelling with laughter as often as a big wave would raise itself over the rail and send one of their number sprawling across the deck. At the table we were as apt to get our soup in our laps as in our mouths, and it was not an unusual sight to see a cabin steward flying down the saloon with our dinner in his outstretched hands, as though he were bent upon going through the bow of the ship. It did no good to call him, for it was utterly beyond his power to stop, so we only laughed at the poor fellow's plight and wondered if the ship's bow would be checked in its downward plunge by striking another billow before our flying steward struck the forward wall of the saloon and frescoed its polished surface with our fricasseed chicken and teal duck with jelly.

It was too wet for comfort on deck that evening, so the ship's passengers amused themselves by holding a mock trial in the saloon, with General Strange in the chair, as the presiding judge, and Sir James Willoughby as the prisoner at the bar. Charges had been preferred, to the effect that "Sir Jimmy" was not a peer of the realm, as he had declared himself to be, and that he was violating a ship's law by carrying concealed weapons. John Ward acted as counsel for the defendant, and Colonel House as prosecuting attorney, while Jimmy Fogarty as Court Crier kept the crowd in such continuous laughter that the trial proceeded with great difficulty. Each witness was sworn not to tell the truth and anything but the truth, so that the evidence was naturally of a startling character. "Sir Jimmy" had been heard to declare he would scuttle the ship, and was known to carry an eight-ton gun in his pistol pocket—several of the witnesses had seen it, and described it accurately; while as to his pretensions to nobility, half a dozen witnesses knew him to be a clerk in the ribbon department at Macy's. Other witnesses, however, testified to the defendant's wonderful tenderness of heart, and still others had been entertained in royal style at his town and country houses in England. "Sir Jimmy" was acquitted with all honor. There was afterwards some talk of bringing Tom Daly into court under "a bill of *lunatico inquirendo*," with Fogarty as "accessory to the crime," but the return and continuation of beautiful weather kept every one outside the saloon upon the decks.

Our only sight of land during our two weeks' voyage from Honolulu to New Zealand was obtained upon the night of December 3d, when we sighted the northward island of the Samoan or Navigator group, made famous during the spring of 1888 by the native war which raged at Apia, and by the destruction in a tornado of the fleet of United States cruisers anchored in the harbor. The trouble was reaching an ugly stage at the time of our visit, though its seat was some ninety miles from Tutuila, the mailing station at which our steamer touched. It had been quite stormy for several hours previous to our arrival. Captain Anson, Ed Crane, Tom Brown, Daly, Fogarty and myself were seated on the lee side of the deck, under shelter of the awning, watching for the first glimpse of a light on shore, or the first appearance of land through the darkness. Shortly after 11 o'clock we suddenly ran under the lee of a mountainous ridge of land, that rose like a black shadow out of the water, and our vessel stopped pitching almost immediately as we glided over waters that rippled gently about our bow, where five minutes before great foam-crested waves had been towering. The transition was so sudden that we all jumped from our chairs and ran to the bow just as the ship was illuminated by a signal light of green from the leeward end of the bridge. Then we saw land, and finally a twinkling light upon the shore nearly five miles away. Slowly we steamed toward it, while signal lights continued flashing their messages between our ship and the shore. We did not attempt to land, but lay in the harbor half a mile out until two boats, one a sloop and the other a little dory that bobbed about us like a cork on the waves, had come out from the dock with the foreign bound mail and two passengers for Auckland. Had we reached these islands in daytime, our ship would have been surrounded with canoes filled with natives, and we should doubtless have been able to bring away many interesting souvenirs. As it was, however, we saw nothing of the country, and caught but a glimpse of the natives as we watched them over the ship's rail. One stalwart fellow with a copper-colored skin and thick, red hair* did clamber up the side to take the purser's receipt for the mail-sacks, and we got a good view of him. He tossed off nearly a goblet full of gin, which the purser handed him, as though it were so much water, and, wiping his lips with his big, red hand, descended into the mail-boat. This was really all we saw of Samoa, for after receiving our passengers and leaving our mail, the "Alameda" moved slowly out of the harbor, and twenty minutes later was again plunging and rolling through the great waves that drenched her decks.

The weather grew cooler after leaving Samoa, and our flannel suits were discarded for clothes of a warmer texture, with light overcoats for use upon deck during the evening. Cricket practice was indulged in every day, and many delightful hours were enjoyed under the light of the southern cross, which was now plainly discernible. But despite the pleasant, lazy life on shipboard, we all began to wish for a bit of dry land to tread upon. Finally, about 3 o'clock on the morning of December 9th, we sighted the revolving light on the first island of the New Zealand group. This light, the man on watch informed me as I came out of my state-room for a solitary smoke, was just eight hours' run from Auckland. All of the passengers were on deck before breakfast, eager to catch sight of the land, that arose in beautiful green hills upon our larboard side, and at the breakfast table Major-General Strange, on behalf of the passengers, presented Captain Morse with a purse of $200 as a testimonial and in recognition of his care and guidance of our good ship upon the voyage. The big captain acknowledged the gift in a brief, though manly and well-worded speech that won him an enthusiastic burst of applause from his assembled admirers. Kind and attentive from the time we had cut loose from our moorings at San Francisco ;

---

* The natives of the Navigator group have a custom of bleaching their hair with lime.

jolly, big-hearted, and an able commander, he completely won the confidence and admiration of his passengers.

Auckland harbor is second only to that of Sydney in point of picturesque beauty, and we had an excellent view of it as our ship steamed her way along a winding channel upon each side of which arose bold, irregular hills, characteristic of all countries of volcanic origin. Pretty sailboats and busy steamers dotted the bay, and upon the sides of the majestic hills were pretty, balconied residences of white stone surrounded

BIRD'S-EYE VIEW OF AUCKLAND AND ITS HARBOR.

by carefully kept grounds. As we neared the dock at the foot of the main street we were struck with the remarkable quiet of the town, and then recalled the fact that we had dropped a day from our calendar upon crossing the 180th degree of longitude, and that it was Sunday morning at Auckland, instead of Saturday, as it would have been but for the change in our calendar. We had expected to meet Leigh Lynch at Auckland, but he was unable to leave Sydney, and sent his cousin, Will

Lynch, who came on board with a big basket filled with bouquets for the members of our party. He was followed by several newspaper men, and one and all poured into our cars a wail of regret that we could not have arrived the day before, when it was reasonably certain we should have had eight or ten thousand people present to witness the game. Usually the steamers stop but a few hours at Auckland, but we were delighted to learn that the "Alameda" could not finish coaling before five o'clock the following afternoon, so we should be able, after all, to play a game in New Zealand. By way of change from steamer life, we accepted an invitation from President Spalding to take dinner at the Imperial Hotel, and the change was delightful, notwithstanding that the cuisine of our good ship was first-class. Indeed, had a Delmonico been our ship's caterer, we should have welcomed any departure from our usual bill of fare. Those who have crossed the ocean will understand this feeling.

They know how to live in New Zealand, even though they be colonists. The beef was delicious, while new potatoes, green peas, fresh from the garden, cauliflower, young radishes, English duck done to a turn, and strawberries, such as Americans have read of, possibly, but have never seen, constituted a dinner all the more enjoyable because its dishes were luxuries with Americans at that season of the year. After dinner, at the invitation of several of the representative newspaper men at Auckland, we mounted two big four-horse coaches and did the city and its environs, finally scaling the sides of Mount Eden, an extinct volcano on the outskirts of the city, and looking into its musty old crater. The country about Auckland is wonderfully rich and beautifully picturesque, and despite the drizzling rain which fell, the drive over the hard roads behind a four-in hand of sturdy English coachers was an interesting one. The clouds cleared away soon after sundown, and the "Alameda's" passengers thronged the big stone dock at which the steamer lay until long after midnight, being eager, all of us, to spend every available moment of our time upon shore.

On the following day I got a better idea of the beautiful country surrounding Auckland. It was scarcely seven o'clock when I was awakened by Bob Pettit, who informed me that a couple of saddle horses awaited us on the dock, and that we had no time to lose.

"How about breakfast?" I asked.

"Bother breakfast," was the right-fielder's reply. "If you'll move yourself in a hurry, I'll give you a breakfast at the end of the prettiest seven-mile ride you ever saw; but there is no time to be lost."

So I tumbled out of my berth, and twenty minutes later Bob and I stood on the dock attired in the pick-up riding costumes we had worn upon our first ride at Salt Lake. Two long-barreled nags awaited us, and on these we were soon riding through the streets of the scarcely awakened city, then on past the parks until we struck the hard white road that led to Manukau Cove. It was a delightful ride, for the country was green and beautiful, the air fresh and invigorating, and our horses anxious to go. We passed quaint English-looking inns and ale-houses, around which groups of New Zealand farmers had gathered for business or idle chat. The "bob-carts" we have read about, driven by square-tiled yeomen, who looked at us curiously as we passed, were frequently met with, and once or twice we stopped en route for a glass of light sparkling ale from the hands of the bright-eyed bar-maids, who, instead of the white-aproned masculine bar-keepers of America, serve customers in New Zealand. Finally turning a bend in the road, we came into view of Manukau, the little village on the shore of Manukau Cove. Nearly all of the inhabitants are seafaring people, and the Manukau Hotel, which faces the Cove, is their headquarters. Without ceremony Bob and I rode into the court-yard of the inn and tied our horses to a couple of staples in the wall.

"You seem to be at home here, old man," I remarked.

"Well, I guess," replied Pettit, with all the confidence of a bred and born Yankee, "this is right where I live, and I only got acquainted last night at that. Come in, and let me introduce you to my family," with which Bob opened a side door and I followed him into the little hotel parlor, and through the doorway across the hall caught a glimpse of the inevitable hotel ale room, which we entered.

There were three people in the room and they were typical samples of colonial life. The first was an elderly, well-preserved old colonist, fat and ruddy complexioned with the ale of his own brewing; the next was a gray-bearded coast skipper, in a fore-and-aft hat and an oilskin jacket; while the third was a colonial innkeeper's wife, fat, forty and

good-natured, and as thrifty and energetic as she was good-natured.
And how well her name fitted her appearance, and her position as mis-
tress of the principal tavern at Manukau, Mrs. Waterman.

Advancing toward Bob and myself with a broad smile of welcome,
she gave the former a hearty slap on the shoulder as she said : " Welcome to ye, me lad ; ye are out a bit early this morning, are ye not?"

" Yes, we came out for breakfast, " said Pettit, "can we have some?"

"That ye can, " was the hearty reply, and after an introduction to the
two old skippers, we turned into the hallway just as two fresh-faced
pretty girls came down the stairs, only to greet, and be greeted by Bob
as though they were old-time acquaintances.   They were the daughters
of our hostess, and each was a typical representative of colonial beauty,
with enough of wit and spirit added to their physical charms, to make
them even a more interesting study for us than were our breakfasts,
hungry, though we were.   Mrs. Waterman sat down with us and
served us from the rich juicy steak that steamed upon the platter, while
we flirted with her two daughters through one of the most heartily
relished breakfasts I partook of on the tour.   After an hour spent over
our sherry and cigarettes in the little parlor, Pettit and I bade a regretful
farewell to our colonial cousins, and turned our horses' heads toward
Auckland for another delightful ride.   We reached the city just in time
to join the party in a visit to the City Hall, where for an hour or more
we were the guests of Mayor Devore.

About 12 o'clock the local band marched down the principal street to
the "Alameda," where it headed a procession of carriages containing the
teams in uniform and two big tally-ho coaches which carried the remainder of the "Alameda's" passengers, as invited guests at the game.   The
drive to the grounds was a pretty one, and the stretch of greensward
within the enclosure as attractive a sight as any we saw in New Zealand.
Our game in New Zealand was of the heavy batting order, and the way
in which a ball rolled whenever it was batted into the smooth, velvety
outfield, would have broken the hearts of a league out-field in a championship game.   A dozen Englishmen sat near me, and as they had never
before seen a baseball game they were completely bewildered.   I explained several of the plays however, telling them how and when the
side had been retired, calling their attention to the fielding, the throwing

to first across the diamond and from the out-field, to double plays, base-running, and sliding, until I had them as deeply interested as ever they had been in a game of cricket. The Englishmen among our passengers who had picked up the cardinal points from the boys *en voyage*, were particularly pleased, and admitted they had never seen such fielding or remarkable base-running.

Two thousand people had assembled to bid us farewell when the "Alameda" left the dock at five o'clock that afternoon, and we watched

THE BOLD HEADLANDS OF THE SHORE OF SYDNEY HARBOR.

the picturesque coast until nightfall. An hour later the "Alameda" turned her nose west by no'r-west, heading for Sydney, 1243 miles away.

On the afternoon of December 14th, after a rough voyage, we sighted the Australian coast. By three o'clock we could discern the shore line, and at five we went down to dinner. We were not long at the table, however. Everybody dined hastily and rushed upon deck, and watched the bold headlands of the shore grow more and more distinct.

Presently we saw a thin trail of smoke across the sky, and soon we discovered the outlines of the pilots' tug as it steamed toward us. Manager Leigh Lynch's face was one of the first we saw as the pilot boat approached, and our big business manager was received with rousing cheers and hearty handshaking as he, with the old gray-bearded pilot, climbed up the ship's side. He admonished us, however, to save our voices, "for" said he, "all Sydney will be in the bay to meet you, and I want you to show them how healthy Americans can cheer."

We soon found that Lynch had but slightly exaggerated the preparations made for our reception, for as we steamed through "Sydney Heads," with schools of graceful dolphins diving about our bow, and hundreds of sea-birds that had flown out from land, as if to welcome us, circling about our masts, we discovered several steamers coming toward us at a speed that cut the water into white sheets upon each side of their bows. Nearer and nearer they drew until we could hear the bands of music with which each steamer was provided, their strains mingling with the cheers that came to us faintly across the water. Then we discerned scores of fluttering handkerchiefs, and eager happy faces, as men clung to the ropes and every other available holding place upon the little crafts and madly waved us welcome, while the ladies—and there were great numbers of them—circled their shawls and bright-colored sun-shades about their heads, determined not to be outdone by their husky-voiced escorts. Steamer after steamer dropped alongside of us, until the "Alameda" had become the centre of a puffing, cheering, banner-bedecked escort, the demonstration causing not a few eyes on board to moisten with joy and gratitude at once more reaching land, the recipients of so glorious a welcome. The lighthouse on the point was draped from top to bottom with red, white and blue bunting, and with American flags, and as we steamed up the beautiful harbor, toward the dock, two flotillas of watermen's boats, fairly covered with the "stars and stripes" and "union jacks," swung into line alongside of us, until our ship was surrounded by an hundred and fifty craft of various characters. Of course we cheered for everything any one among us could suggest, and each cheer was answered by the enthusiastic hundreds who were steaming along beside us. Indeed, no one who has not seen Sydney harbor, and who does not know the generous hospitality of the Australians, can form an adequate idea of our delightful reception. It was glorious! it was soul-stirring! It was in every way a complete surprise, in that it so far exceeded all that we had imagined it might be. Certainly no more picturesque and beautiful scenery, of its kind, exists anywhere in the world than that about Sydney harbor. The waters of the sea extend inland between jutting hills and headlands, until, when viewed from some point high above the sea level, the bay looks like a big glistening star-fish, upon the back of which are moving hundreds of sailing craft of every description. Beautifully-kept private and public parks extend

PANORAMIC VIEW OF SYDNEY AND ITS SUPERB HARBOR.

downward to the water's edge, and quaintly-designed English-looking residences of white stone, with their turrets and tower-capped walls, stand upon the hillsides, partly hidden by a wealth of beautiful foliage. The sight of the picturesque harbor and its beautiful shores was alone a glorious one in the eyes of every passenger on the "Alameda," while the generous demonstration in honor of our arrival made our reception at Sydney the most delightful and noteworthy event thus far upon our tour.

7

Upon the quay at which our steamer was to land stood hundreds of cheering people, and the welcome they gave us was equaled only by that which we had received at Honolulu. Our party with difficulty made its way through the crowd to five four-horse tally-ho coaches, beautifully decorated with the Stars and Stripes, and through the colonial thoroughfares we rode to the Oxford and Grosvenor hotels.

GEORGE STREET—ONE OF THE COLONIAL THOROUGHFARES.

The entire party stopped first at the Oxford, the entrance to which, as well as to the dining-room, had been quite elaborately decorated in red, white and blue bunting, boughs of spruce and evergreen, and swinging colored lanterns. Brief but hearty greetings by U. S. Consul Griffin, Leigh Lynch, and President Spalding followed, and after drinking as many toasts as we thought it advisable to wet thus early in the evening, the boys repaired to their rooms to make a hasty toilet for the formal welcome to Australia arranged for us at the Royal Theatre. The Royal is presided over by "Jimmy" Williamson, a whole-souled and patriotic American, who has made a success of his dramatic enterprises in Australia. Himself and wife were in the caste in "Struck Oil" that evening, and in a farcical hit upon the evils of Chinese Immigration, as an afterpiece. The theatre had been beautifully decorated with American flags, and was filled with a fashionable audience, nearly all of whom were in evening costume. The boys were recognized and heartily applauded as they filed into the private boxes and that section of the dress circle reserved for them. After the closing act of "Struck Oil" our entire party passed through the box aisle upon the stage, where, arranging ourselves in a semicircle, we faced "the house" as the curtain arose, and stood silently for nearly a minute while the applause continued. Then Mr. Daniel O'Connor, a member of parliament and one of the most popular legislators in New South Wales, introduced us, his brief speech being full of kind words for America and everything American, and particularly eulogistic of the party of American ball-players which had come so

MR. DANIEL O'CONNOR, M. P., SYDNEY, N. S. W.

far upon such a mission without any guarantee whatever against financial loss, or against artistic failure, unless, perhaps, their confidence in the beauties of their national game, and in the sport-loving spirit of the Australians, was all the guarantee they wanted.

President Spalding responded in a manner that won him continued and hearty applause, and it is safe to say that when the curtain finally fell, the Royal contained none who were unfriendly to our party. A laughable incident, and one which shows how far a professional ball-player's fame may extend, and how small the world is, after all, occurred as the curtain fell. A voice from the gallery rang out with an unmistakable juvenile ring, "'Rah for Baby Anson." The boy may have been an American lad who had seen many a championship game at home before having drifted to far-away New South Wales, or he may have

HIS WORSHIP, MAYOR HARRIS, OF SYDNEY, N. S. W.

been an Australian reader of our American baseball papers, but whatever his nationality, he was a resident of Australia, and had recognized "Baby" Anson when he saw him.

The ensuing days of our stay in Sydney were filled with pleasant incidents and unlimited entertainment and attentions. At 11 o'clock on the morning after our arrival, we assembled in the office of the Oxford for a formal call at the city hall upon His Worship, Mayor Harris. The big four-in-hand coaches, decorated with the Stars and Stripes, as upon the preceding evening, took us through the principal streets and past enthusiastic throngs of people. not a few of whom stopped to send a cheer after us as we drove by. U. S. Consul Griffin, members of the reception committee and representatives of the Sydney press accompanied us. At the City hall we were received in the council chamber by His Worship, attired in his official robes of purple and ermine, after which we crossed the hall to the mayor's chamber, in the centre of which stood a big table draped with snowy linen and loaded with refreshments, while half a dozen side-whiskered butlers broke the wires upon half a hundred quarts of Clicquot, Mumm and Pomery. The mayor received us with a cheery speech, telling us that Sydney was glad to welcome us, and would doubtless demonstrate, to our entire satisfaction, the interest it felt in the visit of so representative a body of American athletes. He believed that Australians would like baseball, and though he did not understand the game thoroughly himself, he thought well enough of it to predict that in time Australia would herself have a league embracing teams capable of coping with our American professionals. He was personally glad to see us, and tendered us the freedom of the city during our stay. United States Consul Griffin responded happily to the mayor's address, and then His Worship again arose to say that so long as Americans treated Australia with the degree of consideration they had always in the past extended, Australians would make it pleasant for their American cousins while the latter were upon Australian soil. "My reasons for believing that our athletes will emulate your baseball players" said His Worship, in conclusion, "are manifold. In the first place, we have adopted your American ideas of trotting, and we have managed to scrape up material enough to beat your best oarsmen." Here His Worship turned toward oarsman Ned Hanlan, who had quietly entered the room and taken a seat near President Spalding, and the reference was enough to secure for Hanlan a hearty burst of applause from his fellow-Americans. "And," continued the mayor, "if all Americans will yield the palm with as good grace as Mr. Hanlan has done, we will entertain as high an opinion of them as we now do of Mr. Hanlan." The Canadian was loudly cheered when, in answer to a unanimous call, he arose and told us of the warm hospitality of the Australians and his many delightful experiences during his stay among them. Responses to the mayor's address by Mr. Spalding and Leigh Lynch followed, and after drinking to the dozen or more toasts proposed, we withdrew to our equipages, with three American cheers and the inevitable tiger for the Mayor of Sydney.

That same afternoon we played our first game in Australia upon the grounds of the Sydney Cricket Association, and the boys were compelled to admit that, in whatever other respects the Colonies might be inferior to the United States, they certainly possessed athletic grounds so far superior in point of equipment and condition to anything we had in the United States at that time, that there was no room whatever for comparison. The drive to the Sydney grounds is in itself an attractive one, and the playing-field, as level as a floor, velvety with its thick covering of green turf, and surrounded by its sloping lawns and prettily-designed club houses, is a sight to delight the eye of any man who ever played cricket or baseball. Threatening weather doubtless kept many from the grounds, and the great annual foot races at Botany, together with the horse races, affected the attendance at our game to no small extent; still, there were in the neighborhood of 4000 people upon the grounds, and the strict and evidently interested attention paid by the big crowd to a foreign game, with which they were unfamiliar, was a gratifying surprise to the players and a pretty mark of

BASE SLIDING AS AUSTRALIANS SAW IT.
(From the Illustrated Paper published in Sydney, N. S. W.)

respect to our party and to America's national game. Everybody was quick to recognize and appreciate many of the stronger points of play, and all vigorously applauded the base-sliding and running, as well as the good stiff batting indulged in by both teams, all of which were well illustrated in their pictorial papers. The game was a pretty one. It was nip and tuck up to the fifth inning, when Chicago, by the capture of one run, tied the score, and it so remained until All-America sent a man across the plate in the ninth inning, with the winning run. Indeed, had the boys played it to order, they could scarcely have put up a more interesting game or a prettier exhibition of the most attractive features of baseball. During an interval of fifteen minutes at the end of the sixth inning, Lord Carrington, Governor of New South Wales, received the party in the Association club house, where His Excellency, who is a great lover of athletic sports, welcomed us warmly to the colony and wished us every success in our efforts to introduce the game into Australia. President Spalding responded, and, after three cheers for Lord Carrington, Lady Carrington, the Queen, the President, Australia and Sydney, the boys withdrew to finish the game, their reappearance upon the field being the signal for a continued shout of applause from the spectators.

The ride from the grounds was followed by an excellent dinner at the hotels, and then the boys broke away in congenial groups to see something of Sydney after dark. The theatres had all extended general invitations to our party, and each had several representatives present during the evening. John Ward, Ed Hanlan, Jim Manning and myself, under the leadership of Messrs. Allen and Murray, of the *Sydney Star* and *Melbourne Sportsman*, dropped into Larry Foley's gymnasium—the sporting headquarters of Sydney—and witnessed a by no means bad set-to of eight rounds, between two very clever middle-weights. Others of the boys were present at an athletic entertainment at the Sydney Opera House. At the close of the different performances the boys dropped into the various resorts about town, and not a few of us became interested students of that not uninteresting colonial institution, the Australian barmaid, with which no Australian café or drinking resort is unprovided. In most cases they are pretty, in every instance smart, and combining with these qualities·an excellent knowledge of mankind and his weaknesses, they are more valuable to the Australian liquor dealer than our most expert beverage mixers would be, for the Australian, like the Englishman, rarely asks for other than a glass of ale or beer, or a bit of brandy and soda. It is fortunate he is so simple in his tastes, else he would suffer as does the average American who steps into an Australian bar room, expecting to be served as he would be in Chicago, San Francisco, or New York.

Our first Sunday in Australia—the day after our game—was most delightfully spent, the boys dividing into parties of six or eight, to accept invitations extended us for a drive upon tally-ho coaches through the suburbs of Sydney, some driving out to the beautiful Botany Bay

district and others, including myself, going to the bluffs and shores of
Coogee Bay. We drove over sloping hills and beautiful valleys with
their excellent roadways, lined upon each side by pretty vine-clad,
flower-embowered homes of white stone, the names "Edgewood,"
"Myrtle Terrace," etc., being cut into a square block of stone to
answer the purpose of the ugly, unromantic "1922," "1924," etc.,
which we paint upon the transoms of our doorways in America. Our
road lay for the greater part along or near the shore, and we could

FARM COVE—ONE OF THE BEAUTIES OF SYDNEY BAY.

catch an occasional glimpse of Sydney Bay or some one of its many
beautiful coves, to the waters of which the terraced hills descended.
After an hour of such driving we came suddenly in view of the beach,
and finally dismounted at the aquarium on the seashore. Our party
was invited inside, and saw a collection of many hundreds of native
fish—some of them remarkable specimens—in the big plate-glass
tanks, into which the sea water is being constantly injected. Adjoining
the aquarium is the bathing-tank, and into this the boys plunged for a

sea bath that, as Fogarty declared, put them in good trim for a week's ball-playing. After our bath we enjoyed the concert in the pavilion, not forgetting to drink Manager Stafford's health before leaving, and then made our way to "The Point," a great ledge of rocks, around the base of which the sea breaks with impressive grandeur. The view of the ocean from here is magnificent, and down on the sandy beach to the right of the rocks the bathing is particularly fine. The boys were hungry when we got back to the hotel, but not too tired after supper to attend

SYDNEY'S FASHIONABLE BATHING BEACH AT COOGEE BAY.

a delightful concert at the Criterion Theatre, at which we remained until the last number had been given.

None of the boys, I am sure, will forget the first attempt at cricket by the Chicago and All-America teams in Australia. It took place upon the Sydney grounds, between 11 and 1 o'clock, the day after our drive to Coogee, Mr. Spalding, George Wright, Billy Earle and George Wade doing the bulk of the bowling, and the innings ending with a score of

67 to 33, in favor of All-America. Anson, as Captain of the Chicago team, and as one of the greatest baseball batters in America, was accordingly disgusted. All the way across he had been telling what he individually, and a team of his selection, would do at cricket, and had made not a few bets to back his assertion. Consequently, the boys listened to him respectfully as he coached them during the game, and looked upon him with great expectations when he went to bat. When he struck at the first ball bowled at him, however, and was retired on a little pop-up fly ball to Fogarty, some of the boys fell to the turf with laughter and "Anse" looked six inches shorter as he stepped to one side. He tried to "bluff" out of it, but Tom Burns told him to go and sit down, and "Anse" retired to a corner of the field to bat Mascot Duval's bowling. He was crusty enough to snap Tom Burns' head off an hour after when Tom tauntingly asked him if Clarence was "very speedy." Our second ball game in Sydney took place two hours after the cricket game referred to, in the presence of 3000 people, and like the first game, was a pretty exhibition and a close contest, resulting in a victory for All-America by a score of 7 to 5, with Baldwin and Healy as opposing pitchers.

Our first cricket game against Australian cricketers was played the following day, play commencing at 11 o'clock, and ending at 4 o'clock, with the Americans 87 runs in, and the Australians 115 runs in for six wickets, and playing as though they intended making as many more out of the remaining five. The game was brought to a close at this stage, however, to permit of the ball game being played. The latter, although close and hard fought, resulted in another victory for All-America. It was marked by little life, however, the boys being tired out as the result of their hard day's work at cricket.

I asked George Wright that evening what he thought of the showing our men had made at cricket, and he expressed the belief that had they been half as strong in bowling as in fielding, they would have been a match for the Australians. There was many a burst of applause over our fielding, but our batting was very weak, and we had no bowlers aside from Messrs. Wright and Spalding. The Australians gave us the advantage of seventeen men to their eleven.

Although tired out upon arriving at the hotel, the boys changed their uniforms for evening dress, and attended the banquet tendered by the citizens of Sydney at the Town Hall. Two hundred plates were laid, and nearly every seat was occupied. The Reception Hall of the great building, with its palatial dome, great stone columns and stained glass windows, was one gorgeous array of English and American flags. Upon one side of the room was a life-size portrait of Her Majesty, and just opposite was one of the Duke of Edinburgh. The long tables were loaded with every delicacy the *chef's* deft fingers could prepare or his skill suggest, the beauty of the entire scene being enhanced by the soft-colored lights which burned upon the table. The corridors were embowered in tropical shrubbery and trailing vines which only half hid the luxuriant divans and lounges which had been conveniently set about for the use of the guests. Soft carpets covered the marble floors, while on every side, and almost at every step, were banks of cut flowers and plants that filled the air with their delightful perfume. At one end of the hall a raised platform had been erected, and upon this a musical and literary entertainment was given at the close of the feast.

Our trip thus far had been one round of banquets and receptions, but that feast in Sydney was certainly the most elaborate and memorable we had yet enjoyed. The great room in itself, 80 feet from floor to dome and with 125 by 60 feet floor space, its magnificent ceiling of white and gold, its costly paintings, its gorgeous chandelier with two hundred and fifty crystal globes, its wealth of stained glass and its decorations of flags and flowers, was imposing beyond description, and especially so when to these adornments was added the presence of one hundred and fifty gentlemen and ladies in evening dress at banquet. Toasts were proposed, and were responded to by United States Consul Griffin, the Hon. Daniel O'Connor, President Spalding, John M. Ward, Leigh Lynch, Newton McMillan, Mr. E. G. Allen, of the Sydney *Star,* and others. They included: "The Queen," "The President," "The Governor," "Our Guests," "The Ladies," "The Press" and "The Chairman."

Following the responses to the last toast came a musical treat by some of the best amateur and professional talent in Sydney. Among the numbers given was a cornet solo, with piano accompaniment by Mrs. Leigh Lynch. Her execution was a revelation to every one present, and when she played "Yankee Doodle," "Star Spangled Banner," and other popular American airs, the guests arose from their seats and filled the room with a long and enthusiastic burst of applause, while they plucked handfuls of roses from the floral banks upon the table and showered them at the fair musician, who was encored again and again.

This brief reference to the incidents of that memorable evening falls far short of an adequate description of the generous spirit and memorable events of our last hours in Sydney. Sydney people are without doubt among the most hospitable on earth. They did not permit our party to rest an hour after our steamer reached their dock, and certainly no party of Americans ever left a city with more honest regret and kind remembrance than did ours when we took the train for Melbourne the following evening.

There had been no game arranged for the day of our departure, and we put in our time bidding farewell to many friends that each had made. During the morning the boys visited a down-town store, and each secured a neat straw hat with a band of red, white and blue ribbon. An American traveling man whom we met in Sydney also presented the boys with a button-hole badge of the stripes and stars, so that it was not at all difficult for Sydneyites to distinguish the members of our party.

An hour before train time we entered a four-in-hand drag at "The Oxford," and were driven to the "Grosvenor Hotel," where the Hon. Daniel O'Connor had invited us for a farewell to himself and other representative residents of New South Wales. The beautiful dining-room of the hotel had been prettily decorated, and was comfortably filled with the members of our party and some thirty invited guests, and the manner in which we made the walls ring with our cheers as we drank to the toasts proposed, is probably still remembered by the regular patrons of the hotel.

After three rousing cheers for everything and everybody in Sydney, we entered our drag, and were driven to the railroad station, where, thanks to the Railway Department of the New South Wales Government, we took a special train for Melbourne. The English-styled compartment-coaches were novelties to us, and for that reason, probably, we smiled good-naturedly at the discomforts we experienced. The Americans who had made it so pleasant for us at Sydney were down in force to see us off, and nearly all of them brought a package or two, for the boys. The ride out of Sydney is beautiful, and with the comforts of the elegantly-appointed Pullman Sleepers to which Americans are accustomed would have been voted equal to anything at home. The land is rich and fertile, and the hills are thickly wooded, while they are well cultivated and quite generously populated. The roadbed of the railway, which is operated by the Government, is equal in solidity of construction, I think, to any I ever traveled over. We took supper at the little station of Mitagon soon after nightfall, and then the boys stretched out upon the comfortable leather-covered cushions of their compartments, and told stories and exchanged experiences over their cigars while they looked out upon the moonlight-flooded woodlands.

The only unpleasant incident of our journey from Sydney to Melbourne was a change of cars on the borders of the Colony at 5.30 o'clock in the morning, and the examination of our baggage by the Customs Authorities. These gentlemen, fortunately for us, did not think it necessary to examine our luggage very closely, however, so we escaped with but little inconvenience in this respect, and at about 6 o'clock started for Melbourne, which we reached at 11 o'clock. Our train came to a halt in a substantial-looking station at Spencer street, and as we entered, a cheer went up from fully five hundred people on the station platform, apprising us that Melbourne was ready and waiting to receive us. A number of the American residents of Melbourne being members of the reception committee appointed to meet us, and the Victorian Cricket Association also being well represented, we received a most hearty welcome on our arrival at the Victorian capital. Four-in-hand drags profusely decorated with American colors were in waiting, and as our party, wearing their straw hats with the red, white and blue bands, mounted these and drove up Collins Street they attracted general attention and not a few cheers.

We finally drew rein at the Town Hall, where Mayor Benjamin and members of the City Council were to receive us. In front of the imposing building a crowd of between two and three thousand people had assembled, and after elbowing our way across the sidewalk we passed up stairs into the great audience hall, in which has been constructed one of the grandest pipe organs I ever looked upon or listened to. The town organist, Mr. David Lee, treated us to some beautiful music, there being more than one grave face and wet eye among our party as the lovely strains of "Home, Sweet Home," filled the hall. We all arose and removed our hats as the organ sounded "God Save the Queen." We then passed into the Mayor's private room, where a generous collation had been prepared. Among those present to receive

TOWN HALL OF MELBOURNE, AUSTRALIA.

us were the Hon. Mr. Choppin, Consul-General of the United States at the Melbourne Exposition ; Mr. Smyth, Acting Consul ; the Hon. J. B. Patterson, D. Gaunson and Messrs. Chas. Smith and Pierce, with a large number of sport patrons, cricketers and footballers. The Mayor welcomed us in a plain-spoken, hearty speech, referring to the pleasure it gave him to address such a party of Americans, who had come so far for the purpose of making Australians familiar with the game for which so much was claimed in so great a country as the United States. He could assure them of a hearty welcome to Melbourne, and trusted that they would have only pleasant remembrances of the Colonies to take away with them when they returned to their own country. Pleasant words by the Hon. Mr. Smith on behalf of the Victorian Cricket Association, by Mr. Smyth, Acting United States Consul, by Mr. S. P. Lord, who was designated as "an old colonist from America since '53," and a "baseballer," followed; and then Mr. Spalding, after being enthusiastically cheered, properly expressed his appreciation of so cordial a welcome, and expressed a hope that Victorians would take as kindly to our game as they had to its exponents. Captain Ward and Captain Anson were each called upon, and then Frank Lincoln brought down the house, as he always did, by mixing one of his inimitable cocktails. Toasts were drunk to the Victorian Cricket Association, and were followed by brief addresses by Major Wardell, Town Clerk Fitz-

MAJOR WARDELL, SECRETARY VICTORIAN CRICKET ASSOCIATION.

gibbon, Mr. David Scott, and others, and after three parting cheers and a "tigah" for the Mayor and the reception committee, we were driven to our hotel, where we secured much-needed rest and a good dinner. We were quartered at the Grand Hotel, from the doors of which could be seen the Exposition Buildings, and opposite which were the Treasury Building, Parliament Building and the Fitzroy Gardens. In

Melbourne, the Grand, the Federal and other of the most magnificent hotels of the city are termed " Coffee Palaces." They are splendidly equipped, and, in the way of appointments, surpass anything we had met with since leaving Chicago. The boys certainly had little to grumble at in their accommodations at Melbourne.

No plans having been laid for our journey beyond Melbourne—the Victorian Capital having originally been our objective point—we all looked upon it as a temporary home at least, and it was with a feeling of great relief from the almost constant travel of over ten thousand miles that the boys unpacked their trunks in their pleasant rooms at "The Grand." That same evening we accepted an invitation from Mr. Musgrove, a partner of Mr. Williamson, of the Royal Theatre in Sydney, and one of the famous theatrical firm of Williamson, Garnier & Musgrove, to attend the Princess Theatre, where an excellent English company was producing " The Princess Ida." We occupied a full section in the Dress Circle, the fashionable section of all Colonial theatres, and the boys, as they appeared in their evening suits, were certainly a magnificent-looking body of men. At the end of the third act we were called out to one of the reception-rooms, where we met Mr. Musgrove personally, and drank his health in a couple of cases of Monopole. The speechmaking was brief though hearty, and Mr. Musgrove informed us that the doors of his theatre were open to us at any and all times. It was past midnight when we finally reached our rooms at the hotel.

One feature of the Grand Hotel of which I had almost forgotten to speak was the number of pretty Colonial girls employed in almost every department of the big hotel. They answered the ring of one's electric bell, they hovered over one at the table in the dining-hall, they took one's order in the *café*, they did everything and anything, save handling the baggage and filling the duties of a porter. One of the boys—of course, it was Fogarty—made a ten-strike with these maidens within five minutes after his arrival among them, and during the balance of our stay at the Grand he came pretty near getting anything he wanted, from a *café noir*, served in his room, to a lunch at midnight. When he arrived he found, upon reaching his room, that his trunk had not been sent up ahead of him. With characteristic impulsiveness he stepped into the hall and rang every electric bell in sight, with the result that half a dozen

maidens were at his door within a minute after. "Me trunk," exclaimed Fogarty, in a dramatic tone; "me kingdom for me trunk."

"Why! hasn't it come up yet?" inquired a curly-headed bell-boyess.

"In truth, no," replied Fogarty; "and now look here. I am the Star
of this combination—the Star, do you understand? and me trunk I
must have, or there'll be no ball game here on Saturday. Now, do I
get my trunk, or don't I?"

There was forthwith a flutter of skirts and a patter of feet, and five
minutes later the porter stumbled into Foge's room with two heavy
trunks, while the rest of the boys were awaiting theirs in the regular
course of events.

Among the first to meet the Press representatives of our party were
the newspaper men of Melbourne, among whom I saw most of Messrs.
Linck, of the *Sportsman*, McDonald and Kendall of the *Herald*, and
Harry Hedley of the *Age*, all good fellows, and all interested in seeing
baseball established in Melbourne, and throughout the Colonies.

Our first game at Melbourne took place upon the second day after
our arrival, and our professional *début* in Victoria could scarcely have
been a more brilliant and auspicious one. Speaking of the event afterward, with Major Wardell, of the Melbourne Cricket Club, and others,
they informed me that no such large and enthusiastic gathering
of Melbournites had taken place at the Melbourne Oval since the
palmiest days of Cricket in Victoria, and, certainly, I have never seen a
prettier picture on race course or ball field, even in America, than
that which offered itself upon the Melbourne Cricket Grounds on the
occasion of our initial appearance. The sky was of the bluest, and the
turf carpet upon the carefully-tended field was of the greenest. Away
over across the waters of the Yarrow the towers and battlements of
Government House arose in picturesque silhouette against the sky, while
the pretty villas of St. Kilda could be seen further down the stream.
The lawn in front of the Club House was occupied by numbers of
pretty women, dressed in light-colored gowns and carrying bright-hued
sunshades. The Club House balconies were crowded, and two hundred
members, together with their ladies, had found seats upon the roof. The
Grand Stand was packed, both chairs and aisles being full, while the
crowd of people which encircled the field from the far end of the Grand

Stand to the Club House grounds averaged from thirty to forty deep. In short, we played to pretty nearly twelve thousand people, and the degree of interest they manifested in the game was a gratifying surprise to each and every member of our party. The game, though not an errorless one, was of the brilliant order. The base-running would have made even an American crowd of old-time ball lovers grow enthusiastic, and when Fogarty, Manning, Hanlon, Pettit, Carroll and Geo. Wood gave some exhibitions of base-sliding, of which they are so thoroughly capable, the big crowd stood up and yelled itself hoarse, while it waved wildly everything wavable that it could get its hands upon. Baldwin and Crane each pitched a pretty game, the hits standing

GRAND STAND OF THE MELBOURNE CRICKET GROUND.

seven to eight, and the score being tied three and three up to the seventh inning. Chicago finally got a man across the plate in the seventh, as a result of Burns' three-bagger, followed by Baldwin's single, then earned another run in the eighth, as a result of Sullivan's single and Anson's great three-bagger to right centre, "Anse" being put out at the plate by Brown's magnificent throw from the outfield upon trying to make a home-run off his hit. Tom Brown's running, which to me has always been one of the prettiest features of the games in which the Californian takes part, caught the Australians to a man, and many of them expressed a wish that Brown might enter for the foot-racing events there. Altogether, it was a great illustration of the beauties of the American national game, and the newspaper comments, while not altogether eulogistic, were still of a character very gratifying to those of us who had somewhat anxiously awaited the criticisms of the Melbourne press.

If the big, fine-looking fellows of our party had excited interest upon their arrival at Melbourne, they were made far more of after their game than before, for on the diamond the Melbournites had had an opportu-

THE BIG, FINE-LOOKING FELLOWS OF OUR PARTY.
(Photographed at Melbourne.)

nity of seeing the splendid physical development of the boys and their skill as athletes—qualities of manhood which are not valued higher anywhere than in Victoria, and, in fact, throughout Australia. That evening, after their game, the boys were entertained by Mr. Charles Warner, an English actor of note, at that time touring Australia. It was with the desire to meet the boys and do what he could to make it pleasant for them, that he extended to them an invitation to dine at the *Maison Doré*, the Delmonico's of Melbourne, and the dinner was

certainly a charming success in every way. There were some gems in
the way of after-dinner speeches, among which was one by Fogarty,
the centre fielder's native Irish wit leaving every man doubled up with
laughter when he finally took his seat. Of course there were also pretty
references to Americans, to the profession of ball-playing, and to the
character of our visit to Australia, and when, at eleven o'clock, the boys
shook hands with their generous host they had recorded the event as one
of the pleasantest of the trip. Although the dinner had been a treat
indeed, and although Mr. Warner was the prince of hosts, a pleasant
little supplement to the affair, coming unexpectedly, as it did, added
still further to the evening's program. Joe Thompson, by far the best-
known man of his calling in Australia, and well known throughout
England and America as a successful and wealthy bookmaker, invited
a number of Mr. Warner's guests to his rooms at the Grand Hotel,
and, with the assistance of his charming wife and beautiful daughters,
made the "wee sma'" hours memorable ones for each of his
guests.

Shortly after breakfast on the following morning, President Spalding
called the boys together in the big reading-room of the hotel, and
announced to them definitely his intention of returning home by way of
Egypt, the Mediterranean and Continental Europe. Had it not been
Sunday morning, the cheers which filled the boys' throats at this
announcement would have been let out for all they were worth, and even
as it was, the room was filled with bursts of applause, while every man
looked enthusiastically happy. President Spalding spoke frankly and
in a manner that evidently interested all. He told the boys that they
were going to strange countries, and among strange people, and that
they would have to be discreet as to their habits, if only to maintain their
good physical health. He wanted to land the boys in New York sound
and well, and with only pleasant recollections of the tour, and he hoped
that each and every member of the party would coöperate with him to
this end. When the boys finally quit the reading-room they adjourned
to the hotel rotunda and spent the balance of the morning in discussing
the experiences they would probably enjoy during the remainder of the
tour—now to become a tour around the world. The trip to Australia
in itself had been a stupendous affair in the eyes of us all, and now we

stood upon the threshold of an experience that falls to the lot of but a favored few, and it naturally aroused delightful anticipations.

Will Lynch, our advance agent, had left a day or two before for Adelaide, to overtake the P. & O. Line steamer there for Calcutta. He went to look the ground over and determine whether or not it would be advisable for us to go across to India and Bombay, or to cut that country and put in our time in Southern Europe. I met Lynch in the office of the hotel on the afternoon of his departure, and, with Yankee *sangfroid,* he shook hands with me, as he said, "Good-bye, old boy; won't see you again for a while; I'm going over to India to-night." Only a little journey of three weeks, covering sixty-four hundred miles across the Indian Ocean. It is indeed wonderful how time and distance lose their awe-inspiring proportions to the American who has traveled oceans as he has before traveled States in his own country!

Overwhelmed with attentions of all kinds, enjoying courtesies at the hands of the press, and being the recipients of public and private banquets and dinner parties without end, the boys did not suffer for lack of means for enjoyment, aside from their ball-playing, during the stay in Melbourne. Indeed, they gradually fell into the custom of getting into their dress suits every evening about six o'clock, so that they appeared in the hotel corridors for dinner in full evening dress, and were thereafter ready for the theatre or any other form of entertainment that might come up. It was a good departure, and did much, together with the demeanor of the men, to impress Australians favorably. The great Exposition Buildings were not neglected, and though scarcely so extensive or accessible as the Exposition since held in Paris, they were still a grand exhibit which attracted almost every Australian and tourist in the country.

None of us, probably, will ever forget Christmas of 1888, spent as it was in Melbourne, with the temperature standing at 90 degrees, and ourselves, as were all others in the city, attired in suits of flannel or some other equally cool-looking texture. The store windows were filled with displays of toys and Christmas gifts, and all day and evening the streets were thronged with purchasers, just as was, doubtless, the case at home, but amid surroundings so entirely different from anything we had ever experienced that we were struck with the novelty of it all.

Our second game, played the day before Christmas in the presence
of about 6000 people, pleased the crowd immensely.   It was one of
those hard-hitting games that we sometimes see at home during the
Championship season when an opposing team have dropped to the
delivery of an unfortunate pitcher and are pounding him all over the
field.   In this game, however, both pitchers—Ryan and Healy—were
the sufferers, and the batting was exceedingly lively from start to finish.
The crowd showed its appreciation by standing up and cheering when

THE EXPOSITION BUILDING AT MELBOURNE.

the ball was batted into far out-field, or sending up a great roar of
laughter when some of our crack base-runners tore the top off the green
turf for a distance of ten feet or more in a desperate slide to the base.
The boys seemed to partake of the spirit of the crowd and slugged the
ball and ran bases until they were completely tired out.   Following the
game, the " Professor " gave his first ascent and drop with a parachute
on Australian soil.   It was certainly a thrilling exhibition, and caused

the big crowd, which had never witnessed anything of the kind before, to stand in open-mouthed wonder, for Bartholomew was an artist and did his work well. At St. George's Theatre that evening a baseball farce, written for the occasion, was put upon the stage, and all of our party attended. A feature of the performance was the baton twirling and plantation dancing of Clarence Duval, the little darkey being encored again and again, and made the recipient each time of a shower of silver, besides a substantial recompense from the manager of the theatre.

Christmas day we departed from Melbourne for Adelaide. It was one of the hottest days we had experienced in Australia, and the boys turned out about ten o'clock attired in negligé shirts, belts, flannel suits and tennis shoes. We left for the Spencer Street Station at three o'clock, and were delighted to find, instead of the stuffy little English apartment cars we had expected, well appointed "Mann Boudoir cars," provided with all the comforts we could have expected in a railway carriage at home ; riding, therefore, was not only comfortable but delightful. Four hours after leaving Melbourne we stopped at Ballarat, where we were to play after our visit to Adelaide, and found a committee of citizens, together with any number of pretty girls, at the station to

PROFESSOR BARTHOLOMEW.

meet us. Of course the depot rang with American cheers and "tigahs," before our train finally pulled out for the balance of our interesting ride across Victoria and South Australia. We saw no kangaroos along the road, as we had fondly anticipated, but we did see rabbits by the thousands. Rabbits in such numbers and of such sizes as we had never before imagined existed anywhere. As our train proceeded, they jumped out of stone piles, fence corners, clumps of grass and from every conceivable hiding-place, not singly, but in droves, until we could easily understand how these little pests in such numbers had proved a curse to Australian farmers. The country is picturesque and attractive, though by no means thickly settled. Fruit grows luxuriantly, and at every station the boys purchased sacks of luscious cherries and apricots, with which we gorged ourselves until we were sleepy. Ed Crane, who had not thrived under the hot sun of Australia, and the ladies of the party had been left behind us at Melbourne.

We arrived at Adelaide the day after Christmas, about half-past ten o'clock. And was it hot? At first the heat seemed unbearable, but we gradually became accustomed to it and had forgotten it soon after reaching our cool-looking hotels. Upon our arrival at the depot, we were met by United States Consul Murphy and other citizens, and driven directly to the town hall, where we were welcomed to the city by Mayor Shaw. His Worship's address was a warm one, and the response of President Spalding equally hearty. After the hand-shaking was over we were ushered into His Worship's private room, back of the Council Chamber, where a long white-draped table groaned under a load of champagne bottles, sandwiches, Milwaukee beer and baskets of fruit. It was a welcome sight indeed after our long and dusty ride, and we fell to in earnest, winding up with a "shake-down" from Clarence and a bit of cheering that must have convinced Adelaideans that we "had our voices with us." Then we bade good-morning to His Worship and were driven to our hotels, the York, the Prince Alfred and the South Australian, at all of which quarters had been secured.

Our first game took place that afternoon, and it being the opening day of the races in Melbourne, not over 2000 people were present. The Adelaide Oval is equal to those of Sydney and Melbourne so far as the condition of the grounds is concerned, but the buildings do not compare with those on the grounds of the former cities. It is about ten minutes' drive from the hotels, over an even road, past a pretty artificial lake and beyond a well-kept park, a number of handsome residences overlooking the grounds from surrounding hills. The afternoon, though hot, was a good one for ball-playing, and the crowd applauded the batting and base-running—about the only points they seemed to understand. The game was of a decidedly heavy-batting order, resulting in a victory for the All-Americas.

That evening, despite the fact that the boys were all tired out, we accepted the invitation of Messrs. Williamson, Garnier and Musgrove to witness " The Magistrate," by an excellent English Company at the Royal Theatre. The boys, in evening dress, occupied the Governor's Box, a favor rarely extended to visitors, and it is needless to say were the observed of all observers during the evening, the house being crowded, and ladies as well as gentlemen being attired in evening costume.

Perhaps the most delightful experience we enjoyed in South Australia was that of the following morning, when at half-past ten o'clock we assembled at the Town Hall to accept Mayor Shaw's invitation for a drive. A big four-horse drag with a black body and red wheels awaited us, and at eleven o'clock the driver cracked his long whip, the horses started, and the drag with our party bowled down the principal street of the city toward the Sea Beach road. The weather was much cooler, and the delicious breeze, coupled with some of the most picturesque scenery in South Australia, made every rod of our drive an enjoyable one. We sang, cheered, laughed at Fogarty's witticisms and cracked a good-natured joke at the expense of every pedestrian and equestrian whom we happened to pass on the road until, at the end of a ten miles' spin, we drew up at the vineyard of Thomas Hardy & Sons, the largest grape and fruit raisers in Australia. Here we dismounted, partook of Mr. Hardy's generous hospitality, were shown through the citron and almond groves, and then passed through the borders of the extensive vineyard, where bunches of delicious grapes hung upon all sides, and which the boys swallowed by the pound. We saw olives, lemons, oranges and almost every other form of tropical fruit growing in profusion, and finally explored the wine cellars near the house. Down into the great cool vaults we descended, winding about through the stone walls and big bulging casks, until we finally stopped in the " reception room " of the cellar, and drank glass after glass of delicious wine drawn from bottles thick with dust and cobwebs. With our wine were served ripe figs, big juicy globules of fruit, and the finest olives I ever tasted, and down in this wine cellar we gave, in honor of our hosts, three cheers that made the old walls ring, not forgetting to add three more when we mounted our drag and bid the beautiful vineyards

farewell.   From the vineyard we drove to Henley Beach, on the shore
of the ocean, and spent half an hour in picking up the delicate shells
from the wave-washed sands, in quaffing mugs of ale as we sat upon
the balcony of the Beach Inn, and in looking out over the grand old
ocean.   Then we remounted for a delightful drive back to the city, and
for our game of the afternoon.   At our second game the attendance was
better, and the playing was especially marked by some great base-
running.   Fogarty, Ward, Pfeffer, Hanlon, Pettit and Ryan distinguished
themselves by some exhibitions of base-sliding which made the crowd
applaud enthusiastically.   Chicago won handily.

The following day being the fifty-second anniversary of South Australia's existence as a Colony, it was generally observed throughout the
country.   The Australians, by the way, are great people for holidays,
and, like the English, improve every opportunity to indulge in one.   As
we were to leave that afternoon, we played our farewell game in the
morning, beginning at ten o'clock, in the presence of a very good crowd,
the result being an easy victory for Anson's forces.   After the game
Sir William Robinson, Governor of the Colony, who had witnessed four
or five innings of the play, stepped upon the oval and shook hands with
each member of both teams, afterward welcoming them in a neat little
speech, in which he complimented the boys upon their physical prowess
and skill upon the field, and expressed his interest in the game as he
had seen it demonstrated.   After A. G.'s response and our inevitable
trio of cheers, we mounted our drags and drove back to the hotel.

Few days of our journey had been more prolific of events than that
following the day of our departure from Adelaide.   We entered the depot
at Ballarat in the morning at six o'clock, and found a committee of
citizens and a four-horse drag waiting to receive us.   When we were all
in our seats upon the top of the conveyance, A. G., as the boys had
begun to familiarly address Mr. Spalding, missed Tom Daly, and on
going back to the train, found him sleeping soundly in one of the apartment coaches and securely locked in by the guard.   Where he would
have found himself at the end of his nap, had we not found him, it is
difficult to say, but President Spalding, after a deal of hard work, found
a guard to unlock the door and succeeded in getting Tom out upon the
platform.   Probably none of us have since forgotten what a funny look-

ing object the Chicago catcher was as he stumbled out of the depot with his hair awry and with one eye open, making his way to the drag, which, after several vain attempts, he mounted. Tom was not the only one of us who wished that Pullman sleeping-coaches had been introduced into the Colonies before the date of our arrival.

The sun was just coming up over the housetops as we rattled through the streets of the awakening town, and finally drove up to the doors of Craig's Hotel. We made our toilets hastily and repaired to the breakfast room, where the Reception Committee had arranged for us a layout of hot coffee, sandwiches, chowchow pickles, and the inevitable brandy and soda, and in characteristically liberal quantities. We finally endeavored, after making an attempt to cheer our Reception Committee —an attempt, by the way, which ended in a disconnected and very sleepy "Rah-Rah"—to retire to our rooms for a very badly-needed nap, but that privilege was not to be allowed us. The Reception Committee piled us upon the drag again, and we started for the Botanical Gardens. The drive was a beautiful one, and the fresh air of the morning served to awaken us more thoroughly than anything else could have done. Our route lay along the shores of the extensive lake that penetrates the residence district, and then along the borders of the most beautiful public gardens I had ever seen. We dismounted at the main gate and spent half an hour looking and admiring the beautiful groups of statuary and the flowers. Our ride beyond the gardens was in a circle, so that at the end of two hours we were not far from our starting-point. Before pulling up at the hotel, however, we had a bath in the great Ballarat Swimming Aquarium, which refreshed us thoroughly and put us all in the best of spirits. On our return to the Craig a good breakfast awaited us, which we had scarcely swallowed when we were asked to mount the drag for another drive. This time we drove to the Barton Gold Mines, on the edge of the town. After attiring ourselves in overalls, canvas jackets, slouch hats and rough boots, we took a trip to the bottom of the mine, 1100 feet below the surface. Some of the make-ups of our party were indeed laughable: Captain Anson looked like a railway section boss, Bob Pettit like a day laborer, and A. G. like the king of a "white cap" organization. Our rough apparel filled the bill, however; for if there is a wet and slimy place on this earth—or rather, beneath it—it is the

lower end of an Australian gold-mine shaft.   A gold mine is not unlike
a coal mine in appearance, and there was really little to see save the
shadowy forms of the miners, with their ghostly-looking head-lamps, and
the dripping walls of stone and timber.   Still, it was something to have
gone to the bottom of such a cavern, and all of us were interested in
the journey.

From the mine we were driven to the Town Hall.   Ballarat, by the
way, is divided into two municipalities : East and West Ballarat.   Each

THE BOTANICAL GARDENS, THE PRIDE OF SYDNEY, N. S. W.

has its separate town officers and town hall.   We first called upon the
Mayor of West Ballarat, Mayor Macdonald, and enjoyed the same
course of feasting and wine-drinking that we had enjoyed in other Australian cities.   We then bowled through the town to East Ballarat, where
we were the recipients of another "lay-out" and hearty welcome at
the hands of Mayor Ellsworth.   Mayor Ellsworth, however, went still
further : he mounted our tally-ho with us, and drove us to the Ballarat

Orphan Asylum, where we amused ourselves by throwing shilling pieces into the waters of the bath-houses for a hundred little boys to dive for. Then we drank more wine—this time with the officers of the Institution, and finally drove back to our hotel, tired out, but possessed of a fair idea of Ballarat, its people, its hospitality and its environs. President Spalding, by the way, invited all the youngsters of the Asylum to the game, and they attended that afternoon, two hundred strong.

A great crowd for Ballarat—nearly 4500—assembled to see our game that afternoon, and showed their appreciation of it by staying until the last man had been put out. The game was a good one, All-America taking the lead in the sixth inning as a result of a pretty streak of batting that was not thereafter broken. The crowd was quick to discover and appreciate the good points in the fielding and batting, and before three innings were completed, were applauding heartily. The sensation of the afternoon, however, was the ascent and fall of Professor Bartholomew. The light air of the high altitude would not sustain his weight, and the parachute fell with great rapidity for over two thousand feet. It descended in the centre of the business district, the professor striking the cornice of a roof, and gouging himself in a manner that laid him up for a month thereafter. Altogether, he met with a very narrow escape. Our departure was taken at seven o'clock that evening for Melbourne, and the five hours' ride to the Victorian Capital in the English compartment cars was certainly the most fatiguing one we had yet experienced. The boys looked a bit knocked out when they came down to breakfast next morning, but the invigorating cold showers, with which our hotel was wonderfully well provided, had an exhilarating effect, and we entered upon the day's programme, it being Sunday, with avidity.

At eleven o'clock we mounted two big four-horse drags, with the weather as fine as I have ever seen it in Australia, and started upon a twenty-five mile drive to the mountains. A Mr. J. H. Downer, a prominent and wealthy citizen of Melbourne, had asked us to be his guests for the day, and from the moment we left the hotel we were in his hands. Mrs. Leigh Lynch had her cornet with her, and as we rolled along over the country road, the " Tally-ho, tally-ho-ho " from her clear-sounding instrument caused many pedestrians to stop and gaze curiously at our big party in our gay-colored, light flannel suits, and red, white and blue rimmed hats. We saw more of the country surrounding Melbourne on that drive than at any time during our stay. It is rolling, well settled and picturesque until one gets into the bush land, when it is, like all other Australian bush districts, covered with scrub and possessed of no beauty of scenery whatever. The scrub, however, was finally passed, and we then entered the woodland at the foot of the mountains. High upon a hill sat a pretty villa surrounded by rolling lawns and prettily appointed out-buildings, a sort of oasis in the wild wilderness. From the top of one of the buildings floated an American flag, and we gave it a rousing yell as we passed it. Several handkerchiefs fluttered from the balcony of the house, and then a turn in the road hid the scene from view.

After an hour's ride we entered a picturesque rift in the mountains, and soon were sitting on the broad balcony of Mr. Bruce's house at " Fern Glen." A prettier bit of mountain scenery could scarcely be imagined. Giant trees arose on every side of the towering mountain, and Mr. Bruce's house and artistically laid out grounds appeared on the sides of the hill as if photographed there, with the mountain's growth as a frame work. Mr. Bruce, a friend of Mr. Downer, had gladly consented to entertain our party, and a big wagon-load of wines and delicacies had been sent out ahead of us that morning. The long table, with its load of good things, which had been set upon the balcony, was a welcome sight to our hungry crew, and we were not long in getting at it. It was a rich spread, embracing everything from champagne to soda and from roast turkey to sardines, and that we left little of it upon the table it is unnecessary to say. After dinner we took a walk through the beautiful glen above the house, our pathway being arched with great ferns that rose from twelve to fifteen feet high on each side of us, while a mountain stream, of crystal-like water, wound its way between their roots. At the head of the glen we seated ourselves upon a mammoth old moss-covered log, and listened to the " Star Spangled Banner " from Mrs. Lynch's cornet.

An hour later, at the house, Clarence Duval gave us another of his Alabama shakedowns to a guitar and mandolin accompaniment, and then with three cheers for Fern Glen, we turned our faces toward Melbourne. En route, we passed the stock farm of J.

J. Miller, who has undertaken the breeding of American trotting horses from imported mares and sires, on Victorian soil. It was he who had displayed the American flag to our gaze on the way out, and he now sent a messenger to ask us up to the house. It was late, but we could not refuse an invitation so offered. Upon dismounting we were cordially greeted, and were then shown the stock—Architect, by Contractor; Red Wind by Red Wilkes; Lucretia, by Mambrino Boy, Jr., and representatives of other equally celebrated strains. Then we

A JOLLY PARTY AT FERN GLEN.

were wined and toasted upon the broad balconies of mine host's pretty residence. Another exhibition of plantation dancing from Clarence, and more heartfelt cheering, and we bowled down the road, leaving mine host Miller standing at the gate. The "Travelers' Rest," the "Golden Swan," "Bull's Head Inn," and like hostelries were stopped at on our way back, for rest and refreshments, and we finally dismounted at eleven o'clock that evening in front of the Grand Hotel, where we shook hands with Mr. Downer, our host of the day.

An enticing programme had been scheduled for the last day of the year, but unfavorable weather partly spoiled it. The Carleton and St. Kilda Football teams were to play a game of football, Victorian rules, upon the pretty grounds of the St. Kilda's. Then our team was to play a game of ball with a team picked from the Melbourne cricketers, and the programme was to wind up with a game of football between the St. Kilda's and twenty of the Americans. The football game between the Australians proved a most interesting contest. There was a big crowd present, and much enthusiasm was manifested. The rules are a modification even of our most modified American college rules, and contain many points that make the Australian game in every way the most interesting of any football game I ever witnessed. As the fun proceeded our boys realized that we could make little show against the Australians, but they had no opportunity of testing their ability, as a heavy rain put a stop to the afternoon's sport.

ABORIGINAL AUSTRALIAN WOMAN AND BABE.

Two games were scheduled for New Year's day, but only one full game was played—that of the morning. The attendance was light, not more than 2000 people being present, and considering that there were 40,000 people present at the race-track, and as many more at the various cricket and athletic games going on about Melbourne, this attendance for a ball game in Australia was not unsatisfactory. President Moore, of the Victorian

Jockey Club, had invited our entire party to the races, but, as we were unable to procure a conveyance of any kind, we could not accept, and remained at the cricket grounds, where the pure air and beautiful surroundings, together with an elaborate lunch set out for us by Secretary Wardell, of the Melbourne Club, was greatly enjoyed.

After the lunch an exhibition of boomerang-throwing and rope-skipping was given for the entertainment of the crowd and our party by a number of aboriginals, and it was certainly a treat, at least to the Americans present. The degree of skill attained by the black-faced, bushy-haired Queenslanders in the use of the boomerang is certainly remarkable. That afternoon, half a dozen big fellows performed feats with the peculiar Australian weapon which our party had frequently read of, but had never before credited. The light " V "-shaped piece of wood, with its sharp edges, shot from the hands of the natives into the air for a distance of two or three hundred feet, and then, turning suddenly, described perhaps half a dozen circles

ABORIGINAL AUSTRALIAN MAN AND BOY WITH BOOMERANG.

about the head of the thrower, gradually narrowing the circle until it fell almost at his feet. Again it would go out in a direct line and return in a line as direct, passing over the head of the thrower and returning back again to the spot upon which he stood. The skipping-rope performance, with which the natives are wont to amuse themselves, was quite a grotesque and yet clever performance, the per-

9

formers assuming all kinds of queer postures, and yet never failing to raise their bodies from the ground, and at the proper moment, to permit of the rope passing under them at regular intervals. Several of the boys tried their hands at boomerang throwing, and discovered how very little they knew of the use of the Australian weapon. After this exhibition, the Chicago team played an exhibition game with a team composed of Melbourne cricketers, and the crowd enjoyed this about as well, judging from their laughter and applause, as any game we played upon the Melbourne grounds. Rain stopped the play, however, and the players soon after returned to their hotel.

January 5th was the day set for our last game in Australia, it having been decided to sail from Port Melbourne for Ceylon the following Monday afternoon. The intervening time was consequently put in as the boys liked best, and in view of the long trip ahead of us there was much to do in the way of shopping. All articles of clothing are cheap in Australia, compared with our American prices, and nearly all of us laid in a generous provision of flannel suits, underwear and linen. Curios and mementoes characteristic of the country and people also took a fair share of our pocket money and attention. Most of us secured a kangaroo skin, an emu egg, a lump of kauri gum, and photographs of the principal Australian cities. Many of the boys visited the American exhibit at the Exposition, which was quite extensive and altogether very creditable.

The night before our departure, by the way, was an eventful one at the Grand Hotel. The two hundred and fifty guests had scarcely gotten into bed when the interior of the big court was illuminated by a red glow, and cries of "Fire," rang out upon the air. Consternation prevailed; women screamed and men shouted. Manning, of the All-Americas, stuck his head out of the window to learn the trouble and received a champagne bottle on the back of his neck, which cut him badly. Others who followed Manning's example were drenched with water from the upper windows, and it soon became evident that somebody in the building was bent upon making the night interesting for every guest in the establishment. Among the first to hear the cries and be awakened by the lurid glare from the court were Fred Pfeffer and Clarence Duval, Clarence having curled up in a blanket on the floor of

Pfeffer's room. Fred jumped from the bed with one bound and made for the door, but stumbled over Clarence on the way.

"Don't stop to talk, boy," cried Pfeffer, "but get out of here as quick as you can ; don't you see the hotel is on fire?"

At this, Clarence, seeing the glow, became panic-stricken and lost no

A PRECIPITATE FLIGHT ON A FALSE ALARM.

time—though, like Pfeffer, attired only in his abbreviated night robe—in following the second baseman out into the hall and down the stair-case, Pfeffer, doubtless actuated by humanitarian motives, calling "Fire," and pounding at the doors as he ran. Down the stairs went one section of Chicago's stone-wall in-field, seven steps at a time, closely followed by the little African, who was adding his cries to Pfeffer's. The cause, as it turned out, was simply the drunken spree of a couple of young tourists on the upper floor of the hotel, but it threatened for a time to be of a serious character, several ladies fainting and a number of others being greatly terrified by the uproar. When the excitement had finally subsided, and it was learned that the whole trouble had been caused by the burning of a red light on one of the window-sills, accompanied by the howls of the practical jokers, a crowd of angry men in night attire searched the halls, and many of the bed-rooms, for the perpetrators, but finally gave up the effort. Then they eagerly demanded to know who the man was who had gone through the halls yelling fire, and Pfeffer, in night attire like the balance of them, was as anxious as the rest to discover the identity of the villain, although it is said he was inwardly trembling at the time for fear that some one who had seen him as he was charitably arousing the guests from their slumbers by his warning cries, might point him out as the culprit. Clarence Duval was found crouching behind the big water-cooler in the office, trying hard to cover his black legs with a floor-rug. His only comment upon the entire performance was: "Befoh Gawd, I nevah knowed how fass Massah Peffah could run till to-night; he nevah touched de floah fum de top of dem stairs clean to de bottom, an' I knows what I's talkin' about, kase I was mighty cloas behin 'im."

Our farewell game in Australia was played Saturday afternoon, and the assemblage of spectators present, both as to character and numbers, showed the interest which our visit had awakened in the American game. The day was a perfect one for field-sport exhibitions, and when the great crowd of between eleven and twelve thousand had filed through the gates, surrounding the beautiful oval with a living framework of humanity, the scene was indeed brilliant. The programme was a varied one, opening with a two-inning game at three o'clock between the All-America team and a team of cricketers. As in previous engagements, between the Australians and Americans, the superiority of the latter in fielding was plainly apparent. In fact, the Australians were not in the game at all, but they worked hard and evinced the deepest interest in every point of play. At half-past three o'clock, after the completion of two innings between the Australians and Americans, a football game between the Port Melbourne and the Carleton team began, and a prettier exhibition of the kind I have never seen. The Victorians have pruned down and modified the old Rugby rules in a style that has removed much of the danger to life and limb, while it has at the same time increased the opportunities for the display of skill, and has given the game a greater dash and vim than appear in our American college game. I have only one criticism to make of the Australian football teams, and that is this. If they were, as a body, to pay more attention to the selection and designs of their uniforms, they would be a much finer-looking set. The contrast between the becomingly uniformed ball-players and the pick-up costumes of the footballers was much to the discredit of the latter. But they know how to play football, for all that; and I imagine that there is a great deal of truth in the assertion that any football team from England, or America, that can go over there and beat the Australians at their own game, can carry away a cartload of money.

Following the football game, the Chicagos and All-Americas began a five-inning ball game, which was as pretty an exhibition as any we had given since leaving Chicago. Baldwin and Daly, and Crane and Earle were the batteries, and they played ball for all they were worth. When game was called at the end of the fifth inning to clear the field for the long-distance throwing contest the score stood 5 to 0 in favor of Chicago, with not a fielding error on either side, every run of the five having been earned by Anson's men, and but one safe hit scored off Baldwin. The fleetest of the All-America base-runners were unable to steal a base on Daly or Baldwin, and it was equally true that the quickest throwers to bases in the league could not have stopped the Chicago men that day in their thieving practices. Crane and Earle never watched bases more carefully or more accurately, but it was to no purpose—Chicago was out for plunder and got all it wanted, through some of the prettiest base-sliding I ever witnessed. The crowd appreciated many points of the game, which they had not seen or understood at our opening exhibition ten days before, a fact made evident from the applause created over pretty pieces of work, and when Pettit finally ended the game with a great running catch of Earle's long hit to right field, the big crowd

applauded until the players had lifted their caps in front of the grand
stand.

The exhibition of long-distance throwing was not less interesting than
the other portions of the programme, the object being to beat the five and
one-half ounce Cricket Ball, Australian record, of 126 yards 3 inches.
The effort was made by Crane, Williamson and Pfeffer, and was accomplished by Crane, who sent the ball 128 yards 10½ inches. It was a
magnificent throw, and elicited a yell of applause the moment the ball
struck the ground, the crowd seemingly realizing that the record had
been broken, before the measurements were taken. Neither Williamson nor Pfeffer was in shape for throwing, the former failing to reach
126 yards, and the latter falling several feet short of that. The Professor was to have concluded the day's sport with a parachute leap, but had
not sufficiently recovered from his injuries sustained at Ballarat to make
the attempt. It was nearly six o'clock when the crowd filed through the
gates and on through the beautiful Fitzroy Gardens toward town, the
members of our party stopping at the Club House to bid farewell to
Major Wardell and the cricketers, among whom the boys had made many
friends during their stay. Our last evening in Melbourne was spent by
some of the boys at the theatres, by others at Martin Castello's resort,
where there was a L.t of fun with the gloves between middle weights.
Still others dropped in at the parlors of genial Joe Thompson, where
music, Pomeroy Sec, and Joe's generous hospitality made the evening a
memorable one.

On the following morning the boys came down to breakfast attired in
purple and fine linen, realizing no doubt that it would be the last opportunity for a display of their "store clothes" for some time to come.
The rotunda of the Grand was crowded with people all day, many of
them personal friends of the boys who had dropped in for a farewell
chat. The day was beautiful, and some of us improved our time by a
drive through the environs, or a stroll through Fitzroy Gardens, which
were but a short walk from the hotel. The evening for the greater part
was occupied in packing, and the following morning at 10.30 saw our
luggage piled upon the two huge vans required to cart it to the depot. At
three o'clock we drove to Port Melbourne Station, near Princess Bridge,
where we took the train for Port Melbourne dock, seven miles distant.

This port gives superb accommodations for a fleet of fine sailing vessels and steamships, which cluster here from all quarters of the globe. Here lay the " Salier," one of the German Lloyd Steamers, which was to carry us across the Indian Ocean, and we were all soon comfortably settled in our respective state-rooms.   Captain Thalenhorst and the Chief Steward and Purser, with whom we were brought most in contact on board, were affable and pleasant Germans, and had made every preparation for our comfort.   On the "Alameda" the steerage passengers occupied the steerage, and the first cabin and saloon passengers were stationed amidships ; On the "Salier," however, the steerage passengers

THE "SALIER" AT HER DOCK AT PORT MELBOURNE.

occupied the forward deck, and the cabin and first-class passengers were given the entire after part of the boat. The quarter-deck was covered with a big awning, and this furnished a magnificent lounging place, which we enjoyed during our entire voyage through the tropics. It was learned that the " Salier " would probably not sail before daybreak, and some of the boys returned to the city, but the majority remained on the steamer. The scene from the dock that afternoon, with its score or more of big sailing vessels alongside, its red-turbaned, dark-skinned Turks and Hindoos in their queerly-fashioned costumes of bright-colored cloth, together with the warm sun, the blue waters of the bay over which sea birds circled and little crafts moved hither and thither, with the picturesque shores of St. Kilda on one side and the smoke of Melbourne on the other, offered interesting studies for all. We had dinner aboard the steamer. Afterwards we sought the deck, where with our cigars, musical talent, and the company of friends who had come down to the steamer to see us off, we easily managed to put in a pleasant evening.

ON THE INDIAN OCEAN.

The "Salier" sailed from her dock at Port Melbourne at daylight on the morning of January 8th, and steamed slowly down the harbor toward the great Australian Bight. We were now fairly under way upon what most of us remember as the most delightful ocean voyage of our tour. The first week was not so pleasant, for after leaving Port Adelaide, at which we stopped twelve hours, we encountered a cold, raw wind from the South Seas, and the ocean swell was disagreeably heavy. After we had passed this portion of the voyage, however, and began to near the tropics, the air became warm, the sky clear, and the sea smooth, until more delightful sailing could scarcely be imagined. The quarter-deck of the ship, with its open-windowed smoking- and card-room, formed the assembly place of our party from the breakfast hour until midnight, and then, as upon the Pacific Ocean, most of the boys preferred donning their pjamas, and sleeping in the big, easy steamer-chairs, to going to their state-rooms. We were protected during the day by the immense awning, and at night, with a tropical moon lighting the surrounding ocean and making clear everything about the ship, our mandolins and guitars were brought out for a musical soiree on deck, which lost none of its charm for our party because of its originality, or through lack of artistic practice. The officers of the ship could not have been kinder, and it was with real regret that we parted from them when we left the ship at Suez.

There were probably 150 emigrants aboard, embracing Hindoos, Chinamen, Irishmen, Cingalese, Italians and Germans, and it was indeed interesting to take a walk through their quarters, and listen to the babble of tongues that one heard upon all sides. On the forward deck and amidships were located the scullery, the store-rooms and the stock-pens of the ship in which were kept two fat milch-cows, a number of sheep and calves and beeves, which were killed as we needed them for the table during the voyage, to say nothing of porkers, chickens, pigeons, pheasants, quail and all other animals and fowls which the

purser intended for consumption by the four hundred people aboard the ship.

The cooking done on the "Salier" was really excellent, and meals were served in courses, which was at no time attempted on the "Alameda." The waiters were all German, and few of them spoke a single word of English, so that the attempts of some of our boys to make themselves understood at table were laughable. Several of us, however, were German scholars, and managed to help the others in learning sufficient German to make themselves fairly understood. We missed Frank Lincoln on this trip, he having decided to remain in Australia and take advantage of opportunities there offered.

CAPTAIN THALENHORST, OF THE "SALIER."

As there were not over half a dozen first-class passengers aboard in addition to our own party, we, figuratively speaking, owned the ship. The officers were not over-zealous in enforcing rules that might have been obnoxious or annoying to the boys and, in fact, allowed us to do

very much as we chose, so that one was likely to hear a college chorus
on deck at midnight, or to be startled during the quiet of the afternoon
by a simultaneous cheer from a score of the boys in memory, perhaps,
of our homes in far-off America.

During the afternoon of the day of our departure, I took a stroll over
the "Salier" from stem to stern, and made myself familiar with every
corner of our good ship, and at the same time studied her by no means
uninteresting congregation of passengers. In the first-class cabin there
was, in addition to our party, an Australian lady, a resident of Melbourne, who was taking her two little daughters to Germany to be left
at school. There were, also, a couple of young civil engineers, who
were returning home to England after a year's sojourn in Australia.
But by far the greatest character on board ship was a Mr. Theophilus
Green, a portly, middle-aged, red-faced, bald-headed individual, who,
according to his own story, had an ample bank account, no kinsmen,
and no object on earth but to hold himself up as a representative
American among the various countries of the globe, which he visited as
the whim or inclination might suit him to jump from Persia to Egypt,
from Russia to South Africa, or from Iceland to Ceylon. He was a
man possessed of quite a fund of interesting information, and yet his
manner of impressing that fact upon all whom he met was so disagreeable that it detracted greatly, if it did not entirely destroy what
would otherwise have made his companionship delightful. He had
traveled all over the world, had seen everything, had mingled with
almost every race of people under the sun, and possessed what
must certainly have been a valuable collection of photographs of the
different peoples and countries he had seen; but in the midst of an
interesting description of Cairo, or Jerusalem and its people, he would
suddenly break off to tell how smart he had been in evading the thieving and bulldozing propensities of an Egyptian cabman, or a Syrian innkeeper; and, laying his finger upon the side of his nose, would devote
five minutes perhaps to telling how vastly superior was his own cunning
to that of the Cingalese, Neapolitan, or Muscovite beggars who had so
often appealed to him for alms. He never failed, in his conversation,
to impress one with the fact that in every country, and with whomso-
ever he had been brought in contact, he declared himself to be a thor-

oughly "representative American." My chief regret was that our party of magnificent-looking fellows, with their liberal ideas, their love of fun, their fine physiques, and their genial, happy natures, were not going to some of the countries that Mr. Green had visited, so that, in the matter of representative Americans we might have shown those peoples the difference. We left the old fellow at Suez, when we departed from the "Salier" to go to Cairo, but there is a lingering suspicion in my mind that Mr. Green would have been with us all through Egypt and Continental Europe, but for the perhaps too brusquely offered snubbings which the majority of the boys extended. We never saw him afterwards, and he is probably knocking around the Orient at this writing, still posing as a "representative American."

Among the second-cabin passengers were two young Australians, big, broad-shouldered, muscular-looking fellows, of whom we saw a good deal as they paced the deck amidships for their daily exercise. They were bound for Zanzibar in Africa, and were to penetrate as far as possible into the interior upon a hunting expedition, which they intended to extend indefinitely as their health and success permitted. They were well equipped with weapons of modern construction and an unlimited supply of ammunition. They anticipated a great time, but I do not think any of our party, even had the opportunity offered, would have joined these gentlemen in facing the wild beasts and still wilder savages of Central Africa. Think of it! They expected to penetrate for 700 miles at least; to be cut off from all connection of any and every kind with civilization; to take their lives in their hands among savage tribes, who would be as likely to murder them for their weapons as not; to face the dangers of climate and poisonous reptiles, and all for their love of adventure and their desire to slay the King of Beasts in his native lair. We accepted an invitation to break a farewell bottle with them in the cabin before they finally left us at Aden, the nearest point to which the "Salier" could take them in their journey to Zanzibar. I am still anticipating a letter which will tell me of their first month's experience upon the dark continent.

Our mascot, by the way, was a great object of interest to the German waiters aboard the "Salier." On the "Alameda" he had been made to do light chores of different kinds, that he might to some extent pay for his passage, but on the "Salier" the German waiters attended to his wants as though he had been an Indian prince. Indeed, two of them got into a difficulty one evening over a dispute as to which should serve Mr. Duval at the table, and the captain made one of the poor beggars "walk the bridge" all night, by way of penalty. The young African finally began to entertain so exalted an opinion of his own importance, however, that Mr. Spalding quietly suggested to Captain Thalenhorst that it might be a good idea to keep the boy employed. Consequently,

CLARENCE'S HUMILIATION AT THE PUNKA ROPE.

he was set to work pulling the punka rope, which swings the big tapestry fans suspended over the saloon tables ; and thereafter, at meal time, the mascot sat on a chair at the end of the dining saloon pulling the rope, the picture of offended dignity, while the boys further added to his mortification by pegging an occasional ship's biscuit at him on the quiet.

Our only stop between Port Melbourne and Ceylon was that made at Port Adelaide, the second night after our departure. The Port is seven miles from Adelaide proper, a hot-looking little settlement, its buildings and streets apparently unsheltered by foliage of any kind, and we merely stopped to take on a cargo of South Australian wool. We did not finish loading, however, until two o'clock the following afternoon, and during the day employed our time by fishing over the rail of the ship, playing shuffleboard, horse billiards, quoits, and other deck games that we had picked up on the Pacific. The fishing was

AMUSEMENTS ON SHIPBOARD.

not bad sport, and as a dozen of us were leaning over the stern rail, watching the school of mackerel about our hooks, we were suddenly startled by the appearance of a shark, a big fellow, certainly not less than fifteen feet long. He lazily rolled about the stern of the ship as though in search of food, and then passed slowly out of sight. Had there been a shark hook at hand we might have enjoyed some rare sport. Shortly afterward, the black dorsal fin of the shark was seen a hundred feet from our boat as he swam slowly along, and Fogarty, Ryan, Ward and myself got our revolvers and made things so uncomfortable for his sharkship that he quickened his pace for the shore and was soon out of sight. After luncheon, we finished our loading and started on our trip across the Indian Ocean, not again to be interrupted until we had arrived in Ceylon.

The ensuing three days were thoroughly disagreeable. The sky was hidden by low, scudding, lead-colored clouds, the water was lashed into huge waves by a stiff wind, and a ground swell gave our ship a most uncomfortable motion. The ladies of the party, with the exception of Mrs. Williamson, who proved an excellent sailor during the entire tour of the world, did not appear on deck at all. Even Anson was pale and sick for the first time since leaving "Frisco." John Tener, Fred Pfeffer, the "Professor," myself, and the Mascot were the only ones who did not yield to sea-sickness. Fogarty's merry voice was hushed. He lay listlessly on a steamer chair and sighed softly to himself. About three o'clock in the afternoon he began to feel better and called for a cheese sandwich. A waiter appeared in a few moments with a big plate of sauerkraut and some steamed bologna sausages, thinking, no doubt, in the goodness of his German heart, that that which would please his own German stomach would best suit Fogarty's. "Foge" gave one horrified look at it and rolled upon the deck while he begged the Dutchman to take it away. Mrs. Anson fainted, and poor "Woody," Tom Brown, Ryan and Tom Burns all turned an idealic sea green at the same moment. John Tener fortunately happened along, however, and brought relief to the afflicted ones by grasping the tow-headed waiter by the coat collar and the slack of his trousers and hustling him, together with his plate, out of sight. It was rough and the temperature uncomfortably cool for fully four days during our journey through the Australian Bight, but after the ship had changed her course from an easterly to a northeasterly one, it began to grow warmer and the clouds gradually disappeared until the glorious sun of a southern clime warmed our party into life and genial temper. From thence on the weather grew more and more beautiful until, when we finally reached Ceylon, the Arabian Sea, and the Gulf of Aden, it could not possibly have been more delightful.

During our two weeks' voyage across the Indian, we were naturally driven to every recourse for means of passing the time. In view of our journey through Egypt, and possibly through India, the boys devoted themselves studiously to such books of travel as "An Australian Abroad," "India, Historical and Descriptive," "Jerusalem and the Holy Land;" and others of like titles, but one could not read all day, and consequently each man of us utilized what ingenuity he possessed to hit upon some means of diversion. So soon as the weather became pleasant, we divided into groups of four or five and took a trip through the emigrant quarters of the ship, which enabled us to realize, from what we saw, how complete a little world in itself is a big Ocean steamer. There were the cow stables, the pig pen, chicken coops, sheep pens, pigeon coops, and the quarters where our veal and beef supply was kept. The steerage passengers sat about the deck engaged in various characteristic occupations. The German women were knitting, the Italians engaged in mending some gaudy-colored article of clothing, and the red-turbaned Turks were patiently tracing out artistic patterns in colored silk and bead work, which they afterwards sold to the cabin passengers. Anson, with his usual luck, succeeded in winning a handsome silk pillow, beautifully embroidered, which had been raffled off by an old Hindoo at a shilling a chance. The Hindoos, by the way, are an interesting lot for study. There were several castes represented among the dozen aboard, and the rigidity with which the lines of distinction were drawn was remarkable. They would eat nothing cooked by the ship's crew. In their eyes all Europeans are infidels, whose hands must not defile the food of a Mohammedan. They therefore carried their own saucepans and did their own cooking, even killing a sheep every few days with their own hands, which with their own hands they prepared for food. Fogarty early during the voyage christened the forward deck the "Zoo," and he used to show small parties of us through, as though he were the keeper of a menagerie, explaining the habits and origin of the different animals and the different races of people, to the infinite amusement of us all.

Speaking of the Hindoos reminds me that one of them, a merchant of Calcutta, died during the voyage. He had been ill from the time of leaving Adelaide, and gave up the ghost when our voyage across the Indian had been about half completed. With no ceremony whatever he was sewed up in a piece of canvas, with a bar of lead at his feet, and was laid away in his bunk. All the passengers, including those in the steerage, inquired anxiously when the burial was to take place, for all were naturally eager to witness a burial at sea. Their inquiries elicited only unsatisfactory answers, however, and the death had been almost forgotten by the first-class passengers. The following night, however, myself and my fellow newspaper correspondent were smoking a last cigar in our state-room, a few minutes before two o'clock. Through the port holes we could see the waves of the ocean as they rolled themselves into great sheets of silver under the light of a tropical moon, while the ship glided along as it had done without interruption since leaving Port Adelaide. Suddenly the screw ceased to revolve and my friend and myself were startled into silence by the occurrence of so strange an event. Before we had recovered from our surprise we heard a splash in the waters at the bow,—a splash much like that made by a log striking the water,—then all was still. As suddenly as it had stopped, the screw began to revolve again and the "Salier" proceeded on her way. "The Hindoo!" exclaimed my friend; and such it was. By the light of the stars the Hindoo's body had been quietly dropped into the blue ocean, to go down, down, into the dark depths of the sea, to its last earthly resting-place.

The smallest trifles at sea will interest an entire ship-load of passengers. For instance, a pigeon escaped from a coop during the voyage and perched upon the yardarm of the mast. Ever after, that bird was an object of the deepest solicitude to all on board. Water and food were placed within its reach, and after it had flown to the horizon in every direction searching for land, it finally gave up the effort and returned to the ship. After two days of fasting it eagerly partook of the fresh water and cracked wheat that were set out for it. In a few days it became so tame that the first officer succeeded in throwing a net over it, and the fortunate pigeon, no longer fated, as his fellows were, to lie upon a platter surrounded by mushrooms that he might delight the eye and palate of some one of our epicures, was placed in a gilded parrot cage and hung in the officer's room, to be ever afterward the pet and harbinger of good luck to this intelligent though superstitious man.

One afternoon, when it was insufferably stupid, the boys called a mock court in the smoking-room, with Fogarty presiding, and there passed a decree to the effect that, "in view of the excessively warm weather, and through consideration for the comfort and peace of mind of our entire party, Clarence Duval, our chocolate-colored mascot, must take a bath." The object of the decree fled to the uttermost depths of the steerage when he heard his sentence pronounced, but Tom Daly, Pettit, and Mark Baldwin effected his capture, and, despite his cries, thrust him beneath the salt-water shower and held him there until the tank was emptied. Clarence, on being released, went on the war-path armed

with a baseball bat, but was finally dissuaded from his really murderous resolves.

CARRYING OUT THE SENTENCE.

One of the pleasantest reminders of home which we had during our voyage across the Indian occurred during the afternoon of January 22d, when, with our ship steaming along over waters that were perfectly placid and the boys lying about in their steamer chairs, John Ward happened to discover a sail ahead. His exclamation aroused us all. Books were dropped in haste, steamer chairs were abandoned, and our entire party rushed to the ship's rail to gaze upon the stately vessel a mile ahead of us. She lay drifting about upon the waters, but with every sail set. Nearer and nearer we drew to the cloud of canvas until one of the boys read her name with a field glass—"Sam Schofield, Brunswick, Me." Almost at the same moment the stars and stripes were run up from the stranger's deck. The cheer that went up from the deck of the "Salier" as we passed the Yankee made us hoarse for at least two days, and when the cheering had died away, I discovered tears in the eyes of at least half the members of our party.

10

Clarence astonished us all one morning by an act that might have delayed our ship long enough to pick him out of the water, if, indeed, one of the big sharks, which we occasionally caught sight of, had not made a meal of him. It seems that he had made a bet with one of the boys that with an umbrella he could successfully imitate the " Professor's" parachute leap, and that, before the voyage was over, he would jump from the rigging at least thirty feet above the deck and land safe upon the awning. One afternoon, when half a dozen of us were lying about under the awning on the quarter-deck, we were startled by a shadow above us and then a fall, as the canvas gave a foot or two with some object that had evidently struck it on the upper side, followed by a scream of terror. We jumped to our feet and ran to the rope ladders near the smoking-room, and climbed to a point overlooking the awning. There was the mascot, making his way carefully on hands and knees to the rigging, while a reversed umbrella in a badly-damaged condition lay upon the awning.

"What in the world are you doing?" asked Fogarty of the boy. Clarence would not reply at first, but finally informed us that he had " Gist bin practicin'," and that if he had landed all right, it had been his intention to win his bet the next morning. Nothing could induce him, however, to make a second attempt.

The negro game of "craps," introduced by the mascot, soon became a popular pastime in the card room, and in some portions of the vessel, at almost every hour of the day, one could hear the voice of Clarence as, engaged in a game with some of the players, he kept up his calls of, "Come, seben," "Come along dar eight," "What's de matter wid yo nine?" and other like expressions, without which no American negro ever engaged in his favorite method of gambling.

Captain Thallenhorst prepared a pleasant little surprise for us one afternoon after we had been out ten days, by sending the Steward on deck to announce to our half-slumbering party that a ten-gallon keg of German beer, "right off the ice," had been placed on tap below. Ten seconds later there was not a man on deck. The beer keg, however twenty minutes after the announcement, was carried forward in an empty condition.

Such were some of the incidents on the old "Salier," until the morning of January 25th, when we caught our first glimpse of the outlying islands south of Ceylon. Just as the sun came up out of the ocean we saw dimly the coast of Elephant Island, which was in all probability originally a portion of the island of Ceylon itself. At about ten o'clock we sighted the main island, and from that time on until we landed, our interest in the strange country we were approaching was kept keenly alive by all that we saw. Strange-looking, narrow-bodied native boats, called "proas," danced about in the waves and along the beach, paddled here and there by their dark-skinned, naked boatmen, while dolphins plunged and scampered through the water about our bow in great schools, and a hundred sea birds circled about our masts, keeping up their incessant cries as of welcome. We passed Point de Galle, formerly the mailing port of the Island before this distinction was transferred to Columbo, and looked with curiosity upon its ancient walls with their white cement and their background of bending, top-heavy-looking cocoanut trees. Finally, we sighted Columbo, and from three to half-past four o'clock, when we stopped at the entrance of the breakwater to receive the Harbor Master on board, we watched with deep interest the walls and harbor of the city as they became more and more distinct on our closer approach.

There is no natural harbor at Columbo, the city lying upon the open seacoast, and the Government has been compelled to construct an artificial breakwater, a massive stone wall, stretching obliquely away from the shore for a distance of nearly a mile, thus forming a quiet and deep anchorage for vessels of the greatest draught. The Harbor Master's boat, which drew alongside the ship, was manned by black fellows, the upper part of their bodies perfectly bare and the lower limbs but half concealed by a sheet-like robe that hangs from the waist. They were the native Cingalese. We were able to tell this from their long hair, brushed straight back from the forehead and rolled into a knot at the back of the neck, where it was held in place by big tortoise-shell combs. They chattered and gesticulated like a lot of monkeys, and were almost as noisy as the hordes of jackdaws and Cingalese crows which circled around the masts of our ship. No sooner had we dropped anchor than boats of every conceivable character and color put out from the shore and came toward us. There were Cingalese, Malays, and Hindoos of every caste and religion, all talking and yelling and waving their arms and long-handled paddles as they clustered about the "Salier." The queer-fashioned boats, the black bodies of the oarsmen and the red, yellow, green, orange, purple and other brilliant hues of their costumes, with the strangely constructed city and the tall groves of cocoanut palms on the shore, made the scene exceedingly picturesque.

The central object of interest to our party was a little canoe of bam-

THE ODD FISHING-BOATS OF THE CINGALESE.

boo logs upon which knelt four Cingalese boys, the youngest probably eight and the eldest twelve years of age. They paddled their craft about with barrel staves of bamboo and called to us to throw them money. Accordingly, many a sixpence and shilling piece went into the water, and in every instance the seemingly amphibious little animals would dive for them and secure them as soon as they reached the bottom. More than that, they clambered upon the rigging and dived from a distance of thirty feet or more into the water, and then dived under our ship, which was drawing twenty feet of water, and came up upon the opposite side. The "Trow it" of these little fellows, as they looked toward us with their expressive eyes, their long, dark hair dripping and their bodies glistening with the water of the harbor as they called to us to throw our silver at them, was mimicked by the different members of our party for days after we had left Ceylon. Native guards, hotel solicitors, money changers, and natives of other trades clambered over the ship and were soon objects of interest and study for us all. All was babble, confusion, and hurry, and in the midst of it all Mr. Spalding, accompanied by Leigh Lynch, started for the shore just as a drenching rain almost hid the town from view.

IN CEYLON.

At this particular time we were an undecided party. Was the "Salier" to sail at six o'clock in the morning without us, or were we to give up our trip to Calcutta and Bombay? All depended upon the word left for us by our advance agent, Will Lynch. Mr. Spalding had not obtained this when he returned an hour later, but he had made arrangements for the party at the Grand Oriental Hotel. Consequently steam launches conveyed us from the steamer to the dock, a fancifully-constructed, pagoda-like building on the shore, and, after passing through the Custom office, we entered upon the broad avenue that led directly up to the imposing entrance of the hotel, said to be the finest south of the Mediterranean. It is certainly a great structure and admirably adapted in design to the climate of Ceylon. We were shown to our respective rooms, immediately upon going into the hotel, by the dark-skinned servants in their picturesque garments and tortoise-shell combs. The high ceilings, the towering columns, the great dining-hall with its surrounding galleries, in which were Turkish divans for the use of guests, the stone balconies with their adjoining galleries, the latticed, carpetless, polished-floored bedroom—everything one looks upon reminds him of the fact that he is in a country different from any on the face of the globe save India. We enjoyed an excellent dinner. We were fanned by the great swinging punkas which were swayed backward and forward by

the natives outside the walls, while we partook of tender capons, delicious curries, and juicy bananas, but turned up our noses at the foul-
smelling Bombay duck, which seems to be a standard dish on this section of the globe. Our *café noir* was served us as we sat in easy chairs
upon one of the big stone balconies outside the dining-hall, and we
indulged in mouthfuls of tobacco smoke between sips. Then we got
under our bonnets and went out to see the town.

Columbo is quite ancient, but no doubt the buildings with their white
walls and pot-tiled roofs are the most comfortable for the inhabitants,
if they are not as prepossessing in appearance as they might be. The
streets, however, are well laid out, the parks spacious and numerous,
and the people themselves as interesting a study as I had met with on
the trip. The Indian shops under the hotel attracted most of our party
during the best part of the evening. Every imaginable article of Indian
manufacture was displayed for sale. Inlaid boxes, tortoise-shell toilet
articles, sandal-wood boxes, carvings in ebony and ivory, embroidered
shawls, curtains, portières, and what-nots of a thousand names were
purchased, and invariably for one-third or one-fourth the price asked
by the storekeepers. An offer of one pound would be pretty sure to
secure an article marked four pounds, and this rule holds good, I understood, throughout India.

One of the peculiar institutions of Columbo is the "jinrickshaw,"
which answers the purpose of the Hansom cabs of Chicago or New
York. The "jin" is very similar to the Hansom, save that it is smaller
and is drawn by a sinewy Cingalese, who trots ten, fifteen or twenty
miles with you as easily and rapidly as a horse could draw you. The
boys rented a lot of these and drove about town until midnight, finally
ending up with an exciting race down the principal thoroughfare to the
hotel. During the evening advices had been obtained by a visit to the
residence of the American consul, which informed President Spalding
that it would be absolutely impossible, on account of the inconvenient
steamship and railway connections, while it would also be dangerous
because of the unhealthy condition of Calcutta, for our party to make a
tour of India, and it was that evening decided that the "Salier" would
remain in the harbor until five o'clock the following afternoon, in order
to give us time to play a game in Columbo, and that we should then

continue on across the Arabian Sea to the Red Sea and give up our tour across India. Of course all were disappointed at this change of programme, and none more so than Mr. Spalding himself. There was the consoling thought, however, that the abandonment of our Indian tour would give us more time to spend upon the Continent and in England.

We were all up by daybreak the following morning and out upon the street eager to see everything to be seen. I remember that I was

THE JOLLY JINRICKSHAW.

awakened by the cawing of one of the big lead-colored crows, which deliberately flew down upon my railing, hopped in through the window, and, perching upon the back of a chair, startled me from my slumbers by a series of squawks, made all the more effective and discordant by the bare, frescoed walls, which echoed and reëchoed the bird's voice. I threw a boot at the intruder, but he only hopped off the chair and started on a dignified walk for the window, pausing now and then to turn around and screech at me, and, when he had finally reached the window casing, jumped to the balcony railing, and by more frantic screeching brought to his side a dozen of his fellows. I had to get up and go at them before they would disperse. These birds seem to be protected by municipal law, and they are the most impudent, and at the same time the most amusing, bipeds in Ceylon. I saw one sight that would have brought out the pencil of an artist, when, turning a corner of the hotel, I came upon a little bullock, not much bigger than a healthy

BUSINESS BOOTHS ON A COLUMBO STREET.

American calf, harnessed to an immense grass-thatched, two-wheeled cart, standing under the shade of a tree and meekly chewing its cud, while upon his back, standing sleepily upon one leg, was one of these impudent Cingalese crows. It flew to the top of a neighboring palm tree and gave me a severe scolding for shying a stone at it and disturbing its siesta.

Soon after breakfast upon the morning after our arrival most of us

adjourned to a Columbo clothing establishment and purchased from one to three suits of white duck at seven rupees, or about $2.17 per suit. These secured, we added a "cumberband," or bright-colored silk sash, which was draped around the waist and, with the fringed ends hanging over the hip, gave us quite an Oriental appearance. Our straw hats were discarded for cork hats with green linings and a silk "puggery," a sort of silk scarf that passes around the crown, the ends dropping over the end of the hat brim and protecting the neck from the sun. Altogether we looked not unlike a party of returning African explorers. The costumes I have described are worn universally by the higher classes and by all Europeans living in Ceylon and India, and were found very comfortable by our party on shipboard after we had left Ceylon. Before starting out to do Columbo and its environs we were informed at the office of the U. S. Consul that the corvette "Essex," which lay in the harbor, had invited us to pay a visit on shipboard before returning to the "Salier." After appointing one o'clock for our visit to the corvette, we entered jinrickshaws and bullock carts and started upon a tour of the city. Ryan and myself took one district after another, and did it systematically. First we drove to some of the most prominent Indian shops and looked at the big cases of tempting articles on display, embracing everything from a cashmere shawl and a moonstone necklace to a carved ivory watch-charm. On the way we were beset with peddlers and beggars without number; and if there is any country on the globe where the poor have got these professions down to a fine art, it is Ceylon. A peddler will importune you for two blocks, and a beggar will follow you for two miles. "Mastah, mastah," they cry—the Cingalese always address Americans or Europeans as "master"—"Backsheesh,* backsheesh; very hungry, very hungry;" and they will put their hands upon their waistbands, while the youngsters lift up the ends of their little cotton shirts, when they have such on, that you may see how very empty are their little stomachs. The only way to get rid of them is to toss them several Cingalese coppers; and in anticipation of being thus importuned, Ryan and myself had had a sixpence changed into a pocketful of the queer-looking coins, a hatful of which would not equal the value of an English shilling.

---

* Alms.

After inspecting the shops we drove down past the British-India Hotel, and then along the beautiful beach drive to the "Galle Face," a great open lawn that extends along the ocean shore from the military barracks far beyond the Columbo Cricket grounds, until it merges into the tall groves of cocoanut trees in the distance. As we bowled along over the smooth roads and admired the beautiful view that met our gaze everywhere, the thought occurred to me that this splendid stretch of turf would be covered with juvenile ball teams on Saturday and Sunday afternoons were it located in Chicago instead of Ceylon. On the

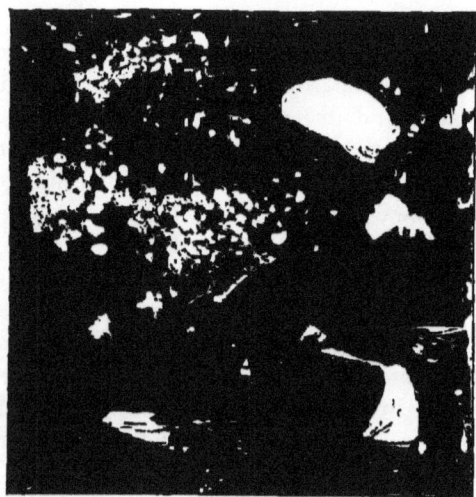

THE CHARMER AND HIS PET.

road we came across a couple of Indian jugglers and snake charmers at work, surrounded by a little crowd of people. We stopped and joined the crowd. The manipulation of the cones and balls by these dusky magicians is certainly wonderful; but what interested Ryan and myself more than anything else was the handling of the thick-bodied Cobra snakes, which spread their terrible-looking hoods and swayed their bodies to the notes of the gourd-like flutes played by the jugglers. Although deeply interested, Ryan and I took good care to stand at a safe distance from both the charmer and his pet.

Our drive through the Cingalese markets and business quarters will never be forgotten. The dusky inhabitants were thicker even than the Chinese in Chinatown, San Francisco, and their incessant chattering, mingling with the yells of the bullock-cart drivers, made the neighborhood a Bedlam. We stopped to look in at the Mohammedan barber shops, laughed at the antics of a lot of monkeys, held our noses as we passed a great pile of "Bombay duck" in one of the stalls, and paused at one of the Buddhist temples, where all good Buddhists of Columbo worship. After looking at its god-bedecked exterior (we were not allowed to enter) we gave our natives the word and were whisked back to the European quarter and to our hotel. At noon we enjoyed a well-served luncheon at the Oriental, and at one o'clock entered the gigs of the corvette "Essex" and rode out to call upon Captain Jewell and the crew. We were cordially entertained on board, the Captain's staff embracing Lieutenants Bignal, Galloway, Gearing and Walling; Ensigns Rodman and Haggatt; and Midshipmen Scales, Hudson, McMillan and Russell. Silence reigned throughout the ship and was followed by an enthusiastic applause when Mrs. Lynch played "America" on her cornet; then the hundred and fifty seamen gathered around Clarence Duval and laughed immoderately while the little African did a plantation shakedown, such as the crew of the "Essex" had probably not seen since they left home three years before. The same gigs that brought us out, rowed us from the corvette to the "Salier," and our boys having donned their uniforms returned to shore.

The native Cingalese gazed in open-mouthed wonder at the teams when they jumped upon the pier in their showy uniforms half an hour later and followed us in crowds to the doors of the Oriental Hotel, where we took, not carriages drawn by gayly-plumed horses, as we had done in America and Australia, but bullock carts and jinrickshaws, and such a scene as the road from the hotel to the Cricket grounds presented I had never imagined, and have never seen before or since. There were hundreds of howling, chattering, grotesquely-arrayed natives, with their red, white, green, blue and orange turbans, sashes and jackets; odd-looking, heavy-wheel carts drawn by ambling hump-backed little bulls, not bigger than an American calf; bare-legged Cingalese darting among the carts with their jinrickshaws; peddlers and beggars without number, and, in short, a state of wild confusion that was as laughable as it was novel to our party. I wondered if we were ever to arrive at the grounds. It certainly looked questionable, but we finally pulled up at the gates of the Cricket grounds and entered. The grounds were situated at one end of the "Galle Face," the beautiful lawn stretching away to the sands of the ocean on one side and a tall grove of cocoanut palms almost encircling it upon the other.

A diamond had been laid out in the centre of the cricket field, and around a big lawn stood 5000 people, the most picturesquely attired crowd, without doubt, that ever assembled to witness a game of ball. The officers and crew of the "Essex" took up a position in front of the Club house and yelled themselves hoarse over the five-inning game which followed our arrival at the grounds. The Englishmen, and seamen too, enjoyed the game as well, but the Cingalese broke into the wildest enthusiasm over the batting. It was laughable to see their desperate efforts to get out of the way when a ball was thrown or batted among them. They flew in all directions, tumbling over each other and chattering like a lot of magpies. During the game the military band, stationed upon the club house balcony, played between innings, and later on some Scotch Highlanders who were present entertained the crowd with their bagpipes.

Horse racing and Scotch games followed the ball game, but our steamer sailed at 5 o'clock, and we saw but little of these latter sports. The journey back to the hotel was almost as amusing as the trip out. The beggars and peddlars were just as attentive and the crowds of blacks, bullock carts and jinrickshaws just as confusing. The crew of the "Essex" cheered us in true American style as we left the pier for the "Salier," which we found again surrounded by hordes of natives. As our steam-launch neared the ship Ed Williamson, Jim Manning and Ed Crane, who had quietly slipped off their shoes, created a sensation by plunging into the water and swimming about in their uniforms among the boat-loads of natives. Our party climbed into the rigging as the screw of the "Salier" began to revolve and sent cheer after cheer to the crew of the "Essex," whose white forms we could see clinging to the rigging as we passed out of sight. The sun sank below the horizon just as we left the harbor and steamed toward the Arabian Sea and the Gulf of Aden.

AT SEA AGAIN.

As I have stated, the most beautiful weather of our voyage from Australia was enjoyed between Ceylon and Egypt. The ocean nowhere had seemed so indolent and so quiet in its great power and grandeur as it did here. The sky was never so blue and the atmosphere never so balmy as it came to us laden with the scent of the spice groves of Ceylon and the coffee plantations of Arabia. There was never a night when the sound of our mandolins and of Ed Crane's excellent tenor voice, as he led our choruses on the deck, ceased before midnight- Our journey, too, was not without incidents of a most memorable character. The evening after leaving Ceylon, Pfeffer, Anson, Williamson, Lynch, Mack and myself were invited down stairs by George and Bob Wilson, our Africa-bound sportsmen, where, in commemoration of the colonization of New South Wales, with the big patriotic Australians, we drank half a case of Monopole and talked with them as to their anticipated experiences in the Dark Continent.

It was late when we got to bed, but very early when we arose next morning, and doubtless our awakening will long be remembered by everybody aboard the "Salier." Indeed, there are those among our party who have not yet, and perhaps never will, forgive Lynch and Fogarty for the cruel practical joke of which they were the authors and perpetrators. Many of the boys were still sleeping when the thundering report of a cannon shook the ship, followed with cries of, "Pirates! Pirates! My God, boys, the Chinese pirates are upon us!" Then came the report of another gun. The effect may easily be imagined. The boys simply fell out of their berths, half-clad and white-faced, and rushed into the cabin in a state of panic. Treasurer John Tener grabbed his bags of gold and backed himself into the coffin-like closet of his stateroom, where he closed the door and tremblingly stood in hope that the bold sea raiders would pass him by unnoticed. Ed Crane left everything of value in his stateroom unnoticed and sprang into the cabin with a pet monkey, which had been given him by the officers of the "Essex." Captain Anson filled his mouth with Mrs. Anson's diamonds, and seizing a baseball bat swung it over his shoulder and stood at his stateroom door, as if waiting for a base hit or a pirate, while he commanded Mrs. Anson to conceal herself beneath her bunk. Ed Hanlon burst into the cabin wearing his hat and holding a pair of trousers in one hand and a valise in the other. Confusion and panic reigned supreme. We could see the smoke descending the stairway in thick

volumes, and most of us got into the cabin just in time to see the flash
and hear the report of the second cannon. Whether the ship was
sinking, was on fire, or had really been attacked, we did not know, but
in our dazed condition we were quite willing to believe that something
terrible had happened, or was about to happen, until we caught sight
of Fogarty galloping around upon the green table cloths that covered
the saloon tables and yelling until red in the face. Then we suspected·
that all was not as it really seemed, and Fogarty confirmed the suspicion by finally falling in a heap upon the dining-room table, convulsed
with laughter.

Upon inquiry, the frightened members of the party learned that the
"Salier's" guns had been simply firing a salute in honor of the Emperor's
birthday, and that Fogarty and Leigh Lynch had improved the opportunity to raise the cry of "Pirates!" There were men enough on board
who were warm enough at the time to string Mr. Fogarty up to the yardarm *sans cérémonie,* and it was fully a week before some of the boys
would consent to smile when the affair was mentioned. We were all
pretty badly frightened, but by far the most terrified of the party was
Clarence Duval. When I came out of my cabin door and into the
saloon, I saw him clinging to the skirts of Leigh Lynch's pjamas, under
which he was vainly endeavoring to hide himself. The whites of his eyes
seemed to have extended over his entire face, and his black skin looked
much as though it had been sprinkled with fine ashes. When Lynch
shook him off and told him he must protect himself, the boy fell to the
floor with a groan, where he sat with chattering teeth until he saw
Fogarty laughing. He then disappeared, and did not show up again
until evening. When asked if he had really been frightened, he said,
"Yes, I reckon I was; I did'n no what *poridges* was, but I made up
mah min' dat whatever dey was, dey was liable to do dis hyah niggah
some h'am, an' I was lookin' foh a place ter crawl inter when I ketched
sight ov dat old Mister Fogaty lafin hisself red in de face, and den I
knowed it was jes one o' his tricks. Some day I's goin' to scar 'at man
so, he'l be gray-headed time he gits to New Yawk."

Mark Baldwin formed a new acquaintance during the voyage across
the Arabian Sea, an acquaintance which, though it at one time promised to assume most intimate relations, eventually changed to a deadly

hatred. At Ceylon the engineer of the ship had purchased a big Indian monkey—one of those tall, long-legged, ring-tailed, evil-countenanced creatures, which seemed to bear an implacable dislike for all mankind. He was a powerful fellow and received Mark's advances coldly as he sat upon the grating of the engine room and glared at the big pitcher from under his shaggy eyebrows. There was a strap around his waist, to which had been attached a rope five or six feet long, and, unknown to the engineer, Mark untied the rope and coaxed the monkey out of the engine room to the deck. The monk was badly frightened at the sight of the heaving ocean and the strange appearance of the deck, and refused to advance further, but Baldwin, holding him by the end of the rope, raced up and down the deck with him, as the monk, bracing himself with stiff legs and paws, slid reluctantly over the surface of the polished floor.

Mark then took him down to the bar room and fed him beer and pretzels, after which he brought him up to the deck again and gave him another race. The monkey in the meantime never lost his expression of terror, and Mark, finally tiring of the sport, took him back to the engine room. Now, the first grating around the big steam cylinders was reached by a narrow iron staircase of five or six steps, and Mark, entering the doorway, descended the steps first. No sooner had his head got on a level with Mr. Monk than the hairy ape, with a villanous shriek, jumped straight at Mark's throat, and but for the pitcher's presence of mind would have probably injured him seriously then and there. As it was, Mark fell backward with the monkey on top of him, and the vicious brute took a mouthful of Mark's leg in his mouth and inflicted a bite that if not dangerous was at least painful. Then, chattering to himself, and his long gray whiskers standing out on each side stiff with rage, he hopped like a great kangaroo over to his corner in the grating and stood glaring fiercely at Mark. Baldwin regained his feet, and after satisfying himself as to the extent of his injuries, made one bound for that monkey. The monkey was quicker than he, however, and jumped from the grating on to the piston rod of the engine, and with every revolution of the screw he would go down into the depth of the hold and then come up again, shaking his fist at Mark and chattering like a fiend at each ascent. Although angry and burning for revenge, the situation was too comical for the Pittsburgher to withstand, and he sat down and laughed at the ape until it finally scrambled up among the crossbars and ironwork of the engine room and watched Mark until he had left the grating. Baldwin laid for the monkey during the entire remainder of the voyage, but the monkey was altogether too watchful and nimble to be caught.

On the morning of February 1st we left the waters of the Arabian Sea for those of the Gulf of Aden, the bluest, I think, of all blue waters upon the globe. We passed the Socotra Islands during the night, and sighted the volcanic groups off the African coast soon after daybreak. Passing these about breakfast hour, we slowly approached Guardafui, the great headland on the northeast corner of the coast of Africa. It rises gloomy and impressive, the waters breaking around its base as it stands looking out over the sea like some great sentinel. Until long after the noon hour we steamed along the forbidding bluff, and then as the sun began to sink we left it in the gray mist that hovered about its peak, miles and miles away. On the afternoon of the following day we sighted the Arabian coast, some forty miles away. Later on we passed an Arabian " dhow," or native sail boat, and gradually the seamed sides of the great bluffs which protect Aden from the gulf winds became more and more distinct. It was nearly dark when we dropped anchor before the little Arabian town and leaned over the ship's rail to watch the boat-loads of chattering, black-bodied fellows who surrounded the "Salier," much as she was surrounded at Columbo. It was nearly supper time, but the boys never thought of that. We wanted to stand on Arabian soil, and consequently three boat-loads of Americans were soon on their way to the shore. Of course we were appealed to for " backsheesh" the moment we landed, but we whacked the beggars with our canes and went on up the lighted street that stretched along the shore for a mile. We raided the shops for curiosities, and found any quantity of them in the way of ostrich eggs and plumes, Indian curtains, portières and handiwork of all kinds, which we brought away as mementoes of our visit to Arabia. John Tener has a cane which is part of a long Arab staff that he bought from one of a group of white-sheeted Arabs on the dock, and which John says is a divining rod for the richest of all his memories of our great tour.

We left Aden at 9 o'clock that evening, in the face of a stiff blow, and were soon on our way to the southern entrance of the Red Sea. The following morning we were startled from sleep by the sound of the gong, and sprang out of bed, not really sure but that we were to have another visitation of pirates. We were informed, however, that we were approaching the Straits of Bab-el-Mandeb, the entrance to the Red Sea, and that all who wished to see them should come up on deck. We all took advantage of the opportunity, and after hastily dressing, congregated upon the deck just as the sun broke upon the gray of the morning.

THE RED SEA.

The straits are about 2½ miles in width. Our ship passed between the coast of Arabia on the right, which arose in great elephantine-looking piles, and at the base of which the billows broke themselves into clouds of spray, and upon our left the Island of Perin, on the shores of which burned the yellow beacons of the lighthouses. Both coasts were barren and uninviting, looking as though no one but the lighthouse keepers ever set foot upon their soils. At ten o'clock that morning we passed the famous city of Mocha, which lay like a city of white walls and glistening towers upon the now far-distant Arabian coast; for the sea had widened as we left the straits behind. We watched it with our glasses until it had faded from view, with other vanished but not forgotten scenes of the many we had passed.

The voyage through the Red Sea was thoroughly delightful, although we had been led to anticipate insufferably hot weather. It was warmer than any we had yet experienced on our way from Australia, but it was by no means unpleasant, and we were sorry rather than glad when, upon the morning of February 7th, we entered the harbor of Suez and slowly steamed in the direction of the little city of the same name, which lay at the southern end of the great canal. The day of our arrival was perfect, and the bright sunlight brought into bold relief the immense bluffs of the Egyptian coasts as they looked down upon the calm waters of the bay and the seemingly limitless desert that stretched away upon the opposite shore. Several large vessels lay in the harbor, among them an English troop ship and an Italian man-of-war. And as we dropped anchor, we were soon surrounded, as in Ceylon, with native

11

boats and a couple of little steam tugs, which towed out to the ship two or three big barges for the reception of our baggage and such freight as we might have for Suez. Again we listened to the unintelligible chatter of a new race of people, and gazed with interest on the remarkable costume of the Egyptian boatmen. After bidding farewell to Captain Thalenhorst and his clever fellow-officers, we descended the companion-way into the little steamer that lay alongside for our trip of two miles to the docks at the city of Suez. On board were several Indian jugglers and fakirs, who entertained our party with their really wonderful feats of legerdemain during the ride.

When we drew up at the pier in Suez, a crowd of Arabs and Egyptians, in long, loose-fitting gowns of blue, white and black, their

THE LITTLE CITY OF SUEZ.

feet shoeless and their heads wound about with white turban cloths, rushed toward our boat, driving before them a troop of long-eared donkeys with queer-looking, gayly-caparisoned saddles and bridles, the latter decorated with brass bangles and bright-colored ribbons. These were the donkey boys of Egypt, whose services we afterward had occasion to employ so frequently in Cairo. We had but a few moments to catch the train for the Egyptian capital, so we mounted these little beasts, none of which weighed over 275 pounds, and with the donkey boys yelling at our heels, trotted off for the railway station four or five blocks distant. What we saw of Suez did not impress us favorably, for of all the tumble-down, ramshackle, dilapidated-looking structures we saw during the trip, those at Suez take the palm. If dirt and general shiftlessness are evidences of antiquity, then surely Suez and its people are the most thoroughly antique of all the antiquities of this nineteenth century.

It was a relief to each and every one of us when the train pulled out from the station, and dodging about through the villages of mud huts, which the Egyptians are either too poor, or too much attached to, to

A PEEP AT THE GREAT SUEZ CANAL.

abandon for more comfortable and modern dwellings, we cut across country into the arid desert region, which extends northward from Suez as far as Ismalia. Our train ran parallel with the canal for a distance of forty-five miles and then branched off westward to Cairo. Gradually the country became more and more pleasant to look upon, until we entered the rich valley of the Nile, where the growth of vege-

tation seems fully as luxuriant as in Ceylon. Great fields of grain and
clover, with here and there a grove of imposing palms or acacias,
stretched away from each side of the track ; flocks of sheep and goats
became a common sight, and along the roadways of the irrigating canals,
which overspread the valley like an immense net, the patient camels
plodded along under their loads of grain or the weight of their Egyptian owners, while groups of water buffalo stood knee-deep amid the
clover. Occasionally we saw evidences of the fidelity of the Egyptians

OX-POWER SHADOOF, OR IRRIGATING MACHINE OF THE NILE.

to the customs and methods of their biblical forefathers. Such, for
instance, as an ox turning an old-fashioned water wheel, which lifted the
water in buckets from the main canal into irrigating ditches. An American pump would have done the work in half the time, but that would
not be the way in which their fathers raised the water, and therefore would
not suit the Egyptian, even of this generation. At every station our carriages were surrounded by Bedouins, Arabs and Egyptians ; the men

being muscular-looking fellows, but servile of manner, and the women veiled to the eyes, their faces disfigured by the characteristic brass ornaments of the Egyptians, which hang from the hood of their outer garment, the "bournous," their figures being thick-set, without the faintest suspicion of contour. Most of them bore upon their heads big baskets

of fruit, oranges and dates, while others carried earthenware jugs of water, from which the occupants of the dusty railway coaches quenched their thirst for the sum of a half-piastre.

Ed Crane's little Japanese monkey sat upon the carriage window-sill in his picturesque scarlet jacket, and greatly amused the ladies by his funny faces and antics. Just at dusk, as we pulled up at a station twenty miles from Cairo, Ryan invented an enlarged edition of Crane's monkey, which had the effect of causing a panic

EGYPTIAN WOMAN WITH BRASS FACE ORNAMENTS.

among the unsuspecting Egyptians. Jim dressed Clarence Duval up in the latter's drum-major coat of scarlet and gold lace; he then put a catcher's mask on the boy's face and tied a rope around his waist, in regulation hand-organ style, and awaited the train's arrival at the station. As at preceding stations, the crowd rushed toward the train, and Clarence sprang through the doorway into the centre of a score of Egyptians, waddling and chattering like an angry monkey. Women screamed and men fell over each other in a wild effort to get out of reach of the terrible-looking ape, which Ryan, apparently with the exertion of great strength, held with difficulty, and finally forced back into the carriage. Then Clarence sat at the window, chattering and making faces as long as we remained at the station, and not a native would come within twenty feet of our coach. One could scarcely

CLARENCE CREATING A PANIC AT THE EGYPTIAN STATION.

blame them, for could a disciple of Darwin have seen the mascot in his impromptu make-up, his heart would have bounded with delightful visions of the missing link.

IN CAIRO.

It was dark when we reached Cairo, and no sooner had we stepped upon the station platform from our coaches than we were beset by an army of black fellows, clad in turbans and elongated night shirts, who laid hold of us and our baggage as though to carry us away bodily. Ed Crane propped one of the heathens under the chin and old Anson sent half a dozen more sprawling by a vigorous shove. Still they came at us as determinedly as ever. We were in a fair way to be smothered or pulled to pieces, when Jimmy Fogarty called out "Step on their trotters, boys, they can't stand that." Happy thought; it was cruel, but it was our only means of relief, and we forthwith proceeded to step on the bare feet of every Egyptian within reach. That settled them, and they kept at safe distance till we had reached our carriages. We were driven quickly to the Hotel d'Orient, where accommodations had been secured for the party. The Orient is not so highly fashionable as "Shephard's" or the " Grand New," but is still a well appointed hostelry, with a table that was not excelled by any that we sat down to during our tour. It faces a big, circular open space from which half a score of thorough-fares diverge like the spokes of a wheel, penetrating every quarter of Cairo.

Opposite is a big public garden in which one of the bands of the Khedive was playing as we drew up to the door of the hotel, and on every hand were booths, cafés and places of amusement without number, from roulette wheels, publicly operated, to French opera and inviting-looking *brasseries* where one can drop in for a puff at a *narghili*, or a cup of chocolate and a cigarette served by waitresses of almost any nationality in Asia or Europe, and possessed of beauty or homeliness to a greater or less degree. All these things we noticed after we had removed the dust of the Desert from our faces and refreshed the inner man with a substantial dinner. One can sit in the Eldorado at Cairo and listen to a French opera, while around him at the tables he will hear the Arabic, Hindostanee, Greek, German, Egyptian, French, Italian and English languages spoken simultaneously. Such a jargon of tongues cannot, I believe, be heard in any other city outside of Continental Europe, unless it be, perhaps, at Constantinople. Before sitting down to post up my diary that evening, I stepped to the balcony of my room, which overlooks the space in front of the hotel, and saw Cairo in the gloom of the night, its towers and minarets rising like shadows among the heavy, white-walled buildings, and the lights of a thousand booths tinting the diverging thoroughfares with a red glow, for the booths and *brasseries* of Cairo seem never to close, and their proprietors never to sleep. In the square below sat the donkey boys watching for some belated pedestrian, and there are scores of these, who might need the services of these hardy and much enduring little beasts. It is a strange land and a still stranger people, and a student of Egyptology finds, ere he has prosecuted his studies to a very great extent, that he has even more than a lifetime of work before him, every day of it filled with research, discoveries and experiences, that grow with interest as he advances.

At the breakfast table the morning after our arrival in the Egyptian capital President Spalding announced that as no arrangements could be made for a game before the day following, the members of the party were at liberty to put in their time as best suited them. Accordingly, a few of us took carriages, but the majority of the boys bestrode the little donkeys and with a donkey boy at their heels covered many a square mile of Cairo during the day. We penetrated the Arabian, Moorish, Turkish, Algerian and Greek quarters of the town, riding through the narrow streets from which the light of the sun was almost excluded by towering walls and overhanging balconies. We handled and admired the rich tapestries and works of art in the bazaars, and listened to the babble of tongues that was kept up incessantly on all sides of us. We crossed the bridge of the Nile to the Khedive's gardens, where the wealth and *élite* of Cairo in magnificent equipages go for an airing each afternoon, and it may be said that on no drive in London, or even in Paris, can so much splendor be seen as here. The foreign ambassadors, Ministers and Government officials possess the finest of Arabian stock, and their carriages are equal to any that I saw in Rotten Row or on the Champs Elysée. The effect is exceedingly Oriental, and ideally regal, as the imposing turnouts sweep down the principal avenue along the river bank, preceded by their gorgeously-liveried *avant-couriers*, attired in costumes of white broadcloth and bright-colored jackets elaborately embroidered in gold or silver, while they hold in their hands the long staffs with which they are supposed to clear the way for their masters' equipages. At the far end of the Gardens is one of the Khedive's palaces, a great imposing building of purely Egyptian style of architecture, surrounded by beautiful gardens, as attractive as art and nature can make them. The Khedive, by the way, has more palaces by half a score than he visits or resides in.

The day passed only too quickly for us all, for with all we had seen, not one tithe of the great district covered by the city, or of the many interesting quarters within it, had been visited. During the evening, French opera at the Eldorado, the Algerian dances at the Byzantine, and the brilliantly lighted shops or the throngs upon the streets afforded us diversion enough. Captain Anson, by the

MACMILLAR AND PALMER MOUNTED FOR A RIDE.

way, managed during the evening to "put his foot in it." He and Mrs. Anson, wishing to see something of Cairo by gaslight, took a carriage and drove in search of the theatre. They drove down past the Grand New Hotel and the French Opera House until a palatial looking structure, its grounds brightly lighted and colored awnings extending from the streets to the doorways, attracted their attention. " Hey driver," called Anson, to the Egyptian on the box, "what is this?",

And the driver, not understanding a word of English, but properly interpreting Anson's question, replied with the single word "*Sirdar.*' Whether it was the rumble of the wheels or the indistinct pronunciation of the Egyptian, I do not know, but at any rate Anson put his own interpretation upon the Egyptian's reply. "The circus, eh?" said he, "well, I guess that is just about our size. Hold on, there!" and stopping the carriage, Anson assisted his wife to alight. They passed under the canopy and by two gorgeously-attired servants who stood at the door. Music came from every direction, and the air itself was filled with the perfume of a score of fountains which spurted forth the most expensive extracts.

"Pretty swell kind of a circus this, isn't it?" questioned the old man of his better half. "I suppose, though," he continued, "that this is the way they do things over here. I have made up my mind not to be surprised at anything I see."

Within, they caught sight of a number of ladies and gentlemen in full evening dress. Still it failed to occur to the old man that he might not have properly understood his Egyptian cab-driver, and Mrs. Anson followed her lord with a confidence born of the belief that whatever he did was perfectly right and proper. Finally, Anson ran squarely against a dark-complexioned, distinguished-looking man, attired in all the magnificence of an Egyptian military costume. He glanced curiously at the Americans, and then stopped as Anson addressed him. "Can you tell me," asked Anson, "where we buy our tickets?"

"Tickets! what tickets?" asked the dark-complexioned man, in a surprised tone, but in very good English.

"Why," said Anson, a bit nervously, "the tickets to the circus here," and he made a sweeping gesture with his right hand.

Then the gentleman in military costume, partly turning away his face to hide a smile, said, "There is no circus here, my friend; this is my private residence. I am Commander-in-Chief of the Egyptian Army and am simply entertaining a few of my friends to-night. I would be very much pleased, however, if you would remain and—"

"Don't say a word, sir," replied the captain of the Chicago Club, looking very much cheaper than lovers of the game have seen him look, when, with men on bases, the Umpire has called three strikes on him.

"It's my mistake, and I hope you will be kind enough to excuse me," with which he bowed himself out, and then had to stand being laughed at by Mrs. Anson all the way back to the hotel.

That evening, in the hotel office, the following bulletin was posted: " Baseball at the Pyramids.—The Chicago and All-America teams, comprising the Spalding American Baseball party, will please report in the hotel office, in uniform, promptly at ten o'clock to-morrow morning. We shall leave the hotel at that hour, camels having been provided for the All-America players and donkeys for the Chicago players, with carriages for the balance of the party. The Pyramids will be inspected, the Sphinx visited, and a game played upon the Desert near by, beginning at 2 o'clock."

The following day, accordingly, witnessed the first professional ball game ever played upon Egyptian soil, and the scenes and incidents of that morning and afternoon rendered the 9th of February one of the most memorable of our eventful tour. Half-past nine o'clock saw twenty of the best known ball players in America in the court of the Hotel d'Orient, in uniform. Every arrangement for the day's programme had been carefully worked out. The dragoman in charge of the camels and donkeys had done his duty, as a glance at the array in front of the hotel indicated. A dozen long-necked camels, saddled and bridled, lay upon the ground, contentedly chewing their cuds, and as many gayly decorated little donks stood patiently beside the reclining travelers of the Desert. At ten o'clock the camels were drawn up in line in front of the hotel, with a line of donkeys before them, and then the fun of the morning began. The crowd of donkey boys, dragomen, guards, and venders of curios and tapestries, and photographs, and earthenware images, and fruits, and goodness knows what not, had increased to fully half a thousand, and every one of them was eagerly looking for a chance to secure, by hook or by crook, a bit of American silver. The dragoman in charge had engaged all the donkeys we needed, but other donkey boys contrived to mix up with those appointed, and succeeded in getting some of the boys upon the backs of renegade donkeys. It was when the players were apprised of their mistake that the real fun commenced, and such a hubbub as was raised in that square I never expect to witness outside of Cairo; donkeys

brayed, camels trumpeted, donkey boys howled and fought and chattered, and scratched each other's faces and tore each other's gowns, and
cried big tears of vexation in their efforts to hold on to their fares,
while above all the noise could be heard the thwack, thwack, of the
bamboo rods, in the hands of the native policemen, as they dusted the
jackets of every thinly-clad Arab and Egyptian that got in their way.
Those of us who had been provided with camels sat upon our reclining
hump-backed beasts, doubled up with laughter, until the police had
finally restored order by the free use of their bamboo sticks.

A CAMEL TRAIN READY FOR A TRIP.

In good time we were all safely mounted, All-America upon the
camels, and Chicago upon the donkeys. Immediately in front of
me, upon the back of a surly old camel, which lay sullenly grunting
under her burden, sat Irving W. Snyder, the fat, good-natured sporting
goods dealer of Nassau street. Just who had persuaded him to mount
a camel I have never been able to learn, and judging from the expression of his face, when I first glanced at him, I imagined he was at that
moment wondering how he could have been weak enough to allow
himself to get into such a box. He had not much time, however, to

devote to reflection, for the order was given for the camels to arise, that the photographer might make a picture of the party. I saw a startled expression cross Snyder's face as the big beast began to stir, and then he pitched forward and flattened his nose against old Sahara's head, as the old girl lifted her rump into the air,—the first in the remarkable series of movements a camel goes through in getting upon its feet. He only retained this position for an instant, however, for the front end of the camel immediately followed the example of the rear end, and Snyder took a tumble in the opposite direction.

When the beast finally settled itself the merchant of Nassau street looked very much as though he had just fallen off the roof of the Hotel d'Orient. Both trousers legs had worked up to his knees, and one end of his collar was poking him in the eye ; but he did not worry over such trifles, even though he must have known that he was sitting for his picture. The sole question agitating his mind at that moment was that of his ability to stay where he was until help came. Alas, however, there was no help, and the incidents of the four miles ride which followed, and during which he clung to those saddle sticks as though they were the only barriers between himself and instant destruction, must be very distinctly engraved upon Mr. Snyder's memory.

Finally we got started, and with the camels and donkeys leading the line, and the carriages bringing up the rear, we moved slowly through the streets of Cairo toward the Bridge of the Nile, attracting no little attention, of course, as we proceeded. We stopped at the residence of the American Minister, and with three cheers for the flag that floated over his quarters, continued on our way toward the Nile, which we crossed, and then entered the Khedive's Gardens. At the further end of the bridge poor Snyder was overtaken by more trouble, and as his animal was just in front of mine, the halter of each camel being attached to the saddle of the camel ahead of him, I obtained an uninterrupted and most interesting view of the performance. A couple of big camels with a load of sawed lumber strapped across their humps, the ends of the twenty-four-foot boards extending out over their heads and beyond their tails, were quietly wending their way, in charge of their Egyptian drivers, along the road which our party took toward the Pyramids. Neither beast of burden noticed our cavalcade until the rear end of the procession overtook them and they caught sight of Snyder. What there was about the merchant of Nassau street to terrify the plank-laden camels I could not discover, and Snyder afterwards told me that it was the only instance in his life in which he had encountered an animal of any kind that had not shown the most marked affection for him. Be that as it may, when the bigger of the two camels saw Snyder he ran his tongue out of his mouth a distance of two feet or more and gave a trumpet that startled every camel within sight into a state of very active interest. The

THE SUPERB BRIDGE OF THE NILE.

Egyptian leading the plank-bearer turned around and endeavored to quiet his beast with a volley of Egyptian oaths and a sudden yank on the halter. The effect, however, was the opposite of what he had antici-pated. The camel gave another trumpet, and then began a waltz with the swearing Egyptian at the end of the halter. A cloud of dust had almost enveloped man and beast within a few seconds after the dance began, and I could see that this miniature cyclone was slowly but surely

approaching Snyder.   Snyder saw it too, and judging from the expression upon his face he must have thought that this time the hour of his
physical disintegration had surely come.   He could only clutch the
saddle sticks and look out of the corner of his eye at the approaching
cloud of dust, while his face grew ghastly with dreadful anticipation.
His suspense, however, was not of long duration.   The waltzing camel
gradually drew nearer until a final whirl brought the ends of the planks

SNYDER IN THE CONTEST OF THE CAMELS.

against the rump of Snyder's camel with a sound like the falling of a
lumber pile.   To say that Snyder's camel was startled would be putting
it mildly.   He was also indignant, for he had been soberly pursuing his
way, wholly indifferent to, if not unconscious of, the antics of the other
camel.   When the planks struck him he let out a spiteful shriek and
shot straight up into the air a distance of about four feet, and for prob-

ably fifteen seconds the air was filled with pieces of flying plank, camel legs, swearing Egyptian and Nassau street merchant, until one was almost at a loss to determine just what character of beast the whole con- glomeration was. The drivers finally succeeded, however, in separating the now belligerent camels, and Snyder rode on, covered with dust and camel saliva, with his hair in his eyes and what was left of his hat on the back of his head, inwardly cursing every four-legged thing in Egypt. He was just beginning to think that after all, camel riding was perhaps not so bad as being seasick or falling off Washington Monument, when the drivers whipped the camels into a trot and Snyder's position was more uncomfortable than ever. He could not get breath enough to command the drivers to stop, and they would not have understood him had he been able to talk, so that he could only clutch the saddle sticks and suffer. Then somebody behind him fired a big, soft, juicy orange that caught him in the back of the neck. Altogether, Mr. Irving W. Snyder's ride to the Pyramids was not a howling success ; but it was funny.

The road to the historic piles is a beautiful one. It runs for some distance along the left bank of the Nile, past the Khedive's palace and the Governor's residence, and then branches off across the rich low- lands of the great river, which, during the annual overflow, are covered with water, until it ends at the desolate-looking sand hills at the edge of the desert upon which the Pyramids have been constructed. Along each side of the roadway stand stately acacia trees, the branches of which meet overhead and form a leafy avenue from the Bridge of the Nile to the sand hills, a distance of eight miles. Half-way out upon the road, at Snyder's piteous solicitation, the procession stopped, and Chicago being desirous of experiencing the novelty of camel riding took the camels, while All-America mounted the donkeys for the balance of the journey. At two o'clock we reached our destination, and after ascending the winding roadway to the base of the Pyramids, partook of the luncheon that had been prepared for us in the brick cot- tage at the foot of old Cheops. While we were waiting, however, for lunch, we were assailed by not less than 150 Bedouins, Arabs and Egyptians, who are a nuisance to every tourist visiting the Pyramids. They besought us to buy musty-looking coins and mouldy copper images, which they explained had been taken from the interior of the big structures. They proved the most persistent beggars we had thus far encountered, not excepting those at Columbo, and we did not escape from them during our stay at the Pyramids.

After lunch we walked past the base of the big Pyramid to the Sphynx, and grouping ourselves about the head, shoulders and feet of the great image, were photographed by the photographer who accompanied the party. Then we passed down the hill until we reached the hard sands of the Desert, where the diamond was laid off and where, in the presence of something like a thousand people, embracing a number of tourists, but more long-sheeted Bedouins, we played the first and only game of baseball ever played in Egypt. The surface of the Desert was hard and firm, not unlike the snow crust of the North, and formed a by-no-means-poor ground for ball playing. Ward's forces were again "out for blood," and though Anson made a good start by the capture of two runs in the opening inning, All-America by good stiff batting piled up seven runs in the second and secured a lead which Chicago could not afterwards approach. The actions of the natives during the game were not unlike those of the Cingalese at our game in Columbo. When a ball was thrown wild or batted into the crowd, the entire aggregation of white-robed sons of the Desert would chase after it, capture it, and crowd around to examine it, utterly indifferent, or thoughtless of the fact that we might want the ball for playing, and as though it was one of the greatest curiosities they had ever seen. In such cases game was suspended until the teams had attacked the mob in a body and rescued the ball. At the close of the game we returned to the Sphynx and the Pyramids and looked over the great masses of stone at our leisure. A couple of Bedouins performed the dangerous task of climbing to the apex of the big Pyramid and down again within ten minutes' time, for a ten-piastre piece, and then Ward, Fogarty and Manning, accompanied by attendants, undertook and accomplished the ascent. The balance of us, however, were content to forego that experience, and soon after we were on our way back to Cairo, which we reached about seven o'clock that evening. I need scarcely say that the camels came back with empty saddles, the boys preferring the carriages and donkeys to another ride on the Egyptian beasts of burden.

12

Macmillan, myself and the Professor started together on three little
donkeys, but the Professor objected to fast riding, and Mac and I soon
left him far behind. Had it been practicable, I am quite sure Mac
would have purchased his donkey and brought him back with him to
New York; for he was an extraordinary donkey in several respects.
His master had taught him to smoke cigarettes, and that the donkey
enjoyed the habit was plainly evident by the enthusiasm with which he

AT LEISURE AT THE FOOT OF THE PYRAMIDS.

went at it. His master, a bright-faced little donkey-boy, would give a
peculiar cry and then take a mouthful of cigarette smoke and start on
a run. The donkey would immediately lay his ears back, whisk his
tail and start after the little Egyptian until he had overtaken him.
Then he would thrust his nose close to the boy's face, while the latter
would blow the tobacco smoke between the donkey's lips. It was
amusing to see the expression of supreme repose and delight that

came over that little brute's face as he drew the white smoke into his lungs and stood there with half-closed eyes wagging his tail and rocking his body to and fro as though he wanted nothing more on earth. It was no trick at all for him to find a pocket-handkerchief in the sand after he had first scented it, and he could reach around with his teeth and unbuckle his saddle strap as neatly and quickly as his master could do it. Then with his foreleg he would paw off his bridle, and thus prepare himself for rest.

THE KHEDIVE OF EGYPT.

Speaking of the Professor starting with us reminds me of an amusing incident that occurred to him during the ball game. When game began, I set my camera upon the sands of the Desert and took a seat preparatory to scoring the game. The Professor happened along at that moment and, feeling somewhat fatigued after his ride, stretched himself out upon his back, and, with his head upon my camera and his hat over his eyes, was soon sound asleep. Pretty soon his hat fell off, but the Professor slumbered sweetly just the same, his sound eye closed and his glass eye staring up at the sky. Presently along came a Bedouin peddler with a trayful of coins, curios, etc., and seeing the Professor reclining upon the sand he knelt down beside him and in broken English began upon an encomium of his wares, offering the Professor his choicest bits, with his most enticing grimaces and at his most tempting prices. For fully five minutes he must have talked to that unfeeling glass eye, and he would probably have continued longer had not a gentle snore from the Professor caused him to look sharply at the sleeper's face, and then

THE DAHABIE, OR PASSENGER BOAT OF THE NILE.

hurry away with his wares. "Prof." awoke fifteen minutes later, without having heard a word of the Bedouin's eloquence.

The following day and night, our last in Cairo, were spent in taking a farewell stroll through the ancient city, most of us visiting the Mosques of Sultan Hassan and of Mohammed Ali. The mosques stand upon the highest point of the city near the citadel, which is now occupied, of course, by English soldiers. Before entering we were compelled to slip our feet into ungainly-looking yellow slippers, lest our infidel heels should defile the marble floors. We tried hard to purchase the slippers we wore, but when we offered ten times the value of the ill-shaped foot-casings, we were met with a determined refusal, on the ground that such a sale would be sacrilegious. The Hassan Mosque, now several centuries old, is fast falling into decay, but the Mosque of Mohammed,

COMMON RIVER BOATS ON THE NILE OPPOSITE CAIRO.

where the Khedive worships, is in an excellent state of preservation. Its great walls of polished marble and alabaster, and the softened light of its beautiful stained-glass windows form as elegant an interior as any in Cairo. The view obtained from the citadel is without doubt one of the grandest in the world. From its walls can be seen Cairo, spread out like a great panorama, with the majestic Nile reaching away up the valley, and the Pyramids of Cairo as well as those at Sakarah, the latter twenty miles distant. One could easily spend six months in Cairo and the surrounding valley of the Nile, and then come away

without having finished what must always remain one of the most interesting countries upon the globe. We managed, however, to cover considerable ground during our brief stay, and most of us doubtless brought
away a fairly good idea of the city, its people, and their peculiar customs.

A NATIVE EGYPTIAN SCHOOL IN FULL OPERATION,

Some of these customs would not charm our American youngsters,
notably that of the private school system, where a few boys (the girls'
education not being of any account in Egypt) are grouped in an out-of-
the-way corner of the Mosque buildings, squatting on the ground as

they pursue their tasks, the stern old teacher sitting over them rod in hand, the petty sovereign of a by-no-means submissive and loyal constituency. The native barber-shops too, were curious in their way, and few of us cared to trust our faces to the tender mercies of their owners.

SCENE IN A CAIRO BARBER-SHOP.

On the day of our arrival in Cairo, President Spalding had, through the American Consul General, expressed to the Khedive his willingness to play a game of ball in the presence of His Highness before we left Cairo. But the Khedive had left the city for his Nile

Palace on state affairs, and sent Mr. Spalding word that, though he would be unable to return to the city, he should be pleased to receive our party at his Nile Palace and witness our exhibition there. To remain, however, would have caused us a delay of fully a week, and as we could ill spare this time we were unable to accept the Royal invitation.

We left Cairo at half-past eleven on the morning of February 11th, our destination being Ismalia, the little city on the banks of the Suez Canal, midway between Suez and Port Said. When our train stopped at the station of Ismalia we were beset, as we had been at Cairo, by natives who insisted upon taking charge of our baggage, in selling us food, or by some other means enriching themselves at our expense. A refusal upon our part had no effect whatever upon their persistency. The entire horde seemed to be under the management of a well-grown Egyptian boy of about seventeen years, and he flew from one group to another urging them on in their persecution of our party and taking the coins which they had succeeded in securing from their sales. It was not until John Healy got at the seat of the trouble, by quieting this fellow, that we were left in peace. John caught sight of him about forty feet away waving his arms and dancing about a group of little Arab boys. Unceremoniously picking up a big yellow orange from the basket of a boy who stood near, the All-America pitcher sent an "inshoot" at the Egyptian with all the speed he could put into it. The orange came in contact with the back of the peddler's neck, just at the base of the skull, and vanished into a million pieces, but it sent the Egyptian sprawling into the middle of his fellows, and he lay upon the ground with his hands to his head, probably in the belief that he had been kicked by an Egyptian donkey. Pretty soon he got up slowly, walked over to the curbing and sat down, where in a half-dazed way he watched our party until we were out of sight, but he hadn't a word to utter.

THE SUEZ CANAL.

At five o'clock that evening we boarded a small steamer and began a five hours' journey of forty-three miles up the Canal to Port Said. The night was beautiful, a full moon lighting up the blue waters of the big ditch, and the barren, weird-looking desert which stretched away on each side of us. A better opportunity for seeing this great artificial waterway could scarcely have been afforded us, and the majority of the party remained upon deck during the entire passage. The canal has a mean depth of 27 feet and varies in width from 250 to 350 feet. At the time of our passage thousands of men and camels were at work widening the canal. It is 87 miles in length, and midway between its terminal points are two natural lakes through which steamers are allowed to run at full speed. In the ordinary channel of the big ditch, however,

HOW JOHN HEALY SETTLED THE EGYPTIAN PEDDLER.

steamers are not permitted to proceed at a speed of more than five miles an hour. I was surprised to learn the rates of toll charged a vessel for passage. The "Salier," for instance, a ship of about 3200 tons burthen, paid a toll of 20,000 francs and half a franc per head on each passenger, thus making her tollage for the round trip from Bremen to Australia something over $8000. The Canal Company have fixed the toll at considerably under the cost of time and money that a vessel would be put to in going around the Cape. Thus, although the toll seems excessive, the expense is not so great as it would be for the vessel to go around Africa by the old route. We passed not less than a score of big steamers en route for the Red Sea, and the sound of our mandolins and guitars and Mrs. Lynch's cornet brought the passengers of most of them to the ship's rail as the big crafts, with their flashing electric lights, steamed slowly by us. At 10.30 we reached Port Said, the northern terminus of the canal, and climbed up the side of the handsome North German Lloyd Steamer "Stettin," where we found a hospitable lot of officers and an excellent dinner awaiting us. An hour later we steamed out of Port Said Harbor upon our journey across the Mediterranean. This voyage was the roughest we had encountered thus far, and we arrived in Brindisi twelve hours late, the result of the storms encountered. The screw of the steamer was out of water every few moments, and we rolled about at a rate that made nearly all of us seasick. The snow-capped island mountains of Crete and Candia were the only glimpses of land we secured upon this voyage. At 12.30, on the afternoon of February 15th, the "Stettin" passed through the river which leads from the bay to the Harbor of Brindisi. Finally her screw stopped before the quaint-looking and ancient little city, and a score of boats, with their Italian oarsmen, rowed out to the dock, with the Customs officers, our mail, and representatives of the various Brindisi hotels. No sight could have been more welcome to us than the big packages of letters and American newspapers which our party received. They were the first we had seen since leaving home, although I believe some of the boys did secure a few ancient copies of *The New York Herald* at the American Minister's house in Cairo. Among the letters received by President Spalding was one from Secretary of State Bayard, requesting American Consuls and Ministers throughout Europe to extend every courtesy to our party. A long letter from Walter Spalding also gave us much baseball news of a gratifying character.

ON EUROPEAN SOIL.

Brindisi is a queer little Italian town, and as we had missed the train for Naples that day, thus being compelled to remain over night at the Grand East India Hotel, we took a stroll through the narrow-winding streets, our ears being met with the sound of the guitar and mandolin at nearly every turn. At supper we were entertained by a trio of typical Italian musicians, one a dark-eyed, swarthy-complexioned, handsome Italian girl and the other two her brothers. They played as only Italians can play. All through Italy music seems to be a gift among the people, common as the gift of language. The big wood fires that burned in our rooms at Brindisi that night were very comfortable, for the raw wind of the storm still swept the coast, and most of us repaired to our apartments at an early hour to talk over the probable events of our tour through Europe. Our arrival upon European soil had put every man of our party in excellent spirits, for it seemed to us all that the greater part of our long journey had been covered, and that we were now really homeward bound.

We took our departure from Brindisi the following morning, at nine o'clock, and after an interesting ride through picturesque Southern Italy, with its vineyards, its fertile valleys and its mountains, we arrived that evening upon the shores of one of the most beautiful harbors in the world—the Bay of Naples. With the exception of four trunks and our hand baggage, all the luggage of the party had gone on to Southampton from Port Said, on one of the North German Lloyd Steamers, so that we were not hampered by the great pyramid of baggage we had carried up to that point.

Anson had the bat bag with him, however, and proposed that it should come under the head of hand baggage. With this purpose he endeavored to take it into the waiting-room of the station from which we were to be admitted to the train, and right here Anson was made to feel the power of the Italian Government. A little five-foot-two-inch, gold-laced railway official insisted that the bag was above the regulation weight, and told Anson that he must have it registered and pay extra fare thereupon. This was exactly what Anson proposed to avoid. The combat between Anson's well-known bluffing abilities and Italian authority was amusing. Here was a funny little old man, twice as aged and not one-third as big as the Captain of the Chicagoes, snapping his fingers in the latter's face. It was a species of kicking in which Anson had never before had any experience, and in which his old tactics did not stand him worth a penny. Anson had good judg-

ment enough, however, to understand that when a traveler in Italy
hits, opposes, or insults a railway official he insults, figuratively speaking, the King of Italy; so the "old man" contented himself with viciously
chewing one end of his blonde moustache for a moment, after which he
picked up the bag as though the bats had been so many matches, and,
with a very red face, slammed it down upon the floor of the Register's
office and demanded to know the amount of extra charge. It was told
him, and he paid it. Indeed, he could do nothing else; but how some
of Anson's old tormentors in America, who delight to sit upon the
"bleechers" and howl with laughter at every misplay or "kick" the big
Captain may make, would have enjoyed the situation could they have
been there.

As we proceeded northward towards Naples the surrounding country
became more and more picturesquely beautiful. We ran through
valleys with their groves of olive and orange trees and their hills
topped by white-walled villages and ancient-looking castles, the turrets
and towers of which reminded one of such history as he had read of
Italy in its feudal periods. During the afternoon we got well up into
the mountains and ran through the first snow storm of the trip. Then
we descended into the valley again, and later on, just as the mantle of
night had enveloped the snow-capped peaks and the pretty low-laying
glades with their flocks and farm-houses, we came suddenly into view
of the Mediterranean coast. Rounding a spur of the mountain, the
Bay of Naples and the beautiful "Palisade City" of the Mediterranean,
Sorrento, burst upon our view with its pyramids of yellow lights and
its background of shadowy mountain peaks. It was an indescribably
pretty picture, and we gazed upon it with many an exclamation of
admiration until a turn in the road hid it from our view. Naples was
not more than thirty miles distant upon the other side of the Bay,
and as we were all awaiting impatiently the first glimpse of its lights,
Fogarty, who sat next to one of the windows of our compartment, in
which were Hanlon, Pettit, George Wright, Mr. Snyder, George Wood
and myself, startled us all with an exclamation of astonishment: "There
she is, boys! There is old Vesuvius, as sure as I am a living man." In
an instant we were all at Fogarty's side in the compartment, and looking through the windows we saw the great volcano standing like a

beacon ; its summit surrounded by a dull red halo and its crater every few seconds belching forth a sheet of lurid flame and lava. It was grand. It was awful to a degree that no description can portray. We looked and looked upon it until the guards had called out "Pompeii, Annunziata," and other historical stations about the base of Vesuvius, and until the walls of Naples itself hid the great mountain from our view.

At the Neapolitan depot we were met by Mr. Spalding and Leigh

THE PALISADE CITY OF THE MEDITERRANEAN.

Lynch, who had come on from Brindisi one train ahead of us. We were all ready for the drive to our hotel, when, much to our astonishment, we found ourselves surrounded by half a score of Italian police in their military cloaks and three-cornered hats. Finally, through the aid of an interpreter, we learned that while en route from Brindisi that afternoon, Martin Sullivan had playfully filched the horn of the guard, by which that official starts the train, a custom like that of the pulling of the bell rope, or a wave of the hand to the engineer by our American conductors. Without any idea of serious consequences, the boys had hidden the horn and had kept the guard in a state bordering upon insanity for perhaps an hour, when the horn was returned. The official's dignity had been offended, however, and he had promptly telegraphed the authorities at Naples, the terminal station of the train, with the result that we found ourselves under arrest when we arrived there. The queer feature of the arrest, however, was that we knew nothing about it until we had attempted to start for our hotel. It took the efforts of two or three interpreters and liberal promises upon the part of Mr. Spalding to straighten the affair out; and after fifteen minutes' delay we finally started for the "Hotel Vesuve," which, by the way, is everything in the way of service, equipment or location that any visitor to Naples could desire. On the way from the depot, which for a long distance led along the Bay's shore, we passed the entrance to the famous Via Roma, or "Toledo," the San Carlos Theatre, the Church of St. Francis, and the Royal Palace; finally turning upon the Bay front again, upon which, just where the "Piazza Nazionale" begins, and in full sight of Castle Ova, the Bay of Naples, and Mount Vesuvius, stands the Hotel Vesuve. We were all thoroughly tired with our long trip from Brindisi, and after a charmingly served luncheon we retired to really magnificent apartments, from the windows of which we secured our first moonlit view of the finest harbor in the world.

The bright light of a Neapolitan sun gilded the waters of the Bay the following morning as the boys stepped out upon the balconies of their bed-rooms, eager for a more extensive view of the city and its famous harbor. Castle Ova arose from the water in front of us, and further away lay the beautiful islands of Capri and Ischia, as the two points of the mainland stretched about them in the shape of a horseshoe. To our right towered Vesuvius, its summit surrounded by a great cloud of dull gray smoke that rolled away, to finally mingle with the real clouds above. We could not dispose of our coffee and eggs quickly enough, and half an hour after arising left the hotel in small parties for different quarters of the town. Some of us started through the Piazza Nazionale to the Aquarium. Others entered the Via Roma and spent the morning in promenading the famous thoroughfare, bril- '

liant with its picturesquely attired crowds and rich shop window displays. Others attended service in the magnificent Duomo, or Cathedral of Saint Maria, while still others secured carriages and drove through the beautiful environs of old Naples, with its ancient church edifices and historical palaces. At six o'clock that evening I met Manning, Pfeffer and Leslie Robinson at the hotel entrance. They had taken a train that morning for Annunziata, and spent the day in climbing to the top of old Vesuvius, approaching as near to its smoking, belching crater as

VIA ROMA, THE LEADING THOROUGHFARE OF NAPLES.

they dared. They were tired out and covered with lava dust, but declared they would not have missed their experience for any consideration.

Of course, every one was at the theatre that evening; some preferring the ballet at Bellini's, while others went to hear Lucretia Borgia at the magnificent San Carlos. Not more than half a dozen of us had assembled in the hotel smoking-rooms at midnight to exchange our

experiences of the day. Where the balance of the boys had gone and
what they were doing I could only conjecture. A bulletin posted in
the hotel office announced that no game could be played until Tuesday,
the fourth day after our arrival. The following day was spent by most
of us at Pompeii, and the scenes we beheld in the ruins of what was
once a great and opulent metropolis, but which is now simply a black-
ened mass of ruins, will linger in our memories for years to come. I
made the trip with a party composed of John Ward, John Tener, Geo.

REMAINS OF THE GRAND AMPHITHEATRE.

Wood, Ed Hanlon and "Mac." We reached Annunziata at 12.30,
having left Naples at half-past eleven o'clock, and took carriages for
the gates of Pompeii, distant about two miles. Here we paid our
admission fee, purchased a printed description of the different objects
of interest within the walls, obtained a guide and began our tour of the
famous ruins. Although at the time of our visit one-third of the
original city still lay buried beneath the ashes belched forth by Vesuvius,

the work of excavation in the other two-thirds has been completed, and gives the visitor a fairly correct idea of the state of civilization, as well as of the customs and methods employed by the people of that unfortunate city, at the time of its destruction.

Pompeii was destroyed in 79 A.D., and at that time, the damage done by a severe earthquake was just being repaired. The shower of ashes probably came down upon the city during the night, for many of the remains recovered were found in their beds. Since the excavations

THE HOUSE RUFFA—ONE OF POMPEII'S PALACES.

began, the Government has erected a museum building near the entrance, and in this have been placed many of the interesting relics collected among the ruins. Others of these relics have been removed to the National Museum at Naples. Perhaps the most interesting of the objects in the Museum are the bodies. Of course, at the time of their discovery amidst the ashes, the flesh had long since turned to dust, but the sifting ashes had closed in around them, preserving the shapes as

13

though the bodies had been of bronze or iron, and when the excavators came upon any of these moulds they ceased work until the impressions had been filled with plaster. After the plaster had hardened, the surrounding ashes and lava were broken away and the plaster casts, in many of which the bones were well preserved, were removed to the Museum. The cast of a dog bent almost double, the muscles convulsed, and the bronze collar still about the neck, indicates the terror and torture the poor beast must have suffered in the agonies of suffocation.

STRADA DE ABUNDANCE—STREET OF PLENTY.

After leaving the Museum we spent several hours among the ruins, strolling leisurely along the principal thoroughfares, such as the Strada de Abundance and the Strada Stabia, and in visiting the Civil Forum, the Triangular Forum, the Temples of Jove, of Isis and of Venus, the theatres, the former homes of wealthy Pompeiians with their marble statuary, fountains and hand-painted walls, and many other points to be seen in this relic of ancient greatness. Pompeii and its history must necessarily be briefly alluded to in this volume, but there is material enough within those historical ruins to fill several volumes. While at Pompeii our party met Fogarty and Carroll. They had finished the tour of the city and were on their way to Vesuvius, bent upon climbing to its crater. I met Fogarty afterward in the Hotel Vesuve, and he told me of his experience in ascending the mountain. A railroad had been constructed up the side of Vesuvius and extended to a point not many hundred feet from its apex, but it recently took fire and had not

THE MOUNT VESUVIUS RAILROAD AS IT WAS.

been reconstructed at the time of our visit. Indeed, it is stated that the Italian guides, who for ages past have carried tourists up the mountain in sedan chairs and "palkas," destroyed the railroad upon finding that it was interfering with their old-established source of income. So Fogarty and Carroll were compelled, as were all other visitors, to make the ascent on foot. I will give Fogarty's account as he told it:—

"Carroll and I started," said he, "upon what did not seem to be such

a big undertaking, but we soon discovered that the farther we progressed the farther away seemed the top of the mountain, while the
steeper and more difficult of ascent it became. Time passed, and we
saw that what we had laid out for half a day was really the work of an
entire day. We kept at it, however, with the perspiration streaming
down our faces, while one of us would every now and then stumble and
fall among the brown rocks and lava ; but we shortened the time by
cracking jokes at the expense of our guides, and lightened the task by
every now and then pausing to look back down the side of the mountain.   Of course, the view of the surrounding country and the Bay and
City of Naples from Vesuvius is very grand.   I cannot begin to describe
it, and will not undertake it, but I would not have missed it, now that I
have enjoyed it, for a great deal. As we approached the summit, the
ashes that had fallen from the crater grew thicker and thicker until our
feet sank almost to our ankles in the drifting cinders, while the air about
us was filled with a fine dust that interfered not a little with our breath-
ing. We got around on the windward side of the mountain, however,
and escaped this annoyance to a very great degree. As we continued
to ascend we could smell the smoke of the volcano, and could distinctly feel the throbs of the mountain as it periodically belched forth
its flames and clouds of smoke. It was awfully hard work, but Carroll
and myself kept on until the guides called to us that we had ascended
to as high a point as visitors usually went. Fred and I laughed at them,
however, and went ahead, the guides remaining in the rear. As we
proceeded, we began to notice little wreaths of smoke coming out from
between the rocks, and further on we could see, not wreaths, but steady
volumes of gray smoke coming out of the ground, much after the manner in which some of the scenes from Dante's Inferno have been illustrated. The mountain now not only throbbed but positively trembled.
The air grew warm, and instead of the dust that had choked us before,
we felt the cinders, of no delicate proportions, as they struck our hands
and faces and fell round about us. Still, we kept on until we reached
what I am sure must have been the outer edge of the crater, for beyond
the edge over which we looked was a great basin of cinders, upon the
opposite side of which I imagined was the crater proper, because we
could see great masses of smoke rolling upward, while every now and

then we could distinctly see the force of the explosion as flame and smoke and pieces of rock were periodically thrown into the air. Was I frightened? Yes, I was; and now that I have gone through the experience, I have no desire to repeat it. I must tell you, though, about our departure and why it was we left very suddenly, as we did. Carroll was standing near me, and we were both wondering as to the causes of the mountain's eruption, when suddenly the ground beneath us began to tremble violently. Carroll excused himself hastily and started for the foot of the mountain. I think I must have been fascinated, how-

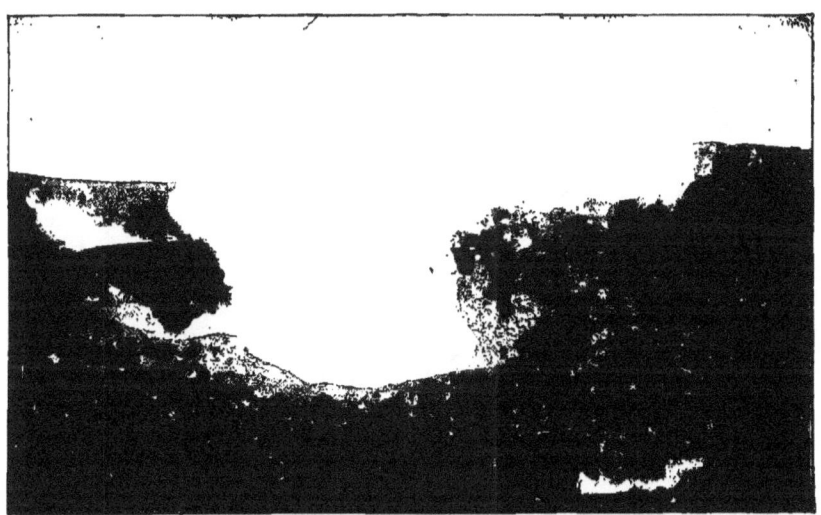

A PHOTOGRAPHIC PEEP INTO THE CRATER OF VESUVIUS.

ever, for I could not have stirred from the spot to save me. I stood there with the cinders flying and the ground trembling, not knowing just whether I wanted to remain or to follow Carroll's example, when I was suddenly startled into immediate activity. The ground seemed to actually rise under my feet. A wave of hot air almost overpowered me and then an explosion, which sounded as though the whole top of the mountain must be leaving its moorings, made me imagine my last hour had come. I did not know which way to run. But when the lava began to fall in pieces as big as my fist, and larger, all about me, I made up my mind that any place was safer than the one I was in. I accordingly started on the run, and, fortunately, having taken the proper direction, had, within a very few moments, put a safe distance between myself and the crater of Vesuvius. I never expect to make the ascent again, but if I ever do, I will not go as near the crater by a thousand feet as I went to-day."

Upon the afternoon of the 19th February we played our first game upon European soil. At one o'clock the boys in uniform entered carriages, and without any special demonstration, drove along the Via Roma and on toward the Campo de Mart, or the "Field of Mars," where the game was to be played. Upon the preceding day, United States Consul Camphausen, who was exceedingly kind and courteous to our party during its stay in Naples, had issued invitations to the members of the different diplomatic corps and to many prominent society people of Naples, and a large proportion of those invited were present. The grounds are beautifully located and are as well kept as any ball park in America. They were not enclosed, however, and there was no such thing as keeping the crowd from pressing upon the very heels of the players in their eager interest to watch every move the boys made. Half a hundred elegant equipages, and nearly as many public cabs containing many richly-dressed ladies and the official representatives of half a score of nations, were gathered upon each side of the diamond, while the crowd, beginning at the home plate, stretched away in two big lines to a point on each side far beyond the out-fielders' positions.

Tener umpired the game, which began with Baldwin and Daly and Healy and Earle in the points. Meantime, the space in which the boys were expected to play had been narrowed down by the encroachments of the crowd until batting was dangerous and fielding well-nigh impracticable. The police force present was entirely inadequate, and, besides, the officers were too deeply interested in the game themselves to admit of their discharging their duties efficiently. Minister Camphausen armed President Spalding with an Italian phrase, which he assured A. G. would have a magical effect upon the crowd, and A. G. accordingly walked up and down the line, calling, "*In di a tros; In di a tros,*" while he waved the crowd back with his hands, but the Italians only laughed at A. G.'s very bad Italian, and pressed more closely than ever about the diamond.

Then the fielders took a hand. When a ball was batted into the crowd the fielders charged after it, scattering people right and left. This had the desired effect for an inning or two, but the crowd closed in again, and just what President Spalding feared, happened in the third inning when a batted ball from Carroll took a big Italian over the eye and laid him out upon the ground. He didn't see any of the remainder of the game, for it had ended before he recovered his senses. Neither side scored a run during the first three innings, but in the fourth, Wood cracked out a single to left, got to second on Baldwin's somewhat unsteady delivery, stole third in good style, and crossed the plate on a passed ball. All-America did not long hold its lead, however, for in the last half of the fourth, Pettit got around the bases on a succession of battery errors and Pfeffer also crossed the plate. The crowd was well-nigh unmanageable when All-America came to the bat in the fifth, but after Hanlon had fouled out to Baldwin, Ward cracked out a three-bagger to centre, Brown followed with a single, and Fred Carroll next took a home run as his part of "the pie." Manning and Earle contributed two more runs, and before the inning closed the boys in blue and white had bettered their score by seven runs. At this period the crowd evidently thought the game was ended, for it rushed upon the field before the nines could change, and as none of our party were good at speaking the Italian language, we could not make them understand to the contrary. Besides, it would have been impossible for us to have handled so large a crowd had we spoken the language like natives. Ward, however, commanded his men to take their positions and claimed the game of Tener, which the latter gave him ; so that, technically, the game stood nine to nothing in favor of All-America.

Our farewell night in Naples was spent by fully two-thirds of our party at the San Carlos Theatre, said to be one of the largest and certainly one of the grandest theatres in Europe. Through the courtesy of the American Minister, a dozen or more of us occupied two of the gilded boxes in the first of six tiers which lined the vast auditorium, and I am quite sure that none of us ever witnessed a more brilliant scene of the kind than we looked upon that evening. The opera was "Lucretia

Borgia." Gayorra, the great tenor, sang, and the magnificent auditorium was filled with the wealth, the beauty and the royalty of Naples, in full evening dress. There is no sham about the production of an opera in Naples. Everything, in costume, in situation, in scenic effect, is genuine, through and through. For instance, in the gladiatorial scene that evening there were not less than 600 people upon the stage, 200 of which were in the ballet and 400 or more of which constituted the spectators seated in the tiers of the gladiatorial arena. A noticeable thing about audiences in Italy, and particularly about that which filled the San Carlos that evening, was their familiarity with music and their readiness to distinguish and recognize creditable and discreditable work by the singers. Those who sat near us and about us seemed as familiar with the music as did the singers themselves, and I discovered more than one pretty Italian woman and her escort keeping time with their fingers to the singing and the orchestra, while they frequently hummed the air as the orchestra played it or as it was sung. Several times, in recognition of successful attempts at difficult executions in solo by Gayorra and his leading lady, the great crowd arose to its feet in a seemingly uncontrollable burst of enthusiasm that found vent in a wave of applause, and then was hushed immediately as the audience gained control of itself and smothered its enthusiasm for fear of drowning the succeeding notes of the singers. I had often heard it said that a singer who could sing in Naples, Venice, Florence, or anywhere in Italy, was not afraid of criticism anywhere else in the world, and after that evening spent in the San Carlos, I understood why this was true. Italians are natural musicians, from little Pepino and Jaquito who play their violins and mandolins upon the street corners, to the great Gayorra, who is wedded to his Naples, and says that he is perfectly content to sing for Neapolitans so long as his voice is left to him. He sings, I believe, three nights in a week, receiving $1600 per night, and invariably crowding the house to its utmost capacity.

We were to have left Naples the following morning at half-past eight, but on arrival at the depot, we found that the commissionaire, to whom Mr. Lynch had entrusted the all-important duty of securing our tickets, had not yet arrived at the station, so we were compelled to see our train depart for Rome with President and Mrs. Spalding, while the balance of us piled our baggage in one corner of the waiting-room, and commissioning Clarence Duval as its guardian, broke away in congenial groups to put in our time as best we might until the departure of the next train, at three o'clock that afternoon. We scattered through out the city for a farewell stroll upon the Via Roma, or a visit to the Aquarium, and a stroll through the Piazza Nazzionale, while some of us took carriages and drove to San Martino, the monastery upon one of the highest eminences about Naples, and from which one of the

THE SUPERB COURT OF SAN MARTINO.

most beautiful views imaginable of the city, its magnificent harbor, and the Islands of Capri and Ischia in the distance, can be obtained. From the monastery most of the boys went for a brief visit to the Naples Museum, which is without question one of the most interesting studies in Europe. It contains within its great halls magnificent collections of marbles, bronzes, antique paintings and articles of gold and silver, embracing in all more than one hundred and fifteen thousand speci-

mens, from which one derives an excellent idea of the manners and
customs of the ancients, as well as of the high state of civilization and
luxury which they enjoyed.

The great building, which one involuntarily stops to admire before
entering, was begun in 1586, and was originally intended for a stable.
It was abandoned, however, and left unfinished until 1610, when it was
assigned to the University of Naples and used for educational purposes. Following the earthquake of 1688, it was occupied by the law

A NOVEL CONVEYANCE IN A NEAPOLITAN STREET.

courts, and during the revolutionary periods of 1701 it was utilized as
barracks for the troops. Later it was again devoted to educational
purposes, and in 1790, by order of Ferdinand IV, the building was
largely added to and dedicated as an archæological museum for all the
specimens found in the excavations at Pompeii, Herculaneum, and
Stabiæ, together with antiquities from the Museum at Capo di Monte,
the collections mainly of Pope Paul III. These invaluable stores of

antiquities were afterward added to by the Bourbons of Naples, who finally declared the Museum to be their private property, but Garibaldi, in 1860, proclaimed the Museum the property of the country, and did much toward enlarging the collections, as did afterward Victor Emanuel the Second. The cursory and hasty glance taken by our party as we hurried through these magnificent halls and paused momentarily before such incomparable pieces of sculptor work as the Farnese Bull and the Farnese Hercules, or silently admired the great paintings of almost every school of art for centuries past, only enabled us to imagine how very many profitable and delightful hours we might have spent in this Museum had more time been at our disposal.

ROME.

At three o'clock our party entered the train at the Neapolitan station, and after another delightful ride through the picturesque rural districts of Italy, we arrived at historic Rome, the city of the Seven Hills, at nine o'clock the same evening. With little delay

THE FAMOUS CORSO OF ROME.

we entered carriages and drove directly to our hotels, the Chicago team going to the Hotel de Alamagne and the All-Americas, together with the newspaper representatives, to the Hotel de Capitol, at one end of the Corso. Rome was very much crowded with tourists at the time of our arrival, and we were exceedingly fortunate in obtaining such comfortable accommodations. The following day Mr. Spalding and Manager Lynch called upon the American Minister at Rome, Judge Stallo, of Cincinnati, and at this gentleman's office the representatives of our party received the first discourteous treatment that we had thus far met with upon our voyage around the world. I learned, from inquiries at Rome, that no more unpopular man ever represented the American Government there than Mr. Stallo, and from what little our party saw of the gentleman, we are quite ready and willing to credit the statement. He declared that he had never been interested in athletics, and did not propose to have his name made use of for mercenary purposes. As there were no enclosed grounds in Rome, and it was absolutely impossible for our teams to give an exhibition for money, there was no occasion whatever for Mr. Stallo to take such a position. Moreover, we had simply called upon him as the representative in Rome of the American Government. He did not, however, extend to us even the common courtesies which, as American citizens, we had the right to expect. Fortunately, Mr. Charles Dougherty, Secretary of the American Legation at Rome, and son of the eloquent Daniel Dougherty, of New York, proved a genial, courteous gentleman, whose efforts in our behalf the entire party appreciated. He gave us much of his valuable time, and largely to his efforts the success of our exhibition in Rome was due. Our game had been arranged for the third day after our arrival, so that we had ample opportunity for sight-seeing.

On the morning after our arrival the party divided into groups of two and three, and, chartering carriages and guides, began the pleasant experiences which most of us had hoped for all our lives, and which all of us had anticipated from the time President Spalding made known his plan to return to America by way of Europe. I think St. Peter's was the most important object of interest with us all. It requires a full day to get even a fair glimpse of the great edifice, its chapels, its galleries, and the Vatican. In the Sistine chapel; in the long galleries of the Vatican with their grand paintings and mosaics; and beneath the dome and towering arches of the great church itself, I met groups of the boys, silent and open-eyed, or inquiring and enthusiastic, as they realized with every succeeding object upon which their eyes rested how inadequate had been the descriptions they had read of this great structure. Volumes, descriptive and historical of St. Peter's, have been written by men famous in literature and journalism, and I shall not attempt even a description of that of which Bayard Taylor, Nathaniel Hawthorne, Mark Twain, and others equally capable, have given such finished word paintings. Some of the more ambitious members of our party, John Tener, Jim Manning, Mark Baldwin, and others, climbed to the ball upon the dome of St. Peter's. From the piazza this big golden globule looks the size of a pumpkin, yet it will comfortably hold sixteen people, and a grand view of Rome is obtained therefrom.

FRONT VIEW OF THE STUPENDOUS ST. PETER'S.

The following day was spent by most of our party in ancient Rome. Mack and myself took a carriage early in the morning, and amidst the ruins of the Forum ; the palace of the Cæsars ; out upon the Appian Way as far as the tomb of St. Cecilia ; at the Catacombs ; in the churches and monasteries ; and everywhere else that we happened to wander, we met members of our party. Every moment of time in Rome was improved by the Spalding tourists. To one who has read anything of the history of the world's great empire, a drive through the districts of ancient Rome is indescribably interesting. All around one are evidences of the incomparable pomp and glory of the fallen city. As one stands upon the steps of the Capitol and looks over the waste of columns and arches and magnificently carved pillars of stone of the Forum ; or stands within the Coliseum and looks upon its great tottering walls; or passes under the Arch of Titus and out over the stones of the Appian Way, the same over which rolled the chariots of the imperial

THE RUINS OF THE FORUM.

rulers of Rome in the days of its splendor, he is confronted on every hand with evidences of the fact that centuries ago there dwelt on this spot a people which, in point of wealth, power, and science, was not inferior to any of the nineteenth century.

We were thoroughly tired out at the end of our second day in Rome, and after dinner, followed by a promenade on the brilliantly lighted Corso, the boys retired at an early hour so as to be ready for the game

in the Villa Borghese the following day. In speaking of the Corso, by
the way, I am reminded that among Americans generally there exists a
quite inadequate conception of Rome as one finds it to-day. It is not
merely a city of ancient ruins and relics of departed splendor, of sand,
and beggars, and unattractive architecture. On the contrary, modern
Rome is an important centre of wealth, royalty, beauty and fashionable
society. Few more brilliant scenes can be imagined than that encountered on the Corso any afternoon from three to five o'clock. It is the

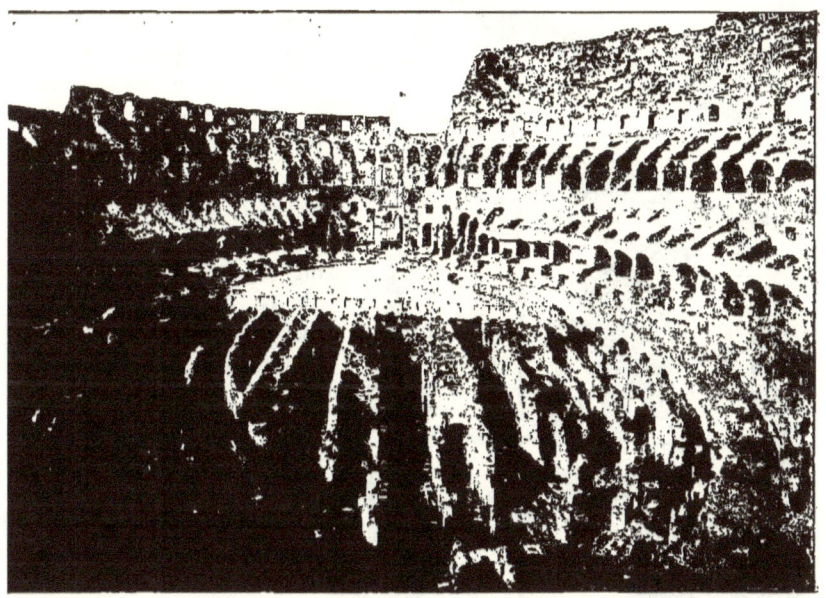

THE GREAT TOTTERING, WALLS OF THE COLISEUM.

fashionable drive and promenade of Rome, and here the wealth and
beauty of the Eternal city may be seen any pleasant day at the hours
mentioned. The shop windows and their contents are marvels of the win-
dow-dresser's skill. The street is barely wide enough for two equipages
to pass and the sidewalks are not over thirty-six inches across, yet I
have seen as much life, as many people, as many magnificent equipages, and as much wealth, royalty and fashion on promenade in this

remarkable thoroughfare as I have ever seen upon the broad surface of the Champs Elysée. Indeed, one sees a very great deal of the world on this little street. For instance, as I stood in front of my hotel one afternoon the carriage of the Prince of Naples, containing the Prince and his uncle—the son and the brother of the King of Italy, passed. The royal livery of scarlet and gold and the magnificent horses and equipage attracted general attention as it swept along. Following was the

THE ARCH OF TITUS.

landau of the widow of a deceased California millionaire, who each winter maintains an elegant establishment in Rome and spends her summers at Nice and Paris. Next came a party of young Englishmen, who seemed desirous of seeing and being seen, and following them in a carriage almost as magnificent as that of the Prince which had just passed was a Parisian adventuress, a beautiful woman, who had won something like a million and a half francs within a week at Monte Carlo. She had taken her winnings and retired to Rome, where she was living in a state of queenly splendor.

One of the pleasantest incidents of our stay in Rome occurred upon the morning of February 22d, when President Spalding accepted for the party an invitation extended by Dr. O'Connell, Director of the American College in Rome, to call at the college and meet the students. Accordingly at one o'clock on the day mentioned Chicago and All-America called at the college in a body, and in five minutes after entering the gates we had all the students, some seventy or more, around us in the college garden. They were big, healthy-looking fellows representing a score of the cities of the United States ; and how glad they were to see us. Ryan and one or two others met old schoolmates among them, and the meeting under such circumstances was exceedingly pleasant to both parties. All of these boys were thorough baseball enthusiasts, and of course were present in a body at our game upon the following day. "We are fond of baseball, if we are studying for the Priesthood," said one fine athletic-looking fellow to me; "and, as I tell Dr. O'Connell, we will make good priests if we never do anything worse than harbor a love and admiration for the good old game of ball. Do we play? Oh, yes ; we get out every Saturday during the summer and have some slashing good games. Have we a good team? Yes, half a dozen of them. But we do not get half the opportunity we would like in which to exercise." After an informal chat, Clarence Duval became the centre of attraction for probably ten

THE ARCH OF SEPTIMUS.

minutes, and his exhibition of baton swinging, together with an illustration of plantation dancing, was plainly a treat to every man in the place. Afterwards we repaired to one of the class-rooms, and with a glass of Bordeaux drank an acknowledgment of the brief but hearty addresses by Bishop McQuade, of Rochester, then on a vist to Rome, Bishop Payne, of Virginia, and Dr. O'Connell, President Spalding also

14

adding a reply.   The class bell finally sounded, and when we said good-
bye to the students, every one promised to be present at our game on
the morrow, and it is needless to say the promises were kept.

Our game in Rome was played upon the afternoon of February
23d.   During the morning, after several desperate struggles with the
Italian language, I had obtained permission of the authorities to have
the party photographed within the Coliseum, and when the boys drew
up in front of the famous structure at half-past one o'clock, we found the
photographer awaiting us.   He grouped us upon the crumbling arches
of the great arena and made a view that must prove a valuable memento

PANORAMIC VIEW OF ROME FROM THE SHORE OF THE TIBER.

Then we re-entered our carriages and drove to the Villa Borghese.   No
more beautiful spot could have been selected than that which we played
upon, through the courtesy of the Prince Borghese.   The Villa itself
is a magnificent private park, which is thrown open to the public
between the hours of two and five on Tuesday, Saturday and Sunday
of each week, and the Piazza de Sienna, where our game took place, is
a picturesque glade, its surface as smooth as any ball park at home,
with ascending terraces on two sides and at one end.   Upon these terraces, shaded by the great forest trees that have stood there for decades,

assembled the representatives of the wealth, royalty and blue blood of Italy. King Humbert drove up quietly when the game was about half over and saw nearly all of the remaining innings, while of the others who remained until the last ball was batted, were the Prince of Naples, Prince Borghese and family, Princess Torlonia, Count Ferran, the Princess Castel del Fino, Count Gionatti, Senora Crispi, wife of the Prime Minister, with her daughters, Secretary Charles Dougherty and ladies, the Class of the American College at Rome, resident and visiting American and English tourists and representatives of the social and artistic circles of the city. As the teams came upon the grounds the boys of the American College gave them three rousing cheers and a "tigah,"

THE APPIAN WAY AND RUINS OF THE GREAT AQUEDUCT.

and then, after fifteen minutes of practice work, they began what was, perhaps, the most remarkable game of the trip. Each team was anxious to win the first professional game of baseball played in Rome. In order to give the spectators a couple of innings of exhibition play, the game was cut down to seven innings. Healey umpired, with Crane and Earl and Tener and Daly in the points. Chicago went first to the bat, but failed to get a man to first base, after which All-America shoved up two runs on a brilliant home-run hit by Carroll that raised the crowd off its feet. Chicago opened the second with Anson at the bat, who sent a hot one to Ward and was retired at first. Then Pfeffer cracked out a pretty

double and scored on Williamson's single, Williamson next reaching
second on Tener's poor throw to first, third on Burns' out, and the plate
on a wild pitch. Double plays, clean hitting and brilliant fielding
marked the next four innings, neither side getting a man past the plate
until Tom Burns sent the ball into far right field for three bases and
scored on a passed ball. All-America failed to better its score in the last half and the victory went to Anson's men by a score of 3 to 2.

The assemblage of 3500 spectators was not only appreciative but critical, and the few errors scored were received very quietly, though the brilliant fielding was enthusiastically applauded, this doubtless being due to the presence of so large a number of Americans. The two innings of exhibition work which followed were as brilliant as the invincible in-field of Chicago and the wonderful base-running of All-America could make it, and a chorus of hearty cheers went up as the boys finally lifted their caps and made their way to the carriages. Our game at Rome was a success socially and artistically.

On Sunday, February 24th, we left Rome for Florence, at 12.30 P. M., not a few of the boys having attended services at St. Peter's and St. Paul's during the morning.

COLUMN OF THE CONCEPTION.

The journey was scarcely an interesting one, for, although the surrounding country was picturesque and beautiful, the day was cold and bleak and we were anxious to reach our destination. At half-past eight we entered the depot at Florence and were soon quartered at the Hotel de Europe, a comfortable inn and only a stone's throw from the right bank of the historic Arno. No one cared to inspect Florence by gaslight, under the circumstances, and all retired soon after arrival. Florence is one of the most interesting and beautiful cities we were to see in Europe, so all the boys partook of an early breakfast the following morning, and were soon after scattered through the city. The beautiful Duomo, or Cathedral of St. Maria, was unanimously voted by

those of us who saw it to possess the grandest exterior of any structure we had yet seen. The Pitti and Uffiza galleries, the latter containing the Venus de Medici; the home and studio of Michael Angelo; the church of Santa Croce in front of which Savonarola was burned at the stake, and which from the time of its construction has been connected with many terrible passages of history; the palace of the Medicis; the quiet flowing waters of the beautiful Arno, and many other celebrated points of interest were gone through rapidly, and I say this with regret, for one would fain spend

GRAND EXTERIOR OF THE DUOMO OF FLORENCE.

weeks where we spent hours, among the works of old Masters, which we had so little time to look upon.

Mr. Leroy de Koven, the scion of an American family of that name now residing in Florence, did much toward making our game in Florence a social success. The teams themselves took care of the artistic part of it, as the score will show. We played upon the Cascine, or race-course grounds of Florence, and, like the grounds of Rome, they are beautifully surrounded, being approached by a charming drive along the Arno and through one of the prettiest public parks in Europe. The game was witnessed by an assemblage which, though small, contained some of the bluest blood in Italy, royalty being well represented in the Marquisa Genora, Marquis and Marquisa Torri Giana, Baron

STATUE OF MICHAEL ANGELO.

and Baronessa Levi, Conte and Contessa Fabricotti, Conte and Contessa Geradesca, Baronessa Von de Heim, Principe Strozzi, Marquisa Balbi and many others, while visiting and resident Americans to the number of three hundred, as well as the members of the Florence Jockey Club and their ladies, embracing many Florentines of wealth and position, completed what was, with little question, the most fashionable assemblage of spectators that we played before during our tour of the world. The game itself was an exceedingly interesting one. Seldom have I seen better fielding, and I am safe in saying that nothing but the consideration which the boys entertained for Mr. Spalding, together with regard for their own good reputations and the presence of so many distinguished people, prevented an outbreak upon more than one occasion. As it was, there was more than one thing said "between the teeth," and many a trick was resorted to upon the field that afternoon which showed how very much in earnest the boys were and how intense was the rivalry between the teams. Chicago tried hard and desperately to win, but Baldwin did not seem to be able to

get the ball where he wanted it, and the All-Americas, who ran bases
like so many fiends, won the game by a score of 7 to 4.

We departed from Florence at 5 o'clock the following morning, for
Nice. The weather was wet and disagreeable as our train pulled out
of the station. With our departure from Florence we practically completed our stay in Italy, and that evening we slept on French soil in one
of the most famous and fashionable resorts of all Europe, Nice. Sara
Bernhardt and the Prince of Wales were both in the city, besides any
number of people prominent in Parisian, London, New York and
Chicago society, for the day following was the day of the Flower
Carnival, one of the greatest of the gala days of Nice. The scenery
en route from Florence to Nice is by far the most picturesque we have
seen in Europe. The road runs along the shore of the Mediterranean
for nearly its entire distance, one moment winding around the edge of
a bold cliff, at the base of which the waters dash themselves into clouds
of spray, and the next plunging into a tunnel, from which we emerged
only to find ourselves upon the side of another cliff with the blue
waters of the Mediterranean stretching away to the horizon.

A few hours out from Florence we entered Pisa, and obtained an
excellent view of its famous leaning tower. At Genoa we stopped for
luncheon, and when we stopped at the next station found that Fred
Pfeffer was not with us. He had been left at Genoa, but followed on
the next train, reaching Nice a few hours after we did. During the
afternoon we passed through the little city of Diana Maria, which was
ruined by an earthquake during the winter of '85, over four hundred
people being killed or seriously injured. There did not seem to be a
building in the city, and there certainly was none in sight of our train,
which was not more or less damaged by the agitation of the earth's
surface. Building after building stood with cleft walls and bare rafters,
just as the earthquake had left it, the scene being one of indescribable
desolation. Leaving this unfortunate city, we rode through some
grand mountain scenery, with little villages clustered in the valleys below
on one side of our train and the sea upon the other. We finally
stopped at San Remo, where lay the late Emperor of Germany during
his fatal illness; and then, as darkness settled down upon us, and
the yellow lights began to gleam in the little harbors along the shore,

we entered the station of Vingt Mille, twenty miles from Nice, on the French border.

Under ordinary circumstances we would have stopped here but twenty minutes. As it was, however, an incident, no less amusing afterward than it was annoying at the time, and similar to Martin Sullivan's experience with the Italian railway guard's horn, delayed us over an hour. It seems that Crane, Fogarty and Carroll occupied a compartment with two over-fastidious Italians, and they took offence when they imagined that the Americans were making them objects of ridicule. Accordingly, when the guard passed through the compartment they called him, and got even with the Americans by informing him that Crane had a monkey in his pocket, which, doubtless, was riding free of charge. The boys, unfortunately, had been having a little fun at the expense of the guard, and he was only too ready to seize this opportunity for revenge. He therefore insisted that Crane should pay fare for the monkey. Crane, of course, refused—indeed, laughed at the idea—for the monkey was no larger than a good-sized rat and was snugly tucked away in the New Yorker's overcoat pocket. The guard said nothing more, and we arrived at Vingt Mille, where our baggage was examined by the customs authorities. When we attempted to re-board our train, however, we were stopped, and while we were indignantly demanding an explanation, which the Italian-speaking officials could not give us, our train started out of the station before our eyes. Finally, we obtained an interpreter in the person of the cashier of the Italian dining-room in the station. We were then informed that the party could not leave the place because one of our passengers had not settled his railway fare. Upon further inquiry, we found that this passenger was Mr. Crane's monkey, and Ed was obliged to fork out seventeen francs for his Japanese pet's passage. Fifteen minutes later the official came back to us, stating that the fare for monkeys was nine francs more than he had charged us, and that he would be compelled to collect this. Crane was angry enough to have thrown the fellow through the window, and indignantly refused to pay another franc, with the result that within five minutes we were again completely surrounded by a cordon of soldiers, and Crane, alternately laughing and swearing at this imposition of Italian rule, went down into his pocket and paid the balance. Then as we were getting upon the train the interpreter mildly informed Mr. Spalding that he owed him twenty francs, or four. dollars, for services as arbitrator, and if the fellow had not gotten out of the reach of Al's foot just as he did, he would certainly have felt its force.

At last we pulled out of the station and sped on toward Nice, past Monte Carlo, past Monaco, until we finally came to a halt in the station of Europe's great pleasure resort. The little city was greatly crowded, in view of the approaching " Battle of Flowers " and it was only after

PANORAMIC VIEW OF THE PRINCIPALITY OF MONACO.

some difficulty that we succeeded in securing quarters at the Interlachen Hotel. The day following our arrival was an exceedingly unpleasant one. It had rained all night and the steady downpour had not ceased for an hour during the entire day. Of course the flower carnival was suspended and the beautiful floral decorations that signaled the approach of the battle in all quarters of the city looked sorry enough. During the afternoon we learned that there were no grounds in Nice suitable

for field sport of any kind and that, consequently, we would be unable
to give an exhibition there.   One would suppose that Nice, above all
other places would be provided with well-equipped athletic grounds,
tennis courts, cricket fields, and the like, but there is not even the
suspicion of a cricket oval, to say nothing of a ball field within the limits
of the city.   The announcement of no game proved a keen disappoint-

THE SUPERB THEATRE OF MONTE CARLO.

ment to two or three hundred Americans who were in the city, but
there was no help for it.

While the festivities of the Flower Carnival had been prevented, or
rather postponed by unfavorable weather, rain did not in any way affect
the attendance in the world-famed gaming halls of Monte Carlo, and
our entire party improved the opportunity to visit them.   I have been
told since my visit to Monte Carlo that there is nothing else like it in

the world, and this I am perfectly willing to believe. The grandeur of the great gambling hall we entered is unequaled by the interior of any theatre or public hall I saw in Europe. Beautiful grounds, made as charming to the eye as the skill of the landscape gardener can make them, and brilliant with a thousand gas jets, surround the building. On the opposite side of the plaza is a sumptuously equipped hotel, and next

ANTE-ROOM OF THE CASINO.

to that is a gorgeously fitted café to which one can escape from the heat of the gambling hall for a cooling ice or a bit of luncheon. Ward, by the way, dropped into this café during the evening and was charged the modest sum of $4.80 for a dish of asparagus, $5.20 for half a cold chicken, and $1.00 for a cup of coffee. Of course he paid it, which was the only thing he could do, but he remarked upon leaving the cashier's desk that the proprietors of the place must certainly have taken him for a gambler, and a very flush one at that.   Such is the basis upon which all things are conducted at Monte Carlo.   Those who have gold seem to regard it as so much dross.   Those who have not gold and who cannot obtain it, too frequently end their lives as not worth the living.

Upon entering the building, one leaves his coat, hat and cane in the ante-room, in charge of a liveried attendant, passes through a magnificent lounging saloon, where gentlemen are smoking and chatting among themselves or with prettily-attired, bright-eyed, attractive-looking French women, and then on into the great gambling hall itself, with its lofty ceilings, crystal chandeliers, moquette carpets, and magnificently decorated walls.   Nine big double tables are in full blast, and about each of these are gathered from 75 to 150 people, representing almost every nation of the globe, making their bets and losing or winning money. Duchess and courtesan, prince and adventurer, gentleman and confidence man, may be found jostling each other as they place their bets. Richly-dressed women, some wrinkled and gray-headed and others fair-faced and lovely to look upon, pass from table to table in search of the luck that comes to but few of them, all seemingly slaves to the one consuming passion of gambling.

I saw a gray-haired, diamond-bedecked, bony-fingered old woman sitting at a table with a pile of gold in front of her, stacked almost bosom high.   Fortune seemed to smile upon her with every bet she made, and her long, slender, colorless fingers plunged in and out among the piles of gold in front of her, while her quick, restless eyes watched every jump of the ivory ball in the roulette wheel.   Whether she lost or won her face never changed its expression.   Opposite her was one of the prettiest, fairest faces I had ever looked upon : that of a young girl, who nervously fingered the few last pieces of money that lay upon the table before her.   The old lady, I was told by my guide, was an English Duchess, who came to Monte Carlo regularly every spring for two or three months' indulgence at the gaming table.   Her winnings had been enormous, and her losings equally great during the past score of years : still she came as regularly as each spring made its appearance. The pretty-faced girl opposite was one of the many pretty creatures who wander in there, lose their little wealth, and then turn to some admiring fellow who is willing to stake them to the extent of his admiration and his pocket book. Many a poor fellow has lost a fortune at these tables, and sent a bullet or a knife through his breast on the marble steps outside. The attendance at the Casino, by which name the great gambling hall is known, for February of 1889, is said to have exceeded, by something like 21,000 people, the attendance for the corresponding period of the year before. The number of suicides is also stated to be correspondingly heavy, nine having been known in that period, to say nothing of those which the police, for reasons best known to themselves, had failed to report. Such examples, however, do not seem to have any effect upon the frequenters of Monte Carlo. They go and come, lose and win night after night, in the face of the realization that the chances of winning are one in ninety, with almost the certainty of a suicide's grave staring them in the face at the end of it all.

Everybody, however, who visits Nice goes to Monte Carlo. An American would no more think of going to the south of France without seeing Monte Carlo than an Englishman would think of visiting America without seeing Niagara Falls, and every one who goes there becomes wicked enough for the time being to gamble, if only just a little. Monte Carlo has a history with which most of my readers are doubtless familiar. It is embraced within the Principality of Monaco and is practically under the protection of the French Government. Still it is an independent principality, as the rule of the Prince of Monaco is almost absolute, and as the greatest source of the principality's wealth is its gambling hall, there is small wonder that the evil is tolerated. It is about thirty minutes' ride from Nice, on the Rivieri, and without question is one of the most exquisitely beautiful places in the world. All of our party during our visit to the Casino wooed the Goddess of Fortune, and some of us quite successfully. Fogarty quit four hundred francs ahead ; Geo. Wood did nearly as well ; and Captain and Mrs. Anson each returned to Nice with a handful of gold. There were others, however, who left within the gilded walls of the Casino a considerable portion of their own cash. President Spalding "quit winner," but the merchant of Nassau street "dropped his little pile," and came away a sadder but wiser man.

The second day after our arrival at Nice, to which the flower festival had been necessarily postponed, was characterized by perfect weather. The sun shone down upon the blue waters of the Mediterranean and warmed the wet verdure and soil into bright fresh life, while thousands of people flocked to the beautiful Avenue des Anglaise, where during the entire day elaborate preparations had been going on for the event of the afternoon. This famous avenue on the shore of the Mediterranean is one of the most beautiful in Europe, and on the day of the carnival presented an attractive picture, with its magnificent private and public hotels and its gaily-decorated booths, extending for a distance of perhaps some twenty blocks. Gendarmes were stationed every twenty feet to maintain order; bright-colored ribbons and bunting were flying from every booth; French women, attired as only a French woman can attire herself, laughed with, flirted and jostled the sterner sex along the walks; while boys bearing huge baskets of flowers circulated among the crowds selling to all who would buy. About three o'clock elegant equipages literally covered with flowers began to arrive, and for two hours these promenaded up and down the avenue, while beautiful women, kid-gloved gallants and brightly-dressed children pelted each other with flowers to their hearts' content. About four o'clock, the drag containing the Prince of Wales and a dozen of his friends, among whom were several pretty American and English girls, whose names I was unable to learn, joined the procession.

PANEL DECORATION IN THE CASINO.

Of course, the Prince was the cynosure of all eyes, and if his taste is to be judged by the size of the bouquets he threw and the method with which he bestowed them, his Highness, though no longer a young man, has still an excellent eye for womanly loveliness; and he had a great array of it to select from that afternoon, for never in my life had I seen a larger concourse of beautiful women or a more brilliant picture of its kind than that of this Flower Carnival.

We all left Nice in the morning of March 1st, at six o'clock, but the majority of our party laid over at Lyons for the night. Ward and myself, however, were too eager to reach Paris to submit to any such delay, and so kept on our way, reaching Paris about eleven o'clock the following morning. There was snow on the ground at Lyons, and it was chilly and disagreeable. When we two entered the environs of Paris the next morning, however, the sun was shining brightly, and

PANEL DECORATION IN THE CASINO.

the air was as balmy and ethereal as we had left it at Nice. From the depot we drove straight to the banks of the Seine, on past the magnificent Hôtel de Ville and Cathedral of Notre Dame, into the Rue Rivoli, and thence past the Louvre into what is the most imposing thoroughfare in the world—the Avenue de l'Opera, finally crossing upon the Rue de la Paix and turning into the Rue Caumartin, where we stopped in front of the Hôtel St. Petersbourg. A. G. and Leigh Lynch met us at the door, and soon John Montgomery and I had removed all evidences of the railway ride. We found, upon arrival, that the heads of the party had experienced much difficulty in obtaining enclosed grounds for an exhibition in Paris, and it was not until we had been there for several days that the Parc Aristotique, on the banks of the Seine and but a short distance from the then unfinished Eiffel Tower, was secured. Meantime, our party saw as much of Paris as American energy and limited time permitted of.

Ward and myself managed to get into trouble before we had been in Paris two hours. On arriving at the hotel, and after having made our toilets, I asked Leigh Lynch where we could purchase some good cigars. "The best place that I know of," replied Leigh, "is at the Grand Hotel; come with me." We did so, and upon arriving at the store (which is, as are all the cigar stores in France, under the control of the Government), I stated the priced goods I wished, and the polite Frenchman, selecting an unbroken box, opened it and held it toward me. I requested Ward to help himself, and then took one myself, and handed the attendant a two-franc piece, the cigars being worth one franc each. He shrugged his shoulders, returned the money to me, laughed, and began to wrap up the box. I laid the money on the counter and followed Ward toward the door. This action brought the Frenchman after us, and he explained, in very indifferent English, that I must take the whole box. The demand was so ridiculous that I laughed; but he was very much in earnest, so I promptly put the cigar back into the box and picked up my money. Upon this, the Frenchman followed me to the sidewalk, and noticing Ward waiting for me, with the newly-purchased cigar between his lips, he walked up to the New Yorker, with true French impulsiveness, and took the weed from between Ward's teeth. Ward was too astonished to speak, but not too much so to act. He grasped the fellow's wrist with a clutch that must have given him an excellent idea of the muscular development of American ball players, and, while holding his hand in a vise-like grip, deliberately replaced the cigar between his lips, and then told Monsieur in French that if he attempted a trick of that kind again, he would find himself in the gutter. The man threatened to call the gendarme, and looked up and down the street in search of one. Ward told him that nothing would please him better, and the fellow, seeing that his bluff game would not go, finally consented to take payment for the cigars.

THE EIFFEL TOWER AS THE TOURISTS SAW IT.

That afternoon and evening we began our tour through the streets of the city, certainly the most beautiful of all the great cities of the world. Its magnificent thoroughfares, its great institutions and beautiful boulevards, its broad public parks, its picturesque environs, with their historical palaces, its public squares, its monuments, its life, its gayety,

15

combine to make Paris wonderfully attractive both to the Parisian and to the visitor within her gates, particularly if he be an American.

Our party arrived in Paris on Saturday. The following Tuesday was Shrove Tuesday, the closing day of the carnival festivities in Paris, and during that evening and the early hours of the following morning none of us had time or inclination for anything more serious than the Bal Masque or the glitter of the big cafés on the boulevards. Our only fear was that we should miss some part of it. We arose at a late

THE COLUMN OF JULY.
Commemorative of the Revolution of July 14th, 1789.

hour on Tuesday morning, having lingered long in the cafés and the variety salons on the boulevards the night before, so that soon after we had breakfasted the fun in the streets, in commemoration of the closing hours of the carnival season, began. Masquers seemed to come from within every doorway, carriages dashed hither and thither with gloriously costumed occupants, horns were tooted, bells rung, and people jostled each other and screamed with laughter upon the slightest provocation. Paris seemed to have gone crazy. The crowd upon the streets resulted in a crush, and I remember that Mark Baldwin, Monsieur St. Claire, of the *Revue des Sportes*—who, by the way, was extremely attentive and kind to our party during its stay in Paris—passed down the Rue de la Paix to the Rue Rivoli, where we had a peep at the

Louvre, and spent an hour in the book and photograph booths with which this thoroughfare is lined. Well-executed copies of the famous paintings in the French galleries can be purchased in these stalls for from ten to twenty francs apiece, and we purchased to the limit of our pocketbooks. Then back up town we strolled *via* the Avenue de l'Opera, which was so uncomfortably filled with crowds of shouting, prank-playing maskers, that it was with difficulty we got through them and turned into the Rue Caumartin, back to our hotel. After dinner Ed Crane, John Ward, Ed Hanlon, Mac and myself deliberately laid out a programme of wickedness, and started out to see Paris on carnival night systematically. First, we drove to the Comédie Français—the home of the drama in France—whose walls have witnessed the débuts and subsequent triumphs of such lights as Coquelin and Bernhardt. We there spent an hour with French Comedy as it can be put on at this famous theatre only, and Ward was so pleased with it that we were compelled to leave him. The remaining quartet drove to the Jardin Bullier, where the students' ball was in progress.

What a crush, what wild hilarity, what exaggerated costumes, and what shockingly short skirts! There must have been five thousand dancers on the floor of that big pavilion at one time, all whirling and kicking amid the glare and heat of two thousand gas jets; yet, despite the crush, all was good nature. Lines of black-tighted students, clasping hands, would go through the crowds of dancers on the run, knocking them in every direction, yet no one lost his temper—that is, no one "kicked," in the sense that the average American baseball enthusiast would use the word. There *was* a "kick," however—a literal kick—and Ned Hanlon will bear me out in the statement. A leg encased in red silk, and belonging to a tall, well-shaped girl, shot upward just behind Hanlon, and Ed's silk hat climbed up among the chandeliers. The girl laughed, the crowd clapped its hands and rushed after Ed's hat, which they finally secured, and returned to him uninjured, but the American had had enough. "Come on," he said in a disgusted tone, "let's get out of here;" and we "got," for the students' ball of Paris is very much upon the rough-and-tumble order, aside from all else that can be said of it.

It was midnight when we reached the Eden Theatre, just off the Rue Caumartin. Here the great masked ball of the evening was shortly to commence, and as we entered, some of the prettiest women we had seen in Paris stood about the foyer, while French gallants in evening dress awaited the reappearance of their ladies from the dressing-rooms. The ball at the Eden was as select and *recherche* as the Bullier ball had been wild and reckless. The interior of the Eden is impressive. The style of the decorations and architecture is Egyptian. The parquet had been boarded over on a level with the stage floor, and a music stand, filled with a hundred musicians, stood under the proscenium arch, room being left for a passage way on each side, while a grand staircase, at a point just opposite the stage, led up to the promenades, cafés and restaurants back of the dress circle. The interior in itself was beautiful, but with the crowds of gorgeously-dressed women and their escorts it became dazzling. Our party took seats in the dress circle—front row, of course—to witness the opening, which occurred a few minutes after twelve o'clock. We had not been seated long before there was a crash of music from the orchestra, two big doors upon the stage flew open, and a hundred girls, in every conceivable costume calculated to show their figures to best advantage, filed out in a long procession, each girl bearing aloft a colored glow ball at the end of her gallant's cane. These constituted the regular ballet corps of the establishment. Most of them were pretty, and all were graceful, and the scene, as they followed their leader on a run across the parquet, up the broad staircase, through the crowds in the cafés and on the promenades, and then down to the dancing-floor again, was a brilliant one.

The programme had thus been opened, and the dancing now commenced in earnest. A dozen quadrille sets were in motion, and all around the borders of the dancing-floor sets of four, two couples, were dancing the Cancan. They evinced as great a spirit of rivalry in their dancing and were as jealous of each other's attainments as were ever two premières of the ballet, and the impulsive, excitable crowds in the room would be drawn from one quartet to another as the applause arose in different sections of the hall over some specially difficult and graceful pirouette of one or more of the dancers. Within half an hour after the dancing commenced, I saw fully half of the American party on the floor, not dancing, but eager spectators of all that was going on. Thanks to the courtesy of our Parisian newspaper friends, we were not long strangers among the assemblage, and as I glanced around I caught sight of Ed Crane, Ed Hanlon, Fogarty, Wood, Tom Brown and the "Professor" bending over the fair heads and the dark eyes of the Parisian beauties who filled the room, and who spoke, according to their own acknowledgment, "Joost a leetle Inglese"—in fact, just enough English to make them all the more interesting. It was three o'clock when the ball at the Eden had ended, and the remainder of the dancers followed those who had preceded them to the cafés on the Boulevard des Italians and the Rue Montmartre, which, when we reached them about the hour mentioned, were a blaze of electric light, brilliant costumes and vivacious women. Revelry, *bon mots*, and a good time generally seemed to be the existing order of things everywhere, until

ARC DE TRIOMPHE.
Commemorative of the Victories of Napoleon I.

approaching daylight frightened the revelers into their carriages and sent them to their apartments. One part of Paris was awaking while another was just retiring, and our party, which belonged most unmistakably to the latter class, wended its way to our rooms in the Rue Caumartin.

Ned Williamson and myself saw much of Paris in each other's com-

pany, and I found the big short-stop an excellent companion. He is
well read, and nothing worthy of notice escaped his eye. Indeed, it is
my impression that had Williamson chosen the journalistic profession
instead of devoting the best years of his life to ball-playing, he would
to-day be as prominent in one as he is in the other. His descriptive
letters of the scenes and incidents of our tour to one or two American
newspapers for which he corresponded were among the most interesting
sent from our party. Mounted upon the big Parisian busses, which, by
the way, is really the best method of seeing Paris, Ned and myself rode
from the Grand Opera House to the Bastile, and from the Grand Opera
House again, past the Madeleine and the Place de la Concorde to the
Champs Elysées, at which we left our conveyance and walked down to
the bridge which spans the Seine, at a point near the Exposition Buildings. Then we took another buss and rode to the Arc de Triomphe,
which we ascended, and from which we secured a view of the French
capital that is not equaled by any other save from the Eiffel Tower.
From the Arc we drove to the Trocadero Palace, and from its balconies
looked out over the terraced gardens and the Seine upon the incompleted buildings of the Exposition.

The others of our party were soon following our example, and,
although we remained in Paris but a week, it is safe to say that we saw
much more of the city than many Americans who have tarried there for
a much longer period. To tell of all the incidents, or half of them, that
made up our experiences in Paris, would require a substantial volume
in itself, and I am not sure but it would make exceedingly interesting
reading. Those who have visited Paris can doubtless imagine how
much there would be for twenty-five able-bodied, fun-loving, much-
traveled young Americans to see and to do, and we were seeing and
doing through every available hour of our time.

The morning before our game, President Spalding and Manager
Lynch, in a personal call, extended to President Carnot an invitation to
attend our exhibition, and the next morning received in reply the following letter from Gen. Brugere, which, translated, reads thus:—

"PRÉSIDENCE DE LA REPUBLIC, Paris, March 7th.

Sir :—I have the honor to inform you that the President of the Republic is warmly appreciative of the invitation extended to him to attend the baseball match at the Parc Aristotique.

He, however, regrets that because of his numerous occupations he will be unable to be present, as he attaches much interest to the development of physical exercise in the education of our youths.

He will, however, be represented by the officers of his military staff.

Accept, sir, every assurance of my distinguished consideration.

GENERAL BRUGERE,

General of the Brigade, Secretary-General to the President.

To Mr. Leigh S. Lynch,

Hôtel St. Petersbourg, Rue Caumartin."

Our game in Paris, which took place on the afternoon of March 8th, was one of the memorable events of the trip. The bright sunshine, the picturesque surroundings, the pretty faces, that grew prettier with excitement and interest as the game progressed, the presence of the large number of Americans familiar with baseball, the assemblage of distinguished spectators and the spirited playing of the teams, all combined to make it so. The park is located on the banks of the River Seine just opposite the Exposition Buildings and within the shadow of the great Eiffel Tower. Walled gardens and big city residences stood high above the field, which, though small, was still large enough for some great sport and a good exhibition. The little grand stand, especially erected, had been profusely decorated with American and French flags and furnished with plush chairs for the members of the President's staff, the American Legation, and other distinguished spectators, while chairs on each side of the stand accommodated all who did not wish to remain standing.

Among those present were General Brugere and Captain Chamin, representing the President; Mr. and Mrs. William Joy, of the American Legation; Miss McLane, daughter of the American Minister to Paris; Miss Urquhart, a sister of Mrs. James Brown Potter; Consul-General Rathbone; M. G. de St. Claire, of the *Revue des Sportes;* Nate Saulsbury, and others of prominence in official, social and theatrical circles. In this game Ed Williamson was injured. He had taken his base on balls, in the second innings, and in attempting to steal second base he fell over a sharp stone, the playing surface being of sand and fine gravel, and tore his knee cap painfully. His little wife, who was among the spectators, hurried to his assistance, and together they left the grounds for the hotel, Baldwin going to first and Ryan covering Wil-

liamson's place at short. No one anticipated that the big fellow's injury
would necessitate more than a few days of rest; but it kept him confined to his room in London for many long weeks, and prevented his
entering upon his duties with the Chicago Club during the greater
part of the championship season of 1889. Seven innings only were
played in Paris, as it was necessary for the teams to depart that night
for London. With the exception of Daly's single in the seventh, Chicago failed to do any hitting, save in the sixth inning, when a home run
by Ryan and a two-bagger by Pettitt, together with a passed ball, netted
them two runs, the only ones scored by Chicago during the game.
Crane pitched a magnificent game for All-America, and his support was
faultless. While the play aroused enthusiasm among the Americans
present, it was "Greek" to the Parisians. All, however, admired the
long hits by Ryan, Carrol, Pettitt, Wood and Crane, and applauded the
base running and the brilliant fielding.

ON THE ENGLISH CHANNEL.

We left Paris at half-past eight o'clock of the same evening for our
never-to-be-forgotten and eventful trip across the English Channel.
We took the long route from Dieppe to New Haven, and it is safe to
say that a thousand dollars would not induce any of us to go through
our experience of that night again. Indeed, we were fortunate in
reaching the shore at all. The Captain remarked, the following morning, that during the thirty-five years in which he had sailed those waters
he had never encountered such weather and such a sea as we had
passed through. Twice during the voyage he was tempted to turn
around and go back to Dieppe, under the belief that it would be impossible for us to reach New Haven in the teeth of such a gale. We
might very well have stopped over in Paris till Saturday, or Sunday
noon, when we would have escaped the nearly all-night ride on the cars
and our unpleasant experience on the Channel. We had expected,
however, to play our initial game in England, at Bristol, the following
day, and nothing but a heavy storm and the overflow of the grounds
there prevented the carrying out of the programme. Even had the
grounds been in condition, however, none of our party would have

been in shape to play ball, for all of them sought their beds at once upon our arrival at the First Avenue Hotel, in London.

We arrived at Dieppe shortly before one o'clock in the morning, and bravely walked down the dock, in the face of the stiff gale, to the little side-wheeled steamer "Normande," where we made ourselves as comfortable as circumstances would permit in the somewhat cramped cabin. Very soon after, we started upon our voyage, and as the ship began to roll, probably five minutes after having left the dock, the steward, a big, ruddy-faced Englishman, came in with an armful of little tin wash basins, one of which he deposited in the vicinity of each bunk. We asked his stewardship if stationary washstands were unknown institutions in England, and were smilingly informed that washstands and the little bowls which were being deposited about the cabin were intended for entirely different purposes. He advised us, however, not to lose sight of the bowls, as we might need them. And we did. Verily, it was a night to remember! Twenty minutes after leaving the dock, the "Normande" was in the gale, and she tossed about much as an air-tight barrel upon the waves might have done. Ton after ton of water poured over her decks as the big waves engulfed us, and we in the cabin below could hear the water rushing over us as we have heard a cataract breaking over its bed in the mountains. Tom Daly, myself and several others were thrown from our bunks by the severe shocks, but all were so sick that we failed to realize the danger we were in, or, if we realized it, were wholly indifferent thereto. Goodfriend and Leigh Lynch went on deck for a breath of fresh air, soon after leaving the dock, and neither of them could get back to the cabin. With the assistance, however, of a couple of strong sailors they reached a rope bin, near the wheel house, and sat there until daylight, with the big seas breaking about them and sweeping the deck between them and the cabin hatch. About three o'clock in the morning we were all startled by a shock, as though the vessel were really going to pieces at last; the shock being accompanied by a crash of timbers and the shouting of men, dimly heard above the roaring gale. We learned the next morning that one end of the bridge had been carried away, but that the lookouts had managed to hold on. Despite the danger of our position, however, the experience was not without its laughable experiences. Mrs. Lynch insisted that she was dying, and begged for her husband; but Leigh, poor fellow, was being tossed about inside the rope bin, on deck, and could not have reached the cabin for his life's sake.

"I guess you won't die, Madam," said the stewardess, and madam did not die, but both she and Mrs. Anson looked not far from dead six hours later, when we arrived at New Haven. Poor John Healy lay upon his face, calling upon all the saints to save him from a watery grave, while John Ward and John Tener went staggering about the cabin in a dazed state, bearing with them the most wretched countenances I have ever beheld. Even Clarence Duval was sick, but not more so than the poor little Japanese monkey, which sat upon Ed Crane's breast, with its funny little head hanging over its shoulder as though indifferent whether it lived or died. Ed himself lay flat upon his back, figuratively "dead to the world."

IN OLD ENGLAND.

But the sun was shining brightly in the little seaport town of New Haven, on the English coast, when we dropped anchor there next morning at 7 o'clock. The air was clear and spring-like, and not a trace remained to recall the perilous voyage of the night, save the wretched appearance of our party—colorless, worn out, and feeling no interest in anything but the prospect of a bed and a much-needed rest. Clarence Duval turned around after having ascended the dock, and with a glance out across the waters of the channel, shook his fist at it and then at the steamer, as he said: "Hi, you Missy English Channel, you tink youself mity smaht, don't ye? and yo' *is* smaht, but you dun did well to have a *extry* good time wid us while you had de chance, 'cause yo' doan neveh get dis boy out dar agen. If eber I git back to Ameriky, I'se gwine to stay dar—yo' heah me?"

It seemed good to hear English spoken again by others than our own party, and we submitted with good grace to the Customs examination, which was hastily made. We then took the train for London town, reaching Victoria station about half-past nine o'clock, where we were met by Mr. Spalding and Mr. C. W. Alcock, of the London *Cricket* and Secretary of the Surrey County Cricket Club. Mr. Spalding smiled as he saw the pale faces that came out of the railway carriages, and was compelled to turn away with momentary laughter as we came up the platform, poor Ed Williamson bringing up the rear on crutches—as sorry a looking procession of representative athletes probably as any that ever landed in England. As soon as he had learned of our experience and Ed's injury, however, he did everything that could be done for our comfort. Drags in waiting rolled us rapidly through the streets of the city to Holborn, where we were soon quartered in comfortable rooms in the handsomely appointed First Avenue Hotel. Mr. Spalding had gone to the expense of having all our baggage shipped to London from Liverpool, whither it had gone on the North German Lloyd steamer from Port Said, so that after a forenoon nap, a raid on the wardrobe and a luncheon, most of the boys began to look themselves again by nightfall.

MR. C. W. ALCOCK.

The spirit of sight-seeing which had clung to us ever since we had left California reasserted itself before we had been many hours in London, and the two days following our arrival were put in by most of us in obtaining, so far as possible, a general idea of the great city. All visitors, so far as I have been able to learn, are, no matter from what quarter of the globe they come, immediately impressed with the vastness and the greatness of London. The famous Strand, one of the busiest of the many busy streets in the metropolis, is but a few minutes' walk from our hotel, and as one strolls along it in the direction of Trafalgar Square, the Victoria Hotel, the Hotel Metropole and the Parliament buildings,

an excellent idea of London street life can be obtained. The absence
of street railway cars and the presence of the big double-decked busses,
as well as of myriads of Hansom cabs, at once strike the American.
Everywhere is London crowded, and no matter in what quarter one may
find himself, London, to the stranger, is greater, grander, more interesting and more impressive than all other cities of the world combined.
I shall not attempt to write descriptively of the world's metropolis. One
might spend a lifetime there, and then not have seen all that would be
well worth writing of. Unfortunately, we reached the city at a most
unfavorable season of the year. It was foggy, cold, damp, penetrating,
and all of us suffered more or less severely with colds, which we seemed
unable to shake off. We were very pleasantly situated, however, in the
First Avenue Hotel, with its luxuriously furnished smoking-rooms,
reading- and lounging-rooms, its excellent table and comfortable apartments.

True to their Yankee training, the boys began bargain-hunting before
we had been many days in London. Clothes, hats, canes, umbrellas,
underwear, linen, and, in fact, every article necessary for a gentleman's
wardrobe can be purchased in London cheaper than in any other city
on the globe, and the boys consequently spent money liberally. Many
of them, however, have since acknowledged that while textures may be
. cheap enough in London, the London tailor is a miserable failure, so
far as his ability to fit an American with a suit of clothes is concerned.
Not only is he unable to fit an American, but also an Englishman, and
it is a noticeable fact, or was to me, that in London, Englishmen seem to
be utterly indifferent to the matter of fit. They seem perfectly willing
to wear their clothes as though they had been thrown at them, and
while brand new and made from the finest cloths, most of the suits that
I saw there would have been promptly sent back to his tailor by the
average American.

Arrangements had been made for a reception and a luncheon to our
party in the Club House of the Surrey County Cricket Club, at Kennington Oval, to take place on the day of our opening game in England.
The Committee appointed to receive the teams on this occasion embraced the Duke of Buccleugh, Duke of Beaufort, Earl of Lands-
borough, Earl of Coventry, Earl of Sheffield, Earl of Chesborough,

Lord Oxenbridge, Lord Littleton, Lord Hawke, Sir Reginald Hanson, Bart., Sir W. C. Webster, Attorney-General, the Lord Mayor, American Consul-General, American Charge d'Affaires, and Dr. W. G. Grace. Tuesday, the day of our opening game, was most disagreeable and thoroughly unsuited for an exhibition of baseball. It was raining when the boys arose from breakfast, and although the down-pour ceased about noon, a typical London fog took its place, a fog which gave the towers and spires of the city a spectral and shadowy look, while but for the noise of rumbling wheels one could almost imagine himself in a community of ghosts, so dim, misty, and shadowy did everything animate and inanimate appear. Indeed, it was questionable whether the day's programme could be carried out, but the fog lifted a little by noon, and it was decided to play the game if possible. The teams accordingly entered the drags in front of the hotel at 12.30, and were driven to Kennington Oval, where, in the Club House of the Surrey County Cricket Club, a generous collation had been prepared and the boys were presented by Secretary Alcock to many, if not all, of the gentlemen named as members of the reception committee, and many prominent members of the Club. Lord Oxenbridge acted as Chairman of the assemblage, and after some of the good things on the board had been disposed of, he proposed the toasts of " The Queen " and " The President of the United States," both of which were enthusiastically acknowledged. Lord Lewisham then proposed the toast of " The American Ball Teams," President Spalding replying to the toast in his characteristically happy vein. Hon. Henry White, United States Charge d'Affaires, then brought the more formal part of the proceedings to a close, by proposing the health of the Chairman which was drunk with cheers. The boys then descended through the crowds that filled the Club House corridors and reception-rooms to the dressing quarters. Meanwhile, spectators kept pouring in at the gates until the immense oval, which is one of the most popular cricket ovals of London, and which is the personal property of the Prince of Wales, was completely surrounded by a living hedge from twenty to twenty-five feet deep, while the Club House windows and balconies were crowded to their utmost limit.

But what a day for baseball! The ground was soft, black and sticky wherever a spike cut through the green turf, and the big reservoirs of the gas company's works, which stood just outside of the walks, looked like spectral balloons in the gray fog, which was so dense that a ball knocked outside the infield could scarcely be seen. The crowd was there, however, with any number of prominent cricketers and representatives of the noble houses of England, and the Prince of Wales himself was expected; so that it was determined to proceed with the game. There was a moment of silence when the boys filed upon the field after having been photographed at the Club House steps, and then applause was tendered from all parts of the ground as the fine proportions of the men were noted. To play good ball under such conditions is difficult, almost impracticable, as almost every lover of the game in America will understand, and yet the exhibition at Kennington Oval throughout the nine innings was an excellent one under the circumstances. Healy and Baldwin pitched for their respective teams, and although the batting by neither side was heavy, many of the hits were clean and well placed, while the base-running was spirited and the fielding really remarkable, when it is considered that the ball could scarcely be seen fifty feet above the ground. At the end of the first half of the third inning a commotion was noticeable about the Club House, and a moment later the well-known face of the Prince of Wales appeared at one of the windows just behind the catcher's box. The boys simultaneously turned, walked to the home plate, and gave three cheers and a tiger for His Highness, while the crowd afterward cheered their approbation of the Americans' action.

At the close of the fifth inning, the teams, accompanied by Manager Lynch and the Press representatives, left the field at the Prince's request and ascended to the room where His Highness was seated. He arose and stood near the table in the centre of the reception room, and as President Spalding introduced the party, shook each one cordially by the hand. There was nothing affected, either in the manner or the attitude of the prospective King of England. He took the mud-stained hands of the players in his own faultlessly-gloved fingers and gave each a good strong, hearty grip and shake. Then he turned and chatted pleasantly with the boys for several minutes, calling Brown, Anson, Ward and others by name, as though he had been familiar with the game and its players a lifetime. He bowed pleasantly to each of us as we left, and then took his seat at the window to witness the remainder of the game. The crowd, understanding the nature of our visit to the reception room, applauded as the boys reappeared and commenced the sixth inning, while the Prince at the window asked question after question as the plays on the diamond were made, and listened attentively as President Spalding explained them.

Soon after the intermission, a representative of the *London New York Herald* asked His Highness what he thought of the game. "Here," said the Prince, "give me a card, and I will write my opinion," and he penciled the following :—

Of course, this was very graceful and very clever, and just what His Highness should have done. He could scarcely have expressed an opinion favorable to baseball, as against cricket, even though he had desired to do so, and the best compliment he could pay the American game was to compare it with the game which England considers so vastly superior to every other field sport. I understood afterward that the Prince, during the morning, had been quite indisposed, and had been advised by members of his household to send his regrets instead

of attending our game. He generously determined, since he had
accepted the invitation, to make his appearance, however, and became
so interested in the play that he remained a full hour at the club-house
window. He was accompanied by Colonel Elliott and Prince Christian.
As to the game, it was closely watched throughout, though, I imagine,
more in the spirit of criticism than of admiration. The fielding, particularly catches of long outfield flies, the base-running and sliding and
the batting seemed to be about the only points understood or appreciated, and these were greatly applauded. The *London New York
Herald*, that afternoon, circulated among spectators hundreds of blanks,
with the request that they pencil their honest impression of the game;
and these, being published the following day, covered almost a page
and a half of that enterprising paper. Many of the criticisms were
severe. Some thought the game "child's play," others "could not
see any sense in it," others thought it "too complicated in its rules to
ever become widely known or popular," and all thought cricket so
vastly superior in every way that there would be no room for American
"diamonds" on English soil. Many, however, applauded the fine exhibition of fielding and frankly acknowledged that English cricketers might
be benefited by emulating their American cousins in this respect. On
the whole, the criticisms were by no means encouraging to our baseball
missionaries, but I am pleased to say that before we left England there
were many among the fifty odd thousand people who attended our games
whose opinions changed materially, and the result of the visit to England of the American College boys, three months after the return of
the Spalding party to America, has been exceedingly gratifying. The
collegians played ball upon the London cricket grounds, interesting in
the game many of London's best-known cricketers.

One of the pleasantest events of the trip, thus far, was the delightful
little supper tendered the party the evening preceding this game by
Miss Grace Hawthorne, Mr. Wilson Barrett, and Mr. W. W. Kelly, Miss
Hawthorne's manager, at the Princess Theatre, in Oxford street. The
teams, by invitation, attended the performance of Mr. Barrett and Miss
Eastlake in "Good Old Times," occupying four of the proscenium
boxes. After the performance, a collation was spread in one of the
ante-rooms of the theatre, and with Mr. Barrett as Chairman of the pro-

ceedings, we spent one of the most memorable evenings of our stay in England. There were musical selections and recitations from a number of clever people, a recitation from Mr. Barrett, as well as a hearty address of welcome and wishes for our success in England, and a charming little speech from Miss Hawthorne herself, which brought down upon her golden head as big a burst of applause as she had ever received from the same number of people during all her professional life. The genial Kelly, too, came in for his share, and, as he afterward put it, was "too thoroughly broken up over it all to say much of anything."

The following morning the party, accompanied by Mr. Henry White, United States Charge d'Affaires, drove to the Parliament Buildings, and were admitted to and shown through the historical structures by the Secretary to the Chairman of the House of Commons, at that time in session, an honor rarely conferred upon visitors. We entered the great hall wherein Warren Hastings and Charles the First were tried, and which had been so badly shattered by the explosion of a dynamite bomb two years before. We visited the Crypt and the Committee Rooms, and were shown the magnificent corridors, their walls decorated with great paintings, executed at a cost of from four to five thousand pounds sterling each. We were next taken through the House of Lords, with its imposing and beautiful interior, and stood before the Woolsack and Queen's Seat, while the seats of the various members were pointed out to us by the Secretary. From the House of Lords we entered the House of Commons, where Sir William Harcourt was speaking upon "The Treatment of Political Prisoners in Ireland." Mr. Balfour occupied a seat which gave us an excellent view of his ambitious and intellectual, yet to me somewhat cold and cruel, face. It was expected that Mr. Gladstone would enter shortly, but we could not wait for even a glance at "the grand old man," and, after listening to Sir William Harcourt for a few minutes, we descended to the corridors, and, still accompanied by Mr. White, crossed over to Westminster Abbey, where we had only time to glance at its beautiful interior before mounting our drags for a drive to the grounds.

There is no question in the world that in England they can give America points on Athletic grounds. They certainly do have beautiful

16

lawns for Cricket, and I thought, as I looked over the velvety turf at
"Lords" that afternoon, of the time when, as I fondly hope, we may
see at least one end of the unbroken stretch of green sward marked by
the runways of a baseball diamond. "Lords" is a grand stretch of turf,
and the manner in which the people poured through the gates that
afternoon was a gratifying surprise to our party. There were fully
seven thousand people present when play began; and what a game
the boys played! It was "away up in G" from the start. All-America
took the lead by capturing three runs in the second inning, and held
it until Chicago, by scoring four in the eighth, as the result of timely
hitting, good base-running and costly errors, forged to the front. Then

THE CLUB HOUSE.

Ward's men, by desperate base-running, which evoked burst after burst
of enthusiastic applause and laughter, jumped in, and, together with the
battery errors of Anson and Baldwin, won the game by one run. It
was just such a game as pleased the Englishmen better than anything
we could have given them, the batting being brilliant, and the base-
running of a character that would have called for hearty applause even
from our best-posted American assemblages. A better understanding
of the game was plainly shown by the spectators, the Duke of Buccleuch,
in particular, being among the first to applaud every clever bit of
fielding and base-running as he viewed the play, together with a party

of friends, from the Club House. That evening our party accepted the invitation of Henry Irving and Miss Terry to occupy boxes at the Lyceum, and we were present in full force. We were invited behind the scenes between acts to enjoy a glass of wine and receive the well-wishes of our host and hostess; after which we returned, some to our seats and others to the hotel.

The following day, March 14th, was the date of our game upon the Crystal Palace Grounds. These grounds, with the great palace of crystal standing in their midst, form one of the sights of London. They are located at Sydenham, some ten miles or more from Snow Hill Station—Sydenham being one of the popular residence districts about the metropolis. Our third game in London took place here, upon the grounds of the Crystal Palace Cricket Club, a beautiful stretch of lawn surrounded by stately old trees and quaint-looking English residences, which stand beyond the boundaries of the park. All-America under the captaincy of Ned Hanlon—Ward having sailed for New York upon personal matters that morning—administered another defeat to Anson's forces, in one of the prettiest games played since leaving Australia. Another big and enthusiastic crowd of over five thousand people were present. The day was fairly favorable for baseball, cool and cloudy, but still dry and fogless, and we had begun to regard even such weather as this in England as wonderfully favorable. The boys dressed in the cosy club house on the grounds, and at three o'clock began the game. More enthusiasm was manifested at this contest than at any other we had yet played in England. Englishmen actually pushed and jostled each other in their excitement, many of them calling out to the base runners, "Run, run, man, or you won't make it." In the eighth inning, when All-America scored by hard batting, the enthu-siasm was such as to remind us of home. Crane cracked out a pretty double, which was finely fielded by Tener in far centre, and started to run.

"He won't get second," exclaimed one Englishman near my shoulder.

"Yes he will, yes he will," shouted another man; "see, he's got it—by Jove, he's got it."

"Yes, and he's going for third," yelled the other, waving his umbrella with excitement. "Oh! ah! look out, look out there, my hearty—you're caught."

Then he joined in the burst of applause that rewarded Tener's quick work and fine throw from the outfield. Hanlon followed with a base hit, and stole second with a slide that awakened the crowd into another burst of applause ; but it was nothing to that which went up when Tom

Brown picked out one of Baldwin's slow balls and sent it out of sight among the tree tops. Brown is a magnificent base runner, and he never showed up before or since that hit, to my knowledge, in prettier style. He was at the plate almost as soon as Hanlon, and Ned was not slow himself in base-running. Such interest and such applause was, indeed, encouraging to our boys, and no doubt spurred Hanlon's forces on to the capture of another run in the ninth inning, which gave them the game by a score of five to three.

DR. W. G. GRACE, ENGLAND'S GREATEST CRICKETER.

AT BRISTOL.

The following morning, at seven o'clock, we left London for Bristol, the home of Dr. W. G. and Mr. E. M. Grace, the most famous cricketers in England. As before stated, it had originally been our plan to play our first game in England upon these grounds, but a storm had rendered them unfit for use. We enjoyed a delightful ride from the metropolis in a big saloon car, especially provided for us, and upon our arrival in Bristol, at noon, were met at the depot by a committee composed of His

HIS ROYAL HIGHNESS, THE PRINCE OF WALES.

Grace the Duke of Beaufort, Dr. W. G. Grace and officials of the Gloucester County Cricket Club. We were driven at once to the Grand Hotel, where, in the parlors, we were presented individually to Dr. Grace and to the Duke. The Duke is certainly one of the finest examples of an old English gentleman I ever met; hale and hearty, yet close on to sixty, he still remains a great lover of field sports of every character. His estate at Badminten, seventeen miles from Bristol, is one of the finest in England, and here he breeds some of the greatest strains of racers extant. He shook each of us cordially by the hand, and then the entire party adjourned to the Windsor Room, where a generously covered table had been set for us. The Duke acted as Chairman, and, after the repast, the usual toasts, "The Queen," "The President," and "The American Baseball Teams," were proposed and drunk. President Spalding excited no end of laughter among our hosts and the invited cricketers present by his humorous recital of some of our adventures abroad. That little dinner and our reception at Bristol will certainly be long and pleasantly remembered by all who shared therein. With three cheers and a tiger for His Grace and our friends in Bristol, the boys left the banquet room and mounted the drags, which were surrounded by crowds of people as they stood in front of the hotel. President Spalding and the Duke of Beaufort drove out in the latter's magnificent private coach. The Gloucester Cricket Grounds are new, having been purchased and equipped but a short time before our arrival, at a cost of twelve thousand pounds sterling. Solid-looking gray walls of stone surround as pretty a stretch of turf as there is in England, and notwithstanding Bristol has but three hundred thousand people against London's four and a half millions, the latter city has no prettier cricket park than that in Bristol.

The day was the brightest we had yet experienced in England, and the grounds in excellent condition for play, yet, strange to say, the game did not show, in a single inning, a tithe of the snap shown in our London game. The boys tried their best to throw some life into it, but for some reason it progressed just as I have seen championship games at home —dead, up to the very last inning. Of course, there was batting and fielding. There was even a pretty double play by Ryan and Baldwin, and there was base-running and base-sliding, plenty of it, yet all of it

seemed listless and draggy. However, the applause was liberal, and
if the Bristolites enjoyed the game, we were all thoroughly glad of it.
His Grace the Duke of Beaufort, with his two daughters, sat upon the
press bench, to one side of the home plate, until the game was nearly
finished, and watched each point of play, asking Mr. Spalding to explain
what they did not understand. On the completion of the game,
which ended in a victory for Chicago, Ryan and Crane, with the
regular Chicago team in the field, sent the ball over the plate, while
Messrs. W. G. and E. M. Grace, together with other prominent cricketers, tried to hit it. When the pitchers put any speed in the ball, not
even the famous Grace brothers could gauge it. When Ryan and
Crane let up, however, the cricketers found the ball perhaps a dozen
times within fifteen minutes, the only safe hit being Dr. Grace's. This
exhibition pleased the crowd even more than the game had done, and
the boys were given a farewell round of applause as they left the
field.

BACK TO LONDON.

Our farewell game in London took place Saturday afternoon, March
16th, on the grounds of the Essex County Club, at Leighton. There
was another big, critical and enthusiastic crowd present, numbering
something over eight thousand people. The score, twelve to six, in
favor of Chicago, would have disappointed an American crowd, but was
declared by the English newspaper men present to be the best game
we had yet played in London. They liked it, as did the entire crowd,
because there had been plenty of hard hitting and base-running.
Crane did not put much speed in his delivery that day, as he was saving
his arm for the long-throwing contest which had been announced to
take place between himself and Bonner, the Australian cricketer, at the
end of this game; and so he was freely hit by Anson's batsmen. At
the conclusion of the game thousands poured upon the field and formed
in a great line, that extended from one end of the oval to the other, in
expectation of seeing the throwing contest. Bonner, however, did not
appear, he having deliberately backed out at the last moment, and
Crane accordingly gave an exhibition of throwing, sending the ball, a
cricket ball, without exerting himself to any great extent, 110 yards,
and following it with a baseball throw of 120 yards 25 inches. Had

Bonner been on hand, the probabilities are that the record would have been broken, as Crane declared himself in splendid condition and in the humor for throwing. On arrival at the hotel that evening the boys changed their uniforms for dress suits and repaired to the splendid buildings of the Niagara Panorama Company, where the stockholders of the institution had prepared a banquet for our party. The good old Duke of Beaufort dropped in upon us, half an hour after we had taken our seats, having come down from Bristol, as he put it, to spend the last evening with this "fine lot of fellows from America." When the toasts had been disposed of, every man of us joined in three cheers and a tiger for the old gentleman, who had been so honestly glad to see us and who had taken such sincere pleasure in entertaining us. On the following morning we fairly commenced our provincial tour in a style that excited comment and curiosity throughout Great Britain.

TOURING IN ENGLAND.

Through the efforts of Mr. S. Stanford Parry, General European Agent of the C. B. & Q. R. R., and Mr. C. W. Alcock, the London and Northwestern Railway Company had fitted our party out with a special train, the like of which had not before been seen in England. We had nine cars, two of which were dining saloons, with a connecting vestibule, two smoking and reception cars, and the remainder sleeping cars, each sleeper accommodating six to eight persons comfortably. The exterior decoration of the train was handsome, the body color being white enamel, with gold and seal brown trimmings, and the Royal Arms in gold and scarlet on the carriage doors. The interiors were even more elaborately equipped than our American vestibule trains, and contained every comfort one could ask. Each carriage was lettered in brown upon both sides, with the inscription, "The American Baseball Clubs," and the train presented a truly royal appearance as it stood beside the platform in the Euston station. It was to take us to Birmingham, Sheffield, Bradford, Glasgow, Manchester, Liverpool and Fleetwood, at which latter point we finally took the Irish Channel steamer for Belfast. There were fully five hundred people present in the station to witness our departure that morning, and with three cheers for Mr. C. W. Alcock and three more for the officers of the London and Northwestern Railway, we started on our journey through England. We were accompanied by Mr. P. G. Lane, the special correspondent of the *London Sportsman*, who was particularly courteous and attentive to our party during its stay in London and our tour through England, and by Mr. Fred W. Thompson, the Special Agent of the London and Northwestern Company, who did everything in his power to make the trip in the special a pleasant one.

BIRMINGHAM.

It was but a short run of three hours to Birmingham, where we were met at the depot by a delegation from the Warwickshire County Cricket

SPECIAL TRAIN FOR THE BASEBALL TOURISTS.

Club, who hurried us to the Colonnade Hotel and expressed their good wishes for us in bottle after bottle of "Yellow Label." Then we partook of luncheon at the Queen's Hotel, and soon after mounted two big drags and were whirled away through the streets of the city to the club grounds, prettily located and well equipped. Three thousand people were present despite the threatening weather, and we gave them a game worth talking about. Chicago opened with the capture of four runs in the first inning and All-America tied the score in the fourth. Neither side afterward sent a man across the plate, game being called at the end of the tenth inning on account of darkness. Englishmen had not seemed to like light-score games up to this point, but they entered into the spirit of this contest, and were heartily disappointed because the boys were unable to play out the game. That evening the boys attended the Prince of Wales Theatre in a body, after which we returned to our sleeping apartments in our comfortable special train.

SHEFFIELD.

We departed from Birmingham the following morning at nine o'clock, and within a few hours were steaming along through the beautiful hills of Yorkshire, at the base of which arise the towers and smoke-stacks of Sheffield, the greatest cutlery manufacturing district of England. At the station we were met by several members of the Yorkshire County Cricket Club, and were conducted to the Royal Victoria for luncheon, then, as in Birmingham, we mounted two big coaches, and with tally-hos sounding, drove to the Bramall Lane grounds, one of the oldest and most famous athletic parks in England. Full four thousand people were present when the game began in the rain. Despite the rain, how-ever, the boys played on, and the crowd, some with umbrellas and some without, stood in the rain and watched every play until the fourth inning, when the grounds were so muddy and the rain was falling so fast that the boys were compelled to leave the field. The players waited an hour for the rain to cease, but finally gave it up and filed through the gates. That evening we attended the Royal Theatre in a body, in response to an invitation extended by Miss Kate Vaughn.

BRADFORD.

The snow was falling heavily when we pulled out of Sheffield, next morning, and started for Bradford. At Bradford we found the weather pleasanter, although the storm of the day before had left the cricket field in a deplorable condition. The grounds of the Bradford Cricket, Football and Athletic Club we found divided into two sections, one being used for cricket and the other for football. The cricket field had a fine turf surface, but the football field was covered with chopped straw and soft loam soil, a combination which no doubt made an excellent playing surface in fair weather, but which, upon the day of our arrival, was little better then so much black paste. To add to the discomfort

of players and spectators, it began to rain while the boys were in their
dressing room, and a chill wind swept the mist in white sheets across
the field.   Still, the people fought and scrambled for tickets at the gate.
In America not ten people would have started for the grounds on such
a day.   In Bradford there were four thousand people upon the grounds
at half-past three o'clock ; even the members' stand being crowded
with ladies in water-proofs and macintoshes.   It seemed folly to attempt
to play ball under such circumstances, but the Cricket Club secretary
stated that three innings, if it was possible to play them, would satisfy
the spectators, and as the players were willing, it was decided to make
the attempt.   So the boys went out and played as pretty a trio of
innings on that black, sticky surface as one would wish to see anywhere.
It was short, to be sure, but it was a fine exhibition, and every spectator
got his sixpence worth beyond doubt.   While sliding a base in the first
innings, Fogarty tore the sole off one of his shoes.   He had no dupli-
cate shoe, and there was no one to take his place in left field for All-
America, so, repairing to the dressing room, "Foge" wrapped the dis-
abled member in a bath towel and played the game out.   At the end
of the third innings we could not get into our drags and back to our
cars too quickly, and in our comfortable saloon smokers we spent a
pleasant evening, while the wind blew and the rain fell outside.

GLASGOW.

When we awoke for breakfast we found ourselves in the London and
Northwestern depot at Glasgow, our train having crossed the border
into Scotland during the night, and had our train borne the Shah of
Persia himself, it could scarcely have been an object of greater curiosity.
Visitors flocked about our carriages by the hundreds.   Even young
women drove up to the station in their carts, took a leisurely promenade
along the platform from end to end of our train, and then drove away.
Until 1.30 P.M.—the hour at which we drove to the grounds—the train
was surrounded, certainly not less than five thousand people having
stopped to look into the windows of our cars during the morning.   At
noon we had luncheon in the London and Northwestern Company's
hotel at the station.   After luncheon, the boys in uniform, but wearing
their heavy coats, for the air was cold and sharp, mounted a big double-

decked, four-horse carry-all, and with nearly a thousand people assembled to see them off, started for the grounds. The West of Scotland Cricket Club's grounds are as well appointed as any outside of London, and happening to be in good condition, with fair weather for baseball, the boys put up an excellent game. All-America, by timely hitting, and by taking advantage of wild throws by Baldwin and Pettitt, won their victory in pretty style, the forty-five hundred spectators liberally according the heartiest applause at the pretty fielding work of Fogarty, Hanlon, Ryan and Pfeffer. Returning to the train, the boys exchanged their uniforms for their dress suits, and adjourned to the Grand Theatre, where, between the acts of "King Lear," they left their boxes to break a bottle of Monopole with Mr. and Mrs. Osmond Tearle behind the curtain.

MANCHESTER.

We reached Manchester for breakfast the morning of the twenty-second, having left Glasgow at midnight. All of our party were more favorably impressed with Manchester than with any Provincial town we had yet visited. In accordance with our usual custom we spent the forenoon in driving and walking about the city and inspecting the principal thoroughfares, then we returned to our train, which, as at other stations, we found surrounded by a curious crowd. After luncheon we climbed to the top of a couple of four-horse coaches and set out for the Old Trafford grounds. When I got the first glimpse of its beautiful stretch of green sward surrounded by pretty pavilions, club houses, and terraced rows of seats, the Old Trafford grounds of Manchester seemed the most beautiful in the world. The air was a bit bracing, but the boys put up one of the prettiest contests of our tour, before as distinguished and fine looking an assemblage of spectators as we had played before since our opening game in London, when the Prince of Wales was present. Had the details been prearranged, the boys could not have fought a prettier battle. In the fifth inning All-America tied the score, which stood five to five up to the time Hanlon's men came to bat in the eighth inning. Manning scored in this inning in dashing style, but Chicago again tied the score in the first half of the last, when Pettitt crossed the plate, the score standing six to six, when Hanlon came to bat for All-America's last half of the ninth. Ned cracked out a pretty single and reached second, risking his neck in a daring and successful attempt at a steal.   The play sent the crowd off into one enthusiastic howl of applause, base-sliding being an entirely new feature of field sport to the majority of the spectators present.   They clapped their hands, waved their handkerchiefs, and called out to Fogarty, when he came to bat, to "Hit it hard now."   "Foge" picked out the ball he wanted, and sent it upon an ideal two-base journey to far left centre.   Away flew Hanlon to third, and touching the bag lightly with his foot sped on toward the home plate, and then to the Club House without ever stopping, the balance of the players picking up their coats and breaking after Hanlon on a tight run, while the crowd stood upon its feet and applauded vociferously.   They had seen a brilliant game, and, what is more, they had appreciated it.   That evening our party was banqueted in the rooms of the Anglo-French Club, as special guests of Mr. Raymond Eddy, the European representative of the house of John V. Farwell & Co., of Chicago.   A score of Mr. Eddy's friends assisted him, Major Hale, United States Consul at Manchester, acting as Chairman. Mr. Eddy proved a typical American in personal appearance, in patriotism for everything and anything American, and in the whole-souled, generous manner in which he entertained our party.

LIVERPOOL.

We departed from Manchester the following morning at seven o'clock, reaching Liverpool an hour later.   Another crowd stood in the depot to see the Yankees at breakfast in their dining-cars, and to stare at the players as they emerged and made their way up town to see the city. Probably because it has so long been visited by so many Americans, Liverpool has an unmistakably American air about it.   Just where or what the existing difference is between it and other English cities, I cannot say, but there is a difference, and it was noticeable to all of our party.   As this was our last opportunity to do any shopping on English soil, the boys put in the morning profitably alike to themselves and to the Liverpool shopkeepers.   We partook of a light lunch at the London and Northwestern Company's hotel at about half-past one o'clock, and then mounted a huge coach with seats for twenty-eight people, and bowled through the streets of the city to the Police Athletic

Club grounds for our game. With the long brass horn of the tally-ho sounding upon every block, and its notes interspersed with the sharp crack of the coach-driver's whip, we created almost as much of a sensation on our way to the grounds as our special train had done at the depot. We found the park already fairly well filled and a big crush of people at the gates. Indeed, the crowd at the gates reminded me much of an American crowd at the gates of a ball park before an important championship game. The pressure of the hundreds upon the outside of the big carriage gate finally broke it from its hinges, and nearly five hundred people swarmed upon the ground before the police could stop them. Between six and seven thousand people had finally packed themselves about the diamond when the programme began.

Five innings of baseball were first ·played by the Chicago and All-America teams, and the only regret of our party, and doubtless of the spectators, was that it did not last longer. Baldwin and Crane were both on their mettle, and how that ball did cut the air about the plate. Neither pitcher wanted to stop at the end of the fifth inning, when the score stood 2 and 2, but other games had been announced and the tie could not be played off. But one hit was made off Baldwin and four off Crane.

After the ball game came the game of "Rounders," which had been arranged between the local club and a team picked from the Chicago and the All-America. None of us had ever seen the game, from which it was claimed baseball sprang, and all were therefore anxious to have it begin. A picked team from the Rounders' Association of Liverpool finally went into the field against an American eleven composed of Baldwin and Earl as battery, with Tener, Anson, Wood, Fogarty, Brown, Hanlon, Pfeffer, Manning and Sullivan. The fielders were stationed much as in baseball, save that there was a fielder back of the catcher, called "long stop," and a fielder back of the third baseman. The batting is done with one hand, and the bat is like a toy cricket bat, or perhaps more like a butter paddle. The ball is the size of a tennis ball, and the bases, instead of being bags, are iron stakes protruding about three feet from the ground. A base-runner could not be retired upon being touched with the ball, but must be struck with it. Moreover, he must run the first time he strikes at the ball, whether he hits it or

not. The pitching is straight armed. In the game they played against
our boys, the rounder players took an unfair advantage in sending our
team to bat first, and, not knowing the rules, the Americans were shut
out with but six runs. The boys soon "caught on," however, and the
two innings played resulted in a score of sixteen to fourteen in favor
of the Liverpool players. This was all we saw of the Rounders during
our tour of the world, and I am quite certain that none of our party
cared to see any more of it.

Following the game of Rounders, the Americans played the rounder
team two innings of baseball, simply to show them the difference. At
the end of the second inning the score stood eighteen to nothing, in
favor of the Americans, and would have been more, had the latter not
tired of running the bases. Baldwin pitched, and after striking out
three of the batsmen, let the other three hit the ball and get thrown out
at first. How the crowd did enjoy this sport. They stood twenty to
thirty deep in the steadily pouring rain, which had begun to fall just as
the rounder game commenced, their hats on the back of their heads,
and they shouting and applauding as though they were witnessing a
horse race on an ideal day in June. A dozen of the biggest cranks in
America could not have been induced anywhere near a ball park in
such weather; and when it was all over, and the boys climbed upon
their drags, the big crowd cheered the teams until we were out of sight.

Our train left for Fleetwood that evening at nine o'clock, yet the boys
managed to accept two invitations after they had swallowed a hasty dinner, some of them going to the Royal Theatre as the guests of Mr. W.
W. Kelley, and others to the Shakespeare Theatre, as the guests of Miss
Litta. Then we hurried to the train, and bidding farewell to Liverpool,
started for Fleetwood on the shore of the Irish Channel. It was but
a three hours' run, and at eleven o'clock we boarded the beautiful
little steamer "Princess of Wales," in which we were to cross to Ireland.

With our experience on the English Channel still fresh in our minds,
none of us looked forward with very much pleasure to crossing the
Irish Channel. Contrary to our anticipations, though, or rather to our
fears, the trip to Belfast was one of the pleasantest voyages of our
entire tour. Even before the breakfast gong sounded, the majority of
the boys were on deck, eager to catch the first view of the Emerald Isle,

and the announcement of breakfast failed to draw many of us down stairs. We were steaming through the Belfast Loch with the beautiful shore of County Down on one side and that of County Antrim on the other. By the time we had finished breakfast, we had entered the river Lagan, and soon after dropped alongside the stone dock in front of the Custom House. Carriages conveyed us to the Imperial Hotel, on Royal Avenue, and, for the first time since leaving Australia, the boys felt a sense of rest and relief from the rapid pace at which we had been trav-

THE JOLLY JAUNTING-CAR OF BELFAST.

eling. It was Sunday, and the players, in parties of three or four, mounted jaunting-cars, and spent the afternoon in driving about the beautiful environs of Belfast. Sunday afternoon was quiet enough to suit the severest Sabbatarian, but Sunday evening Royal Avenue was crowded with pretty girls and their escorts. The bright costumes of the Scotch Highland troops, off duty, added to the attractiveness of the scene. Rain coming up shortly after nine o'clock, however, the boys

17

sought the big comfortable smoking-rooms of Mr. Jury's hotel, where they chatted until bedtime.

The weather on the following day was erratic. During the morning it rained for an hour, and then the sun shone for half an hour, only to be hidden by another downpour of rain, until it began to look really doubtful as to whether or not we should be able to play our game scheduled for Belfast. It cleared up about noon, however, and after luncheon the boys made their way through the crowds about the hotel doors and mounted the drags for the cricket park. The North of Ireland Cricket Club is certainly well provided with grounds. Out on the Ormeau road is a fine stretch of lawn, well fenced in on three sides and its fourth washed by the waters of the river Lagan. Beyond the river is Ormeau Park, and, altogether, the club could not have selected a prettier and more desirable site in Belfast. Despite the condition of the turf, which was too soft for base-running, the boys played one of the cleanest-cut and prettiest games I scored during the trip, and that, too, before an exceedingly attractive and thoroughly appreciative assemblage of spectators. Pretty girls in jaunting-cars, and fine-looking, highly-bred Irish gentlemen, young and old, together with large numbers of Club members and their invited guests, went to make up a crowd of three thousand people, who sat the game out through rain and shine, applauding liberally when good plays were made, and at all times showing the keenest interest. As in Manchester, the game ended beautifully. In the eighth inning it stood eight to seven, in favor of Chicago, when, in the ninth, Wood and Healy each cracked out a pretty single, both crossing the plate on Earl's fine three-base drive to far left field, and thus scoring another victory for All-America under Hanlon's captaincy. That evening the boys were banqueted by the North of Ireland Cricket Club, at the Club House, the Mayor of Belfast presiding.

We left Belfast at an early hour the following morning for Dublin, and it was while the boys were enjoying the soundest sleep of the night, shortly after five o'clock, that they were awakened from their slumbers by a voice in the hallway, which sang out as it passed our doors : " Arf pawst foive ; wudge ye be gettin' oop, surrs ? its arf pawst foive." Oh, the richness of that brogue ! Every man of us will remember it for many and many a year to come. Hanlon rolled out of bed laughing before his eyes were fairly opened, and within two minutes a dozen grinning faces were thrust through bed-room doors into the hall, as the boys asked one another, "Did you hear that? did you hear it, I say?" Like a warden in a graveyard, Pat continued on down the hall, pausing every ten steps to raise his head in the air, and in a voice that seemed to come from his boots, call out, "Arf pawst foive." The mere repetition of that phrase by any member of our party was ever afterward certain to excite a ripple of laughter.

AN OLD IVY-COVERED CASTLE.

Beautifully picturesque indeed is the ride from Belfast to Dublin, where we arrived at eleven o'clock, four hours and a half after our departure. The carefully-cultivated farms, with their borders of stone walls or green hedges and the charming woodlands, with an occasional old ivy-grown castle lifting its towers above the tree tops, more than realized our anticipations of Irish landscape. At Dublin station we were met by U. S. Consul McCaskill and others, and driven to Morrison's

Hotel, famous as the scene of Parnell's arrest. Mr. Spalding had kindly given this day over to such of the boys as wished to visit friends and relatives in Ireland, and there was no game scheduled. Consequently, John Tener, Tom Daly, Jim Manning, and others posted off to Kildare, Kilkenny, Londonderry, and elsewhere, to visit uncles, aunts, and nieces they had not seen for years, and some of whom they had never seen. Indeed, the three mentioned left us at Belfast after the game there.

"I went to Callan, in Kilkenny," said Manning, in talking to me afterward about his trip, "Callan being a little town of about fifteen hundred people, where I have an uncle and several nieces whom I had never seen. I telegraphed my uncle that I was coming, and the 'whole town' met me at the station in jaunting-cars and on foot. Brogue? Well, you should have heard it. I wouldn't have missed it for a farm. Everybody had to shake hands with me. They looked me over as though I might have come out of the clouds somewhere. Then they took me in one of the jaunting-cars, and, completely surrounded by these little two-wheeled conveyances, I was driven to my uncle's home. Almost the first things that caught my eye were a number of pictures on the walls representing myself in costume and as my likeness had appeared in our American sporting and daily newspapers. They asked me all about baseball; wanted to know if it was played like 'Hurley'— an Irish game, something like polo—and could not understand how a man could earn a living salary by playing baseball. Of course I had a delightful time, and everything in Callan, even the scores of pretty Irish girls, was mine."

Tom Daly went down to Kildare, and his two old uncles had the little town in which they resided dressed up in gala attire to receive him. They took him over to their little home, and sat with him upon the balconies, while the town folk dropped in in instalments for a look at their neighbor's American "neffy." The conversation that took place between Tom and his uncles must have been exceedingly funny, as I got it from the Chicago catcher upon his return to the party.

"Phwat is it ye say ye'r afther doing, me boy?" asked one of the old gentlemen.

"I am traveling with the baseball party," replied Tom.

" Phwat's baseball ?"

"Why, it's a game we play in America," replied Tom.

"An is it boi plain' a game that ye make ye'r livin' ?"

"Certainly," said Tom. "We have thousands of people to see us in America, at from two to three shillings a head admission."

"An' it pays ye well, does it ?" still further inquired the old gentleman.

"Yes," said Tom, carelessly fingering the diamond solitaire in his scarf and the diamond-studded charm on his watch chain, and then

PHŒNIX PARK, IN THE CITY OF DUBLIN.

pulling out a $350 chronometer and glancing at the hour. "It is'nt a bad business."

"Faith, an' I guess not," said the old gentleman. "Oive half a dozen of me own Oi would like to send over to yez, if ye consint t' get them inter ther same bisniss."

Tom, like Manning, owned everything within sight during this visit; and handsome John Tener, who ran down into Londonderry on a similar visit, was the lion of the day among the relatives whom he had not seen since childhood. Meantime the balance of our party who remained in Dublin put in their time to good advantage. Some went off on a stroll through Phœnix Park, and others upon jaunting-cars drove through the city and its environs, but the majority of the boys were satisfied to promenade Sackville and Grafton streets, where the crowd was thickest, and where we saw type after type of Irish beauty, such as I am firmly convinced can be seen nowhere outside of Ireland.

SACKVILLE STREET, DUBLIN.

That evening we occupied four large proscenium boxes at the Gaiety Theatre, where an excellent English Company was playing a laughable comedy known as the "Arabian Nights."

The following day was a beautiful one for the ball game, just such a day as we desired for the great game we played before taking our farewell of Old Ireland. The morning was consumed by most of the boys in purchasing black-thorn sticks, "shillalies," and other mementoes of

the "old sod" for Irish-American friends at home. Shortly before noon
we called at the Mansion House, and were received by the Lord Mayor
of Dublin, who expressed his happiness at welcoming such a party of
Americans, and tendered us the freedom of the city. After luncheon
at Morrison's, the boys, in uniform, came down the stairs into the
rotunda, one by one, while half a score of fair guests in the hotel, who
had been waiting for this particular opportunity, leaned over the balus-
trade of the staircase and quietly criticised the boys as they stood

GRAFTON STREET, DUBLIN.

about in knee-breeches. Then into the drags piled the players, and
off we started at a brisk pace for the Landsdown Road Grounds.
Dublin is certainly a beautiful old city, our party passing along avenues
on its way to the grounds that would be accounted attractive in any
city in the world, while from what I saw of Dublin people during our
brief sojourn, I imagined Dublin society must indeed be charming.
Our party were unanimous in awarding the palm for clear complexions,
beautiful faces, and attractive figures to Ireland.

The Landsdown Road Grounds, where our game was played, are more properly tennis and football grounds than cricket or baseball grounds; still they answered our purpose very well indeed, and the boys put up a game that must have fired the blood of every American present. Crane and Baldwin were again "out for keeps," and how they did pitch; while Hanlon, Carroll, Fogarty and Manning ran bases as I had rarely seen them run even in championship games. Cipher after cipher went up on the score board, until each team had six opposite its name. The Dublinites could not understand why eighteen great big fellows like these could not score a run, and when finally Pettitt, by luck and hard hitting, got around the circuit, and by great sliding threw himself upon the plate, just as Pfeffer's sacrifice ball to Brown was returned, there was a noticeable bit of sarcasm in the applause—a sort of " Ah-ha, he has scored a run at last " tinge—whereas in America they would have yelled for a good five minutes. Then All-America scored, tying the game, and Burns and Baldwin also crossed the plate, leading Hanlon's men by two runs. But in the ninth, Earl's three-bagger, Hanlon's base on balls, Tom Burns's fumble of Brown's hit, and Carroll's pretty double settled the game and killed Chicago's chances.

One of the prettiest scenes imaginable was that upon the avenue outside the grounds after the game. Nobby jaunting-cars, with the prettiest of Dublin's girls perched upon them, crowded the thoroughfare, and cabs, coaches, carriages, carts, and people in hundreds made the assemblage a large one. Some of the richest brogue I ever heard and some of the sweetest faces I ever saw it was my pleasure to hear and see in that crowd. It was also distinctly representative of the wealth and intellect of Dublin. Among the notables present were Lord Londonderry, Lord Lieutenant-Governor of Ireland and daughter; Prince Albert, of Saxe-Weimar, commander of the forces in Ireland, and party, in an English drag; the Lord Mayor of Dublin and party; American Consul McCaskill and representatives of other foreign powers.

When we went to the railway station that evening, we found, thanks to the courtesy of the great Southern Railway Company, three elegantly appointed coaches at the disposal of our party. Each plate-glass window of every coach was decorated with an American flag, on which was the inscription, " Reserved for the American Baseball Party." Our train pulled out of the station at eight o'clock, and we arrived in Cork at two o'clock the following morning. We drove immediately to the Victoria Hotel, and after a refreshing sleep of five hours, the majority of the boys tumbled out of bed for a cup of coffee and a picturesque ride in Irish jaunting-cars to the village of Blarney, five miles distant. On the outskirts of the village stands the famous Blarney Castle, majestic, ancient and ivy-grown, and as no good Irish-American visits Ireland without touching the Blarney stone with his lips, Healey, Daly,

THE FAMOUS OLD BLARNEY CASTLE.

Fogarty, Manning, Carroll, Tener, and others of the boys who can trace their lineage back to the green sod, ascended the long winding stairs, and leaning over the parapet, with the assistance of others, went through the performance that is supposed to make an Ingersoll or a Depew of the veriest dunce.

At this castle the party encountered a typical old Irish bogman. The old fellow's costume alone would have been worth a trip to Dublin for

any of our American dime museum managers. He wore a veritable
coat of many colors, and the seat of his ancient trousers sagged downward a distance of a foot. A battered and time-stained hat, with a
pointed peak, sat upon the back of his head, and his " lilac " whiskers
peeked out from beneath the folds of an old gray woolen scarf about his
neck, while a tattered silk vest, that had once been of a delicate canary
hue, the gift, no doubt, of some benefactor, completed his make-up. He
spotted our party immediately as visiting Americans, and we, in turn,

"A FINE OULD IRISH GINTLEMAN."

gathered around him, as deeply interested as we had been in anything
we had met with in Ireland. Fogarty asked him how long he had been
a dynamiter, and this seemed to tickle the old man to death, for he
laughed and slapped his knee and batted his peaked hat from the top
of his head, as he gave a twirl to the white-thorn shillaly he swung
between his fingers.

" How did ye know that ? " he said.

"Ah, I saw it in your eye," said Fogarty ; "I never mistook a dynamiter in my life, and I am always glad to meet 'em," and with that Foge and the Irishman shook hands.

"It's a fine morning," said John Healy.

"Shoore, an' it's a beautiful mornin' for singin'," said the old man.

"Can you sing?" inquired Healy.

"Naw, but I kin dawnce," quickly replied the bogman, and, as if to put weight in his assertion, he commenced a breakdown in the middle of that dusty road, timing himself with a low, crooning rhythm that would make famous any actor who could reproduce it upon the American stage. The finish of the dance was the signal for a handful of silver and applause from the boys, and then Healy told him that if he would sing them a song he could have as much more. The Irishman looked sad for an instant, and then a sparkle came in his eye as he said, "I can never sing unless I be half-slugged."* Then he paused, while his eyes wandered away across the hill to a little red brick house on the roadway. Pointing to this, he said, "Doo yez see thot tavern yonder? Well, Oi'm goin' there now, an' Oi'll be ready to sing in tin minutes," and taking off his battered hat to the boys, he ambled away to the tavern as fast as his legs could carry him.

After a long look at the beautiful view from the tower of the castle, the boys returned to the hotel, and drove to the station where the train left for Queenstown, leaving behind us the quaint old city of Cork, and

> The bells of Shandon,
> That sound so grand on
> The river Lee.

We skirted the lower end of the city and then struck the bank of the river, alongside of which we ran to Queenstown, eleven miles distant—and a beautiful ride it was! No artist, it seems to me, could ever reproduce the picturesque beauty of this river and its shores, with their lovely lawns, their fine old mansions and crumbling, ivy-grown castles. It is the prettiest scenery, by far, that we saw in Ireland. Half an hour's ride took us to Queenstown. The railway station is right at the dock, and it was but a few steps from the train to the little tender which was

---

* Under the "exhilarating influence."

to take us to the White Star steamer in the offing.   While the steamer
was loading with the mail, the boys improved the opportunity to purchase
more black-thorn canes and shillalies and sprays of shamrock, which were
offered by old Irish men and women on the dock.   Just as I had completed the purchase of a fine white-thorn shillaly, I felt a tug at my
sleeve, and turning partly around, beheld a little old Irish woman, with
the most sorrowful expression imaginable.   She had a little basket filled
with sprays of shamrock, the roots attached, and still protected with
clumps of Irish soil.

"Are yez goin' back to Ameriky?" said she.

"Yes," I replied; "can I do anything for you there?"

"Do yez know me boy?" said she.

"What is your boy's name?" I asked.

"Larry Donovan," said she, "as foine a bit of a boy as ever left old
Ireland, and Oi hav'n't 'erd from him foor a year pawst."

"Where is Larry?" I asked.

"Shure Oi don't know," said she, "but if ye wud coome acrosst him,
will ye' take him this bit of shamrock from his old mither, and tell him
that ye got it from her at the dock at Queenstown?"

"Certainly," I replied, fancying, for the instant, how glad I should be
able to make Larry feel, in case I should run across him, at receiving the
bright little memento of his country's soil which his old mother handed
me.   "Certainly, and if I hear from Larry, I will see that he writes to
you."

"May the Saints bless ye," said the old lady, "may the Saints bless
ye," and then, as I turned away, she tugged gently at my sleeve.   "An'
shure Oi knows yez air goin' to leave somethin' for the old leddy, before
ye go."   How could I refuse?   Of course I presented her with the last
English coins I had, and soon we were aboard the steamer.   A moment
later our bow was cutting the waters of Queenstown harbor, and as we
drew near the White Star steamer "Adriatic," the sight of the American
flag at the ship's masthead drew forth three cheers and a "tigah" from
the boys, and these were followed by three more, as the passengers,
including Mr. Spalding's wife and mother, who had embarked at Liverpool, rushed to the rail to welcome us.   Two faces we missed.   Ed
Williamson was still confined to his room in London from the injuries

he received in Paris. He was attended by his faithful little wife, who bravely nursed him back to strength, although alone and three thousand miles from home. Telegrams were received at the steamer from many friends, bidding us "Farewell" and "God speed." On entering the saloon an hour later, we were pleasantly reminded of our London friends by a magnificent floral piece representing a home plate, and bearing upon its face, in immortelles, the inscription : "May you reach home in safety." Attached to this was a broad crimson scarf of silk, which bore the letters, "With compliments of Grace Hawthorne, London, March 27th, 1889, To the All-America and Chicago Baseball teams."

Soon after boarding the "Adriatic" we got under way and started upon the last of our voyages. We encountered exceedingly unfavorable weather, and for two days our ship made scarcely seven knots an hour. The "Adriatic" weathered the storm beautifully. She would bury her pretty nose in many an angry wave that hid the entire forward section of the ship, as it broke into big clouds of spray before her, only to come up again, ready, and seemingly anxious, for the next one.

After leaving Queenstown the boys were feverishly impatient to reach home, and fairly counted the hours. It was rough voyaging, but we bravely made the best of it. Every evening we assembled in the big smoking-room on the hurricane deck for the enjoyment of our after-dinner smoke, and for a turn at poker, yarn-spinning, or Fred Carroll's roulette wheel, which he had purchased in Nice. When Clarence Duval happened in, half a dozen of the boys would start "a-patting," and forthwith Mr. Duval's feet would begin to move, until finally he was dancing a "hoedown" with all his energy and ability. Captain Cameron and Purser Russell did everything in their power for the comfort of our party, and with fair weather our voyage would have been in every way delightful.

Our friends in New York had been expecting us for three days, and the "Adriatic" was sighted off Fire Island at a very early hour Saturday morning, April 6th. By sunrise we were at Quarantine. Meantime the enthusiasts on shore, who had prepared to welcome us to Manhattan Island, had been apprised of our arrival, and just as the sun peeped over the Brooklyn housetops and the sunrise gun on Governor's Island boomed out its accustomed good-morning, the steamer "Starin," with about one hundred and fifty people aboard, cut loose from her moorings at the barge office and steamed down the Bay. The tugboat "George Wood" bore half a hundred more. The party on the smaller boat had picked up a German band on the way down Broadway, and this, together with the steam whistles and the voices of two hundred cheering people, made noise enough to startle every one of our party out of bed and bring them on deck in a hurry. Among those who clung to the ropes aboard the visiting steamers we recognized the faces of Walter Spalding, George Floyd, F. L. Lane, Al Johnson, W. W. Kelly, Marcus Mayer, John W. Russel, Digby Bell, DeWolf Hopper, Joseph Donohue, John Kelly, Nicholas Engle, Henry Anson, J. W. Curtis, James Hart, John Ward, Colonel W. T. Coleman, and many others, including a number of ladies, the wives and daughters of their escorts. Cheering began when the vessels were half a mile apart, and was kept up for fully half an hour. As the "Starin" made fast to the ocean steamer, the cheering was loudest, even the emigrants on the "Adriatic," a thousand in number, joining in the welcoming howl. Whistles blew, the Dutch musicians on the small tugs almost straightened out their horns in efforts to drown the whistles, and hats, canes, handkerchiefs and umbrellas were waved and thrown wildly in the air. Many of the boys were too overcome by the demonstration and their joy in landing to speak, and I discovered tears coursing down the cheeks of not a few of them. Henry Anson, the father of Captain Anson, clasped the big ball player in his arms as the latter climbed upon the deck of the "Starin," and fairly cried for joy. Our entire party boarded the "Starin" and proceeded to the Twenty-first Street dock, from which we were quickly driven to the Fifth Avenue Hotel, where accommodations had been reserved, and it was when we stood in our rooms at the famous old hostelry and looked out over Madison Square that we felt once more at home, and were able to look back upon our great tour of the world as an accomplished fact.

The demonstration which began in honor of our arrival in New York harbor was but the beginning of the series of ovations tendered us until we disbanded at Chicago, two weeks later. Our first evening in America was spent at Palmer's Theatre, where, as the guests of Colonel McCaull, we saw "The May Queen," with De Wolf Hopper, Digby Bell, and other prominent lights of the operatic stage in the cast. The boxes had been elaborately decorated with flags, and from the proscenium arch hung an emblem of all nations, a gilt eagle and shield, with crossed bats, a pair of catcher's gloves and a catcher's mask. Bell and Hopper were irresistibly funny during the evening, and kept the big audience in almost continual laughter by their happy references to the return of the party and their jokes at our expense. There were frequent calls during the evening for Ward and Anson, but both remained modestly in the background, content to let the comedians upon the stage do all the talking.

THE ALL-AMERICA TEAM AFTER THE GAME AT BROOKLYN.

The first game after the return of the tourists took place Monday afternoon, April 8th, upon the Brooklyn grounds. Not more than 3000 people were present, as the weather was cold and unfavorable for ball-playing, but these received the players warmly. All-America won the game by one run. Immediately after the game the boys returned to the Fifth Avenue, and exchanged their uniforms for evening dress, Monday night having been set for the banquet tendered our party by admirers of the game in Gotham.

The supper took place at Delmonico's, and was indeed a notable gathering of representative American manhood and intelligence, in honor of the returning tourists and of the game of which they were the exponents. The decorations, menu cards and souvenirs were beautifully designed and typical of the game. The table of honor had been set crosswise of the room, and from it extended six others, plates having been laid for over 300 people. The walls of the hall had been festooned with American flags, and between them hung large and handsomely framed photographs of the party, taken in Egypt, Rome, Naples, and other foreign cities. The tables were profusely decorated with flowers and large confections, each of the latter being surmounted by the figure of a ball player in action. In the balcony had been stationed a full orchestra, which played almost constantly during the evening. Presiding at the table of honor, sat A. G. Mills, ex-President of the National League and one of the authors of the National Agreement, under the protection of which baseball has attained its present high standard of organization. Upon the right and left of Mr. Mills were seated Mr. Spalding, Hon. Chauncey M. Depew, Hon. Daniel Dougherty, Henry E. Howland, W. H. McElroy, U. S. Consul G. W. Griffin, who represented our country at Sydney at the time of our arrival there, Mayor Chapin, of Brooklyn, Mayor Cleveland, of Jersey City, Erastus Wiman, Mark Twain, Leigh S. Lynch, and the Rev. Joseph Twitchell, of Hartford. At the remaining tables sat representatives of a dozen Yale College classes ; popular members of the New York Stock Exchange ; the presidents and prominent members of the New York Athletic Club, the Manhattan Athletic Club, and other of the crack gentlemen's athletic organizations of New York City and vicinity. Shortly before Mr. Mills arose to call the assemblage to order, the ladies who had accompanied us around the world entered the balcony overlooking the room, and were greeted with a prolonged ovation. Then Mr. Mills, arising, reminded his hearers of the occasion that had brought them together, and during his eulogy of the game, of Mr. Spalding, and of the teams, which followed, was frequently compelled to pause until the applause had ceased.

Mayor Cleveland, of Jersey City, who followed, had his hearers laughing before he had been upon his feet many seconds. He concluded his very happy speech by saying: "Six months ago, these young men went abroad to fight, not like gladiators covered with armor, but covered with their American manhood, and they have come back covered with laurels, to place them on the fair brow of the American girl. Gentlemen, I now welcome home, in the name of the 20,000 residents of the little city across the river, this double team, as I call them, of American athletes."

Mayor Alfred Chapin, of Brooklyn, among many bright and witty things, said: "When we over in Brooklyn receive invitations to banquets, and especially to Delmonico's, we respond with alacrity, and we also make some sort of a speech, in return for a kindly dinner. In looking over the toast list I find that we are seven who will give the welcome, to be followed by a picked nine of intellectual athletes, who might safely make an after-dinner tour around the world and would not find a single foreign team who could catch them in an error."

Mr. Depew was enthusiastically cheered when he arose to his feet and smiled quietly upon the assemblage before him. He said:—

"Representing, as I do, probably more than any other human being, the whole of the American people who were deprived, by a convention that did not understand its duty, of putting me where I belong; and representing, as I do, by birth and opportunity, all the nationalities on the globe, I feel that I have been properly selected to give you the welcome of the world. I am just now arranging and preparing a Centennial oration which I hope may, and fear may not, meet all the possibilities of the 30th of April in presenting the majesty of that which created the Government which we boast of and the land and country of which we are proud, but I feel that that oration is of no importance and sinks into insignificance compared with the event of this evening. Washington never saw a baseball game; Madison wrote the Constitution of the United States, and died without seeing one; Jefferson was the author of the Declaration of Independence, and yet his monument has no tribute of this kind upon it. Hamilton, the most marvelous and creative genius, made constitutions, built up systems and created institutions, and yet never witnessed a baseball game. I feel, as I stand here, that all the men who have ever lived and achieved success in this world have died in vain. I am competent to pay that tribute, because I never played the game in my life, and never saw it but once, and then did not understand it. A philosopher, whom I always read with interest, because his abstractions sometimes approach the truth, wrote an article of some acumen many years ago, in which he said that you could mark the march of civilization and rise of liberty and its decadence by the interest which nations took in pugilism. The nations of the earth which submit to the most grinding of despotisms have no pugilists. The nations of Europe which have never risen in their boasted establishments to a full comprehension of Republicanism, have no pugilists. While Ireland and the Irish people, who can never be crushed, who have poetry, song and eloquence that belong to genius, have the most remarkable pugilists. England, which has a literature which is the only classic of to-day, which has an aristocracy and a form of government which is nearly democratic, has

18

remarkable pugilists, and when you reach the seat of culture in America—Boston—you find the prince of pugilists. Now, that philospher was right on the general principle, but wrong in the game. Civilization is marked, and has been in all ages, by an interest in the manly arts."

In conclusion, Mr. Depew eulogized the returning teams and ended with a brilliant panegyric in favor of the national game.

In response to the toast, "The Influence of Manly Sports," the Honorable Daniel Dougherty delivered an address that won him a burst of applause at the finish. He said, in conclusion :—

"There are no happier moments in the life of man, and especially an American, than when, after a foreign sojourn, he is conscious that he is once more a part of his country and an inmate of his home. Such men a country that holds liberty dear must have, and such men the athletic spirit of the generation is breeding for the future defence of the country against foreign foes. In sports on sea and land we more than hold our own, for an American yacht still keeps the cup, and our boys, who are back with us to-night, have taught new pastimes to the athletes of far-distant lands. I glory in the triumphs of the scholar, yet gladly admit the body has its honors as well as the brain. Open-air sports are conducive to health and hardihood. They give vigor to the arm, fleetness to the limbs, alertness to the eye and nerve to the heart. They ignite the fires of emulation, create thirst for distinction, the longing desire to win a name that will mark them among their fellows. These qualities combined rear a race fit for peace and war. In peace to grapple with the tough adversaries of every-day life, and in war to endure the privations of the camp, the fatigue of the long march in advance or retreat—to do daring deeds, leap into the imminent deadly breach, and, if needs be, fall like the immortal band of Lacedæmonians, who played their gymnastic games on the very spot where the next day they died for their country."

President Spalding was heartily cheered when he arose to give an outline of the tour. He attributed the success of the enterprise to the excellent conduct and ball-playing ability of the players who composed the Chicago and All-America teams. Captains Ward and Anson responded briefly when called upon, but the oratorical gem of the evening was Mark Twain's response to the toast of "The Grand Tour." Beginning in a vein of humor that excited the continued and hearty laughter of his hearers, he concluded his response with a word-painting of the beautiful Hawaiian Islands, so full of poetry and sentiment, and so true to nature as our party had seen it, that the assemblage sat spellbound under the charm of his words. Chairman Mills, in introducing Mr. Clemens, spoke of him as a native of the Hawaiian Islands, and the speaker said :—

"Though not a native, as intimated by the chairman, I have visited the Sandwich Islands— that peaceful land, that beautiful land, that far-off home of profound repose, and soft indolence, and dreamy solitude, where life is one long, slumberless Sabbath, the climate one long, delicious summer day, and the good that die experience no change, for they but fall asleep in one heaven and wake up in another. And these boys have played baseball there!—baseball, which is the very symbol, the outward and visible expression of the drive and push and rush and struggle of the raging, tearing, booming nineteenth century ! One cannot realize it; the place and the fact are so incongruous; it's like interrupting a funeral with a circus. Why, there's no legitimate point of contact, no possible kinship between baseball and the Sandwich Islands ; baseball is all fact, the Islands all sentiment. In baseball you've got to do everything just right, or you don't get there ; in the Islands you've got to do everything just wrong, or you can't stay there. You do it wrong to get it right, for if you do it right you get it wrong ; there isn't any way to get it right but to do it wrong, and the wronger you do it the righter it is.

"The natives illustrate this every day. They never mount a horse from the larboard side, they always mount him from the starboard ; on the other hand, they never milk a cow on the starboard side, they always milk her on the larboard ; it's why you see so many short people there—they've got their heads kicked off. When they meet on the road they don't turn to the right, they turn out to the left. And so, from always doing everything wrong end first it makes them left-handed—left-handed and cross-eyed : they are all so. In those Islands, the cats haven't any tails, and the snakes haven't any teeth ; and, what is still more irregular, the man that loses a game gets the pot. As to dress, the women all wear a single garment, but the men don't. No, the men don't wear anything at all, they hate display : when they wear a smile they think they are overdressed. Speaking of birds, the only bird there that has ornamental feathers has only two, just barely enough to squeeze through with, and they are under its wings instead of on top of its head, where, of course, they ought to be to do any good.

"The native language is soft and liquid and flexible, and in every way efficient and satisfactory—till you get mad ; then, there you are ; there isn't anything in it to swear with. Good judges all say it is the best Sunday language there is ; but then all the other six days in the week it just hangs idle on your hands ; it isn't any good for business, and you can't work a telephone with it. Many a time the attention of the missionaries has been called to this defect, and they are always promising they are going to fix it ; but no, they go fooling along and fooling along, and nothing is done. Speaking of education, everybody there is educated, from the highest to the lowest ; in fact, it is the only country in the world where education is actually universal. And yet every now and then you run across instances of ignorance that are simply revolting—simply degrading to the human race. Think of it—there, the ten takes the ace ! But let us not dwell on such things, they make a person ashamed. Well, the missionaries are always going to fix that, but they put it off, and put if off, and put it off, and so that nation is going to keep on going down, and down, and down, till some day you will see a pair of jacks beat a straight flush.

"Well, it is refreshment to the jaded, water to the thirsty, to look upon men who have so lately breathed the soft air of those Isles of the Blest, and had before their eyes the inextinguishable vision of their beauty. No alien land in all the world has any deep, strong charm for me but that one ; no other land could so longingly and so beseechingly haunt me, sleeping and waking, through half a lifetime, as that one has done. Other things leave me, but it abides ; other things change, but it remains the same. For me its balmy airs are always blowing, its summer seas flashing in the sun, the pulsing of its surf-beat is in my ear ; I can see its garlanded crags, its leaping cascades, its plumy palms drowsing by the shore, its remote summits floating like islands above the cloud rack ; I can feel the spirit of its woodland solitudes, I can hear the splash of its brooks ; in my nostrils still lives the breath of flowers that perished twenty years ago. And these world wanderers who sit before us here have lately looked upon these things ! and with eyes of flesh, not the unsatisfying vision of the spirit. I envy them that ! "

Following the responses to the toasts there was a call for De Wolf Hopper and Digby Bell, both of whom had come directly from the stage to the banquet hall. Both of the popular comedians responded as they only could do, Hopper portraying in verse the troubles of the New York Club in their efforts to hold on to the "Polo" grounds at 111th street, and then, in response to an encore, giving "Casey at the Bat," in his own inimitable style. Digby Bell followed with a description in verse of the arrival of our party in New York harbor, and was compelled to pause between verses for the applause to cease. The lines, written in the rhythm of "Sheridan's Ride," and entitled "Spalding's Ride," ran as follows :—

Up from down town the other day,
Bringing my chambermaid fresh dismay,
Elongated Hopper a message bore,
In a voice that was crossed between grumble
    and roar,
Telling the season was on once more,
With Spalding twenty miles away.

Oh, the excitement that message brought!
Oh, the wild fervor that came unsought!
I cast on my slumbering wife a glance,
And with silence burglarious slipped on my
    pants;
While Hopper impatiently 'gan to prance,
Lest he should be left by the waiting boat.
His broad breast heaved with a wheezing note,
But soon we stood out in the dawning day,
And Spalding was twenty miles away.

Now, there is a road from way uptown,
A good broad highway leading down
To the dock where the waiting tugboat lay,
To bear all the ball cranks down the bay.
And there I beheld a noisy Dutch band,
With boisterous Floyd in proud command,
A temporary baton in hand,
And he gave his stentorian voice such play
That the Dutch wind-jammers were led astray—
But Spalding was twenty miles away.

On the boat we marched with steady tread,
The enthusiastic Floyd ahead.

"Cast off!" the impatient captain cried,
And the boat swung out in the river's tide
With a jerk that unsteady Hopper floored,
And Manager Mayer with excitement roared,
And the Dutch well nigh fell overboard.
But what care we for mishaps to-day,
With Spalding twenty miles away?

We passed down the stream with a mighty
    rush,
That would put Jay Gould's steam yacht to
    blush;
And with every wave's majestic swell,
Our gallant gang, with a lusty yell,
Awoke the rest of the sleeping town.
Steam whistles salute as we pass them down,
And Nature's visage wears never a frown.
And what is the cause of this joy to-day?
Why, Spalding is fifteen miles away.

The Laura M. Starin we overtake,
And soon she is left in our foaming wake.
Our glasses we point through the dawn so
    dull;
On the deck of the tug there's an ominous
    lull,
As we search for the ocean steamer's hull.
She is there, large as life, down at Quarantine!
And each of us makes up in smile serene.
We cheered as we looked where she calmly
    lay,
For Spalding was only ten miles away.

The miles decreased as the moments flew,
And soon the ship's deck sprang into view.
Familiar faces are waiting there,
And cheer upon cheer stirs the morning air,
And the Dutch band brays with its tuneless blare.
We can make out big Anson, and Tener, and
    Crane,
And we yell ourselves hoarse till our vocals we
    strain,
For our two teams of heroes are back again.
There's a blizzard of joy on this breaking day,
For Spalding is only ten feet away.

Hurrah, hurrah for our Spalding bold;
Hurrah, hurrah for his well-won gold ;
And when New York has its baseball ground,
May his statue of bronze on the field be found,
And upon it inscribed : " From the base-
    ball cranks,
Who in manner befitting express their thanks,
To Spalding, who, freighted with ardor sub-
    lime,
Played our national game in every clime
From'Frisco,globe-circling,to New York Bay,
In lands ten thousand miles away."

It was nearly two o'clock when, with a farewell cheer for the friends who had accorded them so generous and hearty a welcome, the boys sought their hotel to rest for the game on the morrow.

Our second game also was played in Brooklyn, in the presence of 3500 people. The game was a rather uninteresting exhibition, Chicago taking the lead at the start and holding it throughout the nine innings. Crane was given poor support by All-America, their errors, without exception, proving costly. We departed the same evening for Baltimore, and played a game upon the Association grounds there the following day. Something over 5000 people were present, the assemblage including many of the most prominent society people of Baltimore, and the teams were given a great ovation when they came upon the field. The game was a most interesting contest. All-America was prevented from tying the score in the final innings only by Bob Pettitt's brilliant running catch of a fly to right field. The crowd was enthusiastic, and, by its liberal applause, incited the boys to some great base-running feats.

At 11 o'clock the following morning we arrived in Philadelphia, where we found a committee composed of the officers of the Philadelphia Club, and representatives of the Philadelphia papers. We were at once escorted to carriages, and were driven down Chestnut street to the South street ferry, where we took the boat for Gloucester. The ride down the river was delightful, and at Thompson's we enjoyed a planked-shad dinner, after which we listened for half an hour to the bright repartee of Messrs. Lynch, Spalding, Chadwick and John I. Rogers, and then re-boarded our steamer for the return ride.

We reached Philadelphia shortly after 3 o'clock, and were driven directly to the grounds of the Athletic Club, where the Athletics and Bostons were playing an exhibition game. The grounds were filled with people, there being 10,000 present. When our party arrived, during the third innings, play was temporarily suspended, and as the returned tourists filed upon the grounds, led by Messrs. Spalding, Reach and Pennypacker, to the strains of "Home Again" by the band, the enthusiasm of the crowd seemed to know no bounds. Ten thousand people stood upon their feet, waving hats and handkerchiefs and yelling at the top of their voices. The Boston and Athletic players had arranged themselves in line, from the home plate to third base, and, with heads uncovered, gave our players three times three cheers as we passed them. The procession moved across the diamond, and, circling about third base, left the field for the grand stand, where seats had been reserved. At the conclusion of the game the party were driven to the Continental, and, after donning evening dress, were escorted to the Hotel Bellevue, where, at 8 o'clock, they took seats at the banquet tendered by the Philadelphia *Sporting Life.*

In addition to the wealth of flowers, flags, and trailing vines in the hall, the dazzling display of cut-glass and silverware upon the table, and the vari-colored glow of a hundred fairy lights, the iron pillar in the centre of the room was surrounded from floor to ceiling with polished bats, catcher's masks, blazers, caps, base bags, and other paraphernalia of the American game all artistically arranged amidst festoons of vines and banks of flowers. The orchestra was hidden behind a pyramid of tropical plants in one corner of the room, and, as the party entered, began the appropriate and familiar air of "The Day I Played Baseball."

Editor Frank C. Richter occupied the chairman's seat, and at his right and left sat Mr. Spalding, Colonel A. K. McClure, of the Philadelphia *Times;* Colonel M. R. Muckle, of the *Ledger;* John I. Rogers, A. J. Reach, and Harry Wright, of the Philadelphia Club; Captain A. C. Anson and John Montgomery Ward; C. H. Byrne, of the Brooklyn Club; President W. M. Smith, of the City Council; and Thomas Dando, President of the *Sporting Life* Company. There were over three hundred guests in all, and it was fully ten o'clock before we had discussed the last dishes upon the elaborate menu card. At that hour the boys lighted their cigars, and until after midnight were entertained by the wit, eloquence, and baseball logic of the speakers present.

After brief welcoming addresses by Chairman Richter, Mr. Dando and President Smith, Mr. Spalding was called upon, and, after the cheers which his name aroused had subsided, first took occasion to thank our hosts of the evening, and then entered into an outline of our experiences abroad. In concluding his address Mr. Spalding said :—

" We found at Honolulu that they had four established clubs ; that baseball was well under way and fully appreciated. If it had not been for an accident, in reaching them on Sunday, we would have had the largest crowd in Honolulu of any at our games since we left home. At New Zealand, I have every reason to believe they will take up baseball, and that it will become one of their established games. It will become one of the games in Australia. While being the most hospitable people in the world, they are also the greatest sport-loving people, and their climate is peculiarly adapted to baseball. They can play the year round. Cricket does not seem to reach the masses. It is a game more for the aristocracy, who have the time, means and inclination to enjoy it. Baseball is for the masses. The requirements for the game are simple, and the grounds necessary are not so elaborate and do not require the same expense of keeping up.

" As to Ceylon, it is of very great doubt whether it will ever become popular, for the climate is very much against them. In Arabia there is no more chance for a game than for a blacklisted player to get to Heaven. In Egypt it is doubtful and in Italy extremely doubtful. We found in Italy and in every country outside of the English-speaking people the uttermost indifference to athletic sports. I think the time is not far distant when baseball will be played in France. I have been asked, ' What do you think of baseball being established in England ? ' I reply that that is a difficult question to answer. An Englishman is a very conservative individual and does not readily take to a new idea, but judging from the immense crowds we had there, and the great attention we received from the press—the comments, in the main, being favorable—I believe in the near future England will have its ball clubs and leagues."

When Captains Ward and Hanlon arose to respond to the toast of "The Chicago and the All-America Teams" they were applauded vociferously. In introducing Anson, Chairman Richter referred to him as " Mr. Spalding's faithful lieutenant, whose fame has grown with our national game, and who is universally recognized as one of the greatest batsmen and ablest captains baseball has ever known." The "Old Man's" reply was characteristically blunt and outspoken. He said :—

" I am proud at being thus honored by my friends in Philadelphia, for I played ball here once, although that was a good many years ago. I began to play here in 1872, and played four seasons, after which, as you all know, I went out to Chicago with Mr. Spalding. As to the tour we have just completed, I don't know that I can say anything Mr. Spalding has not already said. But I wish to pay a compliment to the ball players on the trip. Each and every member has certainly behaved himself as a gentleman. I saw some statements made to the effect that in all probability they would not come back in good condition. Well, I think if you look down along the line you will see that there is no ground for fear."

In introducing Captain Ward, Chairman Richter said :—

"Of course our next toast is to the other half of Spalding's combination, the All-America team, which picked team, without the advantages of long association and preliminary training, won a record that made it the wonder of the baseball world. It seems to me the most fitting to respond is he who so ably welded this team together and so skillfully handled it, Mr. John Montgomery Ward, famous in baseball, famous in literature, and to be famous in law.'

In response Captain Ward said :—

" There is no period in my professional life that I will look back to with more genuine pleasure than upon the six months past. I am glad to have been a member of this pioneer combination and proud to have been a member of the All-America team. In my entire experience as a player I have never been associated with a more companionable lot of boys, and I am sure when the memory of our struggles on the field have faded from us we will recall with affection the many happy hours we have spent together."

"On behalf of the All-America team I wish to thank Mr. Richter, the chairman, the man to whose enterprise and intellect as editor of *Sporting Life* the success of that journal is due. I also wish to thank Mr. Harry Palmer, whose genial and able pen has added so much to the tone of the trip. I should not allow the occasion to go by without saying something of the liberality which Messrs. Lynch and Spalding have shown the players on this trip. It has been a delightful tour."

Colonel John I. Rogers, as a member of the Board of Arbitration and an official of the Philadelphia Club, then held the attention of his hearers in one of the most interesting speeches of the evening. Referring to the unquestioned honesty and integrity of the game, he said :—

" There is no professional sport, there is no game of hazard, there is no athletic exercise which men follow for a livelihood in which there is such an absolute assurance of a game on its merits as in our national pastime. I had a distinguished jurist, Judge Thayer, ask me some time ago, ' How do you know the game is played on its merits ? ' I said, ' Because it is the one unpardonable crime I know of in this wide world—dishonest ball-playing. Arson, murder, highway robbery—aye, treason, may be pardoned, and are pardoned, but for dishonest or crooked ball-playing it has been proven there is no pardon under Heaven.' I said, ' Your Honor, I am a member of the supreme court of baseball, and we have had before us petitions signed by mayors of cities, governors of commonwealths, United States Senators and distinguished citizens, saying that Mr. So-and-so, ten or twelve years ago, in the old order of things, was found guilty of crooked ball-playing; that he has expiated his crime; that he has a family dependent upon him for support, and he has no other means of earning a living ; we ask you for mercy, ask you to restore this man. With all due respect, after due consideration, we respectfully returned the application as denied. And why ? Because the integrity of this game, the honesty of its play, is the foundation stone—nay, the keystone of our arch.'

" We have improved our legislation and reformed abuses. We have not yet reached perfection, but perfection is our goal. We have brought in all the minor leagues, until in all the

States of the Union are clubs formed and banded into leagues and organizations, all of them taking the law and bending their heads to the mandates of the greater organizations for the benefit of this national pastime.

" No man can afford to despise a game that is popular with the people. I have heard that governments, both national and municipal, had aided clubs by the provision of ground and the freedom from taxation, in order to encourage among the people a love for athletic sports, because a sturdy and more manly race will follow. So will it be in America when the great national game shall have established itself so firmly that no American will follow the example of that official in Rome who refused to recognize the representatives of this great institution— who had not time to have baseball talked in his office.

" While the National League only claims to be the pioneer in this work, I believe you will see we shall, with the coöperation of not only every baseball man, but every newspaper man and every citizen, show you that baseball is not the least of American institutions."

Following Colonel Rogers, Mr. C. H. Byrne's stirring address was frequently interrupted by outbursts of applause. He said :—

" I should like to pay to Mr. Spalding the tribute he deserves. The man who conceived and organized and carried out this marvelous enterprise is worthy of all consideration. Aside from him, this venture would have been unsuccessful if he had not been supported, maintained and encouraged in every step by these magnificent specimens of American manhood. They have carried themselves like gentlemen, like American citizens, animated by a purpose and a spirit which has been a surprise to everybody. They have been accompanied by the representatives of the most prominent papers in America, who have watched their career; and I have yet to see one line or word approaching a censure of any of these gentlemen. It is a surprise and a pride to me. I never knew what a legitimate, upright, manly business I was in till Mr. Spalding landed these gentlemen in the city of New York last Saturday night.

" You don't know what you have been doing. You have laid the foundation of something you cannot appreciate as yet. When the sere and yellow leaf comes along, it will be your pride and pleasure ; when the national game is carried out to the extent Mr. Spalding has predicted, when we have the international game, you will say : ' I was one of the band who went around the world and showed the world what the national game was capable of.' "

No more glowing were any of the tributes paid the national game that evening, than was the address of Colonel McClure, of the Philadelphia *Times,* in response to the toast "The Press." The Colonel said :—

" I do not know of any other institution in the country that the American press is so much indebted to, without being compelled to give any return, as baseball. A baseball player is the only man who aspires to any distinction that the newspapers cannot serve. He has to serve himself. In all the other efforts of life where men are constantly struggling for distinction, we are often compelled to make very bad bricks without straw. Any one who knows anything about a newspaper office knows how politicians assail us in every possible way, and appeal and beg, and cajole and threaten, to induce us to make them famous, and we are often very sorry for the things we do. We very often make men, and after they are made we find them disgracing themselves and us. The baseball player cannot be served by the press at all. It is the only line of American distinction in which public notoriety, such as the newspaper gives to many, many men, cannot possibly aid him in his advancement. The baseball man must advance by merit alone. If all the newspapers in the world should undertake to put a man above the standard, or what seems to be the nearest approach to a legal standard, it could not affect the judgment of any one except upon merit.

"That is a very high compliment, indeed, to be paid, which perhaps most of you know, but which I must confess not to have known until it was presented to-night by Mr. Rogers. It is a marvel, indeed, that a great institution in which young men enter with all the energy and ambition that characterize men in every direction of life, that every man enters it to-day with the most perfect knowledge that only by integrity and honest merit can he be promoted. What a frightful clearing-out that would make among the politicians, wouldn't it? I would like very much to get a little of this baseball theory into our politics; I would like to get it introduced into social life—into the churches. I do not know a place or thing, system or class or method that would not be improved by your code of ethics. I am sure that no organization in this country, religious, social or political, could make the assertion that has been made here to-night with reference to the integrity of baseball.

"And then I am delighted with another thing. If it were not for baseball I don't know what the newspapers would do during the summer season. We have presidential elections only once in four years and between times the elections do not catch on. The people do not care about elections and politics. The most of them denounce politics. Here we have a perpetual source of public interest. If we can have a first-class display of a first-class baseball game we are sure to have a very interested community willing to read the newspapers. I regard the movement you have made as one of great significance, and one for which you are entitled to the thanks of every American citizen and newspaper. I bid you Godspeed, for an institution that teaches a boy that nothing but honesty and manliness can succeed, must be doing missionary work every day of its existence. It will not only make a high standard of baseball men, but make the whole world better for its presence. I came here to give you hearty welcome. Having known and heard of you, I say not only welcome, but thrice welcome to the hospitality of Philadelphia."

In response to the toast, "The Rise and Progress of Baseball," Henry Chadwick, the veteran writer upon baseball topics, gave an interesting sketch of the game and its growth in popular favor since 1850. He was followed by President Reach, of the Philadelphia club, Harry Wright, Tim Murnane and Leigh Lynch, after which Fogarty gave a recital of his experiences abroad that kept his hearers in continuous laughter for ten minutes or more. Before adjourning, the following resolution, drafted by Mr. Chadwick, was unanimously adopted:—

"RESOLVED: That the sincere and hearty thanks of all lovers of baseball in America be, and they are hereby, extended to Mr. Charles Dougherty, the present Secretary of the American Legation at Rome, for his kindness and attention to the American representatives of the national game on their recent tour around the globe; that his thoughtful and unselfish friendship, rendered the more conspicuous by the ill-mannered conduct of his superior officer, United States Minister Stallo, shall be treasured as one of the most enjoyable and delightful memories of our tour around the globe."

It was long past midnight when, with three cheers for Editor Richter and *Sporting Life*, the boys shook hands with their generous hosts and departed for their hotels.

The following afternoon, Mayor Fitler received the teams in his office, and after warmly shaking hands with each of the players, said: "I am very glad to welcome you to Philadelphia. I have carefully watched your career as you have traveled around the world, and you have not only done justice to yourselves and your profession, but you have been a credit to your country. I assure you, gentlemen, that so long as I am Mayor of Philadelphia, I will do all in my power to encourage the great game of baseball." President Spalding responded with appropriate words, and after his Honor had accepted an invitation to be present at the game that afternoon, the boys entered carriages and were driven to the grounds of the Philadelphia Club. The spectators present, owing, doubtless, to the threatening weather, numbered only about 3500 people, but a more select crowd had never before been seen at a ball game in Philadelphia. Each player was warmly cheered upon stepping to the plate for the first time, George Wood, Fogarty, Tom Daly and Earle, as Philadelphia players, receiving the lion's share. The game abounded in pretty plays, was closely contested from start to finish, and was, in fact, just such a game as both teams were anxious to put up in return for the generous treatment they had received at the hands of Philadelphians.

The tourists left Philadelphia that evening for Boston, and on arrival at the " Hub " it transpired that catcher Earle had been left upon the platform in Philadelphia while talking with a group of admirers, and as Pettitt and Healy had been granted leave of absence, the party was left short-handed. Sam Wise, however, consented to play first base for All-America, while Carroll did the catching ; and Hugh Duffy, happening to drop around to the hotel, wore Pettitt's uniform and played a good short for Chicago. The game, while one-sided, was not uninteresting. A brilliant triple play by Duffy, Tener and Anson, and a quick double play by Manning and Wise, aroused much enthusiasm. Tom Brown was received with a big volley of cheers when he came to bat, and Ed Crane was the recipient of a handsome basket of flowers, which he received at the plate.

The following evening the party started on its trip westward to Chicago, stopping *en route* at Washington, and then proceeding to Pittsburgh, Cleveland and Indianapolis. The boys were warmly received at every point, and, save at Washington, put up an excellent sample of the ball we played abroad. At Washington, Chicago beat All-America "out of sight;" played a tie game with them at Pittsburgh; beat them again in a pretty game at Cleveland; and were finally beaten by All-America in a hard-fought game at Indianapolis. After breakfast at the Arlington, in Washington, Mr. Spalding was notified of the President's desire to receive the party at the White House. The boys accordingly entered carriages and were escorted to the Executive Mansion by General Williams and Walter Hewitt, the former a personal friend of the President. After shaking hands with Private Secretary Halford and Russell Harrison, the party were invited into an adjoining room and were introduced to the country's Chief Executive, Secretary Halford introducing President Spalding, and he, in turn, introducing each of the tourists. President Harrison expressed his pleasure at meeting the party. Mr. Spalding then extended an invitation to the President to attend that afternoon's game, but the Chief Executive expressed a fear that it would not be possible for him to do so. "I used to go to the games once in a while at Indianapolis," said he, "and also at Chicago. I enjoy seeing a good game, but I do not see how I can spare the time to go to-day. Mr. Halford, however, is a baseball enthusiast, and I am sure will ably represent the Administration." The President then bid his guests good-morning, and the boys, reëntering their carriages, were taken for a drive through Monument Park.

We left Indianapolis, Friday noon, in a special car provided by the officers of the "Monon Route," and reached Chicago the same evening. At Hammond, Indiana, twenty-six miles from the city, we were met by a party of Chicago enthusiasts and newspaper men who had come down from Chicago in a special. Hundreds of questions were asked, and as many answered, as the members of each party came together with hearty hand-clasps and words of welcome, and, before we were really prepared for it, we were rolling into the Union depot at Chicago. Fortunately for us, Mr. Spalding had been notified by wire at Indianapolis, to have the boys attired in evening dress upon their arrival.

We had accordingly made our toilets before reaching Hammond, and so were ready for the programme arranged for us. Not a few of our party had predicted that Chicago would out-do all other places in the welcoming reception it would extend, but not a man among us anticipated anything like the final demonstration made in our honor. The great crowd that filled the railway station could not be controlled by the police or the station guards. As our party stepped from the platforms of the coach, hundreds of cheering baseball enthusiasts swarmed over the iron railings and through the gates, until they picked us up, whether we would or not, and carried us to the carriages in waiting. There were sixty-five of these, and, as quickly as we could enter those reserved for our party, we were driven east to Peck Court and Wabash Avenue, where the lined formed. Finally, the last carriage had been filled and the procession began to move up Wabash Avenue and across Harmon Court to Michigan Avenue, amidst a blaze of pyrotechnics. The great crowd that filled the depot, that crushed about our carriages, that lined the streets along which lay our line of march, and howled and cheered at the sight of each familiar face in line, as well as the music, the calcium lights, the colored torches, and the rockets and Roman candles that burst above our heads, all combined to make the reception tendered us the most enthusiastic ever given any body of athletes upon American soil. When the last carriage had turned into Michigan Avenue, the line stopped until the illuminated procession, embracing sixty-odd amateur ball teams and representative amateur athletic organizations of Chicago, all in uniform, and provided with half a dozen bands of music, filed past us and took the lead. Then, amidst redoubled cheers and fresh bursts of pyrotechnics, our party moved on past the big auditorium building and, via Wabash Avenue, to the Palmer House, where we found the crowd as dense as at the railway station. Inside the famous hostelry we found nearly three hundred admirers of baseball and its players awaiting us, the reception committee embracing Judge H. M. Shepard, Judge H. N. Hibbard, Potter Palmer, John R. Walsh, Frederick Ullman, L. G. Fischer, D. K. Hill, C. L. Willoughby, C. E. Rollins, F. M. Lester, J. B. Kitchen, J. B. Knight, M. A. Fields, Dr. Hathaway, L. M. Hamburger, Louis Manasse, and C. F. Ginther.

The corridors and parlors of the great hotel were filled with guests all eager to shake hands with the arriving "globe-trotters," and bid them welcome home. Half an hour after our arrival we entered the banquet hall—the main dining-room of the Palmer House. This had been magnificently decorated with flowers of every variety, in huge baskets, garlands, wreaths and banks, while designs in flowers and confections, symbolical of the game and its accoutrements, confronted one at every turn. The menu and the wines provided were in keeping with all other details of the committee's work—elaborate and ample; and the menu cards, their different pages emblematic of the various stages of our tour, were the handsomest, both in design and execution, ever seen at a banquet in Chicago. In the body of the hall had been laid twenty-four tables of twelve plates each, and at these sat the players, scattered among their friends. Along the north side of the room, at an elevation of three feet above the tiled floor, stood the speaker's table, at which were seated the Hon. DeWitt C. Cregier, Mayor of Chicago; Hon. Carter H. Harrison, ex-Mayor of Chicago; Rev. Dr. Thomas; James W. Scott, President Chicago Press Club; A. G. Spalding, George W. Driggs, and others. The assemblage was thoroughly representative of the business and commercial interests of Chicago, and of the financial interests, too; for not less than twenty millions of money was represented.

It was, perhaps, ten o'clock when, the last course upon the card having been finished, coffee served and cigars lighted, Mayor Cregier called the assemblage to order, and in an able address welcomed the guests of the evening, not alone as ball-players, but as representatives of free America and the great city of Chicago. President Spalding responded, referring to the many courtesies and attentions tendered us abroad, and complimenting Chicago upon having capped them all with three great receptions—one at the railway station, another upon the streets of the city, and the third in the banquet hall. The party had enjoyed a grand experience, one that its members could refer to with pleasure for many years to come, but all were overjoyed at once more returning to their own country.

The Rev. Dr. Thomas responded to the toast of "Baseball as a National Amusement," and then "His Royal Highness, the Prince of Wales," brought Captain Anson to his feet, amidst a hearty burst of applause. While "Old Anse" was pulling down his décollete-cut vest and sipping a preparatory mouthful of water, an enthusiastic stockbroker proposed "Three cheers for the 'Old Man!'" and they were given with a roar and a wild waving of napkins. Then Anson drew himself up to his full height, and began. He said he was glad of an opportunity to say something pleasant about the Prince of Wales, for the heir to England's throne had treated them most royally, and by his recognition and presence at the opening game in London had, beyond doubt, added greatly to the public interest in our tour through Great Britain. Such recognition, Anson believed, had had the effect of raising the social standard of the national game to the highest point it had yet attained. "Anse" concluded his remarks with an honestly-meant tribute of praise to the habits, conduct and ball-playing ability of both the Chicago and All-America teams.

Major Henry L. Turner followed in a stirring response to "The National Value of Athletics," and then John Ward was enthusiastically cheered as he rose to his feet to talk upon "The World as I Found It." John expressed himself as thoroughly confident that the world was composed of land and water—principally water—as he had never before seen so much of that liquid. That it was round was evidenced by the fact that our party had started from Chicago, and, after traveling west continuously, had finally reached Chicago again. No grander tour had ever been conceived in the history of athletics, and baseball owed much, indeed, to Mr. Spalding's pluck and enterprise in carrying it to so successful an issue.

Ex-Mayor Carter Harrison was warmly received when he rose to respond to the toast, "My Own Experience." He kept his hearers in a broad smile by his humorous comparisons of his own tour of the world with that made by our party. He had gone around the world himself, he said, for the same purpose Mr. Spalding had in view—to advertise Chicago. He had filled all the foreigners he had met full of Chicago, and did not doubt but that the ball teams before him had done the same. He had told Englishmen, Scotchmen and Irishmen about our big fire, about our parks and boulevards, about our unrivaled climate, and about our crack ball team, and Messrs. Spalding, Anson and Ward had gone around the world to verify all he had said in praise of the national game and its great exponents.   Mr. Harrison then gave an interesting account of his own voyages, and finally concluded with a glowing tribute to America and everything American.

"Public Opinion of the Game," "Australia," "The Humor of the Trip" and "The Press," were responded to in an interesting manner by Leigh Lynch, James W. Scott, George Driggs and others ; and then, after an informal commingling and exchange of greetings, the banqueters separated for their respective apartments.

The last game of the tour took place upon the Chicago grounds on the following day, in the presence of eight thousand people.   Tired out with the events of the demonstration on the night before, and impatient to get home to wives, mothers and sisters they had not seen for months, the teams did not put up a very spirited exhibition.   All-America began to size up Baldwin's delivery at the start, and Mark, seeing that Ward's men were bent upon hitting, put the ball over the plate and let them peg away at it.   The result was just twenty-two clean hits for All-America, with a yield of as many runs, the score standing 22 to 9 at the finish.   After the game, the boys shook hands in the club house, and by midnight many members of the Spalding party were on their way to join their respective clubs.

Thus ended a tour the like of which had never before been undertaken, and which probably will never be duplicated.   In conception, it was bold ; in execution, it is worthy of admiration ; and too much can scarcely be said in eulogy of the nerve, the enterprise, the managerial ability and the sound business judgment displayed by Albert Spalding as its projector, and to whom, more than any other, the national game of America owes its present high standard of organization and unquestioned reputation for honesty and integrity.   Much praise is also due the players for their invariable good nature in the face of a thousand and one annoyances attendant upon a journey of thirty-two thousand miles through foreign lands and waters, and for their willingness to play ball under such conditions as, it is quite safe to say, no other ball teams ever played under.   Indeed, the great tour, from beginning to end, must ever remain a credit to its projector and to each and every man who participated in it.

www.ingramcontent.com/pod-product-compliance
Lightning Source LLC
Chambersburg PA
CBHW020902020726
47497CB00005B/1515